**Twelve military heroes.
Twelve indomitable heroines.
One UNIFORMLY HOT! miniseries.**

Mills & Boon® Blaze®'s bestselling miniseries
continues with another year of irresistible soldiers
from all branches of the armed forces.

Don't miss

COMMAND PERFORMANCE
by Sara Jane Stone

BACK IN SERVICE
by Isabel Sharpe

UNIFORMLY HOT!

The Few. The Proud. The Sexy as Hell.

BACK IN SERVICE

BY
ISABEL SHARPE

First published in Great Britain 2013
by Mills & Boon, an imprint of Harlequin (UK) Limited,
Eton House, 18-24 Paradise Road, Richmond, Surrey TW9 1SR

© Muna Shehadi Sill 2013

ISBN: 978 0 263 90331 7

14-1113

Harlequin (UK) policy is to use papers that are natural, renewable and recyclable products and made from wood grown in sustainable forests. The logging and manufacturing processes conform to the legal environmental regulations of the country of origin.

Printed and bound in Spain
by Blackprint CPI, Barcelona

Isabel Sharpe was not born pen in hand like so many of her fellow writers. After she quit work to stay home with her firstborn son and nearly went out of her mind, she started writing. After more than thirty novels for Mills & Boon, a second son and eventually a new, improved husband, Isabel is more than happy with her choices these days. She loves hearing from readers. Write to her at www.isabelsharpe.com.

To my dear friend and fellow author Delores
Fossen, who patiently introduced me
to the fascinating world of the Air Force.

I am very grateful.

1

"I HAD A great time today, thanks, Crystal." Kendra Loner-gan smiled at the attractive middle-aged widow and got a wide smile back. A first! This was good progress. They'd spent the past hour down on Rat Beach tossing balls into the Pacific waves for Byron, the golden retriever Kendra regularly borrowed from a friend for appointments with her dog-loving clients.

"I had fun, too." Crystal bent and stroked Byron's red-dish fur. "It felt good to be on the beach again. Thanks, Kendra."

"You are welcome. See you next week!" Kendra tugged Byron's leash and gave Crystal a quick wave before lead-ing the dog back down the block to the Lexus minivan that had belonged to her parents. For a while now she'd been intending to sell the car and buy something smaller, but she didn't ever seem to have time, and wasn't sure what she'd replace it with. In the meantime, it was a nice—if a bit tough—reminder of the family she'd lost. "Up you get, Byron. I'll take you home now."

She unhooked his leash; Byron bounded into the car and settled on the towel Kendra kept on the backseat. What an amazing animal—she never had any trouble with him. His owner, Lena, Kendra's friend since kindergarten, worked typical lawyer hours and was delighted to have Byron out getting exercise whenever Kendra needed him. Kendra had thought about getting a dog herself, but…she hadn't done that yet either.

The Lexus swung smoothly out of its parking place on Pullman Lane in Redondo Beach; she turned it south onto Blossom Lane, heading toward the Pacific Coast Highway and her hometown of Palos Verdes Estates, a hilltop oasis overlooking the vast urban sprawl of L.A. She was back living in the house she'd grown up in, a temporary situation that had stretched on as the weeks and months passed. The house was much too big for one person, but it was stuffed with memories Kendra wasn't yet ready to leave behind.

Climbing the steeply curving roads of Palos Verdes Estates, windows rolled down to enjoy the cool November breeze, she turned up the volume on a Mumford and Sons song she loved, "Little Lion Man," peeking occasionally at the view of Santa Monica Bay, which became more and more spectacular as she ascended.

She left the view behind and turned onto Via Cataluna, then into the driveway of the house where Lena lived with her husband, Paul. Her cell rang, a private caller.

"This is Kendra." She switched off the engine.

"Kendra Lonergan? It's Matty Cartwright."

Kendra blinked, taking a moment to place the name. Matty Cartwright? From Palos Verdes High School? Whom Kendra had last seen years ago? How typical of a Cartwright to think she'd need no further introduction than her name. "Hi, Matty."

"I'm calling to— Oh, uh, how are you? It's been a long time."

Kendra pushed out of the car, rolling her eyes, not in the mood for friendly small talk. She hadn't seen Matty since her sophomore year, when Matty was a senior, and didn't think she'd ever spoken to her. "I'm fine. What a surprise to hear from you."

"I'm calling about Jameson."

Jameson. Kendra grimaced, opening the car's rear door. Matty's younger brother had been in Kendra's grade from Montemalaga Elementary School through Palos Verdes High School. Not her favorite classmate.

She followed Byron to Lena's front entrance, where she fumbled for the borrowed keys in the pocket of her sweatshirt, not really anxious to be having this conversation. "What about Jameson?"

"I wondered if you could work with him."

Kendra froze. *Work* with Jameson Cartwright? As in *help* him? After the way he'd treated her? Byron whimpered impatiently. She unlocked her friend's door; the dog raced toward the kitchen. "Whoa, back up a second, Matty. Where is he, what happened to him and how did you hear about me and what I do?"

A sigh of exasperation came over the line. Kendra gritted her teeth, tempted to tell Matty where to stick her Cartwright attitude.

"I'm sorry, Kendra." Matty gave a short, embarrassed laugh. "I'm not making any sense. I'm just so upset."

Kendra hung Byron's leash in the foyer closet, feeling an unwelcome twinge of sympathy. "It's okay. Just start at the beginning."

The slobbery sound of Byron lapping water came from the kitchen. Kendra wandered into Lena's airy living room, able to picture Jameson Cartwright as if she'd just seen him the day before. Nordic like his whole family—blond hair, blue eyes, high forehead, strong jaw. Yet she couldn't describe him as severely handsome, like the rest of them, because of his one fatal flaw: a wide, sensual mouth more suited to lazy smiles and lingering kisses than sneering and barking orders. Totally wasted on him. He must hate that mouth every time he looked in the mirror.

All through elementary and middle school he'd harassed her pretty steadily, mostly egged on by his odious older twin brothers. In high school there had been fewer incidents, since Hayden and Mark had graduated, thank God. Senior year Jameson had whipped Kendra for class president, not because he'd run a brilliant campaign, but because she'd been eccentric, brainy and overweight, and he was a Cartwright. *Every* Cartwright sibling had been president of his or her class.

"You know how our family is all in the military." It wasn't a question.

"Air Force, right?" Pilots going back generations, most attaining high rank or managing to be heroes of one sort or another, at least according to the *Palos Verdes Peninsula News,* which had done a rather gushy piece on the family some years back that Kendra had skimmed and tossed.

"Jameson did Air Force ROTC at Chicago University. He graduated last June with the Legion of Valor Bronze Cross for Achievement."

Kendra interrupted her who-cares eye roll. Wait, this *past* June? Kendra had graduated from UCLA and gone on to complete a two-year master's program in counseling at California State by then. "He *just* graduated?"

"It's a family tradition to take a year off before college and travel in Europe. Jameson settled in Spain and…sort of took two. Anyway, after college, he finished basic officer training at Maxwell Air Force Base, a distinguished graduate for top marks in test scores and leadership drills."

My, my. How *lucky* Kendra was that she'd never have to suffer the pain of being so utterly perfect.

She entered Lena's bright yellow kitchen, where Byron was already lying in his crate, tired out from his frantic exercise at the beach. Such a good dog. "Then?"

"Then he was injured his first day of specialty training at Keesler Air Force Base, in Mississippi. He tore the ACL in his right knee and had to have surgery." Matty's voice thickened. "He's back home in Palos Verdes Estates on thirty days of personal leave while he continues recovering enough to go back and recover some more."

"Tough break." Why was Matty telling her this? Jameson needed a Scrabble partner? Someone to read him bedtime stories? Kendra closed Byron in his crate and blew him a kiss. "What do you need me for?"

"He, uh…" Matty mumbled something. It was suddenly difficult to hear her, as if she was speaking through cloth. Kendra pressed the phone harder to her ear. "…accident… with a stray…"

Kendra waited impatiently. Stray what? Bullet? Land mine? Grenade? "Sorry, I didn't hear. Accident with a stray what?"

"Cat." She said the word sharply. "Jameson was injured tripping over a cat. On his way to dinner."

Omigod! Kendra clapped a hand over her mouth to keep Matty from hearing her involuntary giggle. Seriously? Not that she'd wish that miserable an injury on anyone—even Jameson Cartwright—but karma must have had a blast arranging that one.

"What a shame," she managed weakly, barely stifling more laughter. *Latest Cartwright's Journey to Hero Status Cut Short in Fierce Battle. Victim's last words: I tawt I taw a puddy tat.*

"You can imagine what this means to a Cartwright." Matty spoke stiffly. "This could end his military career before it even starts."

But how is the cat? Kendra couldn't bring herself to be wiseass enough to ask. Though she couldn't imagine in a million years making a statement like "You can imagine what this means to a Lonergan." Like they were a rare and special breed of humans the rest of the world could barely comprehend. "I'm sure it's been hard."

"It's been awful." Her voice broke, making Kendra feel guilty for being…*catty*—ha-ha. "Jameson is furious and severely depressed. I've called several times. He only picked up once and would barely speak to me. He won't talk to the rest of the family at all. I don't know if he's eating or anything. I've never seen him like this. Can you help him?"

Kendra's laughter died in the face of Matty's anguish. Depression was not a joke, no matter the cause. Kendra had been paralyzed for months after the sudden deaths of her parents mere days after her graduation from college. "How did you hear about me?"

"I was talking to a friend whose friend recommended you. She said you get referrals from doctors and therapists and hospitals, that your work supplements whatever care they're giving people in various stages of grief. That your methods are unusual but effective. Jameson won't accept traditional talk therapy."

"No?" Oh, there was a big surprise. Cartwright men didn't need some sissy talking out of their feelings. Why would they, when it was so easy to punch or ridicule someone and feel tons better about themselves?

"We…weren't exactly raised on sensitivity and openness."

Well. Kendra raised her eyebrows at the unexpected admission, and at the bitterness in Matty's voice. At least she recognized that much. "I'm not sure I'm the right person to—"

"I know what you're thinking."

"You do?" She doubted it.

"That Cartwrights don't have any whining rights. That I'm being arrogant and overprotective looking for professional help for a guy who isn't suffering from anything more than wounded pride. That he should get over himself and deal."

"Uh…" Darn. That was exactly what she'd been thinking. Except the last part. Telling a depressed person to get over it was not generally effective.

"If it was one of my other brothers or my dad, I'd agree with you. There's no way I'd ask you to try to help one of them. But Jameson is different." Her voice softened. "He's always struggled to fit in. I think life would have been easier for both of us if we'd been born into a different family."

Kendra blinked in astonishment. She didn't know Matty at all, but Jameson? Struggling? He'd always seemed to fit the Cartwright mold to perfection—arrogant, entitled, self-centered…should she go on? "Huh."

"I know, you don't believe me. But he's different from the other guys in the family. And that's why this is hitting him so hard. It's worse than just losing out on his planned future. It's like the final proof that he can't cut it. You know? I don't see it that way, and Mom…who knows… but you can bet Dad and my brothers do."

Kendra stood in Lena's living room, phone pressed to her ear, having a very hard time processing this information, given that it contradicted everything she'd ever thought about Jameson.

"I just know that I can't help him right now, and while traditional doctors and therapists might, he won't go, and he really, really needs help."

"What makes you think he'd let *me* help him?"

"He…knows you."

Kendra gave an incredulous laugh. He knew her? He knew how to typecast her, he knew which buttons to push and he knew how to make her feel loathed and worthless. Thank God her parents had been psychologists and had taken time and care helping her through the pitfalls of childhood with her self-esteem intact. "Not very well. In any case, I'm pretty booked…"

"Please, Kendra. I'll beg if you want me to. You're the first ray of hope I've had in weeks." Matty sounded as if she was about to burst into tears. "I haven't slept all night in so long I forget what it's like."

Oh, geez. Kendra closed her eyes, torn between sympathy for Matty and her instinct telling her she wanted less than nothing to do with men like the Cartwrights ever again.

"Just call him, Kendra. Talk to him. If you think I'm overreacting or it doesn't feel right, then fine, you don't have to take him on. We'll go another route. I just don't know what that would be at this point."

Kendra forced herself into motion, letting herself out of Lena's house. Committing to one call was an easy out, not really saying yes or no, which Matty undoubtedly knew and was exploiting. She was a Cartwright, after all.

Maybe Jameson had grown up some. Maybe Kendra had misjudged him all along, typecasting him as he had her. Hard to imagine, but Matty would know her brother better than Kendra did.

"I'll talk to him." She climbed into the Lexus, started back down the hill toward her house.

"Thank you. Thank you so much." Matty's relief was humble and real, no triumph in her tone. "He's housesitting at a friend's condo. I'll give you the address and his cell. Thank you *so* much."

"Sure." Kendra sighed, feeling both noble and trapped. Lena would have a fit when she told her.

"Um. There is just one more thing."

Uh-oh. "What's that?"

"I'd rather you didn't tell Jameson that I'm behind this. Even though he and I are close, he's...a little sensitive when it comes to family right now."

"Meaning he wants all of you out of his face even if you're trying to help."

"That would be it exactly."

Pretty classic depression symptom. Though if Matty's

description of Jameson as the outcast was correct, he could also be protecting himself from the rest of the family's judgment.

Damn. This was almost intriguing. "Okay. I won't mention you. But I'm not sure he'll buy that six years after our graduation I suddenly want to catch up."

"Tell him you're part of a new program the Air Force is trying out for soldiers on medical leave. Or that his commanding officer or surgeon heard of you through some doctor you work with here. Something that leaves him no choice."

Clearly Matty had thought this through. "So I should lie while I try to gain his trust?"

"Oof." Matty whistled silently. "Do you have to put it that way?"

"Can't you get your commander or some general to write a fake letter?"

"Not me." Matty laughed lightly. "I'm not in the Air Force. I'm an actress."

Kendra brought her car to an abrupt halt at an intersection before she realized there was no stop sign; luckily there was no one behind her. "You're an actress."

"Between jobs I sell real estate, but right now I'm in a musical called *Backspace* at the Pasadena Playhouse. I have a small part, but it's a job." The pride in her voice was unmistakable.

"It's an impressive job." Well, how about that. Her parents must have nearly dropped dead. A canker on the Cartwright family tree! And now Jameson injured and out of his training program? A regular crumbling dynasty. "I'll come up with something."

"Thank you, Kendra. Please stay in touch. And send the bill to me. How much do you charge, by the way?"

Kendra told her.

"*What?* You're kidding."

Kendra was used to surprise and had the explanation for her bargain-basement rates ready. "I want my services available to as many people as possible. I'm not in this to get rich. I like working with people, and I don't want to be limited by fees so high that my clients are thinking every second has to count triple for me to be worth their while."

Happily, money was no problem. Great-Grandpa Lonergan had made a fortune in banking in the early twentieth century, and Kendra's ever-cautious parents had had plenty of life insurance on top of that. She would never have to work, though she knew she'd always choose to.

"How about I throw in two tickets to my show?"

"You're on." Kendra pulled into her driveway on Via Rincon and parked outside the garage, gazing affectionately at the white stucco house with the red-tile roof her grandparents had built into the side of the hill.

"You know, what you do is really remarkable."

"Thanks." Kendra shrugged. It didn't feel remarkable. It was her business, and like any business it could be frustrating, boring, annoying, but overall more deeply satisfying than anything she could imagine doing. For many clients who'd experienced loss, grief and loneliness had become so much of who they were, they didn't want to let it go. Proving they still had plenty of life to live and plenty to offer others was about as good as it got.

She took down Jameson's number, punched off the phone and climbed down from the car. Jameson Cartwright, for God's sake. One of the last people she'd ever imagined seeing willingly again, let alone in a situation where he needed her help.

Following the curving brick path from the driveway, she passed her dad's Meyer lemon tree, heavy with still-green fruit, and the jasmine bush bought by her mom, planted clumsily by Kendra and her brother, Duncan. It would burst into fragrant white blossoms in February. She let herself into the house and headed through the small dining room to the spacious kitchen, her mom's pride and joy. Dropping her bag on the hardwood floor, Kendra dialed her best friend's cell. If anyone would enjoy this story, it was Lena.

"Hey, Kendra, what's up, Byron giving you trouble?"

"I don't think he knows how to make trouble." She helped herself to a can of lemon-flavored sparkling water from the stainless-steel refrigerator and pushed through the sliding glass door out onto the deck overlooking their pool, which overlooked their terraced hill lush with her mom's rather overgrown gardens, which overlooked Redondo Beach and beyond that Los Angeles, the Pacific and the Santa Monica Mountains. "It's a different kind of dog giving me trouble. Remember Jameson Cartwright?"

"*Yes*. Ew. Don't tell me he got in touch with you."

"Sister Matty called me. Jameson was injured on his first day of Air Force training last month." She dragged out a chair from the iron table set her parents had bought soon after they were married and turned it toward the view.

"Last month? What's he been doing all this time? I thought everyone in his family ran to the Air Force as soon as they got out of diapers."

"Nope." Kendra sank into the chair and propped her feet up on the railing. "He took two years off to run around Europe. Spain in particular."

"Two years? No kidding. So what did Matty want?"

"She wants me to work with him."

"You're *kidding!* That obnoxious, bullying… How come? What happened?"

Kendra started smiling before she even opened her mouth. "He's depressed because he tore up his knee at Keesler Air Force Base. Tripping over a cat."

Lena gasped, then her shriek of laughter nearly burst

Kendra's eardrum. "Oh, my God! Another Cartwright hero!"

"I know." She was giggling again, guiltily this time.

"Brought down by a pussy!" Lena snorted and chuckled a few more times. "I know, I know, I shouldn't be laughing. I'm sure it's hell for him. No more Mr. Tough Guy, no more hot uniforms and cool planes. Now who is he?"

"Exactly." Kendra tipped her head back to enjoy the eucalyptus-smelling breeze. "Matty said he's seriously depressed."

"Ugh, I bet. So she wants you to fix up his ego and send him back into battle?"

"Yup." Kendra waited a beat. "Maybe with a squirrel next time."

Another shriek.

Kendra laughed with her. Yes, it was horrible to make fun of someone in physical and emotional pain, but Jameson and his twin brothers…it was sort of inevitable. *Reap what you sow, Cartwrights.* "One interesting fact. Matty never went into the military. She's a working actress. I almost got the impression she had some depth."

"No way."

"What's more, she implied Jameson might have some, too."

"You have to admit, he wasn't as bad as Mark and Hayden."

"Not saying much."

"True. I've told you his dad was a piece of work. We'd hear shouting over there all the time. I don't know if he drank or what, but he had a hell of a temper."

"I remember." Not surprising. Most people who grew up bullies had a first-class role model at home. "I said I'd talk to him."

"Of course you did." Lena sighed. "You can't resist trying to fix everyone. I'm not sure this guy deserves you, though."

"I said I'd talk to him. Then I get to decide what to do. I'm curious, to be honest. Don't tell me you're not. You were madly in love with him."

"Only for a few weeks! Besides, everyone was madly in love with Jameson. He was a jerk, but he was a major hottie."

"Not to me." Kendra shuddered. She liked men whose strength lay in kindness and caring, not muscles and manipulation. Lena had married Paul, a slender, dark-haired fellow lawyer—complete opposite of her plump blond energy—who was gentle, brilliant, funny and the nicest man on the planet. Kendra wanted one of those.

"When are you going to talk to him?"

"When I can stomach it. His sister wants me to make it seem like I'm on official business and leave her out of it."

"Smart. If my brother thought I was trying to force him into counseling, he'd refuse on principle."

"Uh-huh. And honestly, I think he's probably mortified. I mean, really, a *cat?*"

"Oof." Lena started giggling again. "I know, I'm terrible. If it was anyone else it wouldn't be so funny. Call me the second you finish talking to him, okay?"

"I promise." She hung up and sat still for a moment, remembering Jameson in grade school, bringing up his wide, smug smile from her memory bank, that weird nervous snickering he did when taunting her, looking back at his hulking older brothers for validation and support.

In elementary school he'd tripped her in the halls, put worms in her lunch, glue in her hair. In middle school he'd spread rumors that she had mysterious rashes, that she was dating a cousin, that she'd had an abortion in eighth grade, that she was being medicated for a mental illness. In their freshman year of high school he'd asked her to the school dance as a joke—pretending he wanted to date the fatty, ha-ha-ha. Then without lifting a finger, he'd denied her the class presidency she'd worked so hard for.

Why was she even considering helping this guy?

Because she, at least, was a grown-up now. Because he was hurting. Because helping people in pain was her job. Because Kendra knew depression, knew how it could sap your ability to get out of bed in the morning, how the idea of having to live the rest of your life seemed an impossibility, how feeling anything but crushing pain seemed a distant dream, sometimes not even worth going after. Didn't matter what caused the pain, the very fact of its existence meant conquering it should be imperative.

After she'd emerged from the worst of her own grief with the support and help of an amazing therapist Lena had dragged her to, Kendra had decided she wanted to help people out of that same darkness.

For her program, she used the techniques that had helped her the most, starting slow and simple—getting out of the house and back in touch with nature, then gradually resuming favorite hobbies and activities and introducing new ones that had no memories attached. And along with that, listening, compassion and a friendly shoulder—repeat as needed.

Could she offer those things to Jameson Cartwright in good faith? She'd need to make sure she didn't just want to prove he hadn't won. To show him how in spite of him and people like him, she'd emerged with self-esteem intact. To parade her slender self, no longer in thick-framed glasses or drab don't-look-at-me clothes. To show him she had the strength to survive worse than anything he'd ever dreamed of dishing out, a tragedy that put his stupid pranks and arrogance into stunning perspective. To be able to confront him in a situation in which, finally, she held all the power.

Kendra would need to check her baggage and her ego at

his door. If she couldn't be genuine in her approach, she'd do neither of them any good.

A red-tailed hawk circled lazily over a fir tree growing partway down the hill, its uppermost needles at eye level where she sat. The bird landed on the treetop, folded its feathers and stood fierce and proud, branch rebounding gently under him.

When Kendra was in elementary school, she'd found a baby hawk on the fire road below their house—how old had she been, seven? Eight? The creature had broken its wing and lay helpless to move, to fly, terrified of the sudden vulnerability.

In spite of his feeble attempts to peck her eyes out, she'd gotten the creature to the house; her mother had helped her transport it to the Humane Society. Kendra had visited often while the hawk healed, naming it Spirit. The staff had invited her to come along when they rereleased Spirit into the wild. She'd watched him soar into the sky and had felt the deep joy that comes from helping a fellow creature heal.

Kendra had thought of that bird often as she'd struggled through the first year after the crash that left her without family except for the much-older brother she'd never had much in common with who lived abroad. And she'd thought about Spirit when she'd decided on her career path, and when she met people made helpless by grief, and when she was first trying to help people who wanted nothing more than to peck her eyes out. Because she knew something they couldn't grasp yet. That there would be a moment when she could rerelease them into the wilds of a renewed life and watch them soar.

She picked up the phone and dialed Jameson.

2

WE LIVE IN fame or go down in flame. The line from the Air Force song played endlessly in Jameson's head. Torture. As if he needed more.

He was stretched out on his buddy Mike's sofa, staring out the window, sick to death of watching TV. Yeah, he'd gone down in flame. Because this sure wasn't fame, and it could only marginally be called living.

At least Mike had his back, letting him stay at his place so Jameson wouldn't have to crawl to Mom and Dad. As if his humiliation wasn't complete enough, moving back home would have about killed him. He'd met Mike at Maxwell during basic officer training, and in one of those stranger-than-fiction coincidences realized he was living in Jameson's hometown with his wife, Pat, who was with her new-mom sister in Reno. Mike had been assigned to train at Keesler in computer communications at the same time as Jameson, and offered his place after Jameson's accident. Couldn't have worked out better.

His cell rang. Again. He didn't look at it. He hadn't looked at it last time or the time before that. It was Dad or Mom or Matty or one of his brothers or a friend. They'd make stilted conversation, Matty and Mom oozing sympathetic cheer, his male relatives masking their contempt with endless advice about how to recover faster than he was, friends who didn't know expressing shock, Air Force friends going on about all the training he was missing.

He laughed bitterly, throat tight, painful weight in his chest, gazing at the sky. Look out there. No clouds. No birds. No planes. A vast nothing, stretching out over the sea. Perfect metaphor for his days since the accident. Over a month of this limbo, first medical leave, now personal. November 4 today, the accident had happened in early September, then surgery, rehabilitation—felt like forever. And it would be if he was one of the unlucky few who didn't recover post-surgery stability in his knee. The Air Force couldn't use a man who couldn't pass their physical test.

He'd done everything right, everything a Cartwright was supposed to do except want to be a flier. He'd majored in computer engineering at Chicago University, a career field in good demand in the Air Force. He'd excelled in his ROTC training, breezed through basic officer training, in both cases earning the friendship and respect of his fellow officers and commanders. His father and brothers were finally looking up to him, in spite of him being the first Cartwright nonpilot. He was on top, poised to continue at Keesler. He'd ace that, too. What could go wrong?

Everything.

He hadn't seen the damn cat, but he'd sure heard it and felt it. He'd gone down, twisting to one side rather than crush the little bastard, and had torn his ACL—his anterior cruciate ligament, to be precise—clean off the bone, and also damaged his cartilage. Badly. One second in time, a moment he'd take back and redo a hundred different ways if only he could. But, as Dad liked to say, life gave you no do-overs. You had to get everything very right the very first time.

The door buzzer rang, making him jump and curse the intrusion and the surprise. He'd been in town a few days and hadn't seen anyone. Only his family knew he was back, and he'd made it clear he wasn't ready for visits from any of them. This must be one of Mike's friends who didn't know Mike was training at Keesler. Where Jameson was supposed to be. Working hard, moving forward.

Two months of stagnation. Many, many more months to come.

He hauled himself off the couch, thinking a shower and shave were a good idea sometime this month—maybe for Thanksgiving—adjusted his knee brace, and limped through the living room and dining area to the front door, where he pressed the intercom.

"Yeah?"

"Lieutenant Cartwright?" A woman's voice.

He stiffened instinctively. Lieutenant? *Oh, man.* He should not be caught by Air Force personnel looking like such a mess. Why hadn't they called first?

He hadn't been answering his phone.

Crap.

But how had she found him? He'd given out his parents' address here in town.

Dad. Doggone it.

"Yes, ma'am."

"This is Kendra Lonergan."

Jameson did a double take. Kendra Lonergan? From high school? She was in the Air Force? He couldn't imagine it. There must be more than one Kendra Lonergan in the world. "How can I help you, ma'am?"

"Just checking in. I've been sent by Major Kornish."

His orthopedist at Keesler had sent someone here?

"Yes, ma'am." He pushed the buzzer so she could enter the building and hobbled into the bathroom, where he splashed water on his face, combed his dirty hair, cringing at the coarse stubble on his face, and reapplied deodorant, ashamed of how he'd let himself go. That done, he hesitated in the doorway, wondering if he could make it into the bedroom for a clean shirt before she got to his door. He was still slow moving, slower than he thought he should be by now, and didn't want to keep her waiting.

Jameson glanced down. Oh, man. Food stains. Clean shirt was a good idea.

In the bedroom, he'd barely gotten his old one off before the knock came, brisk and no-nonsense, four rapid taps.

Hurry. He yanked the new shirt over his head, part of his physical training uniform, and made it back as fast as he could. Bad sign, this continued pain. He tried not to think about it or what it could mean about the success—or not—of the surgery. Not to mention his chances of staying in the Air Force. Maybe he'd just gone overboard on his home exercises that morning.

"Coming." He reached the door and opened it.

Holy moly, Kendra Lonergan.

No, this couldn't be the same woman.

"Hi, Jameson."

He blinked. The voice was the same. It was her. "What happened to 'Lieutenant'?"

"Doesn't suit you." She stared unapologetically with green eyes he didn't remember being so big or so beautiful. She was also taller. Or at least thinner. And without glasses. Instead of the short ginger hair that looked as if her mother had cut it, she'd pulled back a long mass of auburn waves into a casual ponytail. In place of the drab succession of stretch pants and long shirts, she wore a short flowery skirt under layered tops in bright colors.

Kendra Lonergan was a knockout. And definitely not in any branch of the military.

"You look…different." He hid a wince. Could he say anything more inane?

"Huh." She looked him up and down. "So do you."

Yeah, well, tough. It was unfamiliar and extremely unpleasant to be ambushed like this. He'd been raised to be ready for anything at any time. "What are you doing here? How did you know where I was?"

"Dr. Kornish sent me. I told you."

He narrowed his eyes. "What for? What's your connection to him?"

"May I come in?"

"Why?"

"So I can look around. See how you live, how you're doing." With a flourish she produced a clipboard and a pen from an immense purse that seemed to be made of patches of brightly dyed leathers. "So I can report back."

"To my doctor…"

"Kornish, yes," she answered patiently, peering past him. He moved back as she stepped in, to avoid her getting too close. He was not at his best smelling.

"Why doesn't *he* ask me how I'm doing?"

"Because he'd rather hear it from me." She walked through the dining area to the center of the living room, turning in a slow circle, taking in the TV, the rumpled couch and the state of the coffee table, which made it clear he'd been camped out in this room for quite some time. "Nice place. You own it?"

"I'm house-sitting for a friend. Why does he trust you?"

"I'm a professional." She made some notes on her clipboard and moved toward the kitchen.

"Professional what?" He hobbled after her, trying not to stare at the way the flimsy material of her skirt clung to her very fine rear end.

"I help people recover." She peered into the sink at the pile of dirty dishes. Okay, he wasn't at his best. It was none of her business.

"If you're not a doctor…"

Kendra turned back toward him. "I'm not here for your physical recovery."

"No?" He was immediately hit with an image of her

helping him with his sexual recovery, which irritated him even more. "What, then? Spiritual recovery?"

"Something like that." She moved past him, toward his bedroom. He followed, hoping she didn't do more than glance at the bathroom. It was not pretty.

"My spiritual views are private."

"Nothing to do with religion." She stopped at the bedroom door, flicked him a glance and went inside. Jameson hadn't open the blinds yet. Or made his bed. Or picked up his dirty underwear. Well, she'd invited herself in. He owed her nothing. Though he wasn't wild about a description of this mess going into some report.

This was so effed up. "I wasn't expecting you."

"I called. You didn't answer the phone." She left his bedroom to glance into the master bedroom, still gleamingly neat because Jameson hadn't set foot in it.

"I didn't want to talk to anybody." He followed her back into the living room, feeling like a damn puppy now, more and more annoyed.

"Hmm." She planted herself on the black leather chair next to the sofa, looking as if she was going to stay awhile. "That's a problem."

"Why?"

"Because you have to talk to me." She consulted her clipboard. "First tell me how you're feeling."

He folded his arms across his chest. "If this is therapy crap, I'm not interested."

"Just checking in." She smiled too sweetly, green eyes sparkling. It occurred to him he'd never seen her smile at him. Not that this was a real smile. But damn, it lit up the room even so. "Can I have some water, Jameson?"

"Tell me exactly what you are doing here, what you—"

"Oh, sorry, your knee. I forgot. I'll get it."

"Get what?"

"Water."

Right. He stared after her as she disappeared into his kitchen, keeping his eyes resolutely on the back of her head this time. What the hell? Was she deaf? Crazy?

He made a sound of frustration. No, she wasn't crazy. She was Kendra, as she'd always been, totally sure of herself and incredibly determined. She'd driven him nuts all the way from elementary school through their senior year, simply because he'd never been able to rattle her. Apparently nothing had changed.

Moving carefully, he maneuvered himself onto the big chair she'd left—staking his claim, yeah, but it was also easier on his knee to sit there.

"Now." She came back with the water, stopped to peer at a picture of Mike in uniform with his arm around his wife, Pat, then plopped down onto the couch and drank. Jameson found himself staring at her rosy lips on the glass's rim, the glimpse of white teeth, the pale column of her throat working as she swallowed. Kendra Lonergan was in his apartment, looking like temptation itself. Kendra Lonergan. His brain refused to process it.

Finished, she put the glass down between a coffee mug from four days ago and a plastic tray from a fairly disgusting frozen dinner two nights earlier. She lifted the top page of her clipboard and peered at the sheet underneath.

"I would imagine you're feeling pretty horrible about all this. A big change, not part of your plan at all." Her voice was gentle, concerned. "A threat to everything you've worked for your whole life—a career as an officer in the Air Force."

Her compassion pissed him off even more, because it was so tempting to start whining like a baby. "No, no, this is the greatest."

"Uh-huh." Kendra didn't blink. "You're obviously still in pain."

"Nah."

"You sleeping okay?"

"Never better."

"How is your appetite?"

"Outstanding."

"Any weight gain or loss?"

"Neither."

"Energy level?"

"High."

"Sexual function?"

"Hey." He glared at her, wondering what she'd been scribbling on her sheet. "None of your business."

"Okay." She scrawled again.

"Are we done yet?"

Kendra lifted the clipboard to read. "Subject is exhibiting clear signs of depression, including sleeplessness, minimal appetite, weight loss and lethargy."

Right on all counts. How the hell did she know?

"He is also impotent."

Jameson bristled. "I am *not* impotent."

"Don't worry." She turned that sweet grin on him. This time she was really smiling. It made him want to smile back. Or growl at her. Or kiss her. "I won't tell."

"Kendra…"

"Teasing." Her smile grew wider. "I didn't really write that you were."

"You—" She'd gotten him. Fair game. "Is part of your treatment plan to make me want to toss you off my balcony?"

"If necessary." She capped her pen and tucked it back into the top of the clipboard. "How is your family reacting to your disability?"

"Fine."

"How is your dad reacting to your disability?"

He felt a rush of anger, first at his dad, then at her. She

had no right to question him about any of this. "Dad supports me no matter what."

She held his gaze for a moment, then nodded slowly. "That's what I thought."

Jameson swallowed. He felt a loss, almost a betrayal, as if he assumed she'd be able to see through that lie, too, and offer him—

What? A widdle huggy-wuggums?

For God's sake, get a grip, airman.

"How are your brothers coping with your—"

"Disability. They are also very happy for me." His knee was throbbing. He took hold of his thigh with both hands and swung the leg up to rest on the pile of Mike's *GQ* magazines he'd arranged so he could elevate his injury. "I mean they are also supportive. At all times."

"I remember that about your brothers."

Her tone was quiet, but he sensed the steel in it. A pang of guilt lessened his anger. Kendra knew Mark and Hayden. For years he'd been their puppet, admiring their dadlike toughness and what he'd perceived then as leadership. In college ROTC and basic training he'd learned that a true leader inspired and respected his men. That's the kind of leader Jameson wanted to be in the Air Force. A new kind of Cartwright.

But it looked as if he bloody well wouldn't get the chance for nearly another year. Possibly not at all.

He shifted in frustration, causing a landslide in the pile of magazines under his foot. His leg fell, twisting, onto the table with a thud that shot pain from his knee to his hip.

He was dimly aware of Kendra running from the room. She was back beside him so quickly he wondered if he'd blacked out.

"Here you go. This should help." He felt the chill of a cold pack over his knee, then through the lingering haze of pain, the blessed cool of a wet cloth across his forehead and a warm hand on his shoulder. "Should I call someone? Can I get you meds?"

He shook his head, which was clearing rapidly at her touch. He didn't need baby nursing. "I'm fine."

"Oh, yeah, I can tell. You're in perfect shape." Her voice was exasperated. "Here. Let me at least do this."

She sat on the coffee table and gently lifted his leg into her lap, somehow managing not to hurt him or disturb the cold pack.

"What are you *doing?*" He was unnecessarily snappy from the pain and oddly panicky for some other reason he couldn't identify.

"I'm going to aim karate chops at your knee until you tell me the location of the missing computer chip."

What the—

She didn't, of course. He didn't expect her to. But he also didn't expect what she did do. Carefully but firmly, she began to massage his feet through his socks, which, thank God, were clean that morning.

Her touch was magical, finding and tending to places in his toes, the arch of his foot, his heel, places he didn't realize were in such desperate need of attention. Slowly, the tension and pain in his body started to ease, began to be replaced by relaxation and pleasure.

Wait, what the hell was he doing letting Kendra Lonergan touch his feet?

"Uh, yeah, thanks, that's fine. I'm fine."

"Good." She didn't stop, moved upward, tackling the tight muscles of his ankles, his calves, along his shins.

It was helping. Doggone, it was helping. That spot… *there,* oh, yeah.

But it drove him crazy that she still wasn't listening to him, that he felt, once again, out of control around this woman, out of his element. "You can stop now, Kendra."

"I know." She lifted his leg and put it back on the coffee table, leaving his foot and lower leg tingling from the warmth of her touch, aching for more. He didn't like that she'd come into his house and upended everything about his day and body and attitude in less than fifteen minutes.

He wanted her out of here. He wanted to go back to his bad-assed mood, refining his misery to an art. He didn't want to cope with people who irritated him, seeing his current poor showing as a human being reflected so clearly back to himself.

"You can go now. You should go now."

"You think?" She knelt close to him, smelling flower fresh, and put her hands around his thigh, safely above his knee. She started on the tightness his injury caused in his quads and in his hamstrings, loosening the muscles, increasing the blood flow to his leg. Jameson sucked in a breath. Her hands were strong, long fingered, with clear pink polish.

They were very talented hands.

His cock noticed.

He was wearing sweatpants.

Kendra would notice.

Way more humiliation than he should be expected to bear in one day. "Stop, Kendra. Now."

She stopped, looking up at him with a bemused expression. "We're done, huh."

"Done." He dropped his hands into his lap. She glanced at them as she got to her feet. Of course she'd noticed.

"Better though?"

He nodded stiffly. "Thanks."

"Sure." She sat back down, her color high, picked up her clipboard and stared at it for a moment without seeming to register anything. "So."

"So?"

"We were talking about your family."

"No." He shook his head pointedly. "We were finished talking about my family."

"Ah, yes." Her smile was back. "So we were."

"In fact, I think we're finished talking, period."

"No, not yet." She kept the smile on. This woman did not intimidate easily. She did not intimidate at all. He should know that from their past. He'd been prodded into humiliating this girl more than once, though it hadn't ever quite worked out. Deep down he'd resented his brothers' manipulation, of him and of her. A part of him had cheered when she'd refused to play the traditional role of picked-on student. That same damn part was still admiring her now.

"You're on personal leave, waiting to recover, so you can go back to Keesler and be assigned to a desk job until you can pass the physical exam and be cleared again for worldwide duty. Then you'll be able to resume your specialty training."

He clenched his teeth. If she knew it and he knew it, why bring it up? "Yes."

"If your surgery is unsuccessful, you will most likely be honorably discharged. Since you're planning to be a career officer, how would that feel?"

"Super."

"Uh-huh. I thought so." She scrawled something triumphantly. "Okay, moving on."

"How long is this going to take?"

"You have somewhere to go?"

He held her gaze. "This is an intrusion into my day."

"Of…"

"What do you mean?"

"Your day of what? Pain? TV watching? Brooding? Unbearable waiting?"

"Yes." He spoke through clenched teeth. "It's all I have right now."

"Doesn't have to be that way. What are your hobbies?"

"Oh, for—"

"Okay, okay." Her laughter at his exasperation made him want to smile, too. Instead he glared at her, because that was much safer in a way he couldn't quite comprehend and didn't want to. Not while she was in the room smelling like a flower garden and making him hard with a few strokes of her hands, which none of the PTs at Keesler hospital had come close to doing. "One more question."

"Promise this is the last?"

"Cross my heart." She made a graceful gesture that brought his attention to the dark shadow of cleavage at her neckline.

He must be going completely nuts. "Shoot."

She leaned forward, pinning him with her lovely green eyes. He held her gaze, keeping his cold, impersonal, not wanting her to know how she got to him—a weird reversal of their roles in grade school. "What are you most afraid of, Jameson?"

A laugh broke from him. Oh, no. No way. She wasn't getting that stuff out of him. "That's easy."

"Go on." She looked hopeful, but wary. Smart woman.

"I'm afraid..." He leaned forward to match her posture, ignoring the complaint in his hamstring. "That you'll never, ever get the hell out of here."

To his surprise, she burst out laughing, a musical cascade that shone some light into his darkness and made him feel taller, straighter, lighter himself, though he kept from laughing with her, or even smiling.

Kendra stood and laid a friendly hand on his shoulder on her way past him. "I think that was the first straight answer I've gotten all morning. Except about you not being impotent."

"Could be."

"Okay, you win. I'm off. Don't get up."

"Wasn't going to."

She was still smiling, tall and slender and graceful, her legs shapely and strong looking under the short full skirt, sandals with some sparkly metal on them emphasizing the pretty shape of her feet. "Enjoy the rest of your day."

"You bet."

She tipped her head, looking at him mischievously. "It was very interesting seeing you again, Jameson."

"Surreal."

She nodded once, then walked away, the way she'd said his name lingering behind her. The closer she got to the door the darker the space around him felt. In another three seconds she'd be gone and he'd be back with the pain, the brooding, the agony of waiting, his fate in someone else's control.

At the door, she lifted a hand. He clenched his jaw, stifling the absurd desire to stop her.

Then she disappeared through the door and closed it behind her.

Click.

The room went dead, devoid of sound and light and life.

Jameson hauled himself up and limped into the kitchen, his knee still pissed at him for the thumping he'd given it, mood reverting to its earlier foulness, only now it seemed even less bearable. The reason made him angrier and more frustrated and stir-crazy.

He had no idea when or whether Kendra was coming back.

3

MATTY CROSSED THE alley behind the Pasadena Playhouse and stepped through the artists' entrance onto El Molino Avenue. The show had gone well tonight; she was pumped. The usual stage-door crowd had gathered to see the actors emerge, but given that she had such a small part, Matty put on an impersonal smile and didn't even hope to be asked for her autograph. That way she couldn't be disappointed, and the few occasions she had been asked were a real surprise and pleasure.

The night was cool, mid-sixties, she'd guess, a beautiful night to be out. She had a sudden impulse to drive to the ocean, maybe Santa Monica, which wasn't far from where she lived in Culver City. Hang out on the pier and have a drink. Maybe her roommate and longtime friend, Jesse, would want to come with her.

She was digging in her purse for her cell when it rang. Kendra!

"Hey, Kendra, how are you?"

"Fine. Is this a bad time?"

"No, it's perfect. What's going on?" She tried not to sound too anxious, which was hard, considering she was... too anxious.

"Your brother is definitely having a tough time."

Matty grimaced, stomach sinking. "I know."

"But all is not lost. He's in pain, physically, which will

dissipate, and emotionally, which will be harder. But I think—*think*—he'll let me help him."

"And will you?"

Kendra gave a low, dry chuckle that came from somewhere Matty didn't understand. "Yes. I will."

Relief exploded out of her in a long exhale. "*Thank you.*"

"I might live to regret it."

"No, no, you won't. That is…" She laughed breathlessly. "You *will* live, you won't regret it. What will you do for him?"

"First? Clean up the place and cook him some decent meals. Then we'll try getting out to reconnect with some of the world he knows and introduce a bit of a world he doesn't. See what works. It can be a slow process, but he's not past help."

"Oh, my gosh, Kendra." Emotions jammed in Matty's throat. Hearing that Jameson was not in true despair, that he wasn't going to do something crazy like kill himself… ugh, she couldn't even think about it. That wasn't an option. "I have no idea how to thank you."

"Really, don't be too excited. I haven't done anything yet but piss him off."

"Ha!" Matty nodded sympathetically. "That's not hard these days. Even I can do that."

"We'll see if I can get around the mood. I'll give it a try. For old times' sake."

Matty caught the bite of irony. Hmm. There might be something there. "Kendra…did you and Jameson ever date?"

"*Date?* Jameson and me? *God,* no."

"Huh. Okay, sorry." Matty frowned. Pretty violent denial. The main reason Matty had such huge hopes Kendra could help Jameson was because she'd been sure Jameson

had had feelings for her back in middle and high school.
Maybe she'd been wrong.

"I'll stay in touch and let you know how things are
going."

"Thank you. Thank you so much. I—" Matty rolled her
eyes. "I can't stop thanking you."

Kendra laughed. "Not a problem. Talk to you soon.
Take care."

Matty ended the call and stood, pressing the phone to
her cheek, trying to contain her excitement. This could
be good. This could be really, really good. She wanted
Jameson free of pain, but also free of the family pressure
to be something he might not be. She'd done her medical
research, she knew ACL repair surgery could be unsuccessful, that there was a small chance Jameson could end
up out of a career in the Air Force, the first Cartwright
discharged since God knew when.

But maybe for him that wouldn't be the worst thing in
the world. Maybe Kendra could help him rediscover living
life his own way, as he'd been doing in Spain, working for
a U.S. company, taking art and English courses at St. Louis
University in Madrid and dating a dancer, before their father had reached his patience limit and dragged him back
to the U.S. and the Cartwright Plan for Life.

A hand bumped her arm. She automatically moved
away.

After that, Jameson had—

"Mattingly?"

Matty's head jerked up. Only one person outside her
family ever called her by her full name.

Her eyes met a pair of deep brown ones under a shock
of wheat-colored hair that had gone slightly gray at the
temples. Somehow she managed to stifle a gasp.

"Chris." *Calm. Stay very calm.* As if she'd just bumped
into him a week ago, not wrenched herself away from him

back…how long had it been now? Years. She'd been a senior at Pomona College. He'd been an associate professor. Bad choices had happened. Drama. Pain. Deep love, and the best sex she'd ever had. Not that she was comparing. "What a surprise to see you."

Surprise was putting it mildly. If she didn't make sure to keep breathing, she'd pass out on the sidewalk.

Luckily, being raised by Jeremiah and Katherine Cartwright had taught her how to suppress every vestige of human emotion. Not a good technique on stage, but it could come in damn handy during real life.

"I saw the show." He seemed calm, too. But then, he always did. Except when he was laughing or about to come. "You were great."

Matty accepted his compliment with a polite nod. She had a few solo lines and part of one song—no bragging rights, but she took pride in having been chosen for that much, and in doing her role well. God knew she never took any theater job for granted. "Glad you enjoyed it."

"It was…" He was looking at her too intently, with eyes that were too warm. "It was a shock to see you, Matty, I admit."

"A good one, I hope." She was appalled at the automatic response. *Do not flirt, Matty.*

"Best one I had all week." He smiled down at her and boom, too many memories came rushing back—the nights of passion, the blissful stolen hours together.

What the hell? Had she learned nothing?

"Chri-i-is?" A woman's voice behind them, fake sweet. *"There* you are."

And there she was, slim and elegant in some high-fashion drapey tunic thing she pulled off to perfection. Exactly the type Chris should be with.

"Zoe, this is a former student, Matty Cartwright. Matty, this is Zoe Savannah."

Matty nearly snickered. *Zoe Savannah?* She was perfect. Right down to the leopard-print pants.

Smiling with as much warmth as she could muster, Matty chided herself. Zoe had every right to date Chris. She was closer to his age, for one thing—*meow*. And she was probably a lovely person. Or maybe she wasn't and they deserved each other. Either worked. "Nice to meet you, Zoe."

"Oh, me, too! I *loved* the show." She whacked Chris playfully on the arm with her program and went into gales of laughter for no apparent reason. "And now I see why Chris was staring at you all night. He knows you! I was afraid it was love at first sight."

Actually, it had been.

"No, no, nothing like that." He glanced uncomfortably at Matty, who refused to look uncomfortable.

"You look great, Chris." She wasn't lying, unfortunately. He looked incredible, hair still thick, that new sexy touch of frost at the temple. He'd always reminded her of a cross between Ben Affleck and Russell Crowe: boy-next-door handsome but with powerful masculinity backing it up. "Still teaching at Pomona?"

"They haven't fired me yet."

They should have when she was there.

"Silly." Zoe whacked him again. "You're tenured."

Matty smiled again, for real this time. She was happy for him. He'd wanted that very badly. "Congratulations. A great accomplishment."

"Thank you, Matty." He really needed to stop looking at her like that, half amused, half hungry. It was horrendously unsettling.

"Well!" She glanced pointedly at her watch and lifted a hand in cheery farewell. "I'm due to meet someone for a drink. Great to see you, Chris, and to meet you, Zoe."

Not waiting for answers, she turned and headed for her

red Kia Sportage parked in the lot behind the theater, her cheeks hot, mind whirling. So. Finally, it had happened. She'd seen Chris Hamilton.

For the first couple of years after graduation she'd imagined bumping into him, fantasized about it, actually. How after one glance into her eyes, he'd tell her he'd made a terrible mistake letting her go, that he couldn't live without her, that he loved her desperately and always would and blah blah blah blah.

More years had gone by, six in total by now, and she'd stopped worrying about seeing him. Stopped worrying she'd fall apart, beg him to take her back, stopped worrying about the pain she was sure only he could bring. Because she was over it, thank you very much. There'd been other men since, and no, she was not comparing.

The only really awful part was that after all her efforts, after she'd reached a real understanding of the forces that drove their passion, analyzed that passion to death and accepted not only that it was over, but that its being over was for the best, tonight it turned out Chris Hamilton in the flesh was still dangerously attractive to her. Whatever had pulled them together, in spite of the utter stupidity of professor and student hooking up, that power was still there.

"Matty."

Crap. Matty closed her eyes, considered pretending she hadn't heard him, but he wouldn't buy it. Probably because it was ridiculous.

She whirled to face him. He stopped short, watching her warily. Damn him, why hadn't he put on weight or wrinkled or just turned ugly, for heaven's sake? He looked fabulous. Six feet of good-looking that knew how to do the sheet tango better than anyone she—

No, she was not comparing.

"What do you want, Chris?" Matty bit her lip, shocked

at how bitter and angry she sounded. So much for putting her feelings safely behind her.

"I want to see you. I want— I just want to see you."

"Ha!" The syllable came out without her permission, a mixture of shock, horror and a tiny explosion of pleasure. "How does Zoe feel about that?"

He put his hands on his hips, pushing back his jacket. Stomach still flat. Thighs still long and muscular under casual pants. Darn him.

"Zoe is a colleague."

"Oh, so you're doing those now, too?"

"Low, Matty." The bastard spoke calmly. She could not get to him with insults.

Matty checked herself. She should not *want* to get to him at *all*.

"Sorry. You know me. If it's in my brain, it comes out my mouth." She inhaled slowly to settle herself. "I just don't think getting together is a good idea."

"But…how is that possible?" He looked genuinely confused. "I only have good ideas."

Her laughter was reluctant. Charm as well as sex appeal. Chris had it all, the slime bucket. "No, thank you."

He took a step toward her.

Turn around. Turn around and walk away now.

"You look great, Matty." His gentleness enveloped her. Too much intimacy. "I like your hair long."

"Yeah, thanks." She was not going to tell him how fabulous *he* looked.

"You doing okay?"

"Yes! Fine! Great!" Her voice cracked. He'd notice. He was good at that. And what woman wasn't a sucker for a man who noticed? It's just that *she* hadn't noticed six years ago, that while she had fallen madly in love with him, he was only interested in what lay between her legs. "I'm getting theater work pretty regularly, and I have a side business in real estate that's picking up."

"Good. Good for you." His brows drew down. He pursed his lips, the way he did when he had something uncomfortable to say. "I've thought about you a lot over the years."

Me, too. She stood silent, hands in her jacket pocket clutching her car keys.

"Well." He touched his forehead as if he were tipping his hat and turned away, a gesture at once so familiar and dear to her that tears threatened. *Six years ago, Matty. For God's sake.*

She walked rapidly toward her car, breaking into a run when her steps weren't getting her there fast enough.

Damn it. *Damn it.* What the hell was wrong with her? How could she let him affect her so deeply?

She unlocked the car, wrenched open the door and hurled herself inside, started the engine and peeled out of her parking space.

Santa Monica Pier, here I come. She was going to go there alone and drink herself into a stupor, how pathetic was that?

Very! And it was exactly what she was in the mood for. A long parade of drinks, surrounded by happy partyers and the wild, wavy ocean. She'd sit by herself, looking mysterious and sultry, indulging memories she hadn't allowed herself to call up for years, brooding and wallowing in emotional agony.

Then she'd sleep soundly in the apartment she shared with her best friend and be fine tomorrow. Chris would again be safely part of her past and she could really move on this time, having gotten this first post-relationship encounter over with and ending up unscathed.

An hour later, she was standing at the pier's end, inhaling deeply, pulling her jacket around her for warmth against the stiff, salty wind. Of course she was much too sensible to get drunk. One beer and the crush of bodies around her had gotten annoying, the noise not conducive to proper misery. Her big scene, like most, played better in fantasy than in real life.

But she loved it out here, staring at the black sea, a whole world under there, not one single resident of which had gotten his or her heart crushed by Chris Hamilton.

They'd met in class her senior year. He was teaching a seminar on music and culture in Paris around the turn of the twentieth century. She'd thought he was hot from the first day. In fact, she and her girlfriends—including a new friend named Clarisse—had giggled and oohed and aahed and had a great time dissecting his every word, gesture and look. As crushes went, hers seemed particularly intense, but so what? He was a professor. She was a student. And never the twain shall sleep together.

They'd gotten to know each other through a shared love of all things French, had talked earnestly after class one day, then another, had gone out for croissants and café au lait. Then lunch at a French restaurant he particularly enjoyed…

Later they'd admit that they'd known what was happening, but since they hadn't the slightest intention of doing anything about it, the attraction was harmless. What counted were the ideas they shared, their similar views and tastes and humor.

Ironically, the crossing of the line had happened because of Clarisse's first "suicide attempt," a low-risk grab for attention after a guy dumped her.

Eventually, Matty had realized Clarisse suffered from pretty serious mental issues. Compulsive lying, socio-pathic tendencies and a deep need to screw her friends' boyfriends. But at the time, Matty had been terrified and extremely upset. Who wouldn't be? The woman had tried to take her own life!

Matty had called nine-one-one and ridden with Clarisse to the hospital. When she'd heard Clarisse was going to survive—of course she was—Matty had finally broken down, tears that wouldn't stop. Walking home to her dorm, she'd run into Chris, returning from a Pomona orchestra concert. One look at her face and he'd invited her out for coffee. She hadn't wanted to be out in public looking like hell. No problem, he'd drive her to his apartment, where he'd set up the spare bedroom if she wanted to stay over. They'd shared a bottle of wine. Talked until very, very late.

She'd never made it to the spare bedroom.

The next morning they'd agreed it could never happen again. They weren't that kind of people. He was too old for her—more than ten years older. She was his student. An affair was wrong, and he could lose his job. They'd stay away from each other.

They couldn't stay away from each other.

For the next six months they'd tried to break up, gotten back together, then did both again. All those agonies of longing and pain followed by the joys of giving in to temptation, the guilt, the fear—by the time Clarisse caught on and set her sights on Chris, Matty was frankly exhausted. When she'd caught them together, along with the pain there had been relief. Finally it was truly over. No more temptation. Because Matty understood what he was and how foolish she'd been.

Chris had come after her, he'd explained. He'd laid the blame on Clarisse. It wasn't what it looked like, he'd sworn to her...

Please. It was always what it looked like.

Three weeks later, Clarisse took enough sleeping pills to look ill, but not really threaten her life, and Matty had known it was over for them, too. She'd waited, even tell-

ing herself she shouldn't, but Chris hadn't come looking
for her again.

On the pier now, arms wrapped around herself, squinting into the wind, Matty thought about how she'd come
such a long way since then. She'd built a good, rich life
for herself. Dated a couple of guys seriously, though none
who took her over the way Chris had.

Yes, she was comparing. She'd always been comparing.

But unfairly. Her feelings in college had been intensified by her youth and inexperience, by the lure of the forbidden, by the perfect bubble in which their encounters
took place. She hadn't met his friends, he hadn't interacted
with hers. They'd had no problems to cope with but the
drama of their own taboo passion.

A tear made its way down her cheek. She flung it forward into the sea, sniffed angrily and turned to go home.

Enough. She'd done what she'd come here to do.
Brooded. Remembered. Cried one beautiful tear. The actress side of her had been fed.

Now she'd do her father proud, march home, get up at
0700 hours and take on the next day of her life.

4

KENDRA PULLED INTO the parking lot at Villas of the Pacific, CD player blaring Adele's "Don't You Remember." Villas? Really? She could have sworn they were apartment buildings. Nice ones, yes. But a villa needed a sprawling estate. Jameson didn't quite fit that mold, but he'd also looked painfully out of place in his friend's apartment, which was decorated with modern art, odd sculptures and plants. Jameson belonged in a more traditionally masculine interior, all leather and dark wood, books and model fighter jets, one plant, always about to die...

She found a visitor spot and turned off the engine, sat for a moment in the sudden silence, annoyed at herself for being nervous. Hadn't she been through all this after her visit here the day before? Yes, she had. Going forward she'd continue bypassing Jameson's obnoxious behavior, understanding that it came from his pain and anger. She'd focus only on how she could help him. And she'd ignore the...complication.

Finding herself a teeny, tiny bit attracted to Jameson after all these years did not mean the world was about to end. He was an attractive man. So what? He was also an entitled jerk, who happened to be in a terrible situation and needed Kendra's help. Kendra had agreed to help him because...quite honestly, she was curious. Who was this guy now? Who had he always been? Why had he chosen *her* to make miserable for so long?

One thing she had definitely decided—no more massages. Yikes. Not that his erection had been significant. He was a guy, one who probably hadn't had any in a long time. His reaction had undoubtedly surprised him as much as it had her, especially after so many years of rather juvenile enmity between them.

Out of the car, she took a moment to gaze over the red-tiled roofs and palm trees toward the rust-colored cliffs that dropped to the edge of the vast Pacific. Blue sky today, a good breeze—the sight calmed and filled her as it always did. She could bring beauty and positive feelings and hope back into Jameson's life if he would let her. She'd focus on that. The erection, not so much.

Today's goal: clean the apartment, cook him a healthy meal. Push him gently to talk about his situation. Duck when he threw things at her. Maybe throw a few things back.

Kendra turned to unload the groceries and cleaning supplies she'd brought for this visit, one bag of each. Above all, she'd stay cheerful and brisk in spite of his sarcasm and cranky bad-boy mood, intent on what she was there to accomplish. She was not the same cowed high school kid having to fake self-confidence. She had the real thing now.

At the entrance to Jameson's building, she balanced one bag on her hip and the other on a raised knee, trying to free up a hand to push the buzzer. Her finger had almost made it when a guy pushed out the door and let her in with a warm smile. Well. Looked like she'd catch Jameson by surprise again. She'd called that morning and left a message after another client canceled a late-afternoon meeting, letting him know she'd have time for him today. He hadn't called back to say he wouldn't be in or didn't want to see her, so here she was.

On the second floor she turned right and strode down the cream hallway, enlivened by dark green carpeting and prints of landscape paintings on the walls. At his door she balanced the bags again and knocked, four fast raps, *I'm here, ready or not,* then stepped back to wait, bright smile in place.

Nothing.

Was he home? Had he planned to be out just to annoy her?

A noise inside. Her heart gave a little flip and she scoffed at herself. *Still scared of the big bully, Kendra?*

The door opened.

Whoa.

Jameson had cleaned up. Gone was the stubble, ditto the greasy hair and wrinkled clothes. He looked really good.

Really good.

Unwrinkled navy-and-white Air Force T-shirt over neat khaki shorts. Great legs, scarred on one knee. Awesome chest.

Had she referred to him as an attractive man?

She'd lied. He was smoking hot.

And he was standing there, stone-faced, staring at her. Was she gawking? Well, *yeah,* but she didn't think it was that obvious.

"Come in." He stepped back to let her pass.

"Hello, Jameson." She pushed through the door. First thing that hit her was the absence of crap strewn all over the living room. "Wow, you cleaned."

"Mike has a service." He seemed taller today? Maybe he was just standing straighter. In any case, he already looked 100 percent better, and Kendra hadn't even started her program yet. Matty would be happy.

"Looks like you resumed your human form." She smiled at him, cheerful nurse, big sister, teacher, counselor, whatever kind of person would not want to have wild sex with him all over the apartment. "Did you get my message?"

"What's in the bags?" He took one from her, apparently possessing at least some gentlemanly tendencies.

"That's cleaning stuff, obviously not necessary now. This one is groceries."

"I've got food."

"Not this food." She took the bag into the kitchen, aware of him limping after her.

"So, what, you're taking over my life now?"

"Every bit of it, yes." She put the bag on the counter and started unloading. He was still playing cranky, but his tone didn't sound quite as bitter as the day before. More progress. "How's your knee today?"

"Better than ever."

"Still in pain, huh."

"I love pain."

"*That's* lucky." Always the tough guy. Funny how grief affected people so differently. Some closed up, like Jameson. She called those Turtles. Others, like herself, plunged into activity to alleviate in others what they were suffering themselves. She called those Avengers. Then there were Pancakes, utterly flattened by the experience, and Curators, who turned their memories and memorabilia into museums of those they'd lost, and on and on. "Your home exercises going well?"

"Yes, ma'am."

"Good." She didn't really need to ask. His type would want to get better as quickly as he could. Athletes, military, anyone who depended on his or her body would be driven to stay in the best shape possible and didn't mind the work it took to get there.

She'd just try not to think about how his body was already in the best shape possible—broad shoulders, flat stomach, long legs, no doubt impressive muscles all over…

Ahem. Kendra had a job to do, and it didn't entail stand-ing around imagining Jameson Cartwright naked.

"I'll make you a basic spaghetti sauce. You can eat some, freeze the rest when you're sick of it. You like to cook?"

"Haven't done much lately." He seemed huge in the small kitchen. She'd have to get him sitting on the other side of the counter so she didn't bump into him every time she moved.

"It's easy. I'll show you. You can make this. Anyone can make this."

She pointed to the ingredients neatly laid out on the counter. "Ground beef, carrots, onions, tomato puree, beef broth and cream. Want to chop onions?"

"Chopping onions will help me come to terms with los-ing a year of my life, Kendra?"

She gave him another unreturned smile, not surprised by his sarcasm—she'd heard it all—but shocked by the jolt of sympathy. That was a switch. She'd spent her grade school years, coached by her parents, vainly trying to feel sorry for Jameson Cartwright when she didn't want to, and now she was feeling sorry for him automatically—though she still didn't want to. "I think you'd be surprised what can help."

He shrugged. "You're the expert."

"That is so true." Kendra found a cutting board already out on the counter and selected a knife from the magnetic strip next to the sink. She'd spent last night researching ACL surgery and the recovery process. Long and slow, the worst kind of sentence for a man like Jameson. Nine months, on average, to recover normal use of the knee—though many people were never back to 100 percent—and often pain lingered after that. "You know how to chop on-ions? If you don't, I'll show you."

"I know how."

"Yeah?" She pointed to the chair by the stretch of counter that doubled as a table. "Have a seat there. I'll pass you stuff to do."

"Yes, ma'am." He sat.

"Did you help your mom in the kitchen?" She passed him the board and knife.

"Sometimes."

"She a good cook?"

"Average."

Kendra turned back to the sauce ingredients. Yes, she was getting one-word answers, but at least he was answering, and no sarcasm this time. One of her clients had been so depressed, Kendra would show up at their early appointments and pretty much talk to herself.

"My mom was an amazing cook." She ripped open the red plastic net holding the onions. "Always experimenting with other cuisines. We had Thai food, Indian, Chinese, you name it."

"*Was* an amazing cook?" For the first time, his voice lifted to a normal conversational tone.

"Yes." Kendra put a large onion down on the cutting board in front of him. The news of her parents' deaths had been pretty big locally. Ken and Sandra Lonergan had been active in the Palos Verdes Estates community and in the schools. She would have expected Jameson to hear somehow, even having been away at college in Chicago. But maybe he didn't have long catch-up chats with his parents the way Kendra had had with hers. Or maybe he'd heard and forgotten, since it wouldn't have meant much to his life. Hard to imagine sometimes, since it had pretty much imploded hers. She understood so well when clients said they'd wake up day after day, surprised the sun was still shining. "My mom passed away a couple of years ago."

"I'm sorry." His words were clearly heartfelt.

"Thank you." She couldn't look at him, still found it

hard to speak when she talked about the accident. "Chop the onion whatever size you want. Doesn't really matter."

"Okay."

She set about peeling carrots, feeling his eyes on her, her throat still tight. Music would help. Kendra generally liked an uplifting soundtrack around clients to mitigate silences when they occurred and lessen the pressure to produce constant conversation. "Does Mike have any CDs?"

"Yeah, I think in the cabinet under the TV." He was already on his feet, hobbling into the living room.

Well. Doing something nice for her. Another hint that he was capable of pleasant behavior. Unless he was terrified Kendra was about to do something girlie and horrible, like cry. "Thanks, Jameson."

"Uh-huh."

She turned back to her carrots. Baby steps…though it bothered her he was still limping two months after surgery. Maybe it was the nasty jolt he'd given his knee the day before when she was here, but by now he should be able to—

A horrific blast of death metal came over the speakers. Kendra yelled and jumped, then flung herself toward the kitchen door to peer into the living room. He could not be serious.

The music went off. Blessed silence.

"Uh." Jameson was grinning, crouching in a rather painful-looking position in front of the CD player. "That was not on purpose."

"I am glad to hear that." She put her hand to her chest, this time smiling genuinely instead of in polite encouragement. He was ten times more handsome when he wasn't scowling, though he managed to turn even the grouchy look into an appealing bad-boy aura.

But this…if Kendra didn't already know her heart was pounding from the scare, she might think he was affecting her. But, um, of course it wasn't that. "I think they play that music in hell."

"Wait." He actually chuckled. "You know this CD?"

"God, no."

"It's called *Satan's Soundtrack*." He held up three fingers in a Scout's-honor pledge. "Not kidding."

"Nice." She stepped farther out of the kitchen toward him. "What's the band called?"

"Flagrant Death Meat."

Kendra cracked up. "You aren't serious!"

"I am." He held up the CD, chuckling.

"That is just too weird."

Their laughter trailed off. Their gazes held. He stayed crouched. She stayed in the doorway. A dozen yards apart, they might as well have been chest to chest.

Kendra swallowed. Moments of intimacy with her clients could be important. Sometimes they allowed people the safety to talk about something real. All she wanted to do was hurl herself back into the kitchen to escape Jameson and the strong pull he exerted.

He turned abruptly to the TV cabinet. "I'll find something else."

"Great, thanks." Kendra fled to the sink, shaken by her inability to take charge of the moment. She could not back down from a connection that might prove helpful to Jameson. That was the core of her practice—inspiring trust, creating a safe environment into which clients could dump their innermost fears and feelings.

Instead, Kendra had stared at him as if he were a bug pinned to a foam board.

The smooth strains of an entirely different type of music filled the apartment. The Lumineers. Just the right atmosphere.

"Better?" Jameson limped back into the room and took his seat.

"Much, thank you."

Chopping and peeling sounds filled the kitchen. Kendra took a deep breath, determined to get back on track. "Have you been out of the house since I saw you?"

"'Go outside and play. Get some fresh air.'" He did a high-voiced mom impression.

Kendra cracked up. "Your mother?"

"That's her."

She peered at him over her shoulder. She'd always imagined Jameson as an outdoor type, playing ball with his brothers, building forts, killing things… She couldn't remember much about Katherine Cartwright. Just an impression that she was a good deal younger than her husband. "What did you want to be doing indoors instead?"

"I dunno."

"Yes, you do."

He sent her an annoyed glance. He was chopping the onion with such painstaking care that she almost started giggling.

"Need a ruler?"

"You got one?" He *almost* smiled.

"Tell me what you did inside at home when you were a kid."

This time he didn't bother answering, just looked completely disgusted.

Kendra turned back to her chopping. "Did you listen to music? Write stories? Play with action figures? Watch TV?"

"Not TV. Not in our house."

"No? What, then?" Kendra waited, pushing the carrot peelings down the disposal. Jameson would talk or he wouldn't. At least he was thinking about the answer. "How about I ask you again what you're most afraid of? You seemed to love that question last time."

He made a sound of exasperation. "I'm actually most afraid you'll keep asking me that until you like the answer."

"You can count on it." She rinsed her hands in the sink, dried them leisurely on a San Francisco Giants hand towel.

"I liked to draw."

"Yeah?" she answered calmly, cheering inside. Score one for Kendra. She'd schedule that in as one of their activities. Maybe they could combine a beach trip with a sketching session. "Were you any good?"

"Probably not."

She'd bet he was. Guys like Jameson wouldn't bring up something they were bad at.

"I took art classes at St. Louis University when I lived in Madrid."

"You were enrolled there?" She started searching for a grater in Mike's cabinets, keeping her voice casual, as if she were only politely interested, to keep him comfortable and talking.

"No." His response was quick and tinged with bitterness. "I did AFROTC at Chicago University. But all us kids took a year off to travel before college."

"What a great idea." She opened another cabinet.

"I took two."

"Why?"

"Because I'm so special."

"I knew that about you." Kendra pulled a gleaming box grater triumphantly from the back of the next cabinet. The thing had probably never been used. "Why two years?"

"One wasn't enough."

"I can imagine." She spoke offhandedly, picked up the carrots. "Fun times."

"I wasn't ready to start life yet."

"I see." She set up the grater opposite him on the counter, dying to press him further. Not ready to start life or the Air Force? Why the delay? "What was her name?"

"Marta."

"Wait, really?" Kendra sent him a surprised look. "I was actually kidding."

"I'm not." His voice turned a little wistful. Kendra picked up the carrot and started shredding it viciously, appalled to find herself annoyed. What the hell? She liked to think of herself as the soul of emotional generosity. If Jameson had found the love of his life in Madrid, that was wonderful.

"Onion's chopped." He pushed the board toward her. "What's next?"

"You still in touch with her?"

"You think that's your business?"

"Not in the least." She finished the carrot and scooped the shreds onto the cutting board next to his neatly chopped onion, brought them both over to the stove. "I've never been to Spain. Tell me about Madrid."

"Great architecture, art, food, people. I got a part-time job in an English bookstore, took classes and mostly did what I wanted."

"Big change from high school and living at home."

"Yeah. I loved it too much. Dad had to come get me, to remind me I had a future, which I couldn't spend living in the moment."

"Sounds like a parent." She turned to grab the hamburger as an excuse to see his face. "But for the sake of argument, why couldn't you?"

"Because, Kendra." He held her gaze, his smile growing slowly. "That's not what Cartwrights do."

"I got that impression." Kendra nodded calmly, weighing whether it was smarter to keep pushing now or pull back. And whether she should stand there staring into his blue eyes much longer, because she was going to start thinking about him naked again. She turned and pulled out a large saucepan from under the sink.

"I'm not in touch with Marta."

"As you said, none of my business." She felt herself coloring. A tiny tense spot loosened in her chest. *Kendra, you are strictly forbidden from getting crushes on clients.* "Any idea where the olive oil is?"

"Try that cabinet?" He pointed.

She found the oil and added a glug to the pan, waited until it was shimmering to add the onion and carrot.

"What did *you* do after high school?"

Kendra suppressed a snort. *Recovered from you, you expletive.* "I went on to UCLA, majored in psychology."

"Ah." He came to stand next to her, watching her stir the vegetables. She wished he'd sit back down again. His nearness was so…near. "So you followed in the parental footsteps, too."

Funny, she'd never thought about it like that. "I guess I did. The difference being that they didn't expect or demand it."

"Right." His face shut down. She'd pushed too far there. Matty's assessment of her brother's uneasy relationship with the Cartwright legend seemed accurate.

Interesting.

"So now we add the hamburger and stir until it's not pink anymore. You want to do that?"

He took the wooden spoon she offered. Kendra stepped back, grateful to put distance between them, and watched as he broke up the meat and let it brown, music wafting in, harder to hear with the sizzling on the stove, but a nice atmosphere, warm and good smelling. She hoped he was enjoying it.

Beef browned, she added the tomatoes and broth, put the lid ajar and set the sauce to simmer.

"That'll be an hour or so. When was the last time you left this apartment?"

He put his hands on his hips, looking down at her. "You don't want to know."

"I didn't think so." She wanted to take a step back, but there was nowhere to go unless she could dissolve into a cabinet. "You up for a short walk? It's beautiful out today."

He looked skeptically toward the window, where twilight was threatening.

"There's enough light for a stroll around the grounds here, on good level paths. We can go to the beach another time, when your knee is stronger."

"How many times are there going to be? Why wasn't I told about this?"

She tipped her head back to see his face. "Is hanging out with me that awful?"

For another of those electric moments, he looked down at her without speaking. Kendra felt her control of the situation slipping again into a déjà vu sensation that left her mildly disoriented. Honestly. This was not the way her appointments were supposed to go—or had ever gone. Her job depended on her ability to ask this kind of question without caring so much about the answer.

"It's hell, Kendra." He shook his head slowly. "I've never known such agony as having to spend time with you."

She broke into a giggle. "Call me Satan's soundtrack?"

"That's you."

"It's about time I tortured *you* for a change." She thrust a finger toward his chest.

In a case of painfully exquisite timing, the CD ended and the words she'd blurted out hung in pure silence. *Nice one, Kendra.* First rule of her profession: do not make anything personal or take anything personally. She'd done both.

"Hmm." Jameson's eyes narrowed. His hands crept onto his hips. "I guess you do owe me."

"No, no, of course not." She waved his words away, face turning red. "That was just kid stuff."

"Just kid stuff?" His left brow moved up half an inch; his eyes had taken on a particular…warmth that she responded to by heating up herself. "You think?"

"Of course. What…else?" Instinct told her suddenly and firmly that she did not want to follow this line of questioning. Everything she said was turning intimate in a way she didn't understand.

"I wonder sometimes." He was half smiling now, mysterious and I've-got-a-secret. Once again in control while she struggled with bafflement and confusion.

Kendra turned back to the stove, pretending to check on the sauce, adjusting the flame though it didn't really need to be adjusted, thinking that for the first time since she'd started her practice two years earlier, and despite the experience and confidence she'd gained in that time, she might be in over her head.

5

JAMESON TURNED OFF the treadmill in the apartment complex workout room, grabbed the towel from around his neck and mopped his face. Pathetic that a fast walk could make him break a sweat. Granted, it was too warm in the room, and he'd done the full range of exercises his physical therapist had assigned him plus a few more. Don't overdo, yeah, he knew, but he was itching to get back to full mobility. His knee could almost straighten now, and nearly bend to ninety degrees, but it still hurt like a... thing that hurt a lot.

Research on the internet was not encouraging: pain lasting a year, continued swelling and stiffness, some lack of mobility. Worst case the knee would remain unstable or he'd injure his ACL or meniscus again. Second surgeries were deemed "not as successful," which was doctorspeak for "you're screwed, buddy." He was still having pain from overextending his knee when it fell on the coffee table, in spite of the icing and the rest.

Yeah, okay, maybe not enough rest.

Still, today he felt a little better. A little lighter, a little less as if the weight of the world was trying to crush his chest. Looked like Kendra's "treatments" might be working, though not the way she intended.

He couldn't stop thinking about her. She'd certainly knocked him for a loop when she'd walked into his borrowed apartment two days ago, so cheerful and sweet smelling when he was neither. But last night he'd found himself tempted to back off that anger, to really talk to her, open up, lean a little, confide in her.

Because during the evening as they'd cooked together, he'd found a new piece of the puzzle that was Kendra Lonergan, one he'd tried to figure out all through grade school, when she'd first started fascinating him.

She could be vulnerable.

Her less-than-ideal embodiment of femininity and who-cares attitude had made her an immediate target for him in elementary school, egged on in middle school by his somewhat apish brothers, who'd caught on to his interest, which they'd interpreted as disdain and cheered him for wholeheartedly. But Kendra had confused them, too. She hadn't played the geek role, hadn't been submissive to them or to their arsenal of standard bully weapons against her—chief among them being Jameson.

At that age, like every other boy on the planet, he'd looked up to his brothers and father as male role models. He'd been cruel to Kendra as a matter of course, because they dared him to, because he wanted their approval, because he was insensitive and stupid and bristling with hormones.

But she had never reacted the way he or his brothers had expected, with pain or humiliation, tears or pleas to leave her alone. Neither had she pretended the Cartwright brothers didn't exist. Instead, she'd looked at them with what seemed like genuine pity. In those moments Jameson had been the one embarrassed, ashamed of what he'd tried to do. Instead of stopping, giving up, admitting he couldn't get to her, he'd just tried harder, turned his own suffering into bigger and meaner anger.

Kind of like he was doing now.

Through elementary school, middle school and just over the border into high school, their ongoing battle of wills had become one of the strangest relationships he'd ever had. Sometimes he'd wondered, if she'd once, just once, given any sign acknowledging that he existed as other than a pathetic pain in her ass, he might have stopped, might have approached her differently, as something besides a Cartwright menace.

But she never had given in. By high school, he'd been at least slightly more mature, and getting sick of the game. His brothers, trying one more time, had had him ask her to the freshman spring dance as a joke. He'd agreed, feeling sick inside, and at the moment of asking, promised himself that if she said yes, he'd atone for his cruelty by going through with the date, no matter what it cost him.

She hadn't. She'd laughed in his face. Why would she want to go anywhere with *him?* Then she'd walked off, still laughing, calling to her friend to come listen to the latest.

That had been it. He was done. Mortified and relieved. When Mark and Hayden had called on him to plot their next move, he'd said no and hadn't budged, enduring taunting and a few punches for his insolence. That had been the first time he'd stood up to his brothers, the beginning of his emergence from boyhood.

Unfortunately, he'd been destined—or doomed, was more like it—to get to Kendra once more. Senior year, he'd beaten her for class president. She'd clearly run the better campaign on issues of assigning homework based on GPA—the higher your grades, the less homework you'd have to complete—and other substantive ideas. Jameson had swept to victory on a promise of new vending machines, later curfews for dances and the Cartwright name.

A hollow victory. He'd served that whole year with the

sickening certainty that he hadn't earned and didn't deserve the votes or the presidency.

After all that—Kendra still wanted to help him. She was still a fascinating woman. One he was increasingly attracted to.

Back upstairs, he showered and settled onto the couch with ice on his knee. His workouts took an hour or so out of his day. Meals took another two. The rest—boredom and inactivity, doubly intolerable after the busy, active days of basic officer training.

Maybe he should rent a car. He hadn't bothered because of the pain and the expense, but he might go out of his mind if he stayed between these walls for too many more days.

His cell rang. He peered at the display. Matty. He should answer her call. His dad and brothers were easier to avoid, though he'd mistakenly picked up earlier and spoken to Hayden in Germany, so he'd had to hear about all the friends Hayden knew with ACL injuries who'd been back to 100 percent in about thirty seconds and what was wrong with Jameson's wimp ass?

Thanks, Hayden.

"Hey, Matty."

"Jameson! You've been avoiding me, you pig."

"Sorry."

"I know, you're having a tough time." Her tone reminded him exactly of his mom's when one of her boys got sick. She probably had that same pout-frown on, too.

Drove him nuts.

"I'm *fine*."

"Right! Right, of course. You're fine."

Jameson grinned at her loud raspberry. It was about as easy to B.S. Matty as it was Kendra. Namely, not at all. "So what's going on?"

"Nothing. Getting close to selling a house. Still doing

the show. What's going on with you? Are you feeling better? Any improvement?"

He wanted to tell her about Kendra. She probably didn't even remember Kendra. He just wanted to talk about her. "Nothing."

"Are you checking in with your doctor? Or your PT?"

"No, I figure I can handle this recovery all by myself because I have so much experience." His sister made a sound of exasperation. He could practically see her rolling her eyes, too—blue ones like his. In fact, she had all the standard-issue Cartwright features, but on her the square face and strong jaw became uniquely feminine. "Yes, Matty Mom, I have spoken to both of them. I'll be back at Keesler at the end of the month to start my thrilling life behind a desk until I'm cleared to resume training."

"So you're not working with anyone now?"

Jameson frowned. She'd given him the perfect opening. He took the ice off his knee and stood, needing to pace. "Actually, my doctor did send…someone."

"Yeah? Who is this…someone?"

"Did you know Kendra Lonergan in my class?"

"The name is familiar."

"Apparently she works with people who need… Who could use…"

"The word is *help.*"

"Something like that." Jameson's imagination supplied a picture of Kendra, kneeling at his feet, massaging his thigh, hands warm and skillful, thick auburn ponytail spilling over one shoulder, green eyes bright with concern. He stifled a groan. Not *that* kind of help.

"Did you know her parents were killed in a car wreck two years ago, days after she graduated college?"

Jameson stopped pacing. It was a few seconds before he could speak. "My God, Matty."

"Mom and Dad told me when it happened. It was all

over the papers in Palos Verdes Estates. Poor kid, it was awful. She has one brother, much older, who lives abroad, I think? Her parents were both only children. Grandparents all gone. She's been alone in the world for two years."

Jameson pushed his hand through his buzzed hair, trying to take in the news. Kendra had been close to her parents. How did he know that? He couldn't remember. His mind was whirling, pressure growing in his chest. He could picture two people. The woman with Kendra's hair, tall and slender, the man not much taller, stocky, both young—his mom's age—with gentle smiling faces.

Kendra. The expert on grief.

No wonder.

"Three months later she went on to graduate school at California State as planned. Got her master's in counseling and started her own business."

Jameson felt a sharp jab of protectiveness. All that on her own, all those months carrying a tremendous load of pain and of responsibility. More than anyone should have to bear, let alone a twenty-two-year-old.

Look at him, whining about how his family drove him crazy. They were alive and they loved him and would be ready to support him again—in their own warped and controlling fashion—whenever he was ready.

No wonder Kendra had looked so ripped open, so vulnerable, when she'd told him about her mom the previous night. Where had she been able to go with her grief? Who had supported her? Instead of collapsing into victimhood, she'd gone out and tried to help others who were suffering.

And he'd been selfishly imprisoned by this place and his poor-me attitude, hiding from the world and the people in it because he had a boo-boo on his knee.

Once again Kendra Lonergan had shamed him. But this time he wasn't going to turn that shame into anger. He was going to use it to help her, too.

"SEE YA." MATTY waved to Joe, one of her favorite cast mates, and stepped out into the twilight of a Sunday evening. The matinee had gone well. She'd felt great about her performance. Without so much worry about Jameson, she had more energy and enthusiasm for everything. She'd even finally had an offer over the weekend on a house that had been a particularly hard sell. Tonight she was going home to leftovers of a really good beef-vegetable soup she and her roommate, Jesse, had made the day before, with rolls from her favorite bakery and an excellent four-year-old cheddar. Plus, the rest of a bottle of the Argentinean Malbec she'd discovered, reasonably priced and delicious.

Life was good! After Jameson had finally answered her call the previous week, she now spoke with him nearly every day; he sounded much more like his old self. Kendra was doing something right.

Which reminded Matty, she'd have to ask what night Kendra wanted to go to the show, so she could—

She sensed Chris an instant before he came into her field of vision, dressed down this evening in a casual shirt and jeans, which he still filled out in all the right places, darn him.

"Good show tonight." Casual, calm, as if there was nothing at all weird—practically outrageous—about him approaching her a second time after she'd told him quite clearly to get lost.

"Are you stalking me?"

He shrugged, watching her intently, like a predator waiting for its prey to strike. "I like the show. You're good in it."

"If it's just about the show, why not go straight home?"

"I think you know the answer to that."

She was afraid she did. Bad enough she'd already had to see him once. But she'd handled that perfectly, cried her few tears, processed their meeting through her system and said a firm goodbye. He'd botched this entrance—his part in her play was over.

"Chris, I don't want to see you anymore."

"You could close your eyes."

She rolled them instead at his absurd joke, an unwelcome smile trying to curve her lips. "Okay. You saw the show, you liked it. I'm really glad. Now I'm going home."

"Would you like to have a drink with me first?"

"*No,* I would not like to have a drink with you first." She lifted her arm and let it slap back down. "What on earth do you think I've been saying?"

"That you've missed me. That there is still something between us and probably always will be."

She scoffed at him. "Those are bad drugs you're taking, Professor. I think you need to lower the dose way down."

"Yeah?"

"Do I even need to answer that?"

He shook his head. "Just have a drink with me. There are things we need to talk about."

"Maybe you do." A couple of chorus members passed close by on their way out. Matty lowered her voice. "I'm happy with how we left things."

"I'm an asshole and you're blameless?"

If the shoe fits. She blew out a breath. "Chris, this was years ago. Years. There is no point bringing it up again. Too much pain, too many accusations, it was all so ugly."

"It doesn't have to be." He took a step closer, voice dropping, a touch of vulnerability in his eyes, not something Chris Hamilton showed often. It could still get to her. *Crap.* "I promised myself I would never look for you, Matty. But also that if I ever saw you again, I would take it as a sign to—"

"G'night, Matty!" Dominique, gossip girl of the cast, peered curiously at Chris, giving him the up-and-down once-over, no doubt absorbing details she could then exaggerate and spread around. A few steps past his sightline, she gave Matty an enthusiastic thumbs-up.

Matty couldn't respond, either to her or to Chris. Why was he doing this? It was so much easier to deal with him when he was being Mr. Smooth. This genuine humility and regret—who could turn her back on that?

Worst of all, Matty *wanted* to talk to him. She wanted the closure she'd never gotten. She wanted to understand why, when things had been crazy, yes, impossible, yes, but so, so good between them in a way she'd never found again, he had wanted to dip his dick into someone as obvious and twisted as Clarisse.

After that, after his thing with Clarisse had fallen through and Matty was long gone, what had he done then? Had he gone through one student after another, trading the old one in when the new one showed up? Or had Matty truly been special and Clarisse some bizarre aberration?

Matty needed to know, even if it hurt. In spite of their age difference, in spite of the improbability of their circumstances, she'd been sure Chris was The One. His betrayal had deeply hurt not only her heart but her faith in herself and in her judgment.

She was relenting, she could tell, and it scared her. Yes, it had been six years, but he could still get to her, and she couldn't afford to lose this battle or herself to him again.

Wait. What the hell was she saying? Matty would only lose herself if she allowed that to happen. She was not a twenty-one-year-old kid anymore, and he was not the man the sun rose and set around. He was the Creepy Professor, as Jameson called him, a man into girls way too young for him.

"Can we go somewhere we can talk?"

"Yes," she answered impulsively, held his gaze, searching for smug triumph—if there was even the tiniest flicker of it, she'd change her mind so fast he'd only feel the breeze of her leaving.

There was none. Only surprise, then relief.

"Thank you." His gratitude, too, was real. "Where do you— I don't know this neighborhood…"

"Green Street Restaurant isn't far. About a ten-minute walk. We can get a drink there."

"Or dinner?"

She narrowed her eyes. "Don't push it."

"I'll try." Chris grinned and reached to straighten the collar of her favorite blue jacket. "It's really good to see you again, Matty."

Matty stepped away from his touch, not sure what to say to that. Because aside from all the lingering anger and hurt he'd managed to unearth, it was really good to see him again, too.

Okay. Now that she'd admitted that thought to herself, she'd suppress it for the rest of time.

Talking rather stiltedly, they headed down El Molino Avenue and turned east on Green Street, heading for Shopper's Way, where Green Street Restaurant, a Pasadena institution, had stood since the late 1970s.

Inside, they found two comfortable chairs at the long wooden bar opposite the low curving wall that cleverly separated tables in one area of the dining room. Behind the bar, windows let in evening light that made bottles and glasses glow in rich shades of green and gold.

Chris pulled out her chair, waited until she was seated before he sat and pulled his chair up next to her. She'd always liked Chris's flair for playing the gentleman—grace and respect, not a hint of condescension. He pulled out her chair because he wanted her to be settled and comfortable, not because he thought she was a dainty flower who couldn't manage the task herself.

"What would you like?"

"Oh." She frowned, mind spinning through possibilities. She hadn't thought past the conversation they were supposed to have. "I guess wine?"

"You're right."

Matty laughed. They'd shared a distaste for women who spoke in questions, something Matty didn't usually do. Clearly she was not in her element. "I would like a glass of wine. Stop. Red, full bodied. Stop."

He put on a pair of narrow-lensed reading glasses, which made him look sexy in the intellectual way she was a complete sucker for, and peered at the wine list. "Looks like mostly California. Here's a gigondas from France, how about that?"

"How can I say no to a gigondas?"

"I have no idea, how can you?" He closed the menu and signaled the bartender, who came right over. Chris had that weird power over bartenders. He was also the kind of guy who could find a parking place in front of a train station at rush hour. Or call a sellout concert and score just-returned tickets. Life seemed to arrange itself to suit him. Kind of sickening, to be honest.

They chatted about the show for a few minutes, an obvious delay tactic that made Matty even more nervous. She was about to break in and demand they get it over with when—thank you, Lord—their wine showed up.

"Cheers." He raised his glass to hers. She nodded, inhaled the rich, complex bouquet and took a polite, experimental sip, wanting to gulp a good quarter of it straight down because in these circumstances she damn well needed it.

"Delicious, Chris."

His mouth broke into a smile of pleasure that took her back six years. The way they'd enjoyed food and wine together had been really special. "Yup. Very good."

"So…"

"You want me to get on with it."

"I do." She put her wine down, determined to drink slowly, keep her wits about her.

"Ah, Mattingly." He sighed heavily. "Okay. Where should I start?"

"How about that night I walked into your place and found Clarisse naked?"

"I already explained…" He held up a hand to stop himself. "Sorry. You want me to do it again."

"Yes." Her throat was already thickening. Damn it, why couldn't she have let this go? Let him go? "I'm better able to listen now."

"Okay." He took another sip of wine, cleared his throat. "Let's see. Clarisse came over—I was just back from the gym—and she came over to my apartment all desperate, saying she needed to talk to me. I'd already heard some about her capacity for melodrama, so I wasn't really worried. I figured she was having trouble in class or something. I let her in, made her some tea, and she suggested that since I was still in workout clothes she could wait while I took a shower."

"Then…"

"Then when I came out of the shower, she screamed. I grabbed a towel, ran into the living room and found her lying naked on the couch, completely fine."

"Mmm-hmm." Matty forced her teeth to unclench. "That part I remember."

"Because you walked in right when I was trying to get her to stand up and put her clothes back on. So it looked like I was…" He gave a short, mirthless laugh. "You know what it looked like."

She bloody well did. The image of him kneeling over Clarisse's naked body, her arms wrapped around his bare shoulders, legs spread wide—that lovely picture hadn't left Matty's brain for…

Okay, it still hadn't left.

Chris's story hadn't changed. And one aspect of it still didn't make sense.

"If nothing happened, why did you let me go?" All pretense at not caring was exposed by her husky whisper.

"Matty." His voice was equally raspy, pain evident in his eyes. "I had nothing to offer you. You were miserable and frustrated. We both were. It seemed the decent thing to do, to cut you loose to find someone else. I was hurt that you didn't trust me, but bottom line, we were in an impossible situation."

"You are right about that."

"I thought you'd come back. Sometime." He stared moodily into his wine. "Then I stopped hoping."

No, she hadn't come back. Even after finding out the extent of Clarisse's issues, which meant his story could have been true. Even after Matty graduated and was no longer his student.

"Why didn't you?"

"Because you weren't what I wanted." Matty spoke quietly, but firmly. She hadn't wanted a man eleven years older than she was. She hadn't wanted someone whose class and learning and experience outshone hers by so much. She didn't want a man surrounded daily by young beautiful women who threw themselves at him, whether or not he stayed faithful. And mostly… "I wanted time to discover who I was, apart from the woman my parents wanted me to be. Apart from the woman you wanted me to be."

"When did I want you to be anything but yourself?"

She laughed. "I was twenty-one, Chris. I didn't know who myself was."

He nodded, swirling the rich liquid in his glass. "And now?"

"Now I know."

He raised an eyebrow, devilish and confident again. "You know what that means, Matty?"

"No." She eyed him warily. "But you're going to tell me, aren't you."

"Yup." Grinning now, he reached out and took her hand, drew her fingers between his palms. "It means now is the perfect time for us to try again."

6

KENDRA PULLED HER Lexus into the parking lot north of the Point Vicente Interpretive Center and chose a spot overlooking the ocean. Red-earth cliffs lined this part of the coast, dropping dramatically to a series of coves and beaches for about a dozen miles between Rat Beach to the north and the Port of Los Angeles to the south, where the landscape flattened again.

Jameson sat in the passenger seat; she'd brought him out here for a walk to the whale-watching station. A familiar area, familiar experience, but one that got him out of the house, in ocean air, back with nature. So simple and therapeutic to sit and watch the sea's restless motion, smell the salty fresh air, watch pelicans and seagulls go about the business of living. Most of her clients responded immediately, some with joy, some with hitherto-suppressed tears, some with a release of crippling tension, but very few came away unchanged. She wouldn't risk climbing down to the beach with Jameson today—too many opportunities for knee twisting on the steep, uneven paths—but he'd get plenty from the experience.

"Ready?"

"Sure." He flicked her a glance. Something was different about him today. She hadn't yet figured out what, only that the change made her uneasy.

"Okay." She climbed down from the car—really, she

needed to buy something smaller—and waited for him to come around before they headed toward the path that wound along the sea to the Interpretive Center, which she'd always called "the whale watch place." The Center consisted of a building with a small museum, friendly, helpful staff and a whale-watching station on the outside terrace. December through mid-May during daylight hours, seven days a week, volunteers with binoculars scanned the sea and recorded numbers and types of migrating whales. Farther south, white and proud at the tip of the point, rose the Point Vicente lighthouse.

"So beautiful." Kendra spread her hands to encompass the view and gave a long, blissful sigh. "I couldn't live anywhere else. How about you?"

"For the next twenty years, where I live won't be up to me."

"Twenty." She started walking toward the path that led to the Center, feeling oddly dismayed. "You're staying in that long?"

"That's what Cartwrights have always done."

"After that?"

"Yeah, I'll probably come back here."

She hung back to let a jogger pass, and nearly bumped into Jameson, who'd done the same thing. "What do think you'll want to do then?"

"Oh, probably…circus clown."

"Ah, really."

"Or linebacker for the Packers."

Kendra rolled her eyes. "Uh-huh."

"Then astronaut, most likely."

She snorted. "Okay, smartass."

"All true." Jameson put his hand to his heart. "At least I wanted to be all those things when I was seven."

She glanced at him in surprise. "You weren't born wanting to be a soldier?"

"Airman. Army has soldiers. And no, not me."

"When did that start?"

"Can't really say. Middle school, maybe. When I started clueing into the family history."

Kendra let the silence hang for a few steps, seemingly enjoying the breeze, while she wondered how to phrase her next question. "I guess it would be hard to break a tradition that long."

"Mattingly took care of that."

"Oh, right. She— Mattingly?" She wrinkled her nose. "That's her full name?"

"Uh-huh." He shot her a sideways glance. "We were all named for whiskey. Jameson's Irish, Maker's Mark, Basil Hayden's and Mattingly and Moore."

Kendra laughed, surprised at how comfortable she felt around him today. Sure made a difference when he wasn't snarking at her. "That's hilarious. I never put it together."

"Some do, some don't." He shrugged. "It's Dad's idea of a joke. Where does Kendra come from?"

"Dad's name was Ken. Mom's name was Sandra. They saw Kendra in a baby name book and went 'ooh, perfect!'" She tossed hair from her face, blown there by the stiff breeze, and dug in her pocket for an elastic to control it. "It means knowledgeable."

"Ah, know-it-all, that figures."

"Not what I said." Her hands went through their practiced motions, taming her hair into a ponytail. "What does Jameson mean?"

"Supplanter. When I was little I thought it was something you grew flowers in. I refused to tell anyone."

Kendra giggled, feeling slightly giddy. "What would supplanter mean? Taking someone's place?"

"Yup." He quirked an eyebrow and made quotation marks with his fingers. "Wrongfully or by force."

"Bet you cut in line a lot."

"Nah." His shoulder bumped hers before she could step away. "I think bigger. Maybe a government coup someday."

"Live large, General Cartwright."

"I'm aiming for Colonel by the time I retire."

"Colonel Cartwright has an excellent sound to it."

"Yeah?" He turned his head slowly toward her, grin mischievous, blue eyes warm and alive, utterly transformed from the shut-down guy she'd seen so far into someone boyish and irrepressible. "You grew up fun."

Kendra sucked in a breath. They needed to go on talking. Now. Because she was gazing at him, taking him in, smiling. She hoped she wasn't drooling.

Talk, Kendra.

"My parents used to bring me here a lot when I was a kid." She gestured toward the still-distant lighthouse, aware her voice was too high and silly-chattery. "I used to pretend I knew the names of the whales and their personalities and would tell everyone in earshot all about them, their families, favorite toys, etc. I'm sure the volunteers trying to count them thought it was adorable. And really annoying."

Jameson's smile faded. He put a hand briefly on her shoulder. "I'm so sorry about your parents, Kendra."

Kendra's heart gave an irregular jab. "Thanks."

"I didn't know, when you were talking about your mom, that you lost both of them so suddenly." His voice was deep, sympathetic and absolutely genuine. "Matty told me."

"Ah." Her throat was tight; she stubbed her toe on a rock and nearly stumbled. "Well, thanks."

"It must have been hell."

She could only nod. From the height of giddiness she'd crashed back into grief. Incredible how fast it could happen.

"You have a brother?"

"Mmm." Kendra cleared her throat. "Duncan. He's ten years older. Lives in Wales and herds sheep. We're...different, to put it mildly."

"Did he help out at all?"

She let out a brittle laugh. "Aren't we supposed to be talking about you?"

"Did I sign something saying that?"

"No, but—"

"Did he come home to help you?" There was an odd note in his voice. She struggled to identify it. Not anger, not quite, but almost.

"He came for the service." And left almost immediately after. "He had to get back."

"To his sheep." The disdain was clear enough now.

"No, you don't understand." She tipped her head, eyebrows raised. "He *re-e-eally* likes those sheep."

Jameson cracked up. Kendra's chest loosened. She pointed out toward the spectacular view of Catalina Island. "Look how clear it is today."

He stopped with her, hands on his hips. "How did you manage? Who helped you through all that?"

"Jameson." She laughed awkwardly. "I'm not here to talk about—"

"Did you have uncles? Aunts? Cousins?"

"No. Look, can we—"

"Neighbors?" He swung around to face her, eyes deep with sympathy and something else. "Friends of your parents?"

Kendra turned to keep walking. She could not stand still and stare into those eyes or she'd come apart. "Yes, I had lots of help. Lots of support."

"Uh-huh." He clearly didn't believe her. "Lots. And it was all a piece of cake."

"Chocolate with chocolate frosting."

"So that hell you went through. Alone. That's why you're doing this now for other people. Like me."

"It's definitely part of it, yes." Kendra took a deep breath, trying to regroup. One of the differences between the way she worked with clients and standard talk therapy was that a therapist never—or rarely—brought him or herself into the equation. Whereas Kendra had found that in certain situations, sharing part of her life and experiences could help form stronger bonds of emotional trust. So it should be fine to talk with Jameson about her parents' deaths and her reaction.

It just didn't feel that way.

Immediately her brain started searching for reasons. Because she didn't trust him? Because it felt too vulnerable exposing herself to him? Why?

An answer came surprisingly quickly.

Because Jameson had known her parents, or at least had seen them multiple times, at baseball games and dances and spaghetti dinners and fun fairs. Because in whatever twisted way, he'd been part of her life and her mom and dad's for a long time, and he'd known the three of them as a unit. He was closer to their loss than her clients who were strangers.

Hmm. Not a complete answer, but it was a start.

The path took an abrupt turn to the right after skirting a ravine, and led back close to the sea again. The breeze strengthened as they approached the edge of the cliff, protected by a railing and stern signs warning people not to climb over it. A small flock of brown pelicans rose into view from below the cliff, necks tucked back in flight.

"I guess it must seem strange to you that I'm avoiding my family while you're missing yours."

Kendra shrugged. "Our situations are different, our families are different. I don't judge you."

"You've always judged me."

"Ha! Since when?"

"Since I put worms in your sandwich."

"Um…" She gave him a look, suppressing a giggle. "You thought that wouldn't lead to an opinion?"

"Gosh, no. At least not a negative one."

"Boy logic!" Kendra gave in to laughter. "Hey, I know, I'll ruin her lunch, have people call her 'worm eater' for months and she'll think I'm great!"

"Well?" He sent her a crooked grin. "What's not to love?"

They stopped by the railing to watch the sea heaving in and out, over one hundred feet straight down, wind stiffening now to a good chilly blow. Watching the sea cleared Kendra's mind, the breeze blowing away any lingering sadness.

"Why me?"

"Why you what?"

"Why did you pick on me?"

"Aw, Kendra, why does any kid do stuff like that?"

"Honestly? I can't imagine."

He frowned, shoving his hands into his jeans pockets. "Yeah, good point. For one, you never reacted. It was like nothing bothered you. You were unique."

"So you could get your anger out and not suffer consequences?"

"I wasn't angry with you."

"With your dad. With your brothers." A pair of joggers ran behind them.

"Geez, don't you talk about the weather like a normal person?"

"Nope." Kendra smiled at him, thinking he was like a piggy bank—except for the pink and fat part. If you wanted to get at what was inside him, you'd have to either shake him violently or smash him open. "I talk about you."

"Huh."

"Let's keep walking. Your knee okay?"

"Knee's fine."

Not that he'd admit to pain. She watched him surreptitiously for signs—increased limping, a larger twist to his step, tension in his face. Nothing. Good. She hoped one day he'd tell her if he was overdoing it.

"One time…I don't even remember what I did to you, but I remember your reaction. You looked me straight in the eyes and said, 'People like you feel bad about yourselves, and that's why you need to make other people feel worse.'"

Kendra snorted. "Straight from my parents' mouths."

"It stunned me. I'm serious." He nudged her with his shoulder. "I was supposed to be on the attack, you were supposed to cry. And here you'd flattened me."

"Wait, really?" She turned to see his face, half surprised, half fascinated. "I hurt you?"

His eyes were grave, catching the setting sun, glowing blue. "I have never been with a woman since."

Kendra started to gasp, then, duh, realized he was kidding and burst out laughing. "Stop that."

He grinned. "Maybe one or two."

They approached the Interpretive Center, unstaffed by volunteers at the moment since the whale-watching season hadn't yet started. The light was dimming, sun preparing to sink below the sea. They shouldn't stay long. The park closed at dusk, and she didn't want Jameson walking in darkness in case he stumbled.

Kendra had brought many clients here. With Jameson the view was the same, the lighthouse, the sea, Catalina Island in the distance—all the same, but the place felt different. More as if she was here with a friend, not a client. Odd, since she and Jameson hadn't exactly been buddies. Again, maybe it was their shared history and experiences growing up here.

"Did your parents ever bring you to the Center?"

"Nope." He stared out at the sea, wind making his eyes squint, sexy lines radiating in the corners, the spiky front of his hair ruffling slightly. His jaw was strong, mouth full and serious. Her heart gave a thump.

Yes, Kendra, he is übermasculine and handsome. Get over it.

"Where did they take you?"

"Disney Land. The observatory at Griffith Park. Natural history museum. Baseball games. Basketball games. Los Angeles Air Force Base. March Air Reserve Base. Edwards Air Force Base…"

"No ballet? No symphony? No art or opera?"

"Ha! Uh, no."

"So it was a manly man's upbringing. Where was your sister in all this?"

"Rebelling." He grinned affectionately. "She and Dad were polar opposites."

"Or very similar."

"Maybe that was it. Hey, look." He stepped closer, and pointed out to sea.

"Oh, wow!" Two dolphins, breaking the surface of the water, bounding northward together. The animals gave Kendra a huge charge, no matter how often she saw them. "They always look like they're having so much fun."

"They're free, why wouldn't they be having fun?"

"Free how?" She was so curious about his comment she turned from watching the dolphins to watching him.

"Oh, the questions, Kendra. As Freud is my witness, you do love your questions."

"Don't I?" She blinked sweetly at him. "Free how?"

"Free to be dolphins and do dolphin-y things all day."

"What are Jameson-y things?" She laughed when he started groaning. "How would you fill a day if you could do anything you wanted?"

"Keg of beer and six or seven hot blondes."

"Okay, okay, no more questions. We're done. Let's go home." She turned them back toward the car.

"You hungry?"

His question startled her into hedging. "Not too bad."

"I can make a mean omelet."

"Yeah?" She smiled at him, not that omelets were all that thrilling, but she was still in a smiling mood. "You'll have to show me sometime."

"You busy tonight?"

The wind diminished as the path headed back inland. A beam of sunlight caught him, painting his hair in yellow and rose, throwing shadows and light along his cheekbones, jaw and that sensual mouth. Her heart gave another flip.

Come on, Kendra. Clients had asked to spend extra time with her before if they were lonely. A few had asked her to dinner, and she'd always accepted if she was free. This was completely in the normal range of her treatment.

"I'm not busy." No. She was just confused.

"Good. We can stop at Trader Joe's on the way back and pick up supplies."

"Okay." She walked next to him, feeling rather ludicrously as if she was putting into motion an evening she'd regret. Or as if there was something very wrong with the way she'd accepted his invitation.

It only took her ten more steps and another heart-jumping glance at Jameson's handsome profile to figure it out.

She didn't want to eat dinner with him the way a counselor eats with a client. She wanted to eat dinner with him the way a woman eats with a man.

7

JAMESON STOOD BY the rear of Kendra's Lexus, anxious to get behind the wheel again. His knee was feeling more stable, and he wanted to be in charge of this evening. The idea of inviting Kendra to dinner had been impetuous—the thought of going back alone to the same four walls of Mike's living room had driven him to it—but now that she'd agreed, he was determined to have a fun evening. Show off his cooking skills a little, play some good music, pour some good wine—feel like a normal guy again. Maybe even a normal guy on a date.

If this was her therapy working, she was a genius. But he wasn't sure how much was the therapy and how much was simply being around Kendra. She'd always challenged him, that hadn't changed. But now the challenge was less about proving himself and more about finding out what went on in that beautiful head while she was trying so hard to find out what went on in his. Her reasons might be purely professional—his, not so much.

"Can I drive?"

"Um. Sure." She looked doubtful. "Have you driven yet after the surgery?"

"Oh, yeah, yeah, fifty or sixty times."

"Uh-huh." She tossed him the keys. "Crash my car and I'll hurt you, soldier boy."

"Airman." He caught the keys, feeling better than he

had in…longer than he wanted to think about. "Soldiers, army. Sailors, navy. Marines, marines. In the Air Force we are airmen and airwomen. Get it straight."

"Yes, sir, Lieutenant, *sir*." She saluted briskly and went around to the passenger side.

He entered the car butt first and swung his right leg over as a static unit, successfully avoiding any twisting of the knee, and therefore any pain. From there the movements required of driving were forward and back, similar to the exercise he did every day. No problem. It felt absurdly good to be doing something as normal as getting from one place to another all on his own.

"Nice car."

"Thanks. It belonged to Mom and Dad. A bit much for me, but I haven't—" She laughed nervously and pulled the elastic out of her ponytail, letting that gorgeous hair fall heavy and free.

"Haven't what?" He started the car, adjusted the seat for his longer legs and the rearview mirror for his height. When she didn't answer, he looked at her questioningly. "Haven't…"

"Been able to sell it." She laughed again, folding her arms and clasping each forearm.

"No one wants this car?" That was hard to believe.

"No, I can't make myself sell it."

"That's understandable." He put the car in Reverse and backed out slowly and carefully, not his usual method. Awareness of his injury made him feel as if he was on the verge of having an accident at any time, even though there was nothing wrong with the car or his driving. Probably the same vulnerability older people felt, and why they drove slowly. "Why didn't you want to tell me that?"

"Because…" She gestured impatiently toward the dashboard. "It's just a *car*. It's silly to hang on to it when I want something different."

"Oh, I see." Jameson nodded as if he'd just deduced something brilliant. "So I'm allowed to have emotions that might not make sense around grief but you're not?"

He came to a stop, waiting to turn onto Palos Verdes Drive, and glanced over to find her with her mouth open, for once unable to come up with a retort. *Gotcha.* She was much too hard on herself.

Kendra closed her mouth, still staring straight ahead. "This is *your* counseling."

"True. It is." He spoke gently, her pain causing him to react with tenderness. Funny how even though he hadn't known Kendra in any real sense at school, being with her now felt as if they'd been friends a long time. He reached over and laid his hand behind her head, intending to give her a quick pat, just a comforting touch. But her hair was soft and thick and felt so good under his fingers that he slid them in deeper, rubbed them gently back and forth over her scalp. "But if I can help you, too, why shouldn't I?"

"Why would you want to?" She turned to him, a combination of challenge and curiosity, vulnerability and strength. Her eyes were large and troubled, her mouth soft, lips slightly parted. His fingers stopped moving. Tightened.

He wanted to kiss her.

Kendra's eyes widened. Had he leaned toward her? Brought her head closer? He couldn't have. How had she guessed?

An impatient honk sounded behind him. Flustered, Jameson started forward, then realized a car was coming and had to jam on the brake, sending a shock wave through his knee.

Ow. Doggone it.

"Uh, sorry." A break in the line of cars opened up and he pulled smoothly into it. "Got a little overeager there."

"Uh, yeah...overeager with the car and something else." She was back, voice vigorous and, yes, challenging.

He chuckled, pleased as hell that she took him on. Though she'd never done anything but... "I have no idea what you mean."

"Just focus on the driving, Lieutenant."

"Yes, ma'am." He turned onto Hawthorne Boulevard, then into the crowded parking lot of the Golden Cove Shopping Center, pulling into a space as close to Trader Joe's as he could, composing a shopping list in his head. He had eggs. Spinach, mushrooms, good bread, greens for salad, a good strong white or a relatively light red, maybe a rioja crianza or a pinot noir. Dessert? In Spain he'd gotten to love the combination of Spanish cheeses paired with quince paste or those incredible soft full-flavored fruit bars he missed.

Marta had been the right woman at the right time, sensual, pleasure seeking—not his forever after, but she sure had taught him about food and wine, about self-indulgence and relaxed in-the-moment living, something he'd never encountered at home. He'd immersed himself in the life until Dad came over and yanked him home. A few months in college with the start of his ROTC training had put him back on the goal-focused Cartwright straight and narrow. But it would be nice to taste those concepts again with Kendra, even for a few weeks.

"Ready?"

"Sure." She strode along next to him. He liked that she was tall, five-seven, he'd guess. He liked that she walked with confidence. She'd always walked that way, as if she was absolutely sure where she wanted to go, leaning forward slightly, feet working to catch up to her body. "What are we buying?"

"Food."

"You want me to eat *that*?"

He grinned, wanting to touch her again, but holding back this time. She seemed as keyed up as he felt. Maybe that moment in the car hadn't belonged only to him.

Inside, he grabbed a basket and headed for the produce section, where he picked out fresh spinach and mushrooms for the omelet, mixed baby lettuces, scallions, cherry tomatoes, a ripe avocado and tiny cucumbers for the salad, then red seedless grapes for cheese, since he wasn't in the mood to go on a long search for quince paste.

"You know what you want." She spoke admiringly.

"In Madrid, refrigerators are tiny. People go to shop much more often than we do here. There are outdoor markets everywhere and everything is in peak condition. Bread is fresh every day. It's something."

"I'd love to go there."

"I'd love to take you." He spoke without thinking, then had to cover himself by winking at her startled expression. "Let's find some cheese."

They wandered over to a case holding an impressive collection from around the world. He picked up a wedge of "drunken goat," a semifirm goat cheese soaked in red wine, and a good piece of manchego, remembering the rich nutty flavors he'd come to love.

"You must have had incredible food experiences in Spain." She was looking at him thoughtfully.

"Why do you say that?"

"Because I've never seen you this animated. Or moving this fast."

He wanted to tell her that his energy had more to do with her than food. "I remember telling my brothers about the cheese and sausage shops in Spain. They looked at me, totally unimpressed, and I realized they were probably imagining shelves of plastic-wrapped orange and white rectangles, and a few sticks of pepperoni. It's nothing like that. This food is practically alive."

"Alive. Wow." She was laughing at him, eyes shining. He didn't care. "You lock your doors at night? In case some crawls in with evil intent?"

"You need to be careful." He took her hand and pulled her, laughing, to the bread aisle, where he looked behind and around him. "We're safe here."

She rolled her eyes and picked out a baguette in a brown paper bag. "For dinner and weapon."

"Good thinking."

He picked out wine next, a garnacha, which would be fine with both the omelet and the cheeses—two bottles for good measure.

"You're in your element." She was smiling at him again in that way that made it seem as if she'd just made an amazing discovery.

"I like to eat good food. I like to drink good wine."

"How's the food in the Air Force?"

"Not Spain, but it's not bad." For the first time he could talk about his experience without feeling that desperate sinking in his stomach. His knee was healing. The pain was receding; he could almost walk normally today. He'd go back to Keesler and get on with his life in the Air Force. He felt sure of it. Maybe at some point he'd even be able to look at another cat. "Don't ask me about the hospital food, though."

"That bad?"

"I was too pissed to taste anything." He stopped by a shelf of chocolate. "Are you a dark or milk woman?"

"Dark."

"I like dark, too." He added a bar, feeling as if they'd shared something significant. Oh, yeah, he had a big old crush. "Let's go check out."

She hurried after him. God, it felt good to be walking at a near-normal pace again—somewhere that wasn't a treadmill. He really had shut himself in. A mistake.

"Hey, Jameson."

"Hey, what?" He picked the shortest line and turned.

Kendra was taking her colorful purse off her shoulder. "I want to make sure you let me pay half of—"

"Nope." He cut her off with a raised hand. "My house. My food. My treat."

"Mike's house, my treatment plan, my—"

"Nuh-uh. You're off the clock."

She blinked, holding a twenty in her hand. "What do you mean?"

"I mean, Ms. Lonergan, tonight you are my dinner guest, not my therapist."

"Counselor, not therapist."

"Counselor. So put the twenty away. If it really bothers you, you can have me over some night to your place."

She blinked again. "But that would be like…"

"What?" He started casually loading their purchases onto the belt. "Like we're dating?"

"No." She shoved the twenty at him insistently. "No, of course not."

"Of course not." He held her gaze with a half smile until she turned red and looked away. Tonight was a date, as far as he was concerned. But if she wasn't comfortable calling it that, he wasn't going to push it. He took the twenty. If it made her feel better about it, fine. He'd use it to buy her something. "Thanks."

"Is that enough?"

"Plenty." He nodded to the cashier, who chatted agreeably about the weather and the wave conditions. Fall was a great time for surfing in Southern California, though between the Air Force and his knee, he wouldn't be on a board again for quite some time.

"You surf?" He took the bags and escorted Kendra out to the rapidly darkening parking lot.

"Not me."

"A non-surfing Southern California girl? What *did* you do as a kid?"

"Oh, let's see. Not much." She started counting on her fingers. "I took flute lessons, ballet lessons until they got to toe shoes and I couldn't stay up on the darn things. Swimming lessons, tap dance, jazz dance, voice lessons…"

"Weren't you ever home?"

"At home I read everything I could get my hands on, did needlework, knitted, made my own clothes."

"Good God, do I need to check you for wiring?"

She blew out a breath as if the recitation had stolen too much of hers. "In short, Jameson, I did anything that involved learning a skill and had nothing to do with socializing or school."

He was laughing, not because she'd said anything funny, just because he was having so much fun with her. "C'mon, you had friends."

"I did have friends. But many of my social interactions in grade school were less than ideal." She sent him a pointed stare. "Though I did write for the school paper."

"The Pen."

"That's the one."

They reached the car, opened the back for their haul. "Did your parents push you to do all that stuff?"

"Oh, no." She shook her head emphatically, making that glorious mane ripple around her pretty face, its color enhanced by the evening light. "That was all stuff I wanted to do."

"You make me feel lazy."

She looked at him with scorn. "Only because you are."

Jameson hadn't laughed this much in weeks. He loved the way she could tease him, totally deadpan, and know he'd get it. He had that kind of connection with Mike. His sister. Not many others. "Can I drive home?"

"You've got the keys." She swung gracefully into the passenger side.

Jameson climbed into the driver's seat—without any grace whatsoever—and started the engine. "Home sweet home."

"You looked up any old friends since you've been back?"

"Nope. But I was thinking this morning of going to see my favorite math teacher ever, Mr. Vinely, at Palos Verdes High. Want to come with me?"

Immediately she started hedging.

He just smiled, letting her be all flustered and stutter out reasons not to spend more nonprofessional time with him, and drove straight to the condo.

The omelet came out perfectly, light, tender, fragrant with mushrooms and a pinch of dried thyme. The bread was beautifully crusty with good flavor, the grapes sweet, the cheeses nicely ripe, complementing the deep, smooth taste of the wine.

They were lingering over that garnacha now, their first glass from the second bottle, seated on Mike's balcony, bundled against the chilly air—Kendra looked incredibly hot and sweet in his Air Force hoodie sweatshirt—admiring the distant view of the ocean.

Most important part of the meal was that cooking it together had been a blast. He'd showed her how to shake the pan, stirring, so the omelet cooked quickly and evenly. She'd rolled it onto a plate herself, only slightly clumsy. They'd laughed and talked more easily, less sparring, more sharing.

He liked being with her. A lot.

And right now, softened with wine, she was absolutely irresistible. Her smile slowed, as did her words. Her body had turned languid and relaxed. Jameson found himself occasionally imagining that body tucked against his in sleep. And tucked against his in…not sleep.

"I think I've had enough." She put her wine down on the small glass-topped table between them. "It's so good, but if I keep drinking I won't be able to drive home."

"You know your body." He bit his tongue to keep from saying he wanted to know it, too, and that he thought her inability to drive home would suit him fine. But maybe it was just as well. She was already making him think about sex. If she stayed longer and he had much more wine, he'd be thinking instead about seduction.

Call him old-fashioned, but he thought it was a lot smarter to decide whether to start a sexual relationship with a woman when he was sober. He hadn't followed that advice once, partying here in town the summer after his sophomore year with a girl he vaguely knew who'd attended a neighboring high school. It had nearly taken a restraining order to get her to stop texting, calling and coming by the house. Dad had been livid. *That's what you get for thinking with your dick.*

Kendra blinked sleepily and stifled a yawn. He wanted to gather her in his arms, put her to bed in Mike's room—assuming he could make himself be that much of a gentleman—and cook her breakfast in the morning. Including a pot of brutally strong coffee.

"This has been great, Jamie—Jameson."

Her use of his nickname startled him pleasantly. Only a few people had ever called him Jamie. His mom, his aunts and Matty. The way it had slipped comfortably out of her mouth, then been immediately corrected, intrigued him. She was feeling closer to him. Fighting it.

"I've had fun, too."

"I should go." She spoke regretfully, then didn't move.

Jameson didn't want her to leave either. But he was more sober than she was.

He stood in front of her chair, offered her a hand. She took it and he pulled her to her feet, deliberately not stepping back so she'd end up close to him, too close for normal social contact. Not close enough for him. "You okay driving?"

"Sure." She peered up at him. "Um. You're standing in my personal space."

"You don't like it?"

"No." She shook her head emphatically, then poked him gently in the chest. "I do."

Oh, man. He was going to get hard in another point-oh-two seconds. "Then why—"

"That's the problem, see. God, I sound drunk. Do I sound drunk?"

"Only a little."

"I knew it." She pulled her hair back into a ponytail in one fist, then let it fall. "I better go home before I do something stupid."

He wanted to ask *like what?* But he knew. They both knew. She was tipsy and he was not about to—

Well, maybe.

"Mmm, smell that?" She closed her eyes as a breeze wafted over them and inhaled rapturously, swaying closer. "Eucalyptus. I love that smell."

He gave in. Her lips tasted like sweet grapes, rich wine and Kendra. He could savor that flavor for hours.

But he wouldn't be able to because Kendra's eyes shot wide open. She backed away, tangled with the chair legs behind her and started tipping. He grabbed her waist and hauled her upright, shocked at her pallor.

"You shouldn't have done that."

"Kissed you or saved you from falling?"

"The first."

"You didn't like it?"

"I…" She frowned, holding a hand to her head. "I said you shouldn't have."

"You didn't answer."

"I don't want to."

"I'll try again." He pulled her full against him this time, felt her mouth opening under his, her lips softening, an extremely effective aphrodisiac—except he didn't need one.

"Jameson." She gasped his name. "We should not be doing this. No, *I* should not be doing this."

"Wait. You shouldn't but it's okay for us to?"

"No. No." She pushed his arms away. "None of it is okay. You don't understand."

"If you say so."

"I do." She put a hand to her throat, looking as if she was trying to calm her breathing.

"Hey." He gathered a handful of hair to tug gently. "You want me to drive you home, lovely and slightly drunk Kendra?"

"No, no, no, I'm fine." She turned and sprawled over the chair. He lunged for her too late; they fell in a tangled heap onto the deck.

"Jameson, your knee!"

"Not hurt. I'm okay." He untangled himself and helped her sit up.

"Thank goodness." She burst into a sudden giggle that almost sounded like a sob. "I guess I'm not that fine after all."

"Trust me, you are quite, *quite* fine." He got to his feet and pulled her up. "But because I am an officer and a gentleman, I will take you home and not lay another finger on you."

"No?" She sounded confused.

"No." He guided her through the sliding doors back into the apartment, which seemed antiseptic and stuffy after the sweet night air. "Unless you want me to?"

"I should go home."

He grinned, noticing she didn't answer him that time either. Okay. He'd drive her home tonight, let her sober up and wake alone in her bed tomorrow morning.

But next time they got together, they were going to take the next step in exploring this powerful chemistry that had been between them since they were kids.

Only this time their interaction would be totally adult.

8

KENDRA DRIED HER face at her bathroom sink and drank yet another glass of water, staring at herself in the mirror. The second he'd kissed her tonight, it had all come back. How had she forgotten? She'd dreamed about Jameson in high school. Sexually.

It was after that awful day their freshman year at Palos Verdes High School, when he'd asked her to the spring dance. He hadn't bothered her for a while, not at all that year, so Kendra had been surprised when he'd walked up to her. She'd immediately gone on guard, ready for whatever crap he tried to dish out.

Except, he'd looked more nervous even than she was, nervousness they'd both tried to cover with defiance. She wondered now if his friends or brothers had forced him into the prank, because he had clearly not been enjoying himself. Not like when he'd put glue in her hair.

He'd asked her harshly, rudely, certainly not in any way she could have taken seriously. On the last word, his voice had cracked, he'd glanced to his left, down at his feet. She'd laughed, asked why she'd want to go *anywhere* with him and stalked off, still laughing. Because as she'd watched his face, seeing the cracks in his bully facade, it had come to her that what her parents had been telling her all along was really true. The only power Jameson Cartwright had over her was power she gave him.

A short-lived victory. Because that night she'd dreamed about him in a way that gave him the same power he had over half the girls in school, including her best friend, Lena.

It was the night of the dance, but the dance was over. She was standing alone on the beach in a new dress. It had been dark, warm, the waves quiet, sand soft. Then Jameson was beside her; she'd felt no fear or surprise. It was as if she'd been expecting him. Barefoot, they'd walked to the water's edge, where he'd turned and kissed her, tumbled her onto the wet sand. His hands had begun an exploration that brought her body alive for him with pleasure that shocked her even in fantasy.

She'd woken in a rush of arousal and adrenaline, hand already between her legs, seeking something she didn't yet understand. Clumsily she'd stroked herself, feeling the desire intensify, thinking of Jameson's kisses, of how his hand had traveled briefly to where hers now lay, leaving a burning trail on her skin.

Her body had seemed to rise up, catch fire, and she'd let out an involuntary cry. The force of that first orgasm had stunned her. For days after she hadn't been able to look at Jameson, hadn't been able to reconcile her dread and their enmity with this new awareness of him and of what her body could do.

How could she have forgotten that watershed moment in her sexual development had been caused by Jameson Cartwright? And yet, if she'd had to choose one memory to bury in her subconscious, that would undoubtedly have been it. Easier than keeping it around to analyze, safer than the risk of finding out she could be on the same puppy-love train as everyone else. Not being attracted to him had been a kind of power, and she wouldn't have wanted to give that up.

Kendra gulped another glass of water, wiped her mouth

and launched herself onto the bed that had belonged to
her parents in the room it had taken her a year to move
into after they died, even though it was the best room in
the house, with huge windows facing the sea and the city,
spreading out across the valley to the feet of the Santa
Monica Mountains. She lay on her stomach, arms and legs
spread wide, relieved her head wasn't spinning, though she
was still pretty tipsy.

Jameson Cartwright.

She moved to her side. Her hand slid slowly between
her legs. She was already wet.

Jameson.

With a moan of surrender, she rolled to her back, stroking efficiently now—she was no longer fourteen. Her
breath stuttered in. She lifted her hips as the pleasure rose,
imagining Jameson lying over her, his hard body sculpted
to perfection, his penis searching, finding her, pushing inside. She imagined his pleasure, his groans of ecstasy, his
mouth and tongue finding hers.

The orgasm came quickly, a fierce burst that stopped
her breath, then contractions she panted through, wanting him with her there in bed with a desperation that almost frightened her.

She came down alone, rolled again to her side, pulling up the covers, looking out toward the glittering lights
of L.A. for a long, long time, until her mind calmed, her
breath slowed, eye blinks becoming more leisurely, body
relaxing toward sleep.

Who knew how many hours later, Kendra lifted her
head from her soft cotton pillowcase and blinked blearily
toward the door of her bedroom. Had she heard the front
doorbell?

She stretched under the covers and yawned, peering
at the clock. Seven-thirty. Too early for the mailman or a
delivery. She must have been dream—

Ding-dong.

Huh? Kendra pushed off the blankets and rolled clumsily out of bed, groaning. Who would show up at this hour without calling first? Too early for deliveries. Someone at the wrong house? There'd been workmen across the street. Maybe a new recruit had come here by mistake?

Padding through the small hallway connecting the master bedroom to the rest of the house, she checked in with herself for hangover symptoms, happy not to feel more than a twinge at her temple. Drinking all that water had been a good idea. She crossed the foyer, opposite the sunken living room with floor-to-ceiling windows like the master bedroom.

Ding-dong.

"Okay, okay." She peered through the front door's peephole and—

Ducked.

Oh, my God.

Jameson. She wasn't dressed, she had morning-after breath and bedhead, plus she'd been masturbating over him last night. What the hell was he doing here?

Okay. She was a professional. Her client needed her. She would simply reforget the memories of that erotic dream, and forget for the first time how he'd taken her in his arms and with the mere touch of his lips sent her spinning into a place of new and exciting feel—

Um. This forgetting thing wasn't working.

She opened the door a crack. Jameson was holding a bag from Bristol Farms, the upscale grocery with a store in neighboring Rolling Hills Estates. He was showered, shaved and dressed in a light gray shirt that made his eyes even more dazzling than usual.

"Hi, Jameson."

"Hungry?" He held up the bag. "I wasn't sure what you

liked, so I brought blueberry muffins, orange-cranberry scones, cinnamon rolls and chocolate croissants."

Her mouth dropped open.

Jameson frowned. "Too much?"

"You brought me breakfast?"

"And coffee. And orange juice. And bananas. And raspberries with a carbon footprint the size of Sasquatch's."

Oh, my gosh. Kendra caught herself before she melted all over the doorstep. No one had ever done anything that sweet for her before. At least no one she was dat—

No. They were not dating.

"I'm not dressed. Or showered. Or...anything."

"So? Not like we're dating, right?"

She rolled her eyes. Yeah, where had she heard that recently?

"Besides, you've seen me that way."

Yes. She had. But that didn't mean she owed him her own stink in return. At the same time, she didn't want him thinking she had some girlie need to be attractive to him.

Even though she did.

"Good point." She opened the door and the screen, smiling bravely, hoping her eyes weren't superpuffy or crusted with anything disgusting. "Good morning. Come in."

"Thanks." He stepped into the foyer, instantly transforming the elegant tiled space to a cozy area he dominated. Was he that big? Or just that magnetic? She had a feeling the answer to both was yes.

"Nice." He looked across the living room, the dining room to the right with its full-length marble-topped dining table and modern crystal chandelier that looked like a dense, square collection of icicles. "Quite a place."

"I grew up here." *Yeah, no kidding, Kendra.*

"Kitchen?"

"Through there." She pointed to the opposite end of the dining room. "I'll just go clean up."

"Take your time." He moved toward the kitchen, but not before giving her a devastating smile that made her breath back up in her lungs.

Yes, she needed to shower, but she needed even more to regroup. Jameson had always gotten to her—remembering the dream proved that even more strongly. But not like this. Last night the way he'd kissed her, even in her rather tipsy state—or maybe *especially* in that state—had positively upended her. Desire, absolutely. Lust, why not. But…then this odd tenderness, and an even odder feeling of inevitability, of rightness, that came from somewhere she didn't understand. An extension of the old-friends feeling she'd had at the whale-watching center, with someone who had never been a friend or a lover.

There was no way she could feel any of those emotions rationally. All her dealings with Jameson in her younger days had been negative and she had barely scratched the surface of knowing him as an adult.

The shower was warm and comforting; she scrubbed quickly, aware of her naked body in a way she did not want to be with the man who'd restarted her sex engines the previous night now at the opposite end of the house, which he'd walked into as if he'd been visiting his whole life.

Worse, she'd had to remind herself he'd never been there, it felt so natural to welcome him inside. God forbid she'd repressed more memories. Maybe they'd gotten married junior year.

She yanked the tap off and dried herself quickly, dragging on jeans and her oldest shirt in a rather unflattering shade of coral that clashed with her hair. No makeup.

There. That was how much she cared about attracting Jameson further.

Ha! She'd show him. And herself.

Okay, then.

Halfway to the bedroom door, she let out a growl of

frustration, tore off the top and replaced it with an emerald-green cotton sweater with a flattering scoop neck.

Fine. She was weak. And vain. And shallow. But at least the jeans were awful. And made her butt look fat. And she had no makeup on, so she was pale and teeny eyed.

Right.

Three steps toward the door, she veered right and stomped into the bathroom for a tiny smudge of eyeliner, a quick swipe of mascara and a brush of blush.

So guess what, she was human. Whatever.

Back toward the door, five steps this time, nearly there, almost…

Damn it.

She whirled around, practically growling, kicked the jeans across the room and dragged on a casual black knit skirt that barely skimmed her knees.

Fine. She thought he was hot and after last night she wanted to look that way, too, okay? So shut up.

She smiled brightly as she entered the kitchen. "Hey. I feel better. Thanks for waiting."

"That was quick. And you really did look fine." He was standing by the doors leading out to the deck, next to the wooden kitchen table on which he'd laid out the appetizing fat- and sugar-loaded carbfest. His eyes traveled over her appreciatively. "You still look fine."

"Thanks!" She was jittery, overcheerful, acting like a teacher facing a classroom of hostile faces on her first day. And wishing she had on the jeans and awful shirt. "Wow, you *really* brought breakfast. What did I do to deserve this?"

He was watching her with a half smile that made her feel as if he could see inside her and understand everything she was feeling, which made her wrap her arms around herself to block him. "I wanted to see you. After last night."

"Oh. Last night." She laughed, which made her sound like an awkward and embarrassed virgin idiot.

"Kendra." His blue eyes softened and warmed. She needed to stop this—whatever it was—before it went a millimeter further. "Last night was—"

"A bad idea." She pointed into his face. "A very bad idea. You're injured, depressed and facing uncertain life circumstances. I'm your counselor, in a position of responsibility for your mental health, and charged with gaining your trust and respect. If we took this relationship into a, um, into a new dimension, then I'd be—"

"Wait, wait, let me get this straight." He was positively smirking now. "You think I'm the vulnerable patient falling for his therapist because—"

"Counselor."

"—falling for his counselor because she's the only person who'll listen to me? The only person who understands me in my most painful and difficult hour?"

"Well…yeah." She gestured toward him. "Aren't I?"

He looked startled, but barely missed a beat. "And if anything physical happens between us you'll be abusing your position of immense power over my psyche?"

"Yes, *exactly*." She nodded eagerly, like her worst student had finally caught on to two plus two. "You are a dainty little blossom of a person and if you so much as kiss my cheek again, I will inadvertently bug-squash your soul."

He was laughing now. She couldn't help it, she joined him, and the shared laughter felt intimate, cathartic and really, really good.

"Okay, soul squasher, let's eat breakfast." He gestured to a chair as if he were the host in her house. She liked that.

"But wait." She paused, her butt halfway to the chair. "We haven't agreed on anything yet."

"Nothing?"

"I mean about us. About what…" She was turning red. She hated that. He flustered her now as much as he had in grade school, but for different reasons. "About how we—"

"Do this?" He leaned forward so fast she didn't see it coming and planted a quick, soft kiss on her mouth. Then he pulled away and sat down as if nothing had happened while she stayed frozen, butt still a foot from her chair, tweety birds circling her head.

Damn it. He had to stop doing that.

More to the point, she had to stop liking it so much.

And him.

Because…

For a brief moment, together with him in her kitchen having breakfast as if they'd spent the night shaking the floors, the reason eluded her.

Because why?

Because he was a client. Because he was a Cartwright. Because he was here for another two and a half weeks and then would go back to a life in the military that did not include her.

Those were all good reasons.

She plunked her butt down, grabbed the glass of juice he'd poured her and drank as if it were a lifesaving serum. Delicious juice. She bit into a blueberry muffin.

"Mmm!"

"Good?" He chose a scone and nodded, his own mouth full. "Mmm."

Good Lord. He even made enjoying a scone sexy. She was going to have to think new thoughts now, because hers involved Jameson making that *mmm* noise for an entirely different reason.

"Thank you for this." She pulled her coffee closer and took off the lid, releasing steam and a dark, rich aroma. "It's really nice of you."

"I want to keep seeing you."

"You—" Kendra froze, coffee in hand, blinking at him stupidly while he took another bite of scone. He wanted to... He was just announcing it like that? That he wanted to date her? And then he could go back to eating calmly while he waited for her answer?

No, no, that wasn't it. Geez. He wanted to keep seeing her professionally. What had she been thinking? Thank God she hadn't responded any other way.

"Sure. I don't have an appointment until later this morning, so right now is fine. What's on your mind?"

Halfway through her speech, he started a slow smile that widened into a sexy grin. By the time she finished, he was chuckling. "Kendra..."

"What is so funny?"

"I want to see you romantically. I want us to go on dates, not counseling sessions."

"Oh." Her face must be turning traffic-light red. But okay, she'd encountered this situation before and knew how to cope. She laid a gentle hand on his forearm, smiling, friendly. "Thank you, Jameson. But I can't go out with one of my clients."

He stood abruptly and hauled her to standing. She got a brief glimpse of his amused face before he was kissing her. Like he meant it.

Apparently he really, *really* meant it.

"Well, guess what? I'm not your client anymore."

Kendra had to try twice to speak, hands braced against his chest. "But we're not finished. And Dr. Kornish hired me to—"

"You're the best there is, Kendra. I'm totally cured."

"Ha!" She tried to push away. But whatever they did to airmen in basic training built muscles much too strong for her to budge. "Not even close."

"Look." He cupped the side of her face, tipped her head up to meet his eyes. "I want you, Kendra. Badly. I don't think I'm alone in those feelings. What kind of successful professional relationship are we going to have if all we want to do is crawl into bed together?"

His gaze and his words combined to shoot hot lightning through her. She couldn't think beyond the mental picture of him making his way, stealthily, naked, into her bed.

"I guess I…" Kendra closed her eyes to gather her thoughts, because it was pretty impossible to do that with his arms around her, her lips still warm from his kisses and his gorgeous blue eyes boring into hers. She'd been trained in how to dissuade an interested client; she'd had to smack down a few men in the past couple of years—gently, of course. The psychologists' code of ethics forbade romantic relationships between a therapist and client until two full years after therapy stopped. But Kendra wasn't a licensed psychologist. Nor was she providing traditional therapy. "I need time to think about this, Jameson."

"Sure." His lips landed, warm and lingering, on her forehead. Even that made her whole body shiver. "Think about it. Take all the time you need."

Kendra bent her head gratefully. "Thank you."

"You done yet?"

She cracked up, lifting her head. "Hey. You didn't used to be this funny in grade school."

"Are you kidding? Worms in your sandwich isn't the height of comedy?"

"Uh…"

Jameson's smile faded. "Guess I didn't have that much to laugh about."

"Oh, come on. You Cartwrights owned the school. Maybe the universe."

"Nah. I was the same wreck everyone else was. Just better at faking it." He stroked back hair from her face. "You kept it real, though. I admired you for that. Which is probably why I kept trying to knock it out of you."

"Boy logic." Kendra shook her head.

He kissed her, sweetly, almost tenderly, and her heart did some melting it absolutely should not be doing. Bad enough she was hot for him, but real feelings…out of bounds entirely.

"I should leave so you can get your day going. But you'll think about it?"

She nodded.

"Good." He backed toward the door. "Dinner tonight?"

"Jameson…"

He held up both hands. "Just asking. I'll call you later."

She saw him to the door, noticing the limp was even better than the day before, replaced by a bit more of his masculine swagger. The surgery had worked. He'd be gone soon, flying off to the rest of his career like Spirit the hawk, healed and released, twenty years before he could retire, during which time he could get shipped just about anywhere.

What was the point? If she was sure their relationship would only be sexual, that would be one thing. But she liked him. And like plus sex equaled only one thing.

Trouble.

She closed the front door and ran back into her bedroom to unplug her cell from its charger, glancing at her watch before she dialed Lena. Her friend would already be at the office, unless there was typical L.A. traffic from hell.

"Hey, Kendra."

"You busy?" Kendra wandered out into the hall. "Not that you're ever not."

"I have a few minutes, what's going on?"

"Jameson."

"Ooh, Cartwright drama. You have my full attention."

"He's… That is, he… Well, he wants to…"

"No way! Really? Oh, my God!"

"Uh…" Kendra stepped down into the living room, past

the antique piano only her mother had played. "I haven't even told you what he wants."

"He's a guy, what else could it be?"

Kendra cracked up. "You are good."

She outlined the situation, how Jameson didn't seem to be quite the jerk they'd thought he was, to put it mildly, and then described all the talks they'd had, the fun they'd had, the transformation he'd undergone from miserable and barely speaking to fun and funny and incredibly sexy. Only she didn't admit that last part.

"You know, Kendra, you will think I'm nuts, but I wondered sometimes if he was always bugging you because he was into you."

"Ha!" Alarms went off all over Kendra's body. "No, no. This is not about *being* into me. This is about *going* into me."

Just saying it was true made her feel better.

Lena giggled. "Geez, what a romantic you aren't. It could be more than that. You don't know."

Kendra gritted her teeth. She'd just gotten rid of the alarm bells. "He's a guy."

"Guys fall in love, too. And what would be wrong with that anyway? He sounds like he's grown up a lot. He's hot. He's available. He has a job."

"He's leaving."

"Oh, Kendra." Lena was quiet for a good ten seconds, which didn't happen often. "He's in the Air Force, he *has* to go. I know it's soon after your parents passed, but their deaths don't mean everyone you love will—"

Forget alarm bells, Kendra was approaching panic. "Love? *Love?* We are talking about a nice healthy boinking here. Period."

"Okay, not love. But not just boinking, girlfriend. Listen to how you told me about him. Not just, 'Wow, Lena, this guy has a package the size of Florida!' You told me how much you love talking to him, how funny he is… There's an emotional component."

Kendra's throat thickened. She did not want to hear this. Especially because it might be true. Okay, it was true. A little. But not out of control. She could still keep it from threatening her sanity.

"I'm just saying what's wrong with dating a guy you're attracted to who is also attracted to you?"

Kendra bit her lip, staring over the top of the olive tree in her backyard that her father had planted for one of his and Mom's anniversaries. Lena made it sound so simple. Was it? Was she just afraid of falling for Jameson? Of losing someone she cared for all over again? It had been two years since her parents died. Sometimes it felt as if she'd been alone forever; sometimes it seemed a blink of an eye. As she told all her clients, there was no right time to move on from a death. Everyone at his or her own pace.

Maybe her strong reaction to Jameson had nothing to do with falling for him but was simply her body and subconscious telling her she was ready now?

"Yeesh, I have to get to a meeting. Call me later and let me know what you're thinking."

"Sure. Thanks, Lena. Bye." Kendra punched off the phone, more confused than ever. If she agreed to date Jameson…

Even the phrase made her want to laugh. Date Jameson Cartwright! Her lifelong nemesis.

But oh, a nemesis with hot blue eyes, a dynamite smile, mouth by Cupid, body by Air Force. She'd have to be crazy not to want to explore all of it.

And she'd have to be crazier to actually do it.

And yet, as Lena pointed out—

But then again…

She rolled her eyes and shoved the phone into her pocket, heading to her bedroom to get ready to go. She had a full day ahead, including a visit to Crystal with Byron. Maybe later she and Byron could invite Jameson for a frolic on the beach in safe daylight.

If she decided the daylight would also turn into night, she'd have officially resigned as his counselor.

Kendra stopped dead on her way to the front door.

Oh, God.

She'd have to call Matty to stop the payments. Matty would want to know why.

Gulp.

She could say Jameson was cured. She could say he refused to see her anymore. She could say he was a hopeless case.

Argh. She couldn't lie and retain any professional credibility, not to mention she couldn't lie to a sister about the condition of a brother she loved and live in her own skin afterward.

Which meant Kendra would have to come up with some way to tell Matty the truth: that she couldn't accept further payment for treating Jameson, because after almost two weeks it had become abundantly clear that she was going to have to screw his brains out.

Then she could sit back while Matty either laughed her ass off at Kendra or sent brothers Hayden and Mark over to kill her.

But first she had to decide…

Kendra sagged in defeat. Who was she kidding? She'd already decided.

9

MATTY OPENED HER eyes. Light was already streaming in through the not-quite-closed blinds over her windows, which gave onto a charming view of puce siding on the house next door. Ooh, baby. Well, anyway, the day looked to be sunny, which was always cheering. She stretched luxuriously in the old sleigh bed she'd slept in since girlhood. Her mother had been thrilled to get rid of it, having wanted to update Matty's old room for years. While the rest of their Palos Verdes Estates house had changed with the times, Matty's room remained a quaint anachronism, filled with dark wood antique pieces she'd pounced on as an adolescent when her father's parents had downsized into a retirement home. Sometimes she thought she'd been born into the wrong time period.

She turned to peer at the brass windup clock on her cherry bedside table. Yes, she had her iPhone across the room for backup, but she loved this clock and refused to part with it, even if it gained a minute now and then. Or two.

Ten o'clock.

Adrenaline burned as her sleepiness cleared enough to register the day and its significance. Wednesday, November 13, two weeks before Thanksgiving, the day she was to have a late dinner with Chris after that evening's show. He was going to be in L.A. anyway, he'd said. How about it?

She'd suggested lunch in order to keep the intimacy of nighttime and the inevitable alcohol consumption from leading them into more temptation than they'd have at midday in a well-lit restaurant, but Chris had to teach. With her show schedule, it was rare she got to share an evening meal with anyone during the week.

Honestly, she wanted to see him so badly that she'd said yes in spite of all the voices cautioning her. At least this time she was going in with her eyes wide open. And if he fooled her twice, then shame on her; Matty wouldn't even try blaming anyone but herself.

Across the room, her phone played the opening lines of Gershwin's "I've Got Beginner's Luck." She threw off the covers, jumped out of bed. She'd never been a morning person, not even a late-morning person, though given that she worked until after 10:00 p.m. most nights, her schedule was skewed compared to most people's. But this morning she was wide awake. Was it Chris?

Kendra! She answered eagerly. Jameson had made amazing progress since she'd been working with him, much more than Matty could have imagined. He was not only taking her calls, he sounded cheerful and funny and… she'd say back to his old self, except that he was more cheerful and funny than she'd ever known him to be. Kendra must be a miracle worker.

"Oh. Uh, hey, Matty."

Matty stiffened. Kendra sounded cautious, wary, no sign of her usual dynamic optimism.

"What's going on? How—" She was going to ask immediately about Jameson. Not polite. "—are you?"

"Good, thanks. I'm doing well. Just fine. Thanks."

This was weird. "How are things going with my little brother?"

Kendra made a strange choking sound. "Great, actually. Really great. He's made amazing progress out of depression and into accepting his injury. Faster than anyone I've seen, given how low he'd sunk."

Whew. Matty fell back onto the bed, gazing up at the iron-and-glass ceiling light she'd also pilfered from her parents' house. "This is great news."

"It is. Definitely. He even seems more sure he'll serve out his time in the Air Force."

Matty grimaced. She'd hoped Jameson's experiences with Kendra would help him come around to some understanding of how much their father and brothers' influence forced his decision to sign up. "Good to hear."

"So, um…there is one change."

Uh-oh. Matty sat up again. Apparently she hadn't imagined the anxious undertone in Kendra's voice. "What's that?"

"I…you won't need to pay me anymore."

She frowned. "So you're done?"

"Not exactly."

"He doesn't want to see you anymore?"

Kendra made that strange choking sound again. "Um, no, actually, he does."

"So, what, he thinks you should *donate* your services?" Matty couldn't imagine.

"Not exactly."

Something weird was going on here. "Why don't you just tell me, Kendra."

"Yes. I should. Sorry. The thing is, he wants to— Well, I guess I do, too, but certain ethical problems…" She made a sound of frustration. "I mean, if we keep getting together, not really professionally—at least on my part. Or no, not his part either. *God,* I'm doing this badly."

Matty gasped and thunked a hand to her chest, aghast and fascinated at the same time. "You're involved with him?"

"No. No. No, not at all." She sighed. "That is, not really. Or I mean, not yet. Not completely."

Matty rose from the bed and went to the window, yanked open the blinds—good morning, puce. Kendra and Jameson. She should have seen this coming. "You want to date my brother?"

"Matty, I have never encountered anything like this in my professional life. I mean, I have, but I wasn't interested."

"I take it you're interested now."

"...Yes."

Matty frowned and paced her room, window to dresser and back. Okay. So this was not the worst thing in the world. As long as her brother didn't get hurt. "Are you serious about him?"

"No, no, no." She answered a little too quickly, but she was obviously nervous as hell. "No point getting serious. He's leaving. We both know that."

Hmm. Window. Dresser. Window. This could actually be really good. For both of them.

"Matty, this is totally unexpected. I'm sort of a mess over it."

Matty relented. She even stopped pacing. "You sound it."

"The thing is, I enjoy him. A lot. And he seems to feel the same way. Maybe it's our shared history, I don't know. We just really have...fun."

"Fun is what he needs."

"Yes, I mean, I have fun with all my clients, but this got...very fun."

A grin started to spread across Matty's face. Well, well. "You know one of the reasons I wanted you to do this so badly is that I thought Jameson would trust you in a way he wouldn't trust a stranger, no matter how capable she was."

"So you don't mind?"

"I'm only worried because he's vulnerable right now." A snort came over the line. Matty narrowed her eyes. Oh. Maybe he wasn't that vulnerable. "Does what I think make a difference?"

The silence went on so long that Matty wanted to giggle. Of course it didn't. Kendra was probably too polite to say so. What would Jameson say if he heard Matty was going out with Chris again? Or anyone from college who'd known about the affair? They'd all want to give her a huge whap across the common sense. Would that change her mind? Probably not.

She took pity. "Kendra, when it comes to matters of the heart, you gotta do what you gotta do. It really shouldn't surprise me that you two have found something, whatever it is, however long it lasts. And if it makes my brother happy, then I'm all for it."

"I'll still be taking care of him. Trying to make sure he's doing okay."

Shy tenderness had crept into her voice. Ha! She was crazy about him. Matty relaxed the rest of the way, grinned wickedly. "He's not so bad after all, huh."

"Not *so* bad, no. Not like he used to be. He hasn't tried to trip me in the halls." She was silent for a couple of beats. "But it's less like he's changed fundamentally and more like he let himself out of some box."

"Ah, the Cartwright container."

"Maybe that's it." She laughed nervously. "Half the time I think I'm completely crazy even considering this."

"Tell me about it." Matty pulled up the covers on her bed to neaten them. "I'm thinking of starting up again with an old boyfriend and feeling the same way."

"It's scary." Kendra inhaled slowly. "But also exciting."

Ew. Matty gave her pillow a thump. She did not want to hear how exciting her brother was. "Keep me posted, Kendra. I mean as a friend. If you want to."

"Absolutely. Maybe we could have coffee sometime? I'd love to meet you."

"Why don't you and Jameson come see the show one night this weekend or next week? I promised you tickets."

"I'll check with him." She giggled. "Okay, this is weird."

"Very." Matty would bet everything she owned that Kendra was blushing like crazy right about then. She ended the call and crawled back into bed, turning on her side, hugging the no-longer-neat covers around her. What was that strange power that bound two people together for so many years? Her and Chris, Jameson and Kendra.

When Jameson had been little, the name Kendra had come up over and over. Kendra was smart. Kendra did a great show-and-tell. Kendra was funny in the school play. Kendra was helping organize a food drive. Kendra was running against him for class president.

But every time Matty had tried to talk to Jameson about this Kendra person and a possible friendship, he'd shake his head fiercely and insist she was fat and annoying, words that sounded straight out of their brothers' mouths. So she'd stopped asking, but kept noticing. His victory senior year as class president was the closest he'd ever been to coming clean about his feelings for her.

Matty had been home for the weekend from Pomona when he'd stalked into her room, looking angry and upset. She knew better than to ask, just waited while he roamed around the room, working on her journal entry until he felt like talking. When he did, all he'd said was, "Kendra ran the better campaign."

"Congratulations, you're a Cartwright." Matty hadn't said that the way their dad would.

Jameson had understood the irony. He'd gone on to blurt out how he'd been surrounded by congratulatory friends after the election, and Kendra had made him feel about six inches tall by plowing determinedly through the crowd, congratulating him and walking away. Matty had listened sympathetically, but really, what could she say? If the world was fair, everyone who got ahead would be smarter and harder working and more talented.

Now through a remarkable set of circumstances set in motion by a stray cat, Jameson might finally get his Kendra.

As for herself and Chris, Matty would have to wait to see.

And wait.

And wait—did a day *ever* take this long to pass? She was at the theater half an hour earlier than usual, desperate to escape her apartment and get started on this last block of time before their date. After the show she was out of costume and makeup and into street clothes and her car in record time. The drive to the restaurant would take twenty minutes with no traffic issues.

No traffic issues! She pulled into a public parking lot around the block from the restaurant where they were meeting, the Lazy Ox Canteen, with three minutes to spare. Hurrying across the dark street and down the block, she spotted the glass-fronted entrance and pushed inside.

The place was narrow, bustling, bar on the left, tables in two parallel rows toward the back of the room. Chalkboards on the walls listed the menu options.

It smelled really, really good.

A man rose from a table on her left. She didn't need to look directly at him to know it was Chris. His form was emblazoned so deeply in her memory that even her peripheral vision recognized him in an instant.

She'd planned to be cool, confident, a bit standoffish, all in the name of self-protection, but at the sight of his handsome face and smiling brown eyes all that sensible stuff went out the window and she found herself grinning for all she was worth.

So be it. She'd never been able to fight her feelings for him—what made her hope she could now?

"Hi, Chris." She hugged him quickly, wishing he didn't smell so good and so familiar. It made her want to hold on and inhale. "Thanks for driving out here."

"You had the late commitment. It only made sense." He guided her to their table, pulled out her chair. Matty would never hold it against a guy not to bother with the old-fashioned gesture, but it fit Chris and she enjoyed it. "How did the show go tonight?"

She grimaced, shrugging out of her jacket. "I missed a step toward the end, but otherwise fine."

"Yeah?" He sat opposite her, somehow too close. This was too intense, too awkward; there was too much unsaid hanging between them to relax. She needed a drink. Now. "What happened there?"

Matty pretended to be very involved in adjusting her chair, using it as an excuse to back up just a bit. She'd been thinking of him. Of tonight. Of what might happen after dinner and whether she wanted it to or not. "Mind-body glitch. It happens. My concentration slipped."

"I couldn't keep my mind on anything but you today either."

He spoke offhandedly, as if he'd been praising the restaurant decor. Arousal burned through her. It had always been like this between them. "What makes you think I was thinking of you?"

"Weren't you?"

She smiled and picked up the menu. "Don't let it go to your head."

"Trust me, with you I take nothing for granted." Chris leaned forward as if to whisper, raising his eyebrows. "Any chance you're in the mood for champagne?"

A joke between them. She was *always* in the mood for

champagne. "Hmm. Well…I *guess* so. Are we celebrating?"

"Just drinking champagne."

"I approve."

They spent a few minutes looking over the menu of small plates, discussing which ones to try—difficult choices, since everything looked delicious. They'd just settled on a couple of intriguing vegetable plates and a few heartier selections of meat and fish when the waiter came by with champagne, which Chris had apparently ordered before her arrival.

Matty scowled teasingly. "I thought you took nothing about me for granted."

"Only this." He smiled at her, eyes warm. "You never say no to champagne."

"True." And she never said no to sex after she'd been drinking it. He probably remembered that, too.

After the waiter filled their glasses and took their order, Chris raised his flute to her in a toast. "Here's to stumbling over you again, Matty."

She hesitated, then clinked his glass and drank. The champagne was chilled just right, with a fresh clarity that slid down way too easily. Matty took in a blissful breath. "Oh, that's good. I'll end up taking a cab home."

"I can drive you." He suddenly looked uncomfortable, lined up his fork more exactly perpendicular to the table's edge. "If it comes to that."

Matty dropped her gaze, took another big sip of the wine, knowing they were both thinking about him coming home with her and what might happen there.

"Catch me up on the years, Chris. Still renting the same apartment?"

He shook his head. "I bought a house when I got tenure. Nice three-bedroom on Seventh Street. I have room for my office, and a guest room. I like the space."

"Still got the baseball wall in your bedroom?"

"Absolutely."

She sipped more champagne, watching him over the rim, feeling the bubbles cavorting through her system. He was so, so handsome. She remembered lying in his bed after they'd made love, staring at the autographed poster of Graig Nettles on the wall and wondering if they'd get married, have kids, be together until death.

So young. So naive.

"Did you ever go to Paris, Chris?"

The warmth in his eyes faded to wistful sadness. "No."

"No?" She was dismayed to find herself relieved. They'd planned to take the trip together after Matty's graduation. Matty had been ecstatic. She'd spent her year abroad after high school in London, Scotland and Ireland, but had never made it to the Continent. Paris would belong to her and to Chris. She'd even fantasized that he'd propose there. After they'd broken up, she'd barely been able to think about France, let alone plan to go there without him. Later there had been other more practical reasons of budget and time.

But *he* hadn't gone? Not ever?

"Why not?"

He chuckled dryly. "Paris was supposed to be ours, remember?"

"But it's been *years,* Chris." Emboldened by the champagne, she laid her fingers on the table, their tips just touching his sleeve. "Why didn't you go later? It was your dream destination."

"Mattingly…" Chris put down his champagne and took her hand, eyes filling with a special sweetness, a look she remembered getting many, many times, a look that made her feel adored and desired and as though the world was a uniformly fabulous place—despite all evidence to the contrary. "I don't think you realize how serious I was about you."

She opened her mouth to scoff at him, but couldn't make a sound. How could she know if he was telling the truth or setting the stage for seduction that would ultimately lead to more heartbreak?

"I know that's not what you want to hear right now, so that's all I'll say." He released her hand and sat back. "Did you ever go?"

"No." She developed the same fascination with silverware he'd had not long before, heart still pounding. "Either I didn't have the money or it wasn't the right time."

"Nothing to do with me, huh."

She grinned apologetically. "I put everything I had into getting over you, Chris. After that it was just lack of opportunity."

"I understand."

Waitstaff began arriving at their table, which was soon covered with plates holding small portions of the most amazing-looking food. They tasted everything, exclaimed over one dish, held out bites of another to try, and soon they'd relaxed into conversation involving the growth of Matty's performing career, getting her real estate license, Jameson's recovery, Kendra and the phone call that morning. Then on to Chris, his hopes and victory over the tenure process and changes in the Pomona faculty and administration and in the town of Claremont.

By that time, their food had been happily eaten, the champagne drained, then quick cups of coffee, decaf for her, espresso for him. The restaurant was closing and it was time to go.

"You okay to drive home?" He took her arm and led her out onto the sidewalk. "Where are you parked?"

"In the lot around the corner. How about you? You have a much longer drive. You're not going to fall asleep?"

"Not me." He squeezed her hand. "I'm wide awake. And not just because of the coffee."

"My show schedule has turned me into a night owl."
She wasn't going to admit being with Chris still made
her giddy.

"When can I see you again?"

"Soon as you turn your head."

He snorted and pulled her close, put his arm around her
shoulders. They still fit together perfectly, their steps automatically syncing. "I've missed you, Matty."

She said nothing, didn't think it wise to push the conversation in that direction now, not when they were both
tipsy, it was late at night and they were still under the pull
of this remarkable reunion. She needed distance and so-
briety to analyze the evening with any objectivity.

They crossed into the parking lot, and Matty felt her
tension rising. Good night was coming. God give her
strength if he tried to kiss her...

"Where's your car?"

"Um...there." She pointed to the far end of the lot.

"Mine's here." He gestured to their right. "I'll walk
you to yours."

"You don't have to—"

"I know I don't have to." He walked with her, humming
in his rich, deep voice a tune she vaguely recognized, but
couldn't place. As they approached her car, Matty's nerves
started humming louder than he was.

He'd try to kiss her, of course he would. Would she have
the courage to stop him?

With her body so close, absorbing his warmth, memories of what that body had done with hers clouding her
mind, she suddenly wasn't so sure.

They reached her car. She turned to thank him for the
evening, telling herself to give him a quick hug and re-
treat to safety. He drew her into his arms and began a slow
waltz. Her mind suddenly supplied lyrics to his humming.

Oh, no. She *loved* that song. So tender, sweet and romantic, it was nearly gross.

"Why are you singing that?"

"No idea." He spun her and brought her back to his arms. "It showed up in my head. What is it?"

"'I'd Fall in Love Tonight.'"

"Were they playing it at the restaurant?"

She laughed, losing the battle to keep at least four inches between them. He was such a good dancer. "Hardly. It's from a hundred years ago."

"Then it suits me. What are the words? I can't remember."

"I don't know them."

"Come on." He kept dancing, humming when he wasn't speaking. "You know the words to every song ever written. Tell me."

She took a deep breath, aware of his arm curving around her back, the warm clasp of his fingers, the way their bodies moved so perfectly together. "It's about the singer touching a lover and having it feel like the first time all over again, and really right. Then the singer says if he or she didn't already love the other person, he or she would definitely fall in love with him or her on that night."

"Uh, Matty?" He stopped, holding her an inch away, looking at her with sexy amusement. "What's that, the legalese version?"

She opened her eyes innocently wide. "It was a factual and succinct summary. Highly appropriate to the occasion."

"I see." He went back to dancing, resting his cheek on her hair. "So you didn't want to stand in my arms in the dark and recite a love poem."

"Not really." She was barely able to make sound. "Given our history."

"I really liked parts of our history." He slid his arm all

the way around her until their bodies were touching. "It's probably why my subconscious came up with that song."

"Possibly. But I don't think—"

His head dipped. His lips found hers. Lightly, gently, he tasted her, smelling clean, masculine and so, so familiar. Her body responded as if it was finally where it belonged.

Another kiss, deeper; his embrace tightened. She'd forgotten his strength, forgotten how she could feel so cherished and so safe in those arms. But she hadn't forgotten what his kisses did to her, how no other man had been able to make her feel so much with so little.

She moaned, pressed herself against him, relief she didn't understand flooding her body, a huge release of some tension she'd been holding since she'd finally walked away from him six years before.

He pulled back, pressed her head to his shoulder and rocked her side to side without speaking. Tears sprang in her eyes; her throat thickened.

Chris.

"I'd like to see you again."

"Yes," she whispered.

"Soon?"

"Yes."

He unwound her arms from his neck, kissed her again and stepped back.

She blinked at him uncomprehendingly. Her body was screaming for his, naked and sweaty, tangling up sheets, rocking sofas, overturning chairs—what hadn't they done?

"The only thing I want more than tonight with you is more tonights with you, Matty. A lot more. If I ask to come over now, we'll be going too fast. For both of us. I don't want to crash and burn again. I know you don't either."

Matty nodded mutely, holding back tears as hard as she could. He was doing the right thing for the right reasons. Someday they'd have to talk more about Clarisse.

He'd need to go over it again. And maybe again after that, until she trusted he was telling the truth. But he was right, they needed to rebuild that trust slowly after it had been so thoroughly smashed the first time.

She got into her car, feeling a different kind of relief, this time mixed with longing and wistful regret. "Good night, Chris."

"Call or text me when you get home."

She smiled. Chris had always insisted. Even if she was just walking the few blocks back to her dorm. "I will."

"Sweet dreams." He tapped on the door and stepped back. She backed out of the space and drove off, waving, glancing at him occasionally in her rearview mirror.

Just before she lost sight of him, he tipped an imaginary hat.

10

JAMESON LEANED HIS elbows back on the ancient quilt he and Kendra had spread on Rat Beach—so named not because of rodents, but because it was the beach Right After Torrance. The day was chilly but the sun was warm, and as always the beach was not at all crowded. Frankly, if he could lie next to Kendra on a blanket he would do so even in Antarctica. She was leaning back in the same position he was, her hair a thick curtain between her head and the quilt, making him want to put his hands into it, feel it spreading across his chest…

She'd picked him up after her last appointment and they'd gotten takeout and brought Byron to the beach. They'd been chatting pretty easily during dinner, but there was still underlying tension. There probably would be until they settled into the rules of phase three of the Kendra-Jameson relationship—from grade school enemies to counselor and client to…whatever this was going to be.

Jameson was hanging back until he found out. The chemistry between them had made it pretty obvious maintaining a professional relationship wasn't going to work. He couldn't see her without wanting to touch her, kiss her and…yeah, um, a lot more than that. Hell, he felt that way about her even when she was out of sight.

But this was more than a simple working out of male-female urges. He liked Kendra a lot. He respected her. He wanted to find out more about her life since high school, how she'd weathered the tragedy of losing her parents and what she wanted for her life in the future—whether that could involve a long-distance relationship. And lately he'd found himself wanting to protect her. To keep her safe from the big bad guys of life. To be the one she turned to for advice and support.

Not great ingredients for a casual two-week fling. Yet the thought of ending whatever this turned out to be was nearly as ridiculous as thinking about waiting twenty years to live with her again in the same town.

Behind them Byron let out an impatient woof. Kendra groaned and dragged herself to sitting. "I should let him run around. Why didn't you stop me after I'd eaten enough for three people?"

"I was too busy eating for seven." Jameson surveyed the wreckage strewn around them. Thai food. Decimated. The battle had been long and delicious, starting with tom yum kai soup, a spicy flavorful broth brimming with shrimp, straw mushrooms and cilantro; then fiery, rich red curry with beef; and finally pad thai, rice noodles slightly sour from tamarind juice, rich with peanuts and egg and re-freshed with lime and bean sprouts.

"C'mon, Byron." She got to her feet and untied his leash, then headed for a corner of the quilt. "I have a present for you, Jameson. Want it now?"

"A present?" He pretended childlike eagerness. "Where? What is it?"

"Here. Wait." She reached into her bag and came up with an old chewed-up dog toy.

"Ooh, slobbery tennis ball, thank you!" He grinned at the look she sent him.

"That would be for Byron. This…" She pulled out a sketch pad and a variety of pens, pencils and charcoal.

"…is for you. While I let Byron go nuts off leash, you go nuts on paper."

"Kendra. Wow. Thank you." He took the art supplies from her, admiring the thick sheets of paper, the sharpened high-quality drawing implements. She must have made a special trip to an art store to buy them for him. More touched than he should be, he pretended sudden suspicion. "Wait, this is therapy. I thought you weren't treating me anymore."

She stood with Byron's leash, making the dog shoot to his feet, wiggling all over with excited anticipation. "You don't think friends should help each other?"

Friends? Was that what she'd decided they were? He couldn't blame her, given that he had nothing to offer her but the next two weeks. Yet he couldn't help a sharp jab of disappointment. "I don't want you to do your job and not get paid."

"Oh, yeah? Well, I want you to draw me something." She staggered as Byron pulled in the direction of the water. "Then I think we need to take a long walk and burn off one or two of the sixty thousand calories we just ate. If your knee is up to it."

"Absolutely." His knee had been improving rapidly. Sometimes he wondered if Kendra had affected its recovery as positively as she'd affected his attitude. He only had minor pain now, though he was still careful and did his home exercises diligently, lengthening his stationary bike and treadmill sessions gradually and sensibly, even while his body was yelling at him to push to the limit or he'd fall behind.

But Dr. Kornish had told him horror stories about doing too much too soon. No, thanks.

Speaking of Dr. Kornish, his nurse had called that morning to check on Jameson's progress. When Jameson had praised the work Kendra had done on Dr. Kornish's behalf, the nurse had had no idea what he was talking about.

Smiling, he watched Kendra unhook Byron's leash and race with him down to the water. A sweetness came over him that he hadn't felt in way too many years. Self-consciously, he flipped up the cover of the sketch pad, still squinting at woman and dog and water. Jameson hadn't put pencil to paper since college when he'd designed a publicity poster for a friend's variety show. However, his incredibly sexy ex-counselor "friend," whom he desperately wanted as a lover, had requested he draw for her, so he would.

He let his gaze focus, wander, allowing his artistic eye to take over. Cliffs, palm trees, ocean, surfers and an auburn-haired laughing beauty, legs long, body slender, strong arm throwing a tennis ball into the waves for a crazed canine over and over.

His pencil moved swiftly, a few lines for her torso, the curve of her back, catching her bending to the dog in welcome, skirt blowing in the breeze, hair streaming behind her. Horizon, sea, sky—the page went up and over. Again he drew, this time capturing her larger center frame, stretched in the act of throwing, her body a graceful arc, texture for her hair, her clothes. Up and over. Then again, the strong breadth of her shoulders, the contour of her breasts, the sensual flare of her hips. Up and over. Her head in profile, full mouth stretched in a smile, faintly freckled straight nose ending in a sweet point, cheekbone shaded high, long-lashed eye suggesting joy, brow an expressive slash, hair spilling back in a generous tangle.

She was beautiful. He must have noticed in high school. Beyond the few extra pounds, the heavy dark glasses, the serious demeanor. He must have seen her, internalized her features. How else would he be able to draw this face from memory so easily?

"Can I see?"

Jameson started and hid the drawing instinctively. He hadn't seen or heard her approach. "Not yet."

"You okay for a few more minutes? I want to put Byron in the car."

"Sure."

He watched her walk, hips twisting saucily to gain traction in the sand. His fingers itched to draw her again.

Up and over.

This time he embarked on a full portrait, working the details of a more distant memory. Kendra, cheeks and chin fuller, brows thicker, mouth a line of determination and strength, eyes direct and assessing behind black plastic.

The face he'd encountered many times, most recently after he'd stolen the election from her their senior year. He'd never forget it or how she'd made him feel that day.

A few more details, hair, then the plain collar of a gray shirt.

He glanced over to see her coming back already, down the steep hill from the school parking lot up top. There was no hiding from her. She drew the best from him, goaded him to be his best self. Then and now.

How could he not be falling for her?

She was striding toward him, her smile reaching out. Jameson put away the pad, his instinct to stride over to meet her, scoop her up in his arms and bring her back to the quilt to make love to her. "Can I see now?"

"Later." There was too much of himself and his feeling in the drawings. He wasn't ready to share that yet. "After the walk."

She narrowed her eyes. "Stalling, stalling."

"Can if I want to."

Her giggle at his childish chant made his day. He helped her pack up their leavings, then got to his feet, stretching his right leg, flexing it carefully. His knee still became unwieldy when it had been quiet for too long, but his range of motion was nearly back to normal.

In two weeks plus he'd be back on base. Another three to six months before he could hope to restart his specialty training program, depending on his physical performance and what openings they had for him. He wasn't panicking quite the same way as he used to at the delay. He could probably credit Kendra with that, too.

Trash cleaned up, shoes left behind, they headed barefoot toward the water where the packed sand would make walking easier, then north toward Torrance Beach and the start of the South Bay bike trail, which he used to ride round-trip all the way to Santa Monica, slightly over twenty miles each way. Stunning ride. He'd like to do it with Kendra someday.

Someday. In the brief pockets of time when he'd be back over the next twenty years? They wouldn't have the chance for a someday.

He grabbed her hand because he had to touch her, hold part of her as if to keep her with him. She was so beautiful striding next to him, legs swinging freely over the packed sand, hair flowing out behind her, green eyes catching the rays of the setting sun. Her cheeks were flushed pink and her skin looked so smooth and soft his lips ached for it. "I had an interesting phone call today."

"Yeah? One of your Air Force buddies?"

"Dr. Kornish's office."

"Uh-oh." Her eyes darkened in concern. "What was that about?"

"Just checking on me. Everything seems fine. I thanked his nurse for the fabulous treatment I'm getting from a Ms. Kendra Lonergan they'd never heard of."

"Oh." Her lips twisted. She sent him a sideways look. "How about that."

"Yeah, how about that?"

She wrinkled her freckled nose, looking absolutely adorable but not horribly alarmed, not as though she'd told a horrendous lie and was about to be seriously busted. "I guess I should confess, huh."

"Might be a good plan."

"I'm an impostor, Jameson." She threw up her hands in mock despair. "A fake, a phony, a fraud."

He tsk-tsked, enjoying her melodrama. "How bad is it?"

"I'm really a grief counselor. I really have a practice in Palos Verdes Estates and beyond. I really do work in conjunction with therapists and many doctors. Just not Dr. Kornish. Or the Air Force."

"Who sent you?"

"Does it matter?"

A lightbulb went off. He made a sound of exasperation. Who else would know and care enough to meddle? "Okay, which one?"

She looked at him in confusion. "Which one what?"

"Mom, Dad, Hayden, Mark or Matty?"

"Ah." Her face turned prim but he saw her lips twitch. "Unfortunately, I am not at liberty to disclose the identity of the— Oh!"

He swung her around, pulled her into his arms and kissed her, hard and full on the mouth, dipping her back so she clutched his arm, afraid of falling.

She gasped when he pulled back. "What are you doing?"

"Kissing you." He did so again, longer and sweeter this time, because as always once was not nearly enough.

"I know that, but—"

Twice wasn't enough either. Her mouth was enticing, lips soft and responsive. His body reacted to their touch as if she'd been naked, performing an erotic dance on top of him. What would it be like to make love to her? He probably wouldn't survive the experience. But he'd really, really like to try.

"*Now* are you ready to confess, Ms. Lonergan?"

"I'll never talk. No matter how much you torture me." She lifted her chin in defiance. "Though...you can keep trying."

He grinned and let her stand straight, fitted her body full against his so she'd feel how much he wanted her. She gave a tiny whimper and pressed against his erection, nearly causing him to lose his mind.

Kissing was not going to be enough for long. He bent his forehead to hers and fought down the lust response. Public beach. Stopping was a good idea before he was tempted to take her right here and get them both arrested. And sandy. He took her hand again to continue their walk, making a mental note to turn back soon. To take her back to his place, her place, any place that had a bedroom. And a bed.

He imagined her naked, that glorious hair spread out around her, around them both, and gave a silent groan.

"You okay? Is it your knee?"

"No, no, I'm fine." Oops. Apparently not a silent groan. What had they been talking about? "So some Cartwright committed the mortal sin of wanting to help me."

Kendra pressed her lips together, which pouted them out slightly and made him want to taste them again. "Certainly possible."

"And he or she figured I'd be about as welcoming as a bear woken from hibernation if I knew a family member sent you."

She knitted her brows, sent him a sidelong look. "That is a logical supposition."

"And so this Cartwright decided you should tell me this was an Air Force doctor–led program so that I'd feel I had no choice but to put up with you."

"Well, Jameson." She tapped a thoughtful finger to her lips. "I suppose that would make sense in the abstract, but of course I can't really say."

He shook his head, grinning, and pulled her closer in order to bump her away again with his hip. "It's devious, untruthful and yes, I suppose given the circumstances it makes sense."

"It does. I mean, imagine me showing up when you were so down and miserable and saying, hey, I know! Let's do some counseling! Really, it'll be fun!"

He made a face. "I see your point."

"You were *so* down, and *so* disgusting to be around and so-o-o—"

"Uh, yeah. Right. I get it." He glared at her, dropped her hand then pulled her closer, arm around her waist. "What convinced you to help me?"

"The money."

He forced a laugh, annoyed at himself. What, he'd expected her to say, *Oh, Jameson, you know how you've always been special to me!*

Actually, that would have been great. "Money, huh?"

"It's all I live for." She nudged to show she was teasing. "Really, I was curious. I wanted to see the great and powerful Jameson Cartwright brought low."

"By a cat."

She smiled, eyes sparking mischief, skirt swirling enticingly just above her knees. "You know, that's the first time you've been able to mention that species."

He faked a shudder. "Evil creatures. Demon spawn."

"Have you always felt that way?"

"Nah. I like cats. *Used* to like cats."

They walked on. He sensed her withdrawing into thought, surprised at how easily he could read her moods and body language.

"Actually." She was looking down now, concentrating on the flat sand under her feet. "I've been thinking of getting a dog for a while. Though I hate to give up working with Byron."

"Why don't you get one?"

"I don't know." She frowned as the incoming tide brought a wave close to her toes. "Sometimes...I'm afraid it's because I'm scared."

"Of dogs?" He knew that wasn't the answer, spoke gently to encourage her. Her struggle to confide in him made him want to put his arms around her and make her whole world safe. Twenty years. Damn it.

"Of losing one."

Jameson took time to process that, slowing as the next wave led a mighty charge and sloshed cold water over their feet. She couldn't bear to fall in love with a pet only to have it leave her. Like her parents had left. Like Jameson would, in two weeks.

A frisson of panic climbed his spine. There wasn't enough time. Not enough to get serious. Not enough to lay any claim to Kendra after he was gone. She'd be free to meet someone else when she was ready. Fall in love. Have kids.

The thought was eating him up, and he'd done nothing more than kiss her.

But then, he hadn't been able to think calmly about Kendra Lonergan since he was six years old.

"Give yourself more time. You'll be able to love again someday. Look how your whole life is structured around caring for people. It's in your nature."

"Yes. But I would like to be able to do it now." She sounded vulnerable, shy, totally unlike the Kendra he knew.

"Maybe you can."

"Jameson..."

He reacted on pure instinct, reached for her and locked her in his arms, held her tightly, cold water swirling around their feet, splashing up on their lower legs, pulling at their ankles as it retreated, leaving bubbling patterns in the water and rivulets in the sand.

This time their kiss was different. He wasn't sure how at first, only that it wiped his brain clean, dwindled the world to the two of them and their mouths, their breath, the moisture on their lips and a powerful connection that sprang to life.

Awed—nearly overwhelmed—he pulled back. For a second before she masked it, he saw the same fear and vulnerability on Kendra's face that he'd heard in her voice.

"We're talking about a dog, right?" Her eyes were serious on his.

"Of *course* a dog." He kept his gaze on her, equally serious. "What else would we be talking about?"

The ghost of a smile curved her delicious mouth. "No idea."

He leaned down, rested his forehead on hers again. "Would you like to come over to Mike's place, Kendra?"

"I was going to invite you to mine," she whispered. "I need to take Byron back to Lena's. It's only a few blocks away."

"I'd like that." He straightened, trailed fingers down the side of her face, then turned and walked with her back toward their quilt, thinking about the night to come.

And it occurred to him in a rush of certainty that he'd been in love with Kendra Lonergan his whole life. And that he had only two weeks to prove to her she could love again—and that she'd always belonged with him.

11

THEY DROPPED BYRON off with Lena, who greeted Jameson warmly, chatted cordially and, every time his back was turned, made lewd tongue-hanging-out faces at Kendra, who could barely keep a straight face. Yes, Lena, he was hot. A large part of the reason she'd decided spending tonight together was a good idea. For both of them. Both were in need of human contact and tenderness, and neither would risk much. He had a foot in the military and she'd discovered her parents' deaths had left her with a reinforced steel wall around her heart to keep her from feeling too much. Funny how she hadn't realized it was there for so long. A certain numbness after the initial agony of grief subsided was normal. But she hadn't understood how effectively hers was working until it had faltered.

She loved the way Jameson was so playful and teasing and affectionate. When he'd introduced kissing into their friendship, she'd taken it as a flirting extension of the same. But an hour ago, during their walk on Rat Beach, after she'd been talking about her fears, a friend-to-friend confession, he'd kissed her differently. In response part of her wall had softened. Only a part, only for a short time.

But for that moment she realized how long it had been since she'd allowed herself to feel her own emotions. She'd become so used to—and so skilled at—repressing them in order to concentrate on her studies, and then, in her career, on the feelings of others, that she'd neglected herself.

So many things now made sense. Why she hadn't moved out of Mom and Dad's house. Why she hadn't traded the car, bought a dog, left the area even for a short time—so many steps that would define a true end to her childhood and to her life as a daughter. Steps that would symbolize the embracing of her life as an adult woman. Alone.

All very deep thoughts, ones that would require more analysis and decisions, but as she pulled into her driveway, she decided that serious thoughts could damn well wait, because she was only about twenty yards from her bedroom and beside her was a guy she'd come to like a whole lot, and trust, and feel comfortable with—about as differently as she'd felt about him in high school as you could get.

As long as she made tonight about an extension of the playful fun between them, she'd be safe.

"Home sweet home." She turned off the motor and smiled sweetly at Jameson as if she wasn't planning to have him naked as soon as was decent after they got inside. She figured three or four seconds would do it.

"Nice to be here." Jameson threw her a sexy sideways look as he opened the door. They were going to have fun tonight.

He joined her on the short walk to the house, which was taking forever.

"Lena seems great. I didn't know her in school."

"She's as good as it gets." Kendra's keys were already out. "I would probably have lost my mind over the last couple of years without her."

"Then I like her even more."

The front door was open. They were inside.

Three…two…one…

No! Not yet.

"Would you like a drink?" She tossed her keys nonchalantly onto the table by the door, pretending she hadn't just had a near panic attack.

"Sure. If you're having one."

"I think I will." She strode toward the kitchen, aware of him following closely, wanting to turn and kiss him, but also…not. "Beer? Wine? Something stronger? Whiskey in honor of your father?"

"Got any bourbon?"

"We do. That is, I do." She opened the cabinet that her father had kept well stocked. He and Mom hadn't been big drinkers, but they'd liked their little sips every night, and they'd liked to be able to offer guests whatever they wanted. "Let's see. Maker's Mark, named after your brother, Old Grand-Dad, fortunately not named after your brother and Woodford Reserve."

"Woodford. Excellent whiskey. Thank you. Are you having some, too?"

"Absolutely." She took down the bottle, thinking she could use about a gallon. That kiss on the beach must have unsettled her more than she'd thought. Or maybe she was just nervous because it had been a while since she'd slept with a man. Not that she'd forgotten how.

She assumed.

The last guy she'd been with had been her year-older boyfriend in college, Grant, who'd decided he had to go on to law school unencumbered by anything as distracting as a woman in his life. Last she'd heard he'd flunked out because of too much partying.

Yeah, because that wasn't at all distracting.

She took down two crystal tumblers from the glass-fronted cabinets next to the liquor. Might as well go fancy tonight. It was a special evening.

"Mind pouring for us?" Inspired, she headed for a drawer where her mother had kept candles and selected a few of the small, thick ones that fit into glass cups to shield the flames from the wind. A few Dove dark chocolates in a floral ceramic dish, a blanket her parents had kept in a drawer by the door for just such occasions and she was ready.

Out the back door, they went down the brick steps to the pool level, where chaises were laid out on the concrete deck ringed by trees.

On the table between two chaises, Kendra set up the candles and lit them. The glow was lovely, the air soft. Above them hung a moon, a bit more than a crescent, sharp white against the sky's darkness. Around it a few stars were just beginning to be visible. A hot man who wanted her was settling beside her into a chaise, his long hard body stretching to fill it.

Yes. Kendra was ready now. *Really* ready.

She reached across to clink glasses, tossed back a good healthy swig of Woodford Reserve, loving the sweet burn, the rich smoky aftertaste. "Jameson."

"Mmm?" He was savoring his whiskey properly.

"Would you like a chocolate?"

"Sure." He reached for the bowl; she stopped him with an outstretched hand. "Let me."

He looked at her over the candles, their light flickering across his handsome face. Something in her expression must have communicated itself to him because he shifted in his seat, took in a slow breath, then nodded. "Be my guest."

The air around them turned electric. Distant city sounds and the faint rush of surf traveled from down in the valley. But up where they sat, all was silent except for the occasional whisper of a breeze through the trees.

Kendra got up and slowly unwrapped a chocolate square, peeling back the foil on each corner before exposing it completely. She put the small square halfway into her mouth, lips closed around its middle.

Jameson watched, only his eyes moving over her face, until she took a step toward his chaise. He moved to give her room to sit facing him.

"Kendra." His voice was low, husky, sensual. "That looks *really* good."

She planted a hand on his firm chest and leaned forward, expecting him to bite.

He didn't. He closed his lips over the other half of the square and dragged his tongue across the chocolate, moistening it, melting it, so the rich taste spread between them.

She was finding it hard to breathe, hard to think about anything but the nearness of his warmth, the heat of his body and her need for both.

The kiss deepened; their tongues tasted the candy and each other until the chocolate was liquid, then gone, and they were left only with increasing passion.

Strong arms came around her. Jameson pulled her onto his lap, stroking a line from her shoulder down her side, lingering over her bottom, then back up and across her front, lingering again between her breasts until she was aching for the feel of his fingers on them.

His hands slipped under her top, stroked up her back and unhooked her bra, then traveled around with maddening leisure toward her breasts.

Impatiently, she sat up, yanked her shirt over her head, slid off the bra and tossed it behind her.

"Touch me, Jameson."

His answer was a groan of satisfaction as his palms brushed over her nipples, then closed over her breasts. She arched into his touch, head back, eyes closed, the cool air around them intensifying the warmth of his skin.

He made her feel so beautiful, so alive, so powerfully sexy. As a woman she'd felt strong, capable, skilled and valued…but nothing like this.

She liked this. Increasingly, she liked everything about being with Jameson.

Except that he was still wearing clothes.

Her fingers tugged at the hem of his T-shirt, gray with the Dive 'n' Surf shop logo and colorful surfboards. Nice shirt. Kendra wanted it off. She wanted to feel her breasts pressed against the hard wall of his bare chest.

The shirt flew back over her head. In the dim candle-light his torso was indeed a work of art, warm and male. She lifted to straddle him, feeling the length of his erec-tion hot and hard through the thin material of his shorts and her panties. She leaned forward, rubbed her breasts over the muscled landscape of his chest, loving the stimu-lation, the intimacy, the sheer animal pleasure of skin on skin, of touching and being touched.

Breath escaped him as if releasing it was both pain and pleasure. His hands traveled to her hips, under the elastic waistband of her skirt, finding and stroking her buttocks, moving her over his erection.

"You feel incredibly good, Kendra."

"Mmm." She kissed his neck, inhaling his scent, im-mersed in her senses. "So do you."

"I've wanted this since before I knew what it was."

She giggled, raising herself up to look at him, gently tracing his lips with her finger. "That long?"

"Look at you." He let his head fall back on the chair, pushing rhythmically under her, making her sway. "You are so beautiful."

With him she felt that way, inside and out. So when he sat up, saving her from pitching backward with strong arms on her back, and twisted them over until she was lying beside him on the chaise, then underneath, she went willingly.

This was what she wanted for both of them.

Starting at her calf, Jameson drew one hand up the

length of her leg, stopping to caress her sex through her panties, transferring warmth and pressure that made her feel less in control. Rather hot and desperate, in fact.

He lifted her skirt and wriggled down to kiss the material between her legs, his mouth warm and firm.

"Oh." She closed her eyes, a slight breeze fanning her heated cheeks. "That is amazing."

"So are you." Gently he pulled down her panties, exposing her to the night air. "And you're beautiful here, too."

His finger explored, stroking, touching, barely any pressure. Heat lightning traveled up her body. She forced herself to lie still, wanting to pull his head down to her, wanting him inside her, needing release from the building pressure.

They had all night.

His first kiss was so light she didn't recognize his lips until his tongue traveled up the length of her sex, parting her labia, ending with the lightest touch on her clitoris. Kendra's body jerked in reaction. She forced her breathing to slow, unfisted her hands, made her muscles relax.

Torture. The very sweetest kind.

He took his time, tiny touches and strokes with his fingers and tongue, adding to her arousal incrementally until she thought she'd go out of her mind. No one had ever taken time with her like this, the intensity building until an orgasm was simply inevitable.

"Kendra."

"Yes." She barely recognized the shaky tone as her own voice.

"I would like to make love to you."

"Yes."

The word exploded out of her, making him chuckle. "You don't sound very sure."

God, he was sexy. Looking at her with one eyebrow

quirked in pretend surprise, as if he had no idea what he'd been doing to her.

Then his smile faded. He undid his fly and stepped out of his clothes without ceremony, taking a condom packet from the back pocket of his shorts, rolling it on and sitting next to her, stroking her breasts, her stomach, gazing down at her body and then into her eyes.

"I've thought about this a lot, about how I thought it would feel with you. This is so much better. Better than my wildest fantasy." He waggled his eyebrows. "Some of them were pretty wild."

"Ooh." She drew her hand down the center of his torso. "You'll have to tell me about those."

"This is better because it's real. Of course. But also because it's finally you and me, Kendra. The place we've been heading to for a long time, I think longer than either of us suspects. Out in this garden where we can see the moon and hear the ocean and smell the eucalyptus." He put one hand on her heart, the other on his own. "You and me."

Kendra stared up at him. She could say nothing. What did he mean? He almost sounded as if…

He moved over her. She opened her legs for him automatically, not sure what was happening, why after all this time of good solid clarity, her mind was a whirl of confusion or why she had a sudden urge to cry.

His penis nudged at her sex; she reached down and guided him in, felt him push, stretch her, push farther, in and out until he was filling her completely. Her body responded. Her brain still couldn't grasp the moment or interpret her reaction.

Instinctively, she stopped trying, shut down her thoughts and concentrated on the sensations. The weight and motion of his body on hers, the welcome intrusion of his erection, the occasional caress of the breeze. The sweep of his broad back, the smooth planes of his skin, the swell of his buttocks, contracting and releasing. The climb of desire as he changed his motion, his rhythm, the force of his thrust, as if he was intent on experiencing every angle, every inch of her, inside and out, and had all the time in the world.

Sooner? Later? She couldn't tell. Only that at some point her response gradually changed; her body was no longer content with simple arousal. Her hips moved faster. She tilted her pelvis, squeezed her internal muscles to hold him tighter.

Jameson groaned and dug his hands under her buttocks, thrusting harder. A light perspiration broke out on Kendra's body; she felt her face flushing. She wrapped her arms around him, one hand gripping his side, the other clasping the back of his head.

The orgasm came on slowly, as if from a distance, gathered speed and power, rushing at her. She locked her legs around his, arched her back and let it sweep through her, holding herself rigid through the plateau of ecstasy, aware of Jameson's body gathering itself, as well. As she burst into contractions he gave a low shout, pushed once more and held still.

As if imitating the rise and fall of their climaxes, wind rose, gusted, then quieted again. Something rustled in the garden.

Kendra lay clutching Jameson's head, not wanting to let the moment go, aware of rising emotions that threatened to burst through her control. The steel wall was in danger.

He strained to lift his head; she made her fingers relax so he could, kept her eyes shut, concentrating on the smooth masculine feel of his body over hers, the tiny occasional pulsing aftershocks between their legs, some hers, some his.

This wasn't what was supposed to happen. She should be able to laugh now, to tease him, to smile and feel affection and relief and pleasure. Instead there was again a mass of confusion and conflict she couldn't begin to understand.

"Look at me," he whispered.

She opened her eyes obediently to his, their blue shade muted to gray in the darkness and flickering candlelight.

And then everything was clear.

With his arms around her she felt protected, safe, cared for. For once she was not in charge. For once someone else was taking the lead, watching out for her, keeping her safe.

Kendra enjoyed the revelation for all of about ten seconds, then the pleasure was replaced by the piercing pain of vulnerability, more severe than she'd felt since right after her parents died.

She was falling for him.

"I can't," she whispered, then realized she'd spoken out loud and shook her head, no, no, no. Fear was making her stupid.

"Kendra." His brows drew down in concern. "You can't what?"

"I don't know." To her horror, her voice was thick with tears. God, no, she couldn't cry. He'd want to know what was wrong. She couldn't tell him. She couldn't even begin to tell him.

But the wave of grief was too powerful, too raw to be contained. Tears ran hot down the sides of her face. She pressed her fists over her eyes, as if the torrent could somehow be stopped. He'd think she was a lunatic.

He rolled off her and sat up. She didn't blame him.

"It's okay. It's okay." Strong arms drew her against him; gentle hands stroked her hair. "Go ahead."

His sweetness undid her. She cried until her tear tank was empty, for hours, it seemed. Through it all he held her close, caressing her, murmuring words of support and endearment. Never in her wildest dreams could she have imagined Jameson Cartwright capable of such deep tenderness.

It only made her fall harder.

She clung to him until her sobs quieted, then forced herself to let go, to sit up, then stand. On her own two feet. To stop being a wet blanket weighing him down.

"Jameson." She couldn't begin to imagine what he was thinking. "I'm so sorry I lost it like that."

"Why?" He got up, too, took her hands, then slid his up her arms to cup the back of her neck.

"Well, I mean." She gestured stupidly at the chaise. "We were just... I mean, it's not like we were... It was supposed to be just fun. And playful. Like we are."

"It didn't turn out that way." He started massaging the tight muscles under his fingers.

"No."

"So?" He gave her that lazy smile. "That means there's more between us than fun. Nothing wrong with that."

"But... No, there isn't." She blurted out the words, then didn't blame him for smirking at her. "Okay, maybe."

He bent and kissed her. "I've got two bits of news for you."

"What?"

"One, there is something powerful between us and has been for a whole lot of years. So it makes perfect sense that making love would jar some emotion loose. Because it did in me, too."

"Only you didn't bawl all over me for an hour."

"I didn't lose my parents and have to take care of myself all alone for the past two years."

She scowled at him, but not with any real anger. Just because he was undoubtedly right. "What's the second thing?"

Jameson took her shoulders, looking deeply into her eyes. Her heart started a slow and steady thump. What was he going to say? Something deep. Something romantic and so wonderful she wouldn't be able to handle it.

He jerked his head over her left shoulder. "When you threw them, your bra and panties landed in the pool."

12

"I REALLY ENJOYED the show tonight."

"Thanks, Kendra." Matty grinned at her across their late-night table at Green Street Restaurant, liking her more and more. Granted, she'd only met her for the first time about fifteen minutes earlier, when she and Jameson had come to the stage door after the show, but she was one of those people who instantly appealed.

Not to mention Matty had never seen her brother so relaxed and outgoing and smitten. Around other girlfriends he'd always seemed vaguely apprehensive, as if awaiting judgment day. With Kendra he just looked happy. Matty might have had her last sleepless night over her baby brother for a while, though he and Kendra had a complicated future to work out, with Jameson about to go back to Keesler.

"How's the knee, Jamie?"

"Jamie?" Kendra gave Jameson an incredulous look. "I've never heard you called that."

"Ha!" Matty gestured to her brother with her wine. "There's worse. When he was little, we called him Jam-Jam."

Kendra clapped her hand to her mouth to muffle a snort, then lowered it and blinked sweetly at Jameson. "Jam-Jam... What a *lovely* name."

"Hilarious." Jameson rolled his eyes good-naturedly. "What about you, Fatty Matty?"

"Argh!" Matty clutched her chest. "Not that one!"

"Oh, ouch." Kendra winced in sympathy. "That is horrible. Especially since you're anything but heavy."

"Used to be."

"Ouch again." Kendra lifted her glass. "I'm a member of that club, too."

"Then you know. I think that nickname was one of Hayden's." Matty made her disgust plain. She and her twin brothers got along pleasantly now, but that was about it for closeness. They belonged to another era. "Kendra, what kind of insulting nicknames did you get hit with?"

"There's not much you can do with Kendra. My brother called me Kenny, not that clever, but it annoyed me so he did it. Mom and Dad just used endearments like honey or sweetie or ladybug. At school I got teased for being me." She patted Jameson's arm under the table. "Mostly by your brother."

Matty waved away the comment. "Boys are too dumb to show attraction in normal ways."

"We learn, though." The look he gave Kendra was pure adoration.

Kendra threw him a quick nervous smile and ducked her head.

Uh-oh. What was that? Embarrassed to show her feelings in front of the sister, or she wasn't quite feeling the big love yet?

If it was the latter, silly, silly girl. You didn't take that kind of devotion for granted, because it didn't strike often. No man had looked at Matty the way Jameson had just looked at Kendra for a long, long time. No one since Chris.

"Excuse me, guys, I'll be right back. It's been a long time since intermission." Kendra stood and headed for the restroom.

Matty beamed at her brother. "She's great, Jameson."

"Yeah, she's okay." His smile belied his casual tone. "I hear I have you to thank for siccing her on me."

"Me?" Matty thumped her hand to her chest. "I have no idea what you're—"

"I beat it out of her." He lifted his glass in a toast. "Thanks, Matty. You're a pain in the ass, but your heart is in the right place."

"Thank you, brother dear." She rested her chin on her hand and speared him with a look. "Have you gone over to see Mom and Dad yet?"

"I will." He shifted irritably. "I should, I know. And I will."

"How's Mike doing?" Matty had never met Mike, but would worship him forever because his apartment had saved Jameson from being driven crazy by their mom and dad during his recovery.

"He's loving the training. Working hard, studying hard."

"You'll get there." She watched his face carefully. He wasn't as hard to read as her other brothers, but still a tough one.

"It'll be a long haul. But yeah. They'll probably put me on a desk job until I'm ready to start up again."

"How will you and Kendra leave things?"

"Well, Ms. Nosy." He reached to tweak her nose, knowing she hated it.

"Off me, you pig." She reared back in plenty of time. "Now go on. You and Kendra…"

"Too soon to tell." He was all brisk business again, leaning back, stretching his legs to one side of the table.

"But you'd like to stay together."

"Yeah." He met her eyes, and Matty saw the vulnerability. Oh, gosh. He'd been through so much.

"She feel the same?"

"As I said, it's too soon to tell."

Matty nodded, heart aching. How could Kendra not fall for him? If she broke his heart, Matty would have to take her out personally. "Any chance you'll give up this Cartwright idea of devoting your life to the Air Force?"

"For that, I'll have to say it's too soon to tell." He checked over his shoulder to see if Kendra was on her way back yet.

"Right, right. Shutting up. Butting out." Matty flung herself back in her chair and buried her nose in her wine, gratified when he chuckled.

"You want to have lunch tomorrow? What is that, Saturday?"

"Mmm, I can't, I'm busy." Immediately she started blushing.

"Yeah?" He was watching her closely, which made her blush harder. "Who's this guy?"

"What guy?"

"Matty…"

Matty inhaled slowly. When she'd told Jameson about Chris shortly after they broke up, Jameson had come close to driving to Pomona to beat the crap out of him, more figuratively than literally. She hoped. But she couldn't lie to her younger brother. "Chris Hamilton."

"What?" His face crumpled into disbelief. "The Creepy Professor?"

"It's just lunch."

"What does he want?" Jameson was sitting straight now, all military posture and protective instinct. "How did he find you?"

She shrugged, *why does it matter?* "He came to my show. We talked after."

"Don't trust him."

She raised her left eyebrow. "Do I look stupid to you?"

"No. Sorry." He laughed shortly. "He just totally messed with you."

"Believe me, I remember." She put a finger to her chin as if she'd just thought of something profound. "Gee, kind of like you messed with Kendra in school."

"Oh, come on." He folded his muscled arms across his chest. She remembered when they'd been skinny sticks. "Not remotely comparable."

"No?"

"I was a kid doing stupid kid stuff out of unhappiness I didn't understand. He was a grown man—"

"Doing stupid grown-man stuff. I know. But he still swears nothing happened with Clarisse. And I know for a fact she was psycho."

"Oh, God." A look of horror grew on his face. "He's playing you. He still wants you."

"Am I interrupting?" Kendra approached the table and sat down, looking between them. "Uh. Should I go back to the bathroom?"

"No, no, you're fine." Matty giggled and held up her hand. "Jameson is in caveman mode because a guy who was horrible to me six years ago wants to have lunch."

"Really?" She looked at him curiously. "That horrible? Worse than you were?"

"Much." He glared at Matty, who grinned smugly. "You're going to give him another chance, aren't you?"

"Only if he earns it."

"I gave you one." Kendra nudged him with her shoulder.

"See?" Matty smiled appreciatively.

"It's not the same thing. This guy was her professor. He knew better."

"Excuse me." Matty raised her hand like a kid in class. "I knew better, too."

"He cheated on you with another student."

"Actually, that was just my assumption." Matty spoke calmly to balance her brother's temper. She'd laid it on thick six years earlier out of the horrible pain she was in, painting herself as the innocent victim and Chris as the heartless predator. She could see why Jameson wouldn't buy a new version now.

"She was naked in his apartment!"

"She was a very disturbed girl. He still says he didn't touch her."

Jameson's eyes narrowed. "How many times have you seen him?"

"Twice. We had drinks once, dinner the other night."

Kendra's head was going back and forth following the conversation.

"I can't believe this." He turned to Kendra. "What do you think?"

"Me?" Her eyes shot wide. "I'm not touching this one."

"No, I'm serious. You counsel people. You heard the problem. What do you think?"

Matty watched her, curious, nodding when Kendra turned her gaze to assess Matty's reaction.

"Bearing in mind I know almost nothing." Kendra laid her hand on Jameson's arm. "I'd say give your sister the benefit of the doubt here. I don't know this guy, and it sounds like what he did was a lot more serious than what you did, but I had certainly written you off, Jameson. Now that we're older, I can understand more of what you were going through and how you felt. But you think my father would be happy to find out I'm dating you now, after all the stuff I told him about you, all the times I came home in tears over something you'd done?"

"Woman logic." Jameson rested his head despairingly in his hands.

"She's just having lunch with him." Kendra patted him consolingly, giving Matty a wink. "I don't think that's so awful."

"Thank you, Kendra."

Jameson's head shot up. He glared at Kendra teasingly. "Yeah, thanks."

"I was talking to Mom yesterday." Matty spoke to change the subject, grateful for Kendra's support. "She's already baking and freezing pies for Thanksgiving."

Jameson chuckled. "Trust Mom to have it all under control."

"What's your Thanksgiving tradition, Kendra?" Matty's stomach sank the second the words left her lips. To someone who'd lost her family so recently, it was not the offhandedly polite question Matty meant it to be. "Sorry, that was awful. I wasn't thinking."

"No, no, it's fine." Kendra's smile was strained but genuine. "Last year I spent it with a friend's family. I think I'll just hang out at home this year."

"Come to ours." Jameson stroked her hair back from her face. "Food's great. And maybe Dad will convince you to enlist."

"You can wash dishes while the men watch football." Matty rolled her eyes. She'd given up trying to fight the gender inequity ingrained in her family culture, but it still drove her nuts.

"Oh, *that's* tempting." Kendra snorted.

"I help. Sometimes." Jameson's hand was gently massaging Kendra's neck. "I did once, anyway. I think last year I rinsed a fork."

Matty cracked up. This Jameson was new. She liked him very much. Watching him respond to Kendra's distress, the way he looked at her...

She was just plain envious.

Steady. Matty was not going to let herself jump into a relationship with Chris because she was lonely or because she hadn't been touched tenderly by a boyfriend in a long, long time and she craved it like crazy. Before tomorrow's lunch she'd need to have her list of reasons to go slowly, eyes open, intellect on full alert for a good long time. Only then would she permit herself to soften toward him.

Well, ahem, she'd softened pretty much like butter in the oven last time she saw him. But that was because she hadn't been forewarned or forearmed. Because she'd had champagne, because the night had been clear and beautiful and romantic and Chris was…Chris. Tomorrow they'd have a picnic lunch at Blaisdell Preserve, a public park ten minutes north of the Pomona College campus, emphasis on *public*. Daylight. No alcohol because she had a show that night. Not a setup for getting carried away.

She'd be cool, confident, calm and controlled.

COOL, CONFIDENT, CALM and controlled.

The words rang in her head as she sat behind the wheel of her Kia on her way out to Claremont, home to the Pomona campus and the very sexy Professor Chris Hamilton. The day was cool and hazy here by the coast, but farther inland when she reached the desert, the air would clear and temperatures rise. Southern California had it all.

She couldn't say she was entirely cool, confident, calm and controlled, but she was enough so that she'd come across that way. Machiavelli would approve. Inside she was tense, timid and in turmoil. The memory of the pain Chris had caused her battled with the memory of his arms around her Wednesday night in the downtown parking lot. Every time she thought of his lips on hers, a bolt of adrenaline got her attention in a serious way. A sexual way.

Oof. Maybe Jameson was right and this was a mistake. Matty just couldn't imagine putting her feelings for Chris to rest unless she faced him again and worked through the mess they'd gotten themselves in. Her hope was that, at the very least, she'd reach a place where she'd be better able to give another man her whole heart. The dating she'd done over the past six years had been an exercise in confusion and comparison. Not fair either to the guys she was seeing or to herself.

The trick was to define seeing Chris today as a new, healthy exercise, and let go of the persistent hope that she could give her heart back to the man who still held a piece of it.

She turned up the Patsy Cline CD she had playing and sang along with a Gershwin tune, clearing her mind of any complication. The haze was gradually lifting as she sped west on I-10, sharpening the beauty of the distant snow-dusted mountains, a welcome natural contrast to the traffic and urban sprawl close by. As she'd predicted, the air was warming, too. The temperature sensor on her car read in the low seventies, compared to the sixties close to the coast.

By the time she reached Claremont and had turned onto Harvard Avenue, she had managed to pull herself together internally, as well. She had all the power here. This was Chris's battle to fight. If he wanted her back, he'd have to work hard, regain her trust, prove himself worthy. She could sit back like the emperor at the Colosseum, thumb ready. Up? Okay, she'd give him another chance. Down? Hurl him to the lions!

On Seventh Street she slowed, looking for the right house number, heart pounding again. Normal to be nervous. It meant nothing. Getting close, closer…there. A charming house set back from the street, Craftsman style, painted deep green, with large trees and a nicely landscaped front yard.

Taking a deep breath, Matty swung the car to the curb and parked. Switched off the engine. Closed her eyes and counted to ten.

Then she opened the door and launched herself out, big smile on her face, clutching the container of cookies she'd offered to bring for their dessert—peanut but-

ter–oatmeal–chocolate chip, made that morning while she
sipped her coffee.

She approached the front door, raised her finger to stab
the doorbell.

Cool, confident, calm and controlled.

The door opened, revealing Chris in thigh-hugging
jeans and a loose maroon T-shirt, one hand on the door.
His hair was damp from a recent shower, his eyes were
clear and warm and he smelled like soap and shaving
cream and man.

Crap. *Crap.*

"Hi." The syllable barely sounded. She had completely
fallen apart, victim to a wave of lust so intense the only
thing keeping her from flinging herself at him was that
she'd drop the cookies.

He stepped back from the door; she crossed the thresh-
old, fly into the spider's web, closing her eyes as she passed
him, trying desperately to reconnect with the part of her
that had been so strong seconds before. Where had it gone?
How could she get it back?

Come on, Matty. She needed to break this tension,
jump-start a normal, casual tone, start chatting, comment
on the house, how it was in such good shape and how he'd
done such nice things with it.

His hand took her arm. He turned her toward him, took
the cookies from her stiff hands and laid the glass container gently on a table in his front hall.

She opened her mouth to say something, anything, but
he pulled her toward him and kissed her, over and over,
walking her back until she hit the wall and his body could
press into hers.

Oh, that body. A man's body, fully formed, broadened,
muscled and loaded with life and experience.

She kicked off her flip-flops one at a time, *thunk, thunk,*
and gave in, wrapping her arms around his neck, realiz-

ing deep down she'd known this was going to happen, that this was why she was here, what she wanted more than anything.

Her hands found their way up under his shirt, to his chest, firm and sexy, a man's in the prime of life. He was eleven years older than she, but she had never felt so at home or natural with anyone else.

He had her cream-colored top off in seconds; his face rubbed the swells of her breasts while he unhooked her bra.

It slid off, leaving her breasts cool and sensual, exposed to his sight and his touch.

"Oh, Matty." He gazed reverently, cupping their weight, then took a lingering taste of her nipple, a hot sensation that shot down between her legs.

She whimpered, let her head drop back to rest against the wall, scrabbling her fingers over his shirt, bunching the material to take it off more easily.

The shirt pulled over his head; he straightened, a naked-torsoed god among men, and gathered her in his arms. She laid her head on his shoulder and stood still, listening to his breathing, as rough as hers, absorbing the familiar feeling of his skin on her skin, of her soft breasts pressed against his hard chest.

His sigh was a mixture of ecstasy and relief. Matty understood. She'd had one word running a loop through her brain: finally.

Finally.

"Do you want this, Matty? You're sure?"

"Yes." Her voice came out a husky groan. *"Yes."*

He released her, hands traveling down her sides as he slid to his knees, pressing his face against the flirty cotton knit skirt she'd pulled on that morning, wanting to look casual and sexy for him, but not as if she was trying to do either.

She fisted her hands, breath ratcheting up a notch, wait-

ing for the heat of his mouth on her, the way he could make
her come faster than a speeding bullet, with orgasms more
powerful than a locomotive.

Oh, Chris.

His hands explored her waistband, then yanked the skirt
down, her panties after; he buried his face between her
legs, searching for and finding all the spots that would
send her over the edge.

She lowered herself, spreading her legs, fisted his hair,
urging him on, not that he needed encouragement. His
tongue was driving her wild, bringing her close already.

"Yes." Her breath stuttered; her thigh muscles trembled.
She pushed back against the wall, closing her eyes, brac-
ing herself, waiting. She was close. So close.

The tongue stopped. Her eyes shot open to find Chris
standing, hair disheveled, eyes hot with desire. He stepped
forward and lifted her. She wrapped her legs around his
waist as he carried her into his bedroom, laid her on the
bed and proceeded to take off his jeans faster than it had
ever been done by any human since the dawn of time.

With a small sense of satisfaction, she watched him re-
trieve a condom from a box on a high shelf in the back of
his closet. Satisfaction because she got to watch the fabulous bunch and release of muscles in his back and very nice
ass, but also because he wasn't keeping a big box right by
the bed, available at a moment's notice.

Matty pushed the thought away as soon as she had it.
This was about him and her and right now.

Condom on, he nearly dove back over her on the bed,
making her giggle. "Been a while?"

"Six years."

She blinked in astonishment, then snorted. "Come on."

"Since I've been with *you,* Matty." He lowered his head
and kissed her sweetly, tenderly, then again. "I've never
stopped wanting to be with you."

No, no, no, none of that romantic stuff. They were here to screw each other because they couldn't keep themselves from doing it. That was all. That was enough.

She pulled his head down harder to deepen the kiss, spread her legs and tried to pull him over on top of her.

"Wait. I want to look at you." He put his hand at her collarbone and drew it slowly down her stomach to the hair between her legs, down one thigh, then the other, low as he could reach, following its progress with his eyes. "I've missed you."

"Um. I'm actually up here." She pointed to her head, wrinkling her nose at him, even knowing exactly what he meant, because she'd missed his body, too. And him.

He grinned and moved on top of her. "Trust me. I know where every inch of you is. How it likes being touched. And tasted. And loved."

Not that word.

He slid inside her, watching her face, filling her completely. She closed her eyes, taking deep breaths to keep from crying. She still loved him. She might always love him.

Then he started moving, and she concentrated with all her might on the sensations in her body so she could ignore those in her heart, pushing against his thrusts, savoring his size and shape, not too big, but enough that she knew he was inside her, felt him deep and hard, out and in, long thrusts alternating with smaller, gentle ones, bringing her closer every time.

Slowly, her thoughts were wiped clean; her body's hunger took over. She writhed underneath him, lifted her head, let it drop, sweat breaking on her skin, clutching at his back, panting and gasping for her climax.

And when it came, it bore down on her with astonishing power, a shaft of hot sweetness that built nearly unbearably, making her strangle a scream in her throat. Then the beautiful release, vaginal muscles contracting around his penis. He paused to feel her coming, then pushed again savagely until his body arched and his mouth opened in a silent yell. She didn't have to look. She knew how he came. She knew so much about him.

Except whether he'd break her heart again.

13

KENDRA LAY IN her bedroom, Jameson spooned behind her, his arm draped protectively over her waist. She hadn't slept well, and when she finally drifted off she'd had another nightmare. This time she wasn't watching Jameson be shot by a sniper or exploded by an IED. This one took place on Thanksgiving at the Cartwrights', only the house had become a huge, columned, Southern-style mansion. She'd had to pass between his parents on one side and his leering brothers on the other, one of whom took pictures while the other took her measurements with a tape and called out the numbers with immense disappointment.

At dinner, a sneering servant placed a thirty-pound turkey in front of Kendra, who was expected to carve with an antique sword. Jameson hadn't been there, but as she'd tried to hack pieces off the bird, which slipped and skated around the platter, the Cartwrights' phones had rung in unison with the announcement of Jameson's death—crushed under a load of mashed potatoes tipped from a truck. Driven by a cat.

Amusing, except in the dream the emotions had been very real. Foreigner in a family that didn't belong to her. Panic in a situation she could normally handle—she'd helped her dad carve the turkey once she was old enough for knives. And the wrenching pain of that phone call.

She blinked away tears and screwed her eyes shut, angry at her subconscious for doing this to her.

"Kendra?" The worried whisper was barely loud enough to hear. "You okay? You were making funny noises."

"I'm fine." She tried to speak normally. "Bad dream."

"Yeah?" He stroked her, embrace tightening, hand traveling up between her breasts. It was an effort not to flinch. His arm felt like a vise. "What about?"

"I can't remember." She needed to get up, move around. She'd be fine. It was just another dream. Kendra hadn't yet accepted Jameson's Thanksgiving invitation. She didn't have to meet his family. She didn't have to get into this relationship any deeper than she was already. Jameson would leave in a week and a half. She'd get over him and move on, be fine on her own again, helping people, enjoying her friends. A good, productive life. And when she was ready to get serious about someone, she would. Not now. Not yet. "Be right back."

She wiggled out of his embrace, jumpy and irritable, used the bathroom, then grabbed her short nightie from the hook behind the door and crossed the foyer and dining room into the kitchen to slip out onto the deck.

It was chilly, low sixties probably, maybe high fifties. She hugged her arms around her chest, trying to calm herself, gazing out past the city's twinkling lights toward the blackness of the ocean, imagining its vast, peaceful depths.

The door opened behind her. A flash of annoyance made her close her eyes. It wasn't Jameson's fault. None of this was his fault.

"Hey." He stepped out onto the deck with her, gloriously naked. Lucky neighbors.

"Hi." She gestured out toward the view. "I was just wanting some air."

"What's bugging you, Kendra?"

"Me? Nothing." She shook her head. "The dream was upsetting. I guess I was just feeling—"

"If you don't want to tell me, that's fine. But quit the B.S."

She took in a sharp breath, drawing herself up, opened her mouth for a rude retort, then deflated abruptly. "Yes. Okay. Sorry."

His hands were on his lean hips. She could see in the dim glow traveling up from the night-lights around the pool that his features were drawn with worry. He was so handsome, her naked airman, eyes narrowed, strong chin slightly jutted, full lips compressed. "It's cold out here. You need something warmer?"

"I can't go to your parents' house for Thanksgiving, Jameson."

A gust of wind sent leaves scuttling across the deck. "Okay."

"I don't want to get serious with you."

He jerked back slightly—or did she imagine it? She'd blurted the words out, not even aware they were on their way to her voice box. But maybe if she had to hurt him, it was better to do it sooner rather than later.

Jameson nodded slowly. "Understood about Thanksgiving. And not getting serious, yeah, I get that, too. Easier, actually, since I'll be leaving."

"Yes. Yes, exactly." She should feel relieved. She didn't. If anything she felt more keyed up, angrier, more panicky. "Since you're leaving."

"That it?"

"I think so." She nodded, relaxing a bit, realizing she'd subconsciously expected some kind of battle. Or a strong reaction, anyway. So he hadn't wanted to get serious either. Well, good. That was good. "I mean, yes. That's it."

"So." He folded his arms across his magnificent chest.

"Are you really intent on freezing to death, or can we get back into bed?"

"Jamie…"

He looked surprised, either because of the nickname or the fact that it came out sounding as though she was about to do something desperate.

She wasn't. But she wanted to. Pressure was building in her chest, in her throat. She wanted to do something totally desperate, scream or throw something.

"What is it?" He took a step toward her. Her panic increased, her breathing quickened.

And then, looking up at him, at his amazing nakedness, she knew exactly what she wanted to do.

"I want you to make love to me."

He gave a short laugh. "Kendra, that is never, ever a problem."

"Out here." She turned to the railing, grabbed the wooden bars, flipped up her nightie and bent forward. "Like this."

She heard him mutter under his breath. Then his hands were on her hips; he pressed his pelvis up against the crevice between her legs. "Like this?"

"Yes." All her anger, all her frustration and all her passion were suddenly channeled into intense arousal, intense need for this man and his cock inside her. She separated her feet more, bent down farther. "Now."

He groaned faintly. "I don't have a condom."

"I don't care."

"Yes, you do. I do, too. Hang on."

Hang on. Literally. She pressed her forehead against the wood, breathing hard, body chilling, face hot, feeling the soft breeze tickling her sex. She wanted him this way, behind her like an animal, hard and barbaric, with no chance for her to fall for him any farther than she already had.

His footsteps sounded on the deck behind her. She closed her eyes, waited.

Hands on her hips, fingers spreading her labia, then the strong push inside her, slightly painful, stretching her hard, but good pain, exciting pain, exactly what she wanted. "Yes. Yes, take me. Hard."

He did as she asked, moved forcefully, thrusting, hands pinioning her hips, making her arms work to keep her steady. She closed her eyes, reveling in his power, his masculinity and his control—giving her the ride of her life without real danger.

She wanted danger. "C'mon, Lieutenant. Give it to me."

He grunted harshly, renewed his grip. She reached back, cupped his balls in her hand and squeezed. He was working her hard, erection banging her cervix with the longest thrusts, making her gasp with the sharp pain, then relax into it, increasing her pleasure and the sense of risk.

Along with her arousal, the wildness grew. "Don't come. I don't want you coming. I want you hot and hard and giving it to me the rest of the night."

He gave a hoarse shout, stopped pushing, held still, panting, holding off his climax.

"What's the matter, Jameson?" She pushed back onto him, controlling the movement herself.

"Wait, Kendra."

"I'm not waiting," she whispered savagely. "I'm going to keep you pumping me."

"Wait." He grabbed her firmly, kept her still in spite of her struggle to move, in spite of her hands caressing his balls, in spite of her furious whispering.

Then he gave a low groan and drove into her again and again, breath coming wet and harsh through his clenched teeth.

"Can you feel me, Jamie? How tight I am? Can you feel my muscles squeezing your cock?"

"Yes." He spit the word out, his legs tight as metal rods behind her.

"Don't come. Don't come. Don't come." She reached farther, found the spot under his ball sac, the very base of his penis, the magic spot that would increase his arousal to a point even he couldn't resist.

"Damn it, Kendra. You're going to make me lose—" He stiffened, gave a moan of surrender that turned into a low desperate shout as he plunged viciously inside her, once, twice, again, and came, pulsing, panting, fingers digging into her hips, giving her a fierce sense of power and satisfaction. Yes. *Yes.*

She had control here; she was not the vulnerable one, she was strong and in charge of herself and of her feelings.

Jameson laid his hand on her lower back, his breath slowly returning to normal. A cold, damp breeze swept them, making Kendra shiver. Her back was stiffening. Her sex was raw and throbbing, still aroused.

Oh, God. She was completely losing it.

"Jameson." Her whisper sounded desperate again. Who was in control? Of what?

He pulled out of her gently, helped her straighten, then without missing a beat, bent and threw her over his shoulder. Ignoring her shocked squeal, he strode back through the warm house into her bedroom, where he laid her on the bed and opened her legs, shoved his face between them.

She gasped with the surprise of it, the sudden pleasure, gripping his head as he painted her all over with his tongue, putting in extra time, heat and pressure on her clitoris, fingers pushing gently inside her, searching, exploring.

"Don't come, Kendra. Don't you dare." His fingertips began massaging a spot deep in the front of her vaginal wall.

She made an inarticulate sound, tried to back down,

back away, back off, but his lips, his fingers—she wasn't going to be able to. He shifted the spot; her desire climbed exponentially. She gave up, gave in, gave a short scream, lifting her hips off the bed, the orgasm making her convulse around his fingers and under his tongue, the pleasure lengthening, even as it decreased in intensity. Again and again until she couldn't come anymore.

"Okay." She panted out the word, then started to laugh, slightly maniacally. "Okay. We're even."

"Yeah?" He kissed his way up to her mouth, covering her with his body, covering them with sheets and blankets. "I wasn't keeping score."

"I was. I always do." She put a hand to the side of his face to show she was teasing. Soft, smooth skin, scratchy stubble. A face becoming dear to her. One she'd miss. Dear Lord, what was she doing to herself?

"Good to know."

Kendra laughed again, still sounding crazed, put her hands up to push back her hair, then kept them clamped to the sides of her head. She was going nuts. From sad to restless to depraved, to miserable, to sexual and now... she wasn't even sure what she felt now, other than sexually sated. "I think I have multiple personality disorder. Or, I don't know, what other mental illness has wild mood swings?"

"There's one you should know about."

"Uh-oh." She blew out a breath, lowered her hands. "What is it?"

"Grief."

Kendra let her hands drop, nearly bonking Jameson with her elbow. "Maybe you're right."

"Of course I'm right!"

She giggled, turning toward him, lying close enough that their noses were nearly touching. "I guess I'm not done with that."

"With all you had to cope with, I bet you put some of it off. Maybe a lot of it."

"Stop doing my job." She smiled at him, reached to touch those lovely, sensual lips, fighting another wave of panic at the thought of him going so far away from her so soon.

Not tonight. Tomorrow was another day, as her mom would say. Tonight she had a sexy naked airman in her bed. That would be enough for now.

"Jameson."

"Mmm?"

"Tell me what you're most afraid of."

Jameson groaned. "This again?"

"This again."

He kissed her, started stroking her hair away from her face, hypnotic, rhythmic stroking that made her want to melt into the mattress. "Let's see…"

Kendra's heart flipped. Would he joke again or really answer this time?

"I'm afraid after I leave that you'll have moments of sadness or fear or uncertainty and I won't be here to help you through them."

She caught her breath. Oh, gosh. His worst fear was purely on her behalf. Now she *really* was going to melt into the mattress. "But I'm invincible. Nothing can hurt me."

"And I'm afraid I'll go back to the Air Force and realize it's not my whole life's ambition anymore."

"That's a hard one." She put her hand to his chest. "But you're not locked in for twenty years, right? I mean, you could get out sooner if you wanted."

"It's a four-year minimum commitment. So yes, I could leave earlier."

"Have you considered it?" She tried not to sound hopeful. His life, his decision, and it would still mean he was leaving.

"Yes."

Her chest squeezed tight. "Because of your injury?"

"Because of what you brought to my life, Kendra. And because of you." His stroking moved down her suddenly stiffened back, his fingers warm and sensual on her skin. "Shh, don't panic. Breathe. You have at least four years without me around. I'm handing you your not-serious on a silver platter."

"Huh." She kissed him, sweetly, letting him know with her lips what his words had meant to her. He was just talking, he'd made no decisions. She'd take this as a lovely compliment.

Jameson deepened the kiss, rolled over on top of her. "Want to come with me?"

"To Keesler?"

"You bet!" He nodded, puppy-dog eagerly. "And then wherever they send me for the next four lo-o-ng years?"

She snorted. "*How* is that not getting serious?"

"Oh, right. I forgot. How about instead we get engaged? Tomorrow work for you?"

"Jameson." She cracked up.

"What. You want to get married right away?" He deliberately let more of his weight pin her to the mattress, digging his arms tightly around her. "Geez, give a guy some space, would you?"

"Stop!" She pushed at his dead weight. "Bad Jam-Jam!"

"Don't ever, *ever* call me that." He lifted off slightly, his threat made idle by the laughter brimming in his voice. "Or else."

"Or else what?"

"I'll make love to you until you beg for mercy."

"Oh!" She frowned, pretending to reconsider. "Wait, is that supposed to be punishment?"

"Not tonight. It's late." He rolled off and turned her on her side, curled behind her as he'd been when she first woke from her nightmare, only this time his arms didn't feel threatening or confining, but comforting and secure. "I want you to get some sleep."

Kendra smirked in the darkness. "I hear and obey, oh great and powerful Jam-J—"

"Kendra."

She giggled and adjusted her body against his, checking in with all the places they were pressed together. Calf to shin. Bottom to groin. Back to chest. Skin to skin. "Good night, Jameson."

"Good night, my beautiful."

She took a deep breath and blew out the last of her tension and fear, aware of a growing sweetness in her chest. A contentment like she'd never felt before. And if she wasn't so tired and drained, and if she hadn't had such an emotional workout tonight, she'd probably be panicking all over again.

Because it was a lot harder to keep yourself from being serious about a guy when you were already falling in love with him.

14

KENDRA JOGGED NEXT to Lena down the strip of pavement marking the beginning of the South Bay bike trail in Torrance, the neighboring town to Palos Verdes Estates. On her left the ocean hurled itself relentlessly toward them. On her right, tourists and residents strolled or drove down the esplanade, lined with palm trees, apartments and condos.

"Whoa, honey." Lena touched her arm and slowed, her shorter legs scrambling to keep up. "Are we training to win a marathon here?"

"Sorry." Kendra pulled back. She was pushing her usual pace, hoping to exhaust herself to the point where she could sleep better at night.

"What's going on? You seem tense. Things been going okay with soldier boy?"

"Airman." She corrected her without thinking. "Yeah, they're okay."

"Hmm. I'm not exactly blown away by your enthusiasm."

Kendra stopped herself from speeding up again. "I don't want to get serious with him."

"Given that he's leaving in six days, that sounds reasonable."

"It is. It is totally reasonable."

Lena gave her a sidelong look. "He giving you trouble over it?"

"No." She was startled by the underlying bitterness in her response, and brightened her tone. "No, not at all."

"His sister giving you trouble?"

"Matty? No. She seems fine."

"So?" Lena beckoned more words out of her. "What's the problem?"

"I don't know." Kendra made a sound of exasperation. "I don't know what's wrong with me. I'm a complete mess, mood swings all over the place, impatient one second, crying the next."

"You pregnant?"

"God, no. No, no. I'm on the pill and we use condoms." She snorted. "I think it must be something simpler. Like a brain tumor."

"Oh, there's a nice thought." Lena wiped her perspiring face on the shoulder of her bright red shirt, which fell halfway down her thighs and probably belonged to Paul. "Maybe you're going through something else hormonal. Menopause?"

"At twenty-four?"

"Hmm, guess not." She touched Kendra's elbow. "You missing your parents?"

"Yeah." Her voice choked up. "I bet this fling with Jameson has stirred that up, too."

"Hmm."

They jogged in silence for a while, passing two women with strollers.

"One thing bothers me, Kendra."

"What's that?"

"This thing about not wanting to get serious." She blew at a strand of hair that had escaped her sweatband. "Why would you say that?"

"Because I don't want to get serious? He leaves, he leaves for years. This isn't some brief absence."

"Yeah, but..." They parted company around a pair of

walkers. "If it's right, you could work something out. Tons of military couples do. It sounds like you're being defensive."

"Against what?"

"Oh, I don't know. Maybe the fact that you're falling for him."

"I *am* falling for him." The sentence came out close to hysterical; she forced her voice calmer. "That's the whole problem."

Lena burst out laughing. "Here I was braced for rabid denial. That's great, Kendra. Seems like he's really good to you. And he's not exactly a hardship to look at."

"I don't want to get serious."

"You know, I've heard that about you."

Kendra giggled. "On the news?"

"Do you think he's serious about you?"

"He invited me to his family's Thanksgiving."

"Oh." Lena blew at the strand again. "That is serious. You going?"

"No."

"Why not?"

"Too serious."

Lena cracked up. "We are apparently antiserious! But also maybe…because it's a family holiday and he's got a family, complete with parents. You had a hard time even at my house last year."

"Maybe that, too. I don't know, Lena, that's what is making me nuts. I just don't know. Can we change the subject?"

"No."

"Lena…"

"Okay, okay. How about them Raiders? Think they'll get into the playoffs this year?"

Kendra rolled her eyes. Lena knew she didn't follow football. "I'm sure they will. Unless they don't."

"Here's something I need to tell you…" Lena's voice slowed, became guarded.

Kendra turned to look at her and nearly tripped over a kid chasing a ball onto the pavement. "What?"

"I might not be able to do these runs much longer."

Kendra's stomach dropped. "Why not? Is something wrong? You're not moving, are you? You're not…sick?"

"No!" Lena waved her arms as if to erase what she'd said. "No to both. It's a good thing. Maybe. Maybe someday soon."

Kendra took one look at her friend's face, radiant under her boyish haircut, and gasped. "You're pregnant?"

"Not yet." She patted her abdomen, grinning. "But we've decided to start trying."

"Wow!" Elation filled Kendra, which felt much better than the emotional cesspool she'd been floundering in before. "This is wonderful. Lena, I'm so excited for you. Both of you."

"Thanks. Who knows. It may take a while, but we're ready."

"Will you quit your job when the baby comes?"

"Uh." She held up her hand. "One thing at a time. We only just decided to try."

"Oh, Lena, it's really great. You and Paul will have a family." She jogged three more paces and burst into tears, then started laughing. "See? I've gone completely nuts."

"Honey? Can I say something you might not like?"

"Yes, of course." She sniffed and wiped the tears, struggling for control. "Anyone else I might take out, but you always can."

"I think you're past falling for him. I think you're in love with this guy. As in serious."

"No. No." Even as she protested, something inside her relented. "God, Lena, what am I going to do?"

"Why do you have to *do* anything? Just enjoy it."

"Because I don't want to be involved right now. I'm not ready. It's too soon. He's leaving and it will be horrible and sad and awful missing him. I don't want to miss anyone. I *hate* doing that."

Lena caught Kendra's hand and slowed them to a walk, her brown eyes anxious. "Shh, okay."

Kendra closed her eyes, blew out a breath. She loved him. Of course she did. She had for a long time, maybe even back in school, though she'd been entirely too proud and stubborn to admit it.

"You can't tell your heart what to feel." Lena led Kendra off the pavement, onto the sand, squeezed her hand and let go. "If this guy is right for you, he's right. And maybe he's most right if he's leaving, because then he won't be in your face all the time and you can continue to heal while you have his support."

"But he'll be in the Air Force. He could…trip over more cats." She waited for her friend's shout of laughter. "I couldn't stand to lose him."

"That's what love is, honey. Massive, unbearable vulnerability."

"Well, ick, why does anyone do it?"

Lena gave a blissful sigh. "Because, sweetheart, in all of life, there is simply nothing better."

"You're right. I just wish I could get rid of the fear." Kendra echoed Lena's sigh, but hers wasn't blissful. "I'm being really whiny and annoying, aren't I?"

"Tremendously." Lena led the way back to the path. "Remember when Paul broke up with me the year before we got married? Remember how I was then?"

"Ugh." Kendra made a face. "Unbearable."

"See? You owe me." By mutual consent they started running again. "Have you talked to Jameson about this?"

"All I've told him is that I don't want to get serious. Since then we have just been enjoying each other."

Lena shrugged. "Start with what you feel now, even if it's just laying out your confusion. Don't go farther than that. It's like this baby. We can think about his or her entire life now and drive ourselves into a complete panic... or we can just have a lot of really great sex and see what happens."

"I see your point. Especially about the sex."

"Yeah, you guys do okay, I can tell by seeing you together. Unlike that last guy you dated, what was his name?"

"Grant." Kendra blew a raspberry. "Old Faithful. Same time, same position, same..."

"Do *not* say eruption."

Kendra laughed, feeling more stable, more optimistic and eternally grateful to her friend. "I'll talk to Jameson. Thanks, Lena."

"You're welcome. It's scary giving your heart to someone, but if he's right for you, you'll do it no matter what." She swerved closer to nudge Kendra with her elbow. "So you might as well woman up and admit it."

JAMESON GAVE HIS nervous mother a kiss on her soft cheek and shook hands with his scowling father. The visit, his first since he'd been back in town, had gone well. At least for him. He hadn't squirmed and mumbled under his father's crossfire over his physical therapy routine and gradual return to normal daily activity. He'd answered clearly, honestly and for the first time, his dad's bluster and puffery hadn't bothered him. Dad had done basic training on an injured hamstring? Good for him. Jameson's older brother had recovered completely from shoulder surgery and was back flying within weeks? Hayden was amazing. Jameson was glad for him. Mark didn't think twenty years in the Air Force sounded like enough? Jameson wished him all the happiness in the world. But over the past few days he'd come to see clearly that four would be enough for him.

"Thanks for lunch, Mom. I'll see you Thursday. I'll bring wine." He wished he could say he'd be bringing Kendra.

"Bye, Dad, see you Thursday."

His father nodded curtly, shook his hand and slapped him on the shoulder, his equivalent of a hug. His dad would get over his disappointment eventually. More important, he'd figure out that his youngest son was his own man, sure of what he wanted. Jameson had Kendra to thank for a lot of that. Her crazy questions and her insistence that he get up off his poor-me ass and take a look around him had done more than break his depression. They'd given him the impetus to take a look at his life, too, and to choose what he really wanted to fill it with.

Mostly he wanted to fill it with Kendra.

Jameson nodded to his parents and turned to climb into the SUV he'd rented when he'd gotten sick of having to depend on other people for transportation.

He pulled out of his parents' driveway and headed south on Via Cataluna. An idea had come to him the previous evening, a way he could ease some of Kendra's conflict and get some resolution himself. It might be a colossally bad idea, but he didn't have any others. She seemed caught between what her mouth and words told him—that she did not want to get serious—and what her body and actions told him—that she was falling as far and as hard as he was.

Or so he hoped.

So what should he do? Back off, leave town and send her a how-are-ya email once in a while from Keesler and then whatever base they sent him to next?

There was only one person in the world he could talk to about this. He'd been meaning to call Matty today anyway, to find out how things were going with the Creepy Professor. He'd wanted to call every day, hell, he'd wanted to tag along on their dates with his service weapon…but she was an adult and, like all of them, had her own stupid mistakes to make.

Or not. He hoped not.

She picked up on the second ring. "Hey, Jameson, how was lunch?"

"It was fine. Dad was Dad. Mom was Mom."

"I'm so surprised!"

"I told them I'm not reenlisting after this contract expires."

She gasped. "Jameson, wow. I'm...okay, I'm thrilled. But only if you're sure it's what you want."

"I'm sure."

"How did Dad take it?"

"Pretty much the way you'd expect. But I let it roll over me."

"Good for you, Jamie. I know how hard it is to let Dad roll. But good for you. I'm really happy that you're standing up for—" She gasped again, louder this time. "Is this because of Kendra?"

He smirked. Looked like his segue had just been handed to him. "Are you kidding me? You think I'd change my life for a woman? What kind of wimp do you—"

"I knew it! This is awesome! Have you talked to her yet?"

"That's kind of why I'm calling."

A third gasp. "You asked her to marry you!"

"Who-o-oa, there, Nellie." He did his best cowboy imitation, which admittedly wasn't very good. "She is not in any place to ask right now. She freaked out when I invited her for Thanksgiving. You saw her."

"But if she were in a place to ask, would you?"

He pulled over, parked the car and reclined his seat. "I refuse to answer on the grounds that it's none of your business."

"Which is why you called me to talk about it."

"Oh. Yeah. That." He shoved his hand through his hair, thinking he'd have to make an appointment for a cut before he showed his face back at Keesler. "First tell me how things are going with Creepy."

"Chicken."

"You're having chicken?"

"No, *you're* chicken. I'm having…complications."

"Matty." He struggled upright, not comfortable relaxing when his sister might need him to drive to Claremont and punch someone. "What's going on?"

"We're having nice times, actually. Really nice. Whether or not he's right for me, whether or not I'm a masochistic idiot, there is still something really big going on between us."

He wanted to growl. "Okay."

"But even after all these really nice times…" She sighed.

"You still can't totally trust the bastard."

"Not completely. At the same time, Jameson…" She growled in frustration. "I really need to come up with a way to put this to rest, or I'm going to kill any hope of having something special with this man. Essentially, I'm killing any happiness we might have because of crap I can't stop worrying about that might not even be a problem."

"Or it might."

"Or it might. But guilty until proven innocent is not a good basis for any relationship."

"True." He frowned thoughtfully. Something important was circling in his head, looking for a place to settle.

"I confronted him when we first hooked up again, we've talked it over and he has a logical explanation. Either I have to reject that explanation and leave him, or accept it and leave him alone. This is my crap. I have to own it."

Jameson opened the car door. He couldn't sit still any longer. "Is there anything *he* could do that would help you deal with this?"

"Yes." She laughed dryly. "One thing. About as likely as a solar eclipse."

"What's that?" He knew her answer before she said it, knew that she'd been the right person to call, knew his next stop and what he'd say to Kendra next time he saw her.

"He could tell me he wants to marry me."

MATTY PULLED UP to the small Mediterranean-style house on Oak Avenue in Manhattan Beach and whistled softly. Two million, easy, in this town. Clarisse had done very well for herself. Or found a man who had.

She parked in front of the house and turned off the Kia's engine, wrinkling her nose. This was probably one of the more risky ideas she'd ever had. It could turn out a dozen different ways. She hadn't called to let Clarisse know she was coming. She didn't want to give her former friend any time to prepare for the encounter, or guess any of the reasons Matty was coming. And in case Matty decided this was one of the worst ideas she'd ever had, she wanted to be able to ditch it with no consequences.

Talking to Jameson the day before had gotten her thinking. Saying out loud that she wished she could come up with a way to put her doubts about Chris to rest had made the solution pop into her head. Only one person could corroborate Chris's version of what Matty had seen that day six years ago. The problem, of course, was that Clarisse might still be as unreliable as she'd always been. In which case Matty would be back to square one.

Nothing ventured, nothing gained, as Mom would say.

So it was venture time. She grabbed her purse and got out of the car, self-consciously smoothing the hem of her favorite teal top and fluffing her hair, wishing she'd gotten it trimmed. She laughed at her vanity. As if her outfit or hairstyle would make any difference. What a complication she and Jameson had made of their love lives. How long since their biggest concern was whether Mark and Hayden were cheating at Monopoly?

Someday they'd both be happily married and laugh at these worries, too. She hoped.

Blowing out a breath, Matty forced herself to start toward the front door, telling herself Clarisse could easily not be home, so she might not have to face this confrontation today after all. Her next thought was that Clarisse had better be home, because she wanted this confrontation the hell over with.

On the front step, she made herself jab the doorbell without stopping to think, because otherwise she might stand there agonizing forever.

Two seconds went by.

Clearly Clarisse wasn't home. Matty could just turn around now and—

The door opened.

She was home.

Still beautiful, still slender, the kind of face that drew men's glances, wide-set blue eyes and shoulder-length nearly jet-black hair that spilled over itself in a silky cascade when she tipped her head.

Her lovely dark brows drew down. "May I help— Oh, my gosh, *Matty!*"

"Hi, Clarisse." Matty was suddenly overcome with emotion. Before she'd started to clue in to the depth of Clarisse's issues, they'd had a lot of fun together early in their senior year—midnight beer runs, working out together, seeing movies, writing crazy poetry, trying out for shows on campus, talking until four in the morning.

So when Clarisse burst into tears and went to hug her, Matty did the same.

"I am completely undone. I can't believe you're here." Clarisse sniffed and wiped her eyes with long pink-nailed fingertips. "Come in. Please, come in."

Matty followed her into the living room: exposed beams in the ceiling, hardwood floors, a brick fireplace and an unusual collection of modern paintings. "What a gorgeous house."

"Thanks." Clarisse turned as if seeing the room for the first time. "The art is mostly John's. My husband. I met him— Gosh, Matty, we have so much to catch up on."

Matty nodded, guilty at Clarisse's warmth when she was primarily here to ask if she'd screwed Matty's boyfriend six years earlier. Of course, with Clarisse, you never quite knew what was real. This Clarisse did seem calmer, more self-possessed. And if she'd gotten married, maybe she was doing better. Or maybe her husband was nuttier than she was.

"Would you like a beer?" Clarisse grinned mischievously. "I have our favorite, Sierra Nevada Pale Ale."

"I'd love one." She gave a hyperenthusiastic double thumbs-up, their sign for a good time and place for beer, at the same time Clarisse did.

A few minutes later, Clarisse was back in the living room with a tray on which stood two opened beers—both of them preferred to drink straight from the bottle—a bowl of pretzels, a plate of baby carrots and a hunk of what looked like really good cheddar with some crackers.

"Sit, sit. Help yourself." She put the tray on the spotless glass-topped coffee table and sat on the white couch, her simple red top, diamond solitaire necklace and slim black pants making a stunning contrast. "Matty, I about fell down when I saw you at the door. I've thought about you so many times, thought of picking up the phone, but I figured you didn't ever want to see me again."

"Oh." Matty fingered the label of her beer, then took a swallow. "I'm actually here for a reason besides just catching up."

"Okay." Clarisse abruptly uncrossed her legs and reached for a pretzel.

"It's about Chris."

Clarisse met her eyes, then looked away. She put the pretzel on her napkin. "I thought it might be."

"I bumped into him a few weeks ago."

"Really." She was speaking cautiously, holding her body tight. "When did you last see him?"

"At Pomona. Senior year."

Her face fell; her hand crept to the diamond resting on her chest. "Matty, I...I hoped you'd get back together someday."

"We didn't." She watched Clarisse closely, saw her struggle to keep back tears. "I couldn't trust him after I found him with you."

"But I wrote to you explaining." She got up from the couch and stood by the mantel, three-quarters turned away. "Didn't I write to you?"

"No. Saying what?"

She faced Matty in obvious distress, hand still at her throat. "So many things are still...missing or confusing from that time. I thought I wrote you a letter a month or so after graduation. Or maybe an email. In it I told you about that night and begged you to forgive me."

Forgive what? "If you did, I never got it."

"I don't know, maybe I dreamed it or hallucinated." She laughed bitterly. "Well, that explains why you never answered. I thought you'd written me off."

"I did." She smiled to take the sting out of the words.

"I meant after you found out what really happened."

Matty made herself count to three. "What really happened?"

"You probably figured out I'm bipolar."

Matty winced. No, that wasn't the truth she was after,

but Clarisse was due genuine sympathy. "I'm sorry. I knew you were struggling."

"That's a nice way to put it." She strode back to the couch and sat again. "I'm on meds now. I'm doing really well. But back then I did a lot of really messed-up things that still haunt me. Trying to seduce Chris was a big one."

Matty took a casual sip of beer. "Trying?"

"I was jealous of you." Clarisse lifted her hand, let it flop down on the couch cushion. "I wanted what you had."

Did you get it? She nodded, unsure how else to respond.

"I know it makes no sense, not even to me anymore. But back then in my twisted way of looking at life, it was pure logic."

"I'm sorry to make you talk about all this again." Matty smiled grimly, getting impatient. "But I need to ask—"

"No, no, talking about it is really fine. I feel so much better knowing you never got my letter." She made a face and shuddered dramatically. "If I even *sent* one."

"I'm sure you—"

"Which it looks now like I didn't." Clarisse sighed, shaking her head, hair sliding out of place, then settling back to perfect. "Honestly, Matty, having a mental illness stinks."

"I'm really sorry, Clarisse." She bit her lip. "And I'm so glad you're in a better place now. But I—"

"I'm a new person." She grinned and stretched her slender arms up over her head. "I have my husband, John, to thank for that. He's a remarkable—"

"Clarisse." Matty held up her hand to stop the chatter. "I need to know if he slept with you."

Clarisse gaped in astonishment. "Who, John?"

"No, Chris!"

"Chris?"

"Yes! Chris!"

"No, of *course* not. He didn't even touch me." She looked at Matty as if *she* was the one with a mental illness. "He was crazy in love with you."

15

KENDRA CHECKED THE half turkey breast browning beautifully in the oven. On the rack below it she had sweet potatoes baking. Once the turkey was cooked and resting, she'd bake the stuffing and roast the balsamic and olive oil–coated brussels sprouts she'd combined with onions and chestnuts. Already on the table, whole-berry cranberry sauce flavored with orange zest and potato rolls she'd mixed the day before and baked that morning.

Funny thing about life-changing events. Some of them were huge baseball-bat blows to the head, like her parents' deaths. Some of them were little tickles or itches that you didn't notice changing your life until you gained perspective later on. Then there were those in between, like when you went jogging on the beach with your best friend and she made some astute and challenging observations you didn't want to hear, and you realized the new direction was up to you to put into place.

Kendra was making some of those changes now, preparing for others later. She couldn't go on in this limbo—well, she could, but she no longer chose to—of half her old life and half a new one. She could sell the car and buy one that fit her better. She could get a dog and incorporate him or her into her counseling practice, though she'd feel horribly guilty abandoning Byron to days alone in the house at Lena's. She could talk to Matty about putting the house on the market within the next year or two, maybe find out what she'd need to do to fix it up and start working on that now, then eventually look for a new place for herself.

And she could have a lovely Thanksgiving, a day early, with Jameson, without having to intrude on another family's traditions. Tomorrow Kendra planned to spend the morning on the beach and drive up the Pacific Coast Highway in the afternoon. She could choose how she grieved, what she could let go, what she wanted to keep—all the advice she'd been giving other people and not living herself.

As to what she and Jameson would do in the relationship going forward…she'd take Lena's advice and tell him how she felt, even though she hadn't gotten much further than "play it by ear." Breaking off their relationship when he left would be agonizing, but she didn't feel right committing herself to a long-distance romance when she was only just emerging from the worst of her grief and starting to redefine herself.

For all she knew, Jameson wasn't ready to commit either, which would be fine.

Her instinct rolled its eyes. *No, it wouldn't.*

Yes, actually, it would be.

Liar.

Freedom would make it easier to continue rebuilding the life she wanted.

No, it would totally suck.

Stop.

No matter what happened, she and her instinct were going to enjoy the hell out of tonight and however many other times she saw him before he left on Sunday.

The doorbell rang. Kendra broke into a smile, quickly rinsed and dried her hands, then ran to let him in, her heart lifting into its usual joy at the sight of his unbearably handsome face, faltering only slightly when she noticed he'd gotten a haircut—another reminder that he was leaving.

In the next second she noticed his hands behind his back, which he brought forward to offer a bouquet of red roses and a bottle of champagne. "Hello."

"Oh, Jameson, how beautiful. You are spoiling me with flowers. *And* champagne. You are a sweetheart, thank you."

"You're welcome." He walked in, strong and virile, without any limp, and gave her a sweet, lingering kiss. "Mmm. You smell incredible. Is that…turkey?"

"My newest scent." She took the flowers and wine and led the way to the kitchen. "Eau de Thanksgiving."

"Kendra, wow." He took in the food waiting to go into the oven, the table set with her family's china and silver. "This looks amazing."

She found a vase for the roses and took them to the sink, feeling suddenly shy and awkward. "I thought we could have our own Thanksgiving."

"That is a really nice idea. And a lot of work, Kendra. You should have told me, I could have brought something. We could have cooked together."

"You did bring something. Look how beautiful." She put the flowers on the table, which was transformed by their color and elegance. The perfect touch. "I didn't want us to wear ourselves out in the kitchen."

"No?" He came up behind her, drew her back against him. Kendra closed her eyes. His hard body and masculine scent turned her into a giant lust hormone. "Is there another room you'd rather we wear ourselves out in?"

"Hmm." She moved seductively against him, keeping the mood light, not letting the word *leaving* enter her head for more than a second before it was firmly squashed. "I'll give that some thought."

"I think that's a good idea." His lips found the side of her neck; his hands roamed her waist, eventually finding the hem of her shirt and traveling slyly underneath. "Anything in the oven that would spoil in the next half hour?"

Somehow she kept her breathing under control. "Yup."

"Fifteen minutes?"

"Timer's going off in five."

"I'll take that as a challenge."

"Five minutes?" She started to turn but he held her still.

"Shh." His hand was delicious torture on her breasts. The other started a slow journey down her belly. Kendra let her head loll back on his shoulder, prepared to enjoy his touch, then finding herself enjoying more than just his touch. She enjoyed his solid warmth at her back, the strength of the arms around her, the way his breathing changed, betraying his arousal as he concentrated on hers.

The fingers of his right hand inched lower, under the waistband of her shorts—she'd worn a stretch waistband for exactly this reason—then eased under the elastic of her panties. Her own breathing changed, came out in a small burst as he cupped her sex with his warm palm and held her like something precious he wasn't going to let escape.

"Five minutes, Kendra." His voice against her hair was low and full of promise. His fingers began undulating, as if he were playing a scale on a piano, one finger, then the next, playing her so sweetly.

"Mmm, that is nice," she whispered.

"Yeah?" His fingers rose, fell, playing her again, A, B, then C—his middle finger dipped, parting her labia, stroking back and forth before he moved on—D and E, then did the whole thing in reverse. "Four minutes."

"Keep going," she whispered.

His fingers moved again. This time middle C lingered on her clitoris with gentle pulsing presses that made her inhale sharply and hold still, pushing out her hips, wanting him to touch her there again and again.

"Three minutes," he whispered. His hand moved side

to side, fingers trailing in interrupted sequence across her clit, making her work against the need to move as well so at least one finger stayed where she wanted it to.

"Jameson, stay there. *There.* Keep your finger—"

"Two minutes." His knees bent slightly, throwing her off balance. She sagged against him. He supported her easily, now making lazy circles everywhere but where she *wanted* him.

Her breathing grew frantic. She was desperate with desire, feeling half-foolish to be falling apart like this. "Do you realize what you do to me?"

"It goes both ways, sweetheart. One minute."

"I'm not going to make it unless you—"

"You're going to make it." He bent his knees farther; instinctively she stepped one foot out to stay stable, opening herself to him. "Now."

He pushed a finger up inside her, then two, a rhythm that made her cry out until those same fingers returned to her clitoris, slippery with her moisture, and rubbed in earnest, stopping just as her orgasm gathered to slide up inside her again.

She tightened her buttocks, pushed against his fingers.

"Thirty seconds." His arm released her; he supported her with his strong legs like a human chair. His fingers continued making love to her while his other hand reached around to stroke her.

The orgasm gathered again, faster this time, inevitable. She moaned, straining for it, head pushed back against his strong shoulder, fingers clutching his hard biceps.

Ecstasy burned through her in a blissful, powerful wave, blinding her for a few seconds, then crashing over.

Ding ding ding. The timer went off as if she'd triggered it.

Kendra's giggle mixed with her panting, muscles still contracting deliciously around Jameson's fingers. "Made it."

"I knew you would." He helped her stand, get her legs and hips working again. "Is that the turkey?"

"Yes, it needs to come out." She wobbled toward the range, feeling as if her legs were being tried out for the first time. "Because, you know, if meat stays in my hot oven too long, the juices pour out and then it shrinks."

Jameson cracked up. "Wait, that's a *bad* thing? It sounds pretty great to me."

"Bad for turkeys." She sent a lascivious glance at his distorted jeans and took the half breast out of the oven, burnished beautifully brown and smelling like heaven.

"That is a thing of beauty." He cleared his throat pointedly. "So, um, now that the turkey's out, how long until the next thing?"

"The turkey should rest." She threw him a smile, turned up the temperature, slid in the pans of stuffing and brussels sprouts and tossed her oven mitts across the room, where they landed neatly on the counter. "Half an hour."

"I'm thinking a glass of champagne." He crossed to where she'd stood the bottle on the counter.

"I'm thinking the same." She took down flutes from the cabinet near the door to the deck. She'd miss this house. But a new one would be fun to make her own, to fill with her own memories.

A place to share with Jameson when he was in town?

Yeah, sharing tidbits of vacation for the next twenty years. She might as well face it, there was no way they could continue this with anything but frustration and pain. Stop.

She handed him the flutes with a determined smile. Fun now, serious conversation later.

"I wonder, Ms. Kendra." He twisted off the cork with a loud pop, tipping the bottle to keep the champagne from rushing out. "If you have any objections to drinking this champagne in bed."

"How could *anyone* have objections to drinking champagne in bed?" She picked up the glasses, gave him a come-hither look over her shoulder and headed for her bedroom, hearing him follow, at first at a distance, then closer and closer until she broke, giggling, into a run. "In a hurry?"

He set the bottle on her nightstand, grabbed the glasses from her hand, then tumbled her down on the bed. "Yes."

"What about my champagne?" Her protest was lame; she welcomed him on top of her, closed her eyes, her mind and her heart to how much she would miss him, how deeply she felt about him, and kissed him, wrapping her legs around his thighs, pulling his erection close, feeling it warm and insistent between her legs. She wanted to please him. She wanted him inside her, going crazy from how much he wanted her, how desperately he wanted to come.

And she wanted him to love her, just a little, as she loved him, just a little, even knowing it would make Sunday that much more painful when it came.

No matter what they decided, she'd make sure their parting was beautiful and dignified and something he'd always remember fondly. A tear, a smile, a heartfelt wish for his future happiness, and then she'd hold herself straight, waving until he was out of sight.

After that, she could break down for a while, wallow in her brokenheartedness and then get over it. One thing about surviving tragedy—after the first time it happened to you, and after seeing it happen to so many others, you knew it was not only possible but inevitable to move on and thrive and find happiness again in new and sometimes unexpected places. Spirit the hawk, reborn.

Jameson undressed her slowly, reverently, kissing every inch he uncovered, lingering in places they both liked best. Naked, she pushed him onto his back and did the same to him, dragging her breasts over the firm planes of his chest, her hair over the long hardness of his thighs and her hands and lips over the jutting pride of his erection.

He lay back as she expanded the range of her kisses, across that chest, down his belly, let her mouth hover tantalizingly over his penis before she drew it into her mouth, fisting the base, swirling her tongue around its tip. Jameson's breathing became harsh, labored; his head rolled to one side, eyes closed, brows down, full, sexy lips parted ecstatically. She wanted a picture of him like that to keep by her bed.

Except whomever she made love to next might not appreciate it.

She didn't want to make love to anyone else.

Stop.

She took him all the way in, sucking hard, up and down, a furious denial of her feelings, even knowing there was little point denying them except to make their separation easier.

Jameson clamped a hand on her shoulder, holding her still, then pulled away from her mouth and hauled her up next to him, breathing deeply. "That was close."

"I wouldn't have minded."

"*I* would have minded. We have half an hour. That would have been about three minutes."

"Mmm, good point." She nuzzled his neck, trailing her fingers gently down the soft skin of his penis, loving that contradiction, the erection so hard and masculine and the skin velvety soft and so very sweet.

He lay back again while she idly stroked him, his eyes closed, lips curved in bliss. She studied his face, the high slope of his forehead under the short spikes of his hair. The straight Cartwright nose and high cheekbones, the strong Cartwright jaw. And that soft full mouth, so finely shaped, that called him out of the mold, gave him the look of sensuality his brothers and father lacked.

She'd miss him.

Stop.

She drew her hand up his chest, over to his shoulder, then pushed herself up to straddle him, sliding her sex up and back, pressing his penis flat against his abdomen.

His breath came out in a soft groan. Impressively muscled arms came around her and pulled her down against him; he kissed her hair, her mouth, a long, sweet kiss that made Kendra wrap her arms around his neck and give herself over to it, kiss after kiss, lips clinging, exploring, slow and lovely, involving way too much of her heart.

She loved him.

Oh, hell.

In self-defense she unlocked her arms from around him, rose onto her hands. "Condom?"

He opened his eyes slowly, their clear blue a sudden contrast with his golden skin and the white bed linens around him. "We could go without, Kendra. You're on the pill."

"Pills don't protect against—"

"I tested clean after my last lover."

"I did, too, but there are viruses you can't test for that—"

"Kendra."

Something about the way he said her name stopped her midsentence, made her climb off and sit facing him. "What is it?"

"I want to make love to you. Not just today but for a long time into the future. I'd like us to stay together. I'd like to give this a real shot."

Me, too.

No, it was crazy. But there was no more calling *stop*. They were going to talk about this now, with her Thanksgiving dinner nearly ready and the champagne still untasted.

As if he'd heard her thoughts, Jameson got up, poured them two glasses and handed her one. "Here. Either way you answer, having met you again calls for celebration."

Answer? He hadn't asked her anything. He must mean her reaction to his announcement that they should stay together.

It was impossible.

It was so tempting.

She sipped her bubbly, vaguely noticing the wine was delicious, not able to concentrate fully on enjoying it.

"My future plans have changed."

Kendra was so startled she aborted her next sip. "What do you mean?"

"I'm not extending my commitment to the Air Force."

She stared at him. "What does that mean?"

"It means I'm out after four years. I can come back here to live."

Kendra's heart started beating faster. Four years. That was a lot shorter than twenty. But *four years.* Anything could happen in that time. "You're coming home."

"And I'll be back as often as I can be in the meantime. Depending on your answer."

Answer again. To which question? Would she like that? Would she still be here for him when he visited? Was she happy he was shortening his commitment?

She didn't know. "Jameson, this is a huge change. What does your family think?"

His jaw set. "They'll get over it."

She had to smile. Good for him. Good for Jam-Jam, telling his family what *he* wanted instead of just doing what they did. "I'm proud of you."

"Thanks." He grinned that irresistible grin, sitting naked in her bed, holding a bubbling champagne flute, behind him through huge windows the vista of L.A. and the ocean.

She could keep seeing him. They could turn this relationship into something serious.

No. She didn't want to be serious.

Why not?

She wasn't sure anymore.

"I will never regret the years serving my country or forget what the Air Force has done for me. It's my family I've served for much too long in too many ways." He posed ridiculously, an overbright smile on his face. "This is the start of *me* time!"

Kendra cracked up, nearly spraying champagne over her sheets. "Don't ever say that again."

"Sorry." Jameson gazed at her, his smile gradually fading into something darker and warmer that began a serious spring thaw in her chest. He toasted her with his glass, drained it, then took hers over her protests and put them both on the bedside table. He grabbed his pants and began rummaging in the pocket.

Good boy. Condom. They could put this confusing and uncomfortable conversation on ice while they—

It wasn't a condom he'd pulled out.

Unless they put condoms in jewelry boxes now and she hadn't gotten the memo.

"Kendra."

She sat there, blinking, unable to comprehend what was happening. Maybe it was a necklace? A bracelet? Earrings? A friendship ring?

Depending on her answer. To what question?

"We met under strange circumstances. Twice. The first time was in elementary school when a serious, chubby girl sat next to me and said hello and I threw a spitball at her. The second was in Mike's apartment, when I opened the door to this incredibly funny and beautiful woman and nearly drove her off with my bad mood.

"Matty was right. I've been telling you I love you my

whole life. But I'd like to tell you again, in two different ways. The first is to say it. I love you, Kendra. And the second way is to show you that I always will." He opened the box.

Not earrings.

A ring. A stunning ring of diamond and sapphire chips set in a delicate curve. It was the most beautiful thing she'd ever seen. Her breath came shallow; spots flew in front of her vision. She forced herself to relax, forced her breathing low. The spots cleared.

"This ring symbolizes my promise to you, Kendra. I promise I will always come back to you. I promise that I will work hard to make you proud and I promise that someday I will ask you to be my wife." His mouth curved in a devilish smile. "If you've stopped freaking out by then."

"What?" She jerked her head up from staring at the ring. And freaking out. "I'm not out. Freaking. No."

"You had hard work to do getting me out of my bad mood when we met this second time. I promise also to be that understanding and that determined with you." He touched her cheek, his eyes filled with so much love she could barely look at him.

"Which means, Kendra, when I ask if you'll wear this, I won't let you get away with saying anything but yes."

16

MATTY DROVE EAST on I-10 toward Claremont, having just finished the Wednesday night performance of *Backspace*. She had the next day off for Thanksgiving, which, if tonight went as she hoped, she'd be tempted to skip at Mom and Dad's. Her brothers were bringing girlfriends. This batch of females could surprise her, but so far Mark's and Hayden's judgment of a woman's worth had been based on breasts over brains.

So be it. She'd go of course, if only because she couldn't leave Air Force–ditching Jameson to the wolves by himself.

If tonight went as she hoped.

Part of her was not happy with the chain of events that had led to her change of heart. Part of her felt she should have been able to trust Chris implicitly, and that when he'd insisted nothing had happened with Clarisse six years ago, she should have been able to believe him. But she had been a college kid, on pins and needles from the illicit circumstances of their affair, underexperienced and overwrought. Now, too much pain and time had passed for her to throw it all behind her.

Her relief at finally hearing from Clarisse's mouth the same truth she'd heard from Chris's was so great that she couldn't call it a mistake. Finding out she'd had been in the wrong all these years was remarkably freeing. Going forward, which she desperately hoped they would, she would do whatever she could to prove she trusted Chris now.

A glance at the speedometer made her push her Kia a little faster. She couldn't wait to get to Chris's house and issue a heartfelt apology. And give him the present she'd decided on for both of them. And drag him into bed. And…mmm.

Half an hour later, nearly trembling with excitement, she pulled up opposite his house and switched off the engine, took a little time to sit and think about this moment, six long years after their initial relationship, and how wonderful it was to finally cast off doubt, to stop fighting her feelings for this man, to realize he'd loved her all this time and that it had nearly cost him his sanity to let her go, thinking that doing so would be the best thing for her.

Which, actually, given the possibility of such a happy ending now, it might well have been.

Heart brimming, she patted her jacket pocket to make sure the paper was still there, even though she'd put it in herself an hour earlier and hadn't touched it since. Out of the car, she gazed around her, then up at the stars, inhaling deeply, trying to take everything in, impress each detail onto her memory bank so she could return whenever she wanted.

Heels tapping on the front walk, the sound echoing in the silent neighborhood, she hurried to his front door and rang the bell, unable to keep the smile off her face.

Chris opened, scowling, did a double take, froze in what looked like horror, then swore viciously.

Matty's eyes shot wide. Whatever she'd expected, that wasn't it. "Um. Nice to see you, too."

"I'm sorry, Matty. But my God. Fate is seriously effed up sometimes."

"Chris." She stared at him, taking in his features, his

pallor, the beginnings of fear waking in her system. Was he ill? "What do you mean?"

He looked at her a moment with pain in his eyes she didn't understand. Then he stepped back and gestured her inside.

A woman. A girl. Beautiful. Brunette. Not naked, but sitting on the couch wearing a low-cut clinging dress short enough to get her arrested.

"Jenny. This is Matty, who I was just telling you about. Matty, this is Jenny, who decided to stop by tonight because Satan must have told her you were coming to surprise me, so he could try to ruin my life for the second time in a decade." He gestured in frustration, hair a rumpled mess, as if he'd been trying to tear it out all night. In a weird déjà vu moment, she remembered his reaction the first time around, with Clarisse. He'd sounded the same. Not guilty, not anxious, just pissed off. How had she missed it?

The problem wasn't with Chris. The problem was with circumstances and with her.

"Hi, Jenny." Matty kept her voice gentle. Her lips curved into a smile meant to terrify. Judging by Jenny's deer-in-the-headlights reaction, it was working. "It's awfully late to be visiting your professor on a school night, isn't it?"

"I needed to talk to him. He didn't answer his phone."

"Because you never called me." Chris's voice had calmed some. She glanced at him and saw in his eyes what she might have been able to see if she'd spared him a glance six years earlier, if she'd done anything but pour all her fear and frustration and insecurity over their affair into anger and blame. Excusable? Yes, actually. Naked women in your boyfriend's room didn't make cheating an unlikely conclusion. But she could have taken a second look.

In an ironic flash of insight she recognized now that the

trip to see Clarisse had been a waste of time. Matty would have come to this same place on her own.

She turned back to Jenny. "What did you need him for? Can I help?"

Jenny shook her head, scowl almost as black as Chris's.

"Is there someone else who could help you?"

"I guess."

"Maybe you could go find that person." She smiled even more sweetly. "Right now."

Jenny stood and flounced past them, giving Chris a pleading look on the way out that six years ago would have reduced Matty to furious ash in three seconds. Now she just wanted to roll her eyes.

The door slammed behind her.

"Seems like a lovely girl." Matty turned and gave Chris a thumbs-up, nodding as if they'd just decided to purchase a new car. "Nice legs."

"Mattingly." He closed his eyes and gave a bitter laugh, shaking his head. "I can't tell you what went through my mind when you came to the door."

"Let me guess. 'Uh-oh'?"

"A little stronger."

"I heard some of that."

"Right." He stood straight, hands on his hips, looking so hot in jeans and a blue shirt that she wanted to pounce on him. "She's a nice kid. Bad family situation. I was kind to her. She thought there was more to it than that, apparently."

"Plus you are *so* irresistible."

"Ha." He blew out a shaky breath, looking at her, head tipped to one side. "What's going through your mind, Matty?"

"I wish last time I'd taken a moment to calm down and pay attention. I wish I'd trusted my instinct that what we had was strong instead of wondering how you could ruin it."

"You were young. Too young. I was old enough to take responsibility for how stupid we were being. I should never have let it go so far."

She shrugged. There was no point in blaming anymore. "We were both in it. But yeah, I wouldn't have wanted to keep having to sneak around."

"That was awful."

She nodded, gazing at him, thinking that in a strange sense tonight's timing couldn't have been better. She'd been able to show Chris her trust in a way that would mean a lot more than just telling him.

"So with that hell out of the way, hello, Matty." He dropped a kiss on her mouth, then another, then took her into his arms and kissed her soundly.

"Hi." She sounded like a breathless, ridiculously in love person. Which she was.

"I wasn't expecting you tonight." He kept her close, kissed her temple. "This was a nice surprise."

"I went to see Clarisse."

"Huh." His body stiffened. He took a step back. "Would you like a drink? Because I could use a double."

Matty giggled. "A drink would be really nice."

"Cognac?"

"Perfect."

He strode over to his liquor cabinet in the dining room, poured two healthy shots into balloon glasses and offered her one, gesturing to the couch where Jenny had arranged herself so seductively. "Cheers."

"Cheers." She sipped the fiery sweet liquid. Not yet her favorite, but a lovely indulgence to be drinking with Chris.

"So." He cleared his throat, put his arm along the back of the couch behind her. "What did Clarisse have to say?"

"What I should have known all along. What you kept telling me. That you loved me. That you were never a cheater. That it cost you to let me go, but that you did it for me."

"Thank God." His face relaxed; he closed his eyes briefly. "I was afraid she'd still be lying."

"I shouldn't have had to talk to her." Matty swirled her Cognac, then resolutely met his eyes. "Tonight I would have reacted the same way whether I'd gone to see her or not. It's not nearly enough, but Chris, I am truly sorry I didn't trust you."

"It wasn't our time, Matty." His voice was low, controlled, but the hope in his eyes nearly tore her in half.

She put her glass down and took out the folded paper in her pocket, was about to hand it to him when he took hold of her shoulders.

"I want this to be our time."

She met his kiss, melting into his arms when he wrapped them around her and pulled her into his lap. His mouth was hungry, demanding. Matty answered that hunger and made it clear her body was making demands of its own.

In five minutes their clothes were off and they were straining frantically to join their bodies, giggling when the angles weren't quite on target, when she wasn't quite ready at first, then sighing blissfully when they got it right, when he found her and sank slowly inside. Their eyes met and held, communicating everything they felt for each other.

He moved inside her slowly, holding back, letting their arousal build gradually until they were once again frantic for each other. Matty met and absorbed his thrusts until her own need to come was so strong she couldn't delay anymore, even to keep this beautiful lovemaking going longer.

They'd have time. Years and years…

"Chris," she gasped. "I'm going to come."

He moaned and ground himself into her, pushing her over the edge, then gave the hiss of breath that let her know he'd gone over with her.

Yes. This was their time.

They came down together, releasing the tension, laughing from the sheer physical and emotional joy of what they'd shared. Matty gazed up at him and the words she'd been holding on to for so many years came out as naturally as if she'd been saying them all along. "I love you."

"Aw, Matty." He rolled to one side and pulled her to him tightly. "I've thought about saying that to you again every day for the past six years."

"Say it now."

"I love you." He said it twice more, kissing her, then said it again, "I love you."

"Hmm." Matty grinned at him. "I think this is what happiness feels like."

"I think you're right about that." He pushed back her hair, eyes warm and loving. "And I think you were trying to give me something when I jumped you."

"Oh! Yes!" She struggled up to look around them. "I took it out of my jacket. Where is it? A piece of paper."

"I don't know. Is that…no."

"Did you take it from me?"

"I don't think so." He sat up next to her, scanning the room and their clothes strewn around it. "Maybe it's… No, not here either."

"We'll find it."

"Tell me what it is." He stroked up and down her back.

"A coupon I designed. For a trip för two to Paris." She was brimming with triumph and the pleasure of surprising him. "I sold two houses last week. And we've always wanted to go."

"Matty." He looked stunned, exactly as she'd hoped he would. "That's too much."

"What, you don't want to go to Paris with me?" She shrugged, *oh, well*. "Okay. I can ask someone else."

"Wait, wait, I'll go, I'll go." He shook his head, grinning at her. "If you let me help."

"I want to do this for us."

"But Matty, that's a huge amount of—"

"I know how much it is and I know how much I can afford. Take it or leave it."

He stared at her for a moment, clearly exasperated, then his face cleared. "I'll take it. On one condition."

Matty narrowed her eyes suspiciously. "What's that?"

"That the trip is our honeymoon."

"Our…" She blinked, barely able to take in that he'd just given her all the reassurance she'd ever need, all the love she'd ever want with the only man she'd ever wanted it from. "You…"

"Matty Cartwright." He slid off the couch, got down on his knees and clasped her hands in his, stunningly naked, her man from now until forever. "I have never loved anyone the way I love you. Will you marry me?"

"Yes. Yes. Oh, my gosh, yes." She wrapped her arms around him, pulled his forehead up to hers. "I've always wanted a Paris honeymoon. And I've always and only wanted you."

17

KENDRA STARED GLUMLY at the ceiling, splayed out on her couch with the TV still on. Happy Thanksgiving to her. Nearly noon. She'd been awake from her last fitful doze since six. Hadn't been to the beach. Hadn't organized for a drive up the Pacific Highway. During the past six hours, she had accomplished a couple of trips to the bathroom, one tooth-brushing session, quantity ingestion of junk food and a whole lot of quality angsting.

Jameson had left the beautiful—so, so beautiful!—promise ring in its box by her bed, saying he wanted it staying there to tempt her. Yes, it had tempted her, jumping out of its box and onto her finger about once every ten minutes, until she'd gotten out of bed, driven to the 7-Eleven and bought every type of disgusting, unhealthy food she could find, then returned home and stalked into the living room, determined to escape the diamonds and sapphires taking over her brain.

She wanted to accept the ring. Of course she did. But committing to eventual marriage was a huge step, and she didn't feel she'd known Jameson long enough.

They had fun together, they had similar taste, humor, outlooks, incredible sex. Jameson made her feel beautiful and smart and cherished and sexy as hell. They handled disagreements with care, respect and humor. He made it safe for her to take risks, if that made any sense. In the brief time since she'd known him again she'd realized how much of herself she'd held back, how much she'd been looking to the past instead of the future. Now she was ready to sell her car, get a dog and think about moving out of this house that she loved, but that had never and would never feel as though it belonged to her. Wasn't that enough for commitment?

Yes? No?

Jameson seemed completely sure of her answer, which irritated her. How the hell did he know so much about her and what she wanted and what she was feeling? *She* didn't even know.

Mom and Dad would know. They'd have sensible, practical advice that would make her worries and uncertainty seem silly. They'd say she was overcomplicating a simple yes-no situation. They'd tell her to follow her instinct. And when she told them her instinct was voting both pro and con, they'd insist one side was instinct and one was fear, and help her find out which was which. But Mom and Dad weren't here. Which was probably just as well right now, because they'd have a fit at what she'd been eating.

Not to mention she wanted to be left the hell alone.

The doorbell rang.

Oh, the irony.

She shoved a handful of barbecue-flavor potato chips into her mouth and scowled at the front door.

The doorbell rang again.

"Go away."

Who the hell would show up at her house on Thanksgiving? Lena was with her own family at her sister's house in Santa Monica this year—she was the only friend who'd feel she had the right to show up unannounced on a major holiday. Kendra's clients didn't know her home address.

Jameson was...

Oh, no. Not with her looking like the walking dead. And smelling worse.

She got up and tiptoed to the door just as he started pounding.

"Kendra. It's me, open up."

Kendra groaned. Mr. Macho Military would probably break down the door if she didn't answer. Her car was in the driveway; it didn't take much to figure out she was home.

Wait, she could be on a long walk…

"Kendra." He pounded again. She heard him muttering about going around to look for her in back.

Fine. She opened the door. "Hi."

Jameson turned abruptly and ran back up the steps, his grin widening. He was carrying another beautiful bouquet for her: mixed flowers today, in autumn colors, burgundy, rust and gold. "Happy Thanksgiving, Kendra. You are beyond gorgeous this morning."

She grunted, absurdly glad to see him, but cranky and embarrassed to be caught looking like hell. "What are you doing here?"

"Visiting my true love." He was entirely too cheerful. She might have to slug him. "What are you doing here?"

"Nothing." She took the flowers, stepped back and gestured him in, resigned to him seeing her pigsty.

Oink.

Jameson strode in, then stopped, hands on his hips, and surveyed the living room. Several crushed soda cans littered the coffee table along with the barbecue chips, a Pop-Tarts box, a half-eaten package of Oreos and an empty bag of peanut M&Ms.

As he stared, a throw pillow tumbled off the couch, as if it couldn't bear being seen in such humiliating circumstances.

Kendra knew how it felt.

Jameson turned to her, chuckling. She really would have to slug him. "Have a good night?"

"Best I've had in a while."

"I can see that."

She glared at him. "What are you so happy about?"

"It's Thanksgiving. I'm grateful for many things. My knee recovering, choosing what to do with my life and having the most wonderful woman in the world dying to marry me."

Her hands plonked on her hips. "I am not dying to marry you."

"No?" He drew his brows down. "Well, hey, I know! Let's *talk* about it!"

"I don't *want* to talk. I want you to leave me to my stench."

"Is the living room a good place, do you think? Or the kitchen?"

"Jameson, I think you should—"

"Yeah, I like the kitchen, too, it's brighter." He strode toward it without looking back.

Kendra shuffled behind him, rolling her eyes. He was the most wonderful and annoying person on the planet, and how was she supposed to be dying to marry him when technically he hadn't even *asked* her? He was breaking all rules of politeness and consideration, shoving his way in, talking over her, not listening to what she was saying.

But he looked damn hot. Eyes bright, body filling out neat black pants the way pants should be filled out. His shirt was a rich dark green with a subtle black stripe, his shoulders broad, movements confident and graceful.

Yum.

She laid the flowers on the table, grabbed a vase from the cabinet and arranged them in fresh water. They were gorgeous. And he was sweet to have brought them, especially since he'd only just brought her roses. And she'd been very ungracious to him about it.

"Jameson, I'm—" She broke off at the sight of him sitting calmly at her kitchen table with two stacked pads of paper and a pen in front of him. "What are you doing?"

"Sit." He gestured to the chair opposite. "I have a few questions. I can't stay long, about five more minutes. I promised to help Mom in the kitchen."

"What questions? What is this?" She scowled her way to the chair he'd indicated and slouched into it, scratchy and hot.

"Tell me what you're feeling." He looked up, all impish seriousness, pen poised to record her answer.

Kendra narrowed her eyes. "Are you making fun of me?"

"Yup."

"You have no clipboard."

"I know." He shook his head in disgust. "I'm an amateur. But a serious amateur. Feelings?"

"Okay." She thunked her elbows on the table, chin flanked by her fists. "Troubled. Confused. Lethargic."

"Appetite okay?"

"As long as the food isn't healthy."

"Sleeping well?"

"No."

"Sexual appetite?"

"Um. That seems to have perked up lately."

"How lately?"

"Like…in the last five minutes."

A brief smile sneaked onto his face. "Hmm. We'll take that into consideration."

"We?"

"Me and my questions. Let's see…any major gifts of jewelry recently?"

She snorted. "Yes."

"Any urges to buy a pet?"

"Yes."

"Desire to trade in your current vehicle?"

"Yes again."

"Uh-huh. Uh-huh." He tapped the pencil against the

pad. "I think I'm getting the picture. Oh, and speaking of pictures, I brought the ones I drew on Rat Beach."

"Jameson, thank you." Pleasure jolted her out of her bad mood, at least temporarily. She was curious to see what he'd done.

"I'll leave them with you since I need to go. But before I do, I have one more question. Very important."

"Uh-oh." She narrowed her eyes. "What's that?"

"Kendra Lonergan." He leaned forward, touched her cheek gently. "What are you most afraid of?"

JAMESON PUSHED BACK his plate, leaving his last few bites of pecan pie untouched. He'd had enough—of food and family. As usual his father and brothers had dominated the meal, while Matty and Mom had listened in annoyance, amusement or some combination. His brothers had hooked up with a new crop of women beautiful to look at and tedious to listen to. Every now and then one of the men would get in some "funny" dig about Jameson not making a career of the Air Force. Matty and Mom would look uncomfortable. The boobsy twins would laugh. The topic would change, then return.

A few weeks ago the teasing would have made him miserable. Now? He just nodded, smiled, acknowledging the jokes but not commenting or defending himself. He didn't have to. He no longer cared what they thought of his life decisions. He could love his family without being victim to their...Cartwrightness.

And he had somewhere else to feel accepted as he was.

The burn in his chest that had become his constant companion became stronger. Thrill and fear. For all his supposed confidence that Kendra would stay with him, for all his belief that their love was the real thing and would survive the next four years and on until death, he could answer that favorite last question of Kendra's easily now, the one he'd turned on her.

His biggest fear? That she wouldn't give them a chance. That she'd need someone right here, who could reassure her every day in his arms, in his bed that he was not going to leave her, not going to disappear.

Jameson couldn't offer her that now. And he couldn't ask her to pick up her life and hard-won practice and start over now and every other time the Air Force moved him.

The doorbell rang, stopping Mark from recounting every detail of some reality show he'd been watching the night before.

"Who could that be?" Katherine rose from the table.

"Aunt Bea?" Hayden suggested.

Jameson groaned silently. God, no.

"She's in Missouri with a friend who isn't well," Jeremiah announced.

"Oh, yes, yes, hello, come in. Nice to see you." Katherine's voice grew louder from the foyer. A musical female voice answered her.

Jameson stood, eyes trained on the dining room door, aware that everyone at the table was staring at him.

Kendra. She stepped into the dining room and so far into his heart that he thought it was going to stop beating.

"Hello, everyone." She gave a huge smile, looking cool and beautiful in a room of stuffed, bored and lethargic people. About as far from the way she'd looked at home that morning as she could get. It even seemed she'd brought in fresher air. Her gaze met Jameson's; her smile widened. "Sorry to interrupt your dinner."

He shook his head, trying to communicate his pleasure at seeing her without making his brothers start gagging. "I was just finished."

"Would you like some pie, Kendra?" His mother was already at the china cabinet looking for another plate.

"No, no, I already ate, thank you." She winked at him, knowing he was picturing Pop-Tarts, then went around the room introducing herself, charming each of the men in his family. Hayden cracked up. Mark blushed. His father took her hand and held it longer than was appropriate. Even the girlfriends smiled approvingly. Matty gave her a huge hug, beaming. Jameson was happy for Matty, though he still owed Chris a punch in the face. Maybe at the altar.

"I get it now." Dad brought his hand down on the table. "This beautiful woman is the reason you're quitting the Air Force, Jameson."

"I'm afraid I am." Kendra laughed easily. "In four years we plan to join a commune in North Dakota to raise goats and llamas. I'm already carrying his triplets."

Her smile continued to shine through the atmosphere of sudden horror in the room. Finally Matty couldn't suppress her laughter anymore; eventually, even the boobsy twins got it.

Jameson walked to Kendra and put his arm around her. "We do have news."

He felt her stiffen. "What are you doing?"

Jameson squeezed her shoulder. "About another commitment I've made."

"Jameson." Her furious whisper made him chuckle.

"I promised to spend the afternoon with Kendra at her place." Beside him Kendra went limp with relief.

"You won't stay for pie?" Jameson's mom had finally found a plate.

"No, really, thank you, Mrs. Cartwright." Kendra smiled brilliantly and kicked Jameson in the shins. "I just came to kidnap your son."

"Well, all right." His mom grinned at him, looking much younger than her fifty years, and walked them to the door amid a chorus of goodbyes and wishes of happy

Thanksgiving. Jameson didn't think he'd ever left his family feeling so warm and fuzzy.

Kendra was a miracle.

The door closed behind them. Four steps later, Kendra turned and threw herself at him at the same time he threw himself at her. Their kisses were deep and desperate, arms tight around each other, pelvises pressed close.

One of the windows in the dining room grated open.

"Hey, get a room." Hayden's voice, booming out into the front yard.

Jameson chuckled and gave him a brotherly finger, then pulled Kendra down the front walk toward her car.

"Your brothers are charming as ever," Kendra said dryly.

"Aren't they?" He followed her around to the driver's side and pressed her against the door, kissing her with more appetite than he'd had for his dinner. It had to mean something that she'd shown up today. That she'd introduced herself to his family. That she seemed so cheerful and calm, all while carrying triplets. He wanted to ask what she'd decided—hell, he wanted to demand she marry him right now. But this was her kidnapping, so he'd let her take the lead.

"Where are you taking me to?"

"My house."

"Yeah?" He leaned back slightly to get a better look at her green-eyed, auburn-haired beauty, keeping his hips pressed tightly to hers. He was still half-erect from their passionate kisses. "What are we going to do there?"

"You'll see."

"I think I'm going to like this."

"I think you are, too." She tipped her head back; her eyes went past him. Her breath caught.

"What is it?" Jameson peered into the sky and saw a red hawk swooping over their heads.

"Nothing." She laughed softly. "Reminds me of an old friend."

"You have bird friends?"

"Don't you?" She snapped out of her trance and opened her car door. "Let's go. Silly to drive less than a mile, but I wanted to get you back fast."

"Ah, so this is urgent?" He slid into the passenger side.

She flashed him a sultry-eyed look that made his half erection go for three-quarters. "Very."

"I understand. I'm pretty sure I can help you with whatever you need."

Kendra squeezed his hand, then put the pedal down and drove like a wild woman until they reached her driveway, where she bounced to a stop.

"I'm going car shopping tomorrow. Want to come?" She opened the door and jumped down.

"Absolutely." He was already out, hurrying her to the front door, both of them giggling like idiots.

Inside, their mouths joined; they moved together toward her room, shedding clothes along the way.

Naked, they fell onto the bed, tangling their limbs, touching and writhing to be closer, then closer still.

Crap. He pulled his mouth off hers. Immediately Kendra started in on his neck. "No condom."

She pulled away slightly, started exploring between his legs with her hand, fisting his cock, reaching past it to stroke his balls. "Don't need one."

His brain went blank. No, no, he had to think...

"Why don't we need one?"

"Because I say so."

He rolled his eyes, grabbed her hands, pinned them above her head and lunged over her. "Really? Is that how things will be from now on? How *you* say?"

"Uh-huh." She blinked sweetly at him. God, he loved her. "For instance. You're going to slip inside me right now just the way you are, and feel me around your cock, all naturally hot and wet."

Jameson swallowed. "Ungh."

"Then you'll start moving and be able to feel me gripping you." She lifted her head and dragged the tip of her tongue slowly across his lips. "Really tightly."

He shifted on top of her, breathing hard, the tip of his penis planted at the juncture of her tightly closed thighs.

"Then I'll whisper what I want you to do to me tomorrow, and the next day, until you can't take it anymore and explode inside me."

"Yes." He sounded desperate. Because he was.

She spread her legs slowly. Jameson lifted to look down at her sex, so sweetly formed and so inviting, all reddish-brown curls and lush pink lips. He couldn't get enough—wouldn't get enough for a long time, if ever. Not using a condom must mean she'd decided to accept the ring and all it symbolized. He wanted to hear her say it.

But he'd play this game her way.

Slowly he slid inside her, and without the barrier of the condom her flesh was as slick and warm as she'd promised and embraced him like the world's most sensual glove.

Within three minutes he knew he was not going to be able to last, that he was going to come too soon for her to be ready. He gritted his teeth and held on to her buttocks, forced his body to go still.

"What is it?"

"I'm too close."

"Yeah?" She started pushing up and down, then lifted one leg nearly up to his shoulder, increasing the pressure.

"Kendra." He was practically going blind from lust. "If you do that—"

"Oh, but I *am* doing that, Jameson."

She was. It was too much. He groaned and thrust into her; the orgasm swept him like a hurricane, leaving him flattened and powerless, overwhelmed by the physical and emotional power of what lay between them. She had to know how he felt.

"I love you." He murmured the words into her neck. He didn't care if she didn't answer, he just wanted her to know.

She was doing something. He couldn't tell what. He couldn't lift his head. It was all he could do to keep breathing.

"Jameson," she said softly. "Look."

He dragged himself up to peer at her, blinking stupidly, then followed her gaze.

His ring. She was wearing his ring.

Energy flooded back into his body. He held her hand, gazing at the stones, so perfect on her slender finger. "Kendra."

"I love you too, Jameson." Her eyes were sweet green, shining, melting him. "I'll be proud to wear this."

He kissed her, holding her, tasting every inch of her beautiful lips until finally, remarkably, he wanted to talk to her more than he wanted to kiss her. "What changed your mind?"

"Two things, actually. First, that picture you drew of me in high school." She tipped her head, looking at him with awe. "You really saw me. You remembered me. That was…amazing."

"I've kept you in my head all these years." He traced her beautiful mouth with his finger. "I've loved you all my life."

"I didn't know."

"Worm sandwich, Kendra…" He laughed with her, happier than he could ever remember being. "And reason two?"

"Believe it or not, that question, what did I fear the most. I'd been going back and forth and over and under our situation, making myself crazy. But once I was able to sit alone and really consider my answer—it was so obvious." She touched his face tenderly. "My greatest fear was losing you. I realized that if losing you was my worst fear, then the only thing I should be worried about was keeping you."

He kissed her, kissed her again and again, lowering her back down to the mattress to kiss her better. And then even so soon after his climax, he started adding hot thoughts to the loving ones and moved down to make sure she enjoyed this time in bed as much as he had. This time and every time, stretching ahead for four tough years apart—but then the rest of their lives together.

As his tongue entered her and he felt her shuddering response, he knew she was made for him and he was made for her.

Afterward, they lay in a blissful haze of joy, stroking, touching, planning, daydreaming about their future.

"Will you come with me to the Humane Society in the morning, Jameson? I've decided in order to survive your absence I need company in the house."

"Sure, of course." He'd walk on coals for her—but the Humane Society would be less painful. In fact, he loved the idea of doing a domestic errand with her. "What kind of dog were you thinking about getting?"

"Well…" She stretched luxuriously against him, a mischievous smile growing on her gorgeous face. "I've given it a lot of thought, what kind would work with my lifestyle and how Byron would feel about being replaced. It wasn't until last night when I sorted myself out about you that I realized. This animal would belong to you, too. Then the obvious solution came to me."

"What's that?"

She reached to squeeze his injured knee gently, grinning sweetly. "I'm going to buy us a cat."

* * * * *

The man did crazy-good things to her...

Macy had no desire for anything complicated. As long as they were discreet, no one in town would know. Friends with benefits. She'd never really had one of those.

"Why are you looking at me like that?"

She blinked and realized she had been staring at Blake. "Uh...you're very handsome."

That sly grin spread across his face. "Okay."

He turned back to the computer, but continued to grin. He knew.

"You do bad, bad things to me, Mr Marine." The grin grew bigger.

"I haven't touched you," he said, his eyes still staring at the screen.

"Oh, but you don't even have to," she whispered. Maybe she had had one too many glasses of wine with the dinner. The room was too warm...

That made him turn.

"Ms Reynolds, are you coming on to me?"

"Yes, sir. I believe I am... So what are you going to do about it?"

HER LAST BEST FLING

BY
CANDACE HAVENS

First published in Great Britain 2013
by Mills & Boon, an imprint of Harlequin (UK) Limited,
Eton House, 18-24 Paradise Road, Richmond, Surrey TW9 1SR

© Candace Havens 2013

ISBN: 978 0 263 90331 7

14-1113

Harlequin (UK) policy is to use papers that are natural, renewable and recyclable products and made from wood grown in sustainable forests. The logging and manufacturing processes conform to the legal environmental regulations of the country of origin.

Printed and bound in Spain
by Blackprint CPI, Barcelona

Award-winning author and columnist **Candace "Candy" Havens** lives in Texas with her mostly understanding husband, two children and three dogs, Harley, Elvis and Gizmo. Candy is a nationally syndicated entertainment columnist for FYI Television. She has interviewed just about everyone in Hollywood, from George Clooney and Orlando Bloom to Nicole Kidman and Kate Beckinsale. Her popular online writer's workshop has more than two thousand students and provides free classes to professional and aspiring writers. Visit her website at www. candacehavens.com.

For those in the military
and police and fire departments,
who put their lives on the line for us every day.

1

AFTER NINE MONTHS of hell in the Middle East—stuck in a hot, dark cave—Blake Michaels welcomed the deluge pounding his windshield. Heavy rain might keep the curious townsfolk from showing up at the Lion's Club. His mom had moved the party when she discovered a good portion of Tranquil Waters wanted to be there for the hero's return.

He was no hero.

He was a man who served his country, and happened to be in the wrong place at the wrong time.

The gray, wet weather mirrored Blake's mood. He wasn't fond of crowds, at least since he'd returned to the States. The time away had changed him in ways he'd only begun to explore.

He appreciated the thought of a party in his honor, but being around that many people at one time was enough to give a guy the cold sweats. His doctors had promised the anxiety would eventually pass. Almost a year in solitude with only a guard, who never spoke for company, had left him with a few issues.

Once, in the hospital afterward, the nurses had found him huddled in a corner of his room. He never wanted to repeat that night.

He'd had a complete blackout, an "episode" they called it, and it scared the hell out of him. That was when he started to take the therapists more seriously.

As he came around a curve on the highway, a flash of white popped up before him. Brakes squealed as his Ford slid to a stop. His breath ragged from trying to steer away from the woman and the giant animal struggling against her. She held the animal while simultaneously trying to push its hindquarters with the toe of her candy-red high heels into the backseat of her car. This was a problem as her tight pencil skirt only allowed her leg to move to a certain height.

Crazy woman.

The dog outweighed her by at least fifty pounds. She'd have better luck putting a saddle on the black-and-white creature and riding to wherever she wanted it to go.

If they didn't get off the two-lane road fast, someone would plow into them. No way would Blake allow that to happen.

A dog isn't worth her losing her life.

He paused for a second.

Dang if he wouldn't have done the very same thing. He loved animals. Scotty, the therapy dog at the hospital, gave him hours of companionship while he went through the hell the docs called physical and mental therapy.

Straightening his truck on the shoulder, Blake hopped out.

"Here," Blake said as he shoved the beast into the back of the Ford SUV.

As he did, the woman teetered on her high heels and fell back. He caught her with one hand and pulled her out of the way. Slamming the door with his foot so the dog couldn't get out, he steadied her with his hip. Pain shot through his leg, and he sucked in a breath.

"Are you okay?" He kept her upright with his hands around her tiny waist. The sexy librarian look with the falling curls hiding her face, nearly see-through, rain-soaked blouse and tight skirt over sexy curves did dangerous things to his libido.

Down, boy. Down.

"Thanks," she said as she glanced back at the dog. "I'm fine. I better get Harley back to the shelter. This is the second time this week she's broken out. Her owner passed away, and she keeps trying to go home. If you ask me, it's the saddest thing ever to see an animal suffer." She waved her hand. "Well, there are worse things in the world, but it's sad that she doesn't understand that he's gone."

"You could have been killed," he said through gritted teeth, although more from the pain in his leg than being upset with her.

Stiffening, she turned slowly. When their eyes met, a clap of thunder boomed. She jumped and stumbled. He held on to her to keep her from falling down.

Tugging out of his grasp, she raised an eyebrow. "Yes, I'm aware of the danger." Her chin jutted out slightly. "Which is why I stopped to get the dog. She was a danger to anyone else who might cross her path. Thank you for your assistance."

He'd offended her without meaning to. The nurses were right, surly had become his natural state. "I— uh…" He wasn't sure if he should apologize. With his luck, he'd only make it worse.

"Mr. Clooney's rooster Pete says the thunderstorms are going to be pretty bad the next couple of days," she said as she climbed into the vehicle. "And that darn rooster is never wrong. Perhaps you should think about staying inside so you aren't tempted to help poor defenseless animals."

With that, she slammed the door shut.

Did he just get the brush-off?

Mr. Clooney's rooster? Wait, how was that annoying creature still alive?

He remembered when his brother poured half a bottle of cold medicine in the rooster's feed so they could sleep in one morning during the summer. If anything, the somewhat drunk rooster crowed even louder the next morning.

The SUV sped off toward town.

Yep, that was definitely the brush-off.

It'd been a while since he'd spent time with a woman. Well, besides, the doctors and nurses at the hospital. He'd done four tours in a row, only taking a few months off occasionally to see his mom while trying to forget everything he'd gone through the past two years.

This final tour was one he couldn't put on the "man shelf." That's what his therapist, a woman who was exceptionally bright and never let him get away with anything, had called his ability to shove things that upset him to the back of his brain. Every time he tried to redirect the conversation away from his recent past, she called him on it.

Blake shoved a hand over his newly shorn hair. He'd let it get longer in the hospital, but his mom didn't like it that way.

And hell if he wasn't just a big ole mama's boy. Blake and his brother, J.T., would do anything for her. She'd held their family together after their dad died when he and J.T. were teens.

He might not like the idea of the party, but eating home-cooked meals his mom made was high on his list of favorite things. He could suffer through any inconvenience for that.

Thunder hit again, and the black-haired woman's heart-shaped face popped into his mind with those almost-translucent green eyes that had seen too much of the world. He wondered if the thunder might be an ominous sign that he should stay away from her.

He grinned.

Nope, that wasn't going to happen. The last thing he needed was to chase some skirt, but there was something about her. She'd been dressed sexy, but she didn't suffer fools gladly.

That was something he admired.

He liked a challenge. This was a small town, and he was about to be at a party with some of the best gossips in Texas—and that was saying something in this state. A type like the sexy librarian would surely be a topic of conversation. His mom hadn't mentioned anyone moving into town during their chats, so the woman had to be fairly new to Tranquil Waters.

After parking the truck in front of the Lion's Club,

he ripped off the wet shirt. He had an extra hanging in the cab. Once he was dressed in his blues, he steeled himself for the oncoming tide of good wishes.

"For he's a jolly good…" voices rang out as he swung open the door and stepped inside. In other circumstances, he would have run back to the truck. But he smiled and shook hands, all the while thinking about that woman with the raven hair and killer red heels.

Perhaps having half the town at his party wasn't such a bad thing.

Facing the blue-haired gossip brigade, he gave them his most charming smile.

"Ladies, you haven't changed a bit," he said. "If I didn't know better I'd guess you were selling your souls to keep that peaches-and-cream skin of yours."

His mother rolled her eyes, but stood on tiptoes to give him a hug.

"You're up to something," she whispered.

Oh, he was definitely up to *something*.

"BRAN MUFFINS AND fake butter. That was one knight in shining armor," Macy complained to Harley as she wrapped wire around the lock on her cage. She never swore around the animals in the shelter as she believed they'd been through enough trauma, without listening to her temper tantrums. So when she wanted to use angry words, she thought about foods she hated.

"Doesn't it figure that ten minutes after I vow no more men forever, he shows up?"

The dog made a strange noise that sounded like

"yes." Great Danes did have their own language. And she bet Harley understood every syllable she said.

"Oh, no. He has to be so hot that steam came off of him. And me." She fanned her face. The heat from the encounter still on her cheeks.

"Here he comes galloping on his horse to the rescue." Macy's last two relationships were nonevents, except for the part where they'd cheated on her. Three weeks ago she'd discovered the man she thought she might marry was having what he called "a meaningless relationship" with an intern at the paper.

Well, it had meant something to Macy.

Harley made a strange sound.

"Fine, it was a truck he galloped in on, but still."

The dog whined again.

"Lovely girl, I'm sorry. I've been going on and on about me, when you have much more to be sad about." She squatted as much as her skirt would allow and petted Harley through the kennel.

The handsome face of the knight was one she recognized. Though his dark brown hair had been cropped close to his head, it was those dark brown, almost-black eyes she couldn't forget. The marine, who'd been captured in Afghanistan, had returned home. She'd been headed to the welcome-home party to cover it for the newspaper. That wasn't the kind of thing publishers did at larger papers, but this was a small town. Darla, the reporter assigned to the story, had to pick her kid up from school and take him to the dentist. And the other two reporters had the flu.

Thinking that it would be a quick in-and-out, Macy had decided to cover the party.

Well, until she found Harley soaked to the skin.

She loved animals. They weren't as judgmental as humans. Since she was sixteen, she'd been volunteering at various shelters around the world. Every time she took a new job, that was one of the first things she did. Well, except for when she was in the Middle East. She didn't have time to breathe then, let alone help anyone else.

In the newspaper business, one had to move a lot. There was constant downsizing and she had to go where the jobs were. That was how she'd landed in Boston—until the fiasco that was her almost-fiancé throwing their comfortable life into the proverbial toilet.

Harley nudged her.

"I promise as soon as the fence guy gets done, you are moving in with me. If this rain would stop, they could finish." This was the first pet she'd ever adopted. The old girl had one green and one blue eye. The sorrow in them tore at Macy's heart. She was an orphan, too, and she'd bonded with the dog ever since she'd caught her trying to get back home the first time.

Her great-uncle Todd, who had been Macy's only remaining relative, had willed her the town's newspaper. For months she'd been trying to sell it with no luck. When she walked in on her ex and his meaningless plaything, she decided moving to a small locale wasn't such a bad idea. Along with the paper, her uncle had left her a beautiful house overlooking White's Lake. She'd decided to put an eight-foot fence along two of the four-acres of the property so Harley would have a place to roam.

"Great Danes need a lot of space." She smiled and scratched the dog's ears.

"Hey, I thought you went to the party," said Josh from the door as he slipped booties over his shoes for sanitary purposes. He was the local veterinarian who donated his services to the shelter.

"I was on my way, but Miss Harley got out again. I caught up with her on the highway."

Josh tickled the dog under her chin, his fingers poking through the cage. It was a large eight-by-eight-foot space, but it wasn't big enough for the hundred-and-seventy-five-pound dog.

"Nice knot with the wiring there. Do you sail?" He pointed to the impenetrable knot she'd devised to keep Harley in.

She shrugged. "Something I picked up from my dad. In the summer we'd go sailing." Those weeks were some of the happiest of her life. Her parents were journalists, so it was in her blood, but it meant they traveled the far ends of the earth, leaving Macy at home.

"So are you heading over to the hero party?"

Feeling as if she'd stood in a rainstorm for an hour, which she did, she decided she'd be better off going home. "No, I'm heading back to my place to change."

She noticed Josh wasn't meeting her eyes. He did everything he could not to look at her.

She glanced down. Her white blouse was completely sheer and she was cold.

Great. Wonderful. Lovely.

"Well, Cecil is up at the front, so I guess I'll be going," she said as she made a quick exit.

Josh was a nice guy. They'd even tried to date once. But discovered there was absolutely no chemistry, which was probably why he was doing his best not to look at her nipples protruding through the sheer fabric of her shirt and nude-colored bra.

Unless she wanted to be the fodder for more town gossip, there would be no party in her future.

The lovely scent of wet dog pervaded her senses as she made the short drive home.

Five minutes later, she turned on the fireplace in the main family area. The front of the place had a Gothic Revival exterior. The back was full of windows. She loved the water. Living near it made her feel close to her dad.

After constantly chasing the next big story, the pace of Tranquil Waters nearly killed her at first. But she'd grown accustomed to the quiet. Her whole life she'd heard Texans were incredibly kind, and they were— However, the ones here didn't trust outsiders, especially Yankees, of which she was one, having spent most of her formative years in the Northeast.

A hot shower was in order. Then she'd bundle up and see what Mrs. Links, the housekeeper who worried that Macy was wasting away, left in the fridge for dinner. The housekeeper came in three times a week, even though Macy was perfectly capable of cleaning up after herself.

Mrs. Links was another part of her strange inheritance from Uncle Todd. He'd provided for her weekly allowance until the time she no longer needed employment.

Macy didn't have the heart to ask the nearly seventy-five-year-old woman when that might be. For someone who made a living by asking the tough questions, Macy had a soft spot when it came to animals and her elders.

As the warm water sluiced across Macy's body, her mind drifted to the marine. Those biceps under her hands were of a man who wasn't afraid of hard labor. Marines had to stay fit, and she had a feeling he'd have washboard abs, as well.

Men with great abs were her weakness.

You swore off men.

The smell of his fresh, masculine scent. Those hard muscles, the warm smile, even after all he'd been through.

The blood thrummed through her body.

She hadn't been with a man in what felt like forever. That was all. He was hot, and any other woman would feel the same way after looking into those sweet chocolate-brown eyes.

Turning down the water's temperature to cool her body, she wondered how long she'd be able to resist the marine.

2

VIOLENT THOUGHTS CROSSED Blake's mind as Mr. Clooney's rooster crowed, waking half the town—so much for the extra rest. Shoving the pillow over his head, he closed his eyes and willed himself back to the dream about the woman in the red heels. The rooster crowed again.

"I'll kill that bird some day," he growled as he rolled out of bed. Too many years in the military had him up, showered and sipping coffee ten minutes later.

His mother had taped a note to the fridge that said, "Muffins are in the warming drawer. Love, Mom."

At five in the morning, she'd probably already been at the feed store for at least an hour. She liked to get the paperwork done before the place opened. Even though she didn't need to be there anymore, she'd insisted on keeping the books and visiting with customers when they came in. She'd built the business from the ground up while his father traveled the world with the military. She believed in having roots and wasn't much for leaving the town she'd been born in. Their relationship worked, because when they were together, they treated each other as if no one else existed in the world. Well, except for Blake and his brother.

Their parents made certain their boys had an idyllic childhood in the town centered between two lakes. They lived on the edge of town, which had exactly four stoplights, a couple of grocery stores and various shops on the rectangle, as they liked to call it. When the town was first built, there was no real plan. When they finally decided they needed a courthouse it was built in the heart of the rectangle of shops and businesses.

But Tranquil Waters had changed while he was deployed. He remembered laughing about the letters from his mom talking about how the town council had decided that they could have a Dairy Queen and a McDonald's on the same side of the highway.

They also—thanks to the lakes and artists and writers who populated the town—had a good tourist industry year-round. It was almost Halloween and he hadn't seen a house yet that hadn't been decorated. There were several haunted B and B's and even a large corn maze on the Carins' pumpkin farm.

Everything seemed so simple in a small town. It didn't take a CIA spook to find out that the woman he'd run into on the highway was the new publisher of the town newspaper.

"That Yankee girl just doesn't understand our ways," complained Mrs. Lawton. "She reported that old Mr. Gunther was thrown in jail Saturday night.

Well, everyone knows he's spent every weekend in that jail cell for the last twenty years. Ever since his sweetheart of a wife, Pearl, passed—God rest her soul—he's just been longing for her. Poor man. What he needs is a new woman, a younger one to keep his mind off his troubles."

While she had glanced around at the other women in her circle, Blake had a feeling she wanted to be the new woman to occupy Mr. G's thoughts. Blake grinned as he sipped his punch. Didn't matter that she'd just turned eighty-five and Mr. G had to be nearing a hundred.

"She has that huge house, darn near a mansion," Lady Smith chimed in. Her name was Lady, and for some reason everyone in town called her Lady Smith. Out of respect, and the fact that she was a friend of his mother's, Blake had once called her Mrs. Smith when he was about ten. She'd scolded him and told him she was a Lady, and he'd do well to remember that in the future.

The town was full of oddballs, and he'd been one of them. As a kid, he'd run around dressed like Davy Crockett for two years and no one had said a word. Apart from his brother, who was more a Spider-Man fan.

"She's got more money than she knows what to do with. Imagine, putting the paper on the inter— whatever those kids use nowadays," Lady had complained. "People here like to hold a newspaper in their hands. And she doesn't seem to understand that there are some stories that just aren't fit to tell. I've written countless letters to the editor, but she never prints or listens to them." Lady waved her hand in the air dismissively.

"Darn Yankee."

How dare she tell the truth about Tranquil Waters. The nerve of the woman. Blake found himself chuckling as he rinsed his cup in the sink.

His mother probably didn't need his help at the feed store. But he didn't want to sit around stewing. It almost always sent him in the wrong direction.

He wondered where Macy—he'd finally learned her name—might be. Likely still in bed, if she were smart. Any sane person would be at this hour of the morning. Pulling the truck out of the drive, he saw something run past.

Blake blinked a few times and followed the blur.

"It can't be."

The monster dog he'd recently stuffed into a car sat on the porch of a white-framed house with a for-sale sign in the yard. The spot was about five blocks from his mom's house.

The way Harley stared at the door, as if willing it to open, broke his heart. Blake had seen a lot of awful things through the years, but kids and animals in distress were his weaknesses. He'd do anything to protect them.

Macy was right. Unlike a human, the dog couldn't understand her master was gone.

Exiting the truck slowly, he stepped up the stone path. She glanced back at him, with the saddest puppy eyes. One of the eyes was blue, the other green.

He hadn't seen her eyes when he'd been dealing with the hindquarters.

"Hey, pretty girl, what's up?"

He held out his hand, but she turned away from him. Lifting a large paw, she hit the doorknob.

Damn dog. His heart lurched. Not sure what he should do, he sat down on the top step next to her. He could drag her to the truck, but he didn't have the nerve. If he gained her trust, maybe she'd go willingly. He had a feeling being at the house was about more than just returning to where she felt safe.

"I'll sit here with you until you decide what you want to do next," he said softly. He didn't have anything better to do.

The dog pawed at the door again and growled.

Blake leaned back against the railing. He could have sworn the dog said, "Let me in."

I am losing it. Now dogs are talking to me.

"Did you just say, let me in?"

The dog pawed his shoulder.

Yep, he was crazy.

"Oh, girl, sorry, I don't have a key. I'd let you in if I could, but I don't have one. And I have a code I live by. Breaking and entering isn't an option."

She barked and then leaped off the porch.

As quick as his sore leg allowed him, he got up and followed her around the side of the house.

When they reached the back porch, she pawed at the door handle and attempted to open it with her mouth. She snarled when it didn't budge.

"Well, we tried," he said.

She cocked her head, and he swore she rolled her eyes.

Taking off to a chipped birdbath in the middle of

the lawn, covered with dirt, she pawed the rocks sur-
rounding the base of the concrete fixture and barked.
Blake limped out to the fountain, more to appease
her than anything.

There on the ground was a key.

"Okay, dog. Now you're freaking me out." If she
had had two legs instead of four, she could pass for
human. And she had to be one brilliant pup to relate
the key to the door.

As he unlocked the door, he noticed someone
peeking over the fence.

He pointed an accusatory finger at the dog. "Fine,
but if we get arrested you're taking the rap." He patted
her on the head. Before he could turn the knob and
open the door himself, she nosed it open and stood in
the small kitchen, as if waiting for him to come inside.
Once he was in, she closed the door with her nose.

Blake had never seen such a thing. The few dogs
he'd had when he was a boy could sit and lie down,
but that was about it.

Harley woofed and trotted to the living room,
where she sat in front of a wingback chair. She nodded at him, as if she wanted him to sit down in it.
More out of curiosity than anything, he did. A paw
shot out and pushed so hard on the chair he worried
he'd go head over heels.

But he didn't fall.

The dog ducked beneath the chair and tossed out
several stuffed animals, a ball and chew bones that
had seen better days. Once she had her stash from
under the chair, she moved the items one at a time to
the charcoal-gray sofa. The booty soon became a pil-

low as she lay atop her toys, sighing as if she'd been on a long journey.

"Poor girl," Blake whispered. The sight of her relaxing choked him up.

"That's the first time I've seen her sleep since he passed," a feminine voice whispered.

Head snapping around, he took in Macy Reynolds's tight jeans, pink hoodie and those furry boots women wore when the thermometer dipped below seventy. The town was having an unusually cool October, and the temperature hung around the fifty-degree mark. A sleepy angel with no makeup, and more beautiful than she'd been the day before.

"I saw her running past my mom's house when I left this morning and I decided to follow." He held up a hand. "I swear she made me unlock the door. She showed me where the key was."

"I believe it. Evidently the drama was about her missing toys. I don't blame her," Macy continued to whisper. "I'm kind of fond of my stuff. I don't have that much, but what I do have is precious to me."

Odd since he'd learned she inherited her uncle's house. He assumed she had tons of stuff.

"What?" She checked her clothing as if she might have missed a button.

"Nothing. I...heard last night that you inherited your uncle's new mansion."

She scrunched her face. "Yes, he— Yes."

"For the record, I haven't been stalking you. Some of the gossips at the party were talking about it."

She smirked and moved to the sofa to sit beside Harley.

"Is there an expiration date or something on being the subject of town gossip? I've never lived in a place where other people were so in your business. Usually, as a reporter, I'm the nosy one. It's disconcerting. And I don't think they like me very much, although I'm doing my best to turn their local into a paper that resembles more than tractor reports."

He laughed, and the dog opened an eye and glared at him.

"Unfortunately, until the next interesting person moves to town, it'll be all about you."

"Yes, but the hero has returned." She nodded in his direction. "Can't you be the subject of conversation for a while?"

"Nah. I'm not nearly as interesting as a Yankee woman who wears pencil skirts and sky-high heels. And according to the gray hairs, you have a scandalous past where you combed the world reporting on everything from celebrities to wars. Some man broke your heart, and you're here hiding away."

Her eyes opened wide. "Wow. They are good. I wish they'd be as generous with their words with me. Honestly, I know heads of state who give more in an interview than people in this town."

She hadn't bothered to deny any of what he'd said, so it must have been true about combing the world and the man who was in her life. He wondered if that relationship was really over. He shrugged. "Give it some time, they'll come around."

"Will you talk to me?"

He frowned. "I thought that was what we were doing."

"No—I mean, yes." She waved her hand. "In an interview. The *Tranquil Waters News* should do a feature on the town hero."

That was the last thing he wanted.

"There isn't a lot these folks don't already know. I've been gone for about seven years. I'm back, a little worse for the wear but alive. There isn't much more to tell. I was doing my job but happened to be in the wrong place at the wrong time."

She sighed, not unlike the suffering sound the dog had made. "I should have known. You're no different than the rest."

The disappointment in her voice forced him to do something he promised he never would.

"All right, if you want to talk, that's cool, but not right now. I need to get to the feed store to help my mom." Small white lie, but he had to stall to gather his thoughts. "I was on my way there when I saw Harley." At least that part was true.

She glanced from the dog to him as if she were trying to discern the truth. "We could do something a little less formal, if that would make you more comfortable. How about tonight? I could make you dinner at my place."

He almost laughed at the look on her face as if she couldn't believe she just asked him to dinner.

"If food is involved, I'm there. If you're sure?"

She nodded. "How about seven-thirty?"

"See ya then." He stood.

"Don't you need the address?"

He chuckled. "The house is where the old Gladstone farm used to be, right?"

"Yes. It overlooks the lake."

"Trust me. I know that area very well." More than once, he and his friends had thrown a party at the old barn, which had been torn down years ago.

"Do you need help with the dog?"

"No, I'm going to go grab my laptop and work here so she can rest. I have a feeling she'll follow those toys wherever I take them."

"Okay, see ya later." He patted the dog and walked out the front door.

He had a date. Well, it was technically an interview, but he was practiced at giving nonanswers. He'd done it his entire military career. All of his assignments were classified, so he couldn't share anything.

Hope she won't be too mad when she finds out I'm as tight-lipped as the rest of Tranquil Waters.

He started the truck engine. The last thing he wanted was the sleepy angel mad at him.

"WHAT WAS I thinking?" Macy blurted into the phone. "You don't invite people you're interviewing to dinner."

"Yes, you do. It's just the dinner's at a restaurant most of the time," her friend Cherie chimed in. "Chill, girl. You're going to have a heart attack. This guy must be superhot to make you so nervous."

Macy slipped on a pair of flats. After his comment about the heels, she realized she'd been trying too hard. Except for those over sixty, this was more of a jeans and T-shirt town. She was perfectly comfortable in that attire.

It wasn't until her breakup with Garrison that Che-

rie, her nearest and dearest friend, forced her to leave
Boston and took her for a makeover in Manhattan.
They tossed out everything she'd owned and decided
to start fresh with a sexy new wardrobe. Add a brand-
new haircut that was perfect for her shoulder-length
curls. And a newfound passion for accessories. Cherie had convinced her that shoes and purses were
really works of art.

She didn't have to twist Macy's arm very hard.

But if Macy wanted to fit into the landscape of
Tranquil Waters, she'd have to scale back on the big-
city wardrobe, etc.

"*Superhot* doesn't cover it," she said honestly.
"*Scorching* might come close. He puts that gorgeous
action-adventure star Tom Diamond to shame."

"Wait. Hotter than Tom Diamond? The man who
will be my husband someday, even if I have to shoot
him with a tranq gun and stuff him in my trunk? I
think it might be time for me to visit Texas."

"You are welcome anytime. I certainly have the
room. And yes he's that handsome, and he's sweet to
dogs and loves his mother. You know how tough that
is for me. He's like a triple threat. But I have to keep
this professional. The last thing I need in this gossip-
hungry town is to date its hero."

"So you want to date him. Hmm."

"Stop analyzing me and putting words in my
mouth," Macy complained. Cherie never stopped
being a psychiatrist, but it was her only vice so Macy
put up with her.

"You said the words. I'm just placing them in the
proper order for you."

"Privacy is impossible at any of the restaurants in town. I'm sure that's why I came up with making the dinner. I wanted him to feel comfortable, to share as much as possible."

"He's a war hero, you know there's not much he can say," her friend warned.

"This isn't my first time." She'd been to almost every war zone in the world the past five years. It had only been the past twelve months that she'd decided to take a permanent position out of the line of fire. Little did she know it was just as dangerous at home.

She'd been shot at, kidnapped twice by insurgents and lost in the middle of the desert. None of that had been as bad as her ex's betrayal.

"Stop thinking about that jerk. He's not worth it."

"How did you know?" Macy laughed at her friend's incredible insight.

"He called here looking for you again. For a hot-shot newspaper publisher, he's not very good at finding people."

Macy snorted. He was one of the best reporters ever, and if he truly wanted to find her, he would. But she'd told him if he did, she'd only turn him away again. It was the truth.

"Of course, I told him to stuff it up his—"

Lights flashed across her bedroom window. "Oh, man, he's here early. Darn those marines and their punctuality."

Macy stared down at the melee of clothing on her bed and picked up the frilly black blouse on top.

"Put down the black, and choose the red. Men love red."

"That was scary. Fine. Red it is. I love you and I wish you'd come see me. It's a nice town but—I still feel very outsiderish."

"Oh, girl, don't you worry. They'll love you as much as I do. Just give them some time and the chance to get to know you. Charm the pants off that marine. That will be a great start."

The doorbell rang and Harley barked twice.

The big dog had settled in just fine. Macy had even bought the dog her own couch for the family room. The fence had been finished that afternoon, and they'd reinforced the gate with two different kinds of locks.

She turned off the phone.

Harley sat patiently at the door waiting for their guest.

Shoving her curls out of her face, Macy took a deep breath and turned the knob.

Oh, shoot, the man is beautiful.

Dressed in dark jeans, cowboy boots and a dark blue button-down under a leather jacket, he was way beyond scorching.

Her normally agile mind couldn't think of the word, but she knew there was one.

This is work. This is work. This is work.

He cocked his head and stared down at Harley.

"Did she run away again?"

"What?" Macy forced her hand to stay still even though she wanted to wave it in front of her own face, which was suddenly too warm even though the temperature outside was in the low fifties.

"Harley? You know the dog?"

He smiled at her as if he were humoring her.

"Uh, sorry. I'd been on the phone and I'm a little—uh—" *Hot for you.* No, that wasn't right. "Out of sorts. Please come in. And Harley lives with me now. She would have been in here days ago, but the rain kept the ground too wet for them to finish putting the fence in."

He handed her a colorful bouquet of chrysanthemums in a vase. "These are a present for your new home." In his other hand he held a large paper bag. "I didn't know what you were cooking so I brought a couple bottles of wine, some dark beer and, er... green tea."

She took the flowers and led him to the kitchen. "Thank you, these are beautiful, but you didn't have to bring anything."

He shrugged and sat the bag down on her quartz countertop. "It's the south, if you don't bring a housewarming gift on the first occasion you visit, or to any party you're invited to, they'll talk about you for years."

"I'll have to remember that," she said. Not that she'd been invited to anything, but maybe some day.

"I probably should have mentioned my kitchen skills are somewhat limited. But I make a mean beef stew. I put it on earlier today, so it should be ready in a few minutes. And I have bread and salad."

"Sounds good to me. In general, I like food, so it doesn't matter too much what it is. After C-Rats, I can, and have, digested everything from guinea pig in Machu Picchu to some weird toad in Africa. I'm

not sure that last one didn't lead to a night of hallu-
cinations."

She laughed. "I'm pretty adventurous when it
comes to food, but I've never eaten either of those."

"You get to a point where just about everything
really does taste like chicken." He smiled and her
heart did a double thump.

Oh, heck, I'm in trouble.

She forced a smile.

"Now I feel like maybe I should have tried for
something more exotic." She examined the wine bottles he'd brought. He'd surprised her with his choices.
She didn't know much about wine, but neither bottle
was cheap. "Do you have a preference?"

"Whatever you want is fine with me. I'll be drinking the tea."

At her quizzical look, he explained. "The docs are
weaning me off the painkillers for my leg. It's best if
I don't drink as it can create an allergic reaction. Although, me and my buddies at the hospital suspected
they only told us that so we don't find out how the
painkillers are with alcohol. They deal with a lot of
addicted vets there."

"We can't have that. Tea it is. The last thing I need
is alcohol. It tends to loosen my tongue, and I'm not
the one who needs to do the talking tonight."

She caught the tightening of his lips before he
turned away. "I don't mind," he said. "If you want a
glass of wine. It won't bother me."

"No," she said lightly. "I've grown fond of tea since
moving here. Cracks me up that they drink it iced
even in the dead of winter."

"Staple of the South," he said, pulling a large plastic pitcher with a lid out of the bag. "Usually it's black tea. I have this friend from China who told me that green tea has healing properties. It also clears away some of the fogginess from the drugs."

"I've heard that, too." She'd forgotten about his injuries. Except for a small limp, he didn't seem to be in much pain. But she'd met plenty of marines and she knew how tough they were. If he had to take drugs, the injuries were severe. The journalist in her wanted to know specifics, but it would wait.

"Before we eat, would you like to see the house? Actually, most of it is my uncle Todd's taste. But I have a few touches here and there."

"I like the stonework on the outside mixed with the pale brick. It blends into the rocky hills behind the house."

"Yes, that was one of his ideas—for it to blend into the landscape. Though, I think it's kind of fun that he added a Gothic touch with some of the windows and the roof alignment.

"Did you know my uncle? I mean, you've been gone awhile, but before?"

"I didn't know him. I probably heard his name around town, but I wasn't much interested in the newspaper when I was a kid. And some might say I was a little self-absorbed back then. I like to say, I was a teenager."

They laughed.

She took him through the family area where Harley plopped down on her sofa. The television was on

Animal Planet, which seemed to be the dog's favorite along with anything on PBS.

He smiled. "She's made herself at home there."

"Oh, that couch is hers. I even had them put extra down in it and then had that wrapped in plastic and an outdoor fabric. Great Danes have joint and bone aches most of their lives. I wanted Harley to have a soft place to rest. Just a minute, I need to change the channel for her."

Picking up the remote, she set it on one of the PBS *Nova* specials. Harley grunted her agreement.

She'd learned about the dog's television preferences earlier in the day when she'd sat with her at her former home. If Macy tried to watch a channel Harley didn't like, the dog would voice her displeasure.

Not that she was spoiled or anything.

The house was a Texas T shape. The various hallways fed into the center area, which was the main entertaining space. "Down that hall are two bedrooms. There's another guest bedroom down that hall—" she pointed "—and the master bedroom and study are down that hall," she said.

It didn't seem appropriate to take him to the bedrooms. "There's a loft upstairs with two more bedrooms. But it isn't really worth the trip up. Let me show you the study. There are a lot of Civil War antiques in there. My uncle was a collector." The rest of the house had been furnished in rich warm tone-on-tone colors. It was a comfortable place to relax at the end of the day. The only room that was slightly feminine was the master bedroom and bathroom, which Macy had decorated.

Macy opened the door to the study and smiled when Blake muttered, "Wooooee. This is a museum."

His eyes traveled over the glass cases filled with small items and guns from various Civil War battles.

She'd had the estate appraised and this room alone was worth a couple of million. The study had been outfitted with special equipment that would protect it from fire and anything else Mother Nature might throw at it. The whole house was a bunker of sorts, concrete surrounded by stone. The windows could withstand an F-5 tornado. That was good because in this part of the country hurricanes and tornados happened at least once or twice a year.

"I don't have the heart to auction off these things. Other than the newspaper, this was my uncle Todd's only passion. I can feel his spirit in here, and I just can't let go of his stuff."

Blake blew out a whistle. "I'm no expert, but even I know this is one incredible collection. There are people who'd pay big money for it, but I understand how you feel. My dad collected baseball caps and cards. We still have an entire wall of his hats, some are from teams that no longer exist, and a few are hats his dad had given to him. There's an original Yankees cap in the bunch, but my mom hides that one when her friends come over.

"It was never even a question if we'd keep them. And I feel the same way about them, as you do."

She smiled. "Sounds like you really loved your dad."

Flipping off the light switch, he followed her out the door and to the kitchen.

"Has the interview started?" His voice had changed and he sounded as if he suspected her of trying to get him to talk about his past.

"No. Mere curiosity. I thought I'd feed you before grilling you." She winked at him.

"Then, yes. My dad was a hero to my brother and me. He's the reason I went into the military, albeit he was air force. He was a pilot until he decided to retire and help Mom with the feed store. He was a tough old goat, and my brother and I didn't get away with much when we were kids."

"I met your mom when I first arrived. I had to get a lawn mower and other gardening tools."

He chuckled.

She served up the bowls of stew. "Your mother found me frowning as I checked out the lawn mowers. She dug around in her pockets and handed me a card that had the number of a teenager who does yards. Her exact words were, 'He's a good kid. For four acres it'll be about a hundred dollars a week. If he tries to charge you more, tell him I'll knock him upside the head.'"

Blake laughed. "Yep, that's my mom."

"I loved her. She was one of the few people who was genuinely kind to me. I'd heard Texans are a friendly bunch. And, okay, everyone has been nice to my face. But I get the strangest looks. And as I mentioned earlier, they haven't been exactly welcoming."

He carried both of the bowls to the other end of the counter where there were stools and place settings. "Like I said earlier, soon someone will move to town and then you'll be one of the gang. Just give them more time."

She smiled. "My friend Cherie told me the same thing. I'm not sure why it bothers me so much. I never knew any of my neighbors when I lived in New York, Paris or anywhere in the Middle East. Most of the time I lived out of hotels."

At the mention of hotels, his jaw tightened. She'd read what she could find on him, and knew that he'd been in Africa when he sustained his injuries. He was protecting a visiting American ambassador there. He and most of his men were hit by enemy fire, but they'd saved the ambassador and other dignitaries that day. The soldiers had earned Purple Hearts.

"Don't be too worried about it," he interrupted her thoughts. "Small-town life isn't always what it's cracked up to be. Eventually, you feel like a part of the community when everyone knows your name. It can be a wonderful thing, or a curse." His eyebrow rose.

"A curse?" It hadn't been that bad.

"Oh, yes. And especially if a certain high school girl's dad finds you in the barn with her, um, counting hay straws. He calls your dad, who gives you the I'm-disappointed look in front of the entire town when he finds you later at Lucky Chicken Burger sharing a box with your friends." He looked to the heavens. "People still talk about how he watched as my mom dragged me out by my ear. One of the most embarrassing days of my life."

She nearly sputtered her stew, she laughed so hard. "I can't imagine your mother doing that. She talks so highly of you. She's so proud."

"Now she is. That day, not so much. I was grounded for six weeks after that and wasn't allowed to go on dates alone with a girl until I left for college. If we didn't go in a group, I wasn't given permission to go. I had to write letters of apology to the girl, her parents, my parents and our minister."

He shook his head as she started to laugh again. "Sure, it sounds funny, but back then—my friends and my brother never let me forget it. I ran away to college so fast, it was no joke. Joined the marines to help pay for my bachelors and MBA.

"I was determined I would never come back to this place, but I'm a mama's boy. I probably shouldn't admit that. I missed her and dad so much by the end of that first semester, I hitched a thousand miles to get home by Christmas Eve. Of course, my mom read me the riot act because I could have been killed on the road."

"Still, I bet she was glad to see you."

He nodded. "It wasn't long after that my dad got sick. So I was grateful we had that Christmas together."

A chunk of carrot caught in her throat as she watched the memories pass across his face. There'd been a deep family love there. She envied him that. He grew silent.

She swallowed and had a drink of tea. "My parents traveled a lot for their jobs. We didn't get to have many holidays together. I kind of envy you that."

"What did they do?"

"Journalists. My mom wrote for magazines, my dad was on air for different TV affiliates."

"Are they still at it?"

Macy bit her lip. "No. They were killed in a small-plane crash on their way to report on a new orphanage in India. Happened about eight years ago. Uncle Todd was my last living relative. It's just me now."

Blake frowned. "Sorry. I didn't mean to bring up such painful memories."

She patted his arm. Her fingers tingled from the contact. "You didn't. We were talking about family. I just wish I had what you had and have with your mom. I believe the world would be a better place if more parents were like yours.

"I'm lucky that I have great friends all over the world. They helped me when I lost my parents. I was doing an internship in Bosnia with a newspaper and the military guys I'd been following arranged for me to get a flight home on one of their transports. One of them even flew with me and stayed until Uncle Todd could get to the base. I never forgot that. Kevin Donaldson was his name. He had two kids and a wife who adored him. Anytime I was stateside, they insisted on me coming to visit.

"Wow. Look at me telling you my whole life story. Who is interviewing whom, here? I never talk to anyone like this."

He winked at her. "It's the green tea. Has mystical properties in it."

They both laughed.

"Do you want another bowl?"

"Sure. The stew is good. I miss home cooking."

She handed him another full bowl and shoved the plate of French bread at him so he could reach it. "I—I did some digging. As I mentioned, I've covered the military for years for various assignments. I know you can't tell me exactly what happened, although I do know about the ambassador. That's a matter of public record. And that you guys saved him and the others who were investigating the ammunitions camp someone had discovered in the Congo."

"You have done your research." His voice was guarded again.

"I don't want to ask you anything I know you can't answer. What I would like to know is how it happened. Several of your men were hit, but luckily everyone survived."

He sat his spoon in the bowl and stared down at it.

"Some were luckier than others," he whispered.

Her brow furrowed. "Do you mean the injuries?"

"Yes, and the nightmares. Some of us are having a tough time letting go what happened there."

"What did happen?"

His deep brown gaze cut to her. "You know I can't give you details."

She sighed. "Was it an ambush? From what I've figured out so far, you guys had a peaceful week there until you were getting ready to leave. Then all hell broke loose."

As if Harley had sensed the tension, she nudged between them and put her head on his thigh.

He sucked in a breath.

"Is she hurting you?"

"No. It's just sore, like a bruise. Mind you, her head is like a ton of bricks."

"It is very large. She accidentally bumped my nose earlier with her head when I put food in her bowl, and I thought for sure I'd have black eyes."

He smiled, but it was weak.

Stupid. As professional as she was, it bothered her to realize she'd triggered such old memories—hurtful ones from the look of concern on his face.

That was it. He wasn't just a hero. He was a man. That would be her story. No one needed to read about his nightmares of that terrible day, or the darkness that clearly haunted him. How often had she told that story? Heroes deserved to be recognized, but maybe she could focus on who they were after they came home, rather than who they were then.

So many soldiers were affected by the experiences they'd gone through. Some—not in a good way. But some said that it made them more aware of how small the world could be.

"I have chocolate chip cookies for dessert. Actually, I was going to show you the best way to eat them."

"Well, I thought you ate cookies with your mouth." He gave her an odd look, and she rolled her eyes.

"Ah, where is your sense of food adventure? In fact, I'm going to take that adventuresome nature of yours to a whole new level."

"Bring it on, Macy. I can take whatever you've got."

The seductive, whiskey sound of his voice and his choice of words did all kinds of naughty things to her.

Be careful.

But it was too late. She'd already crossed the line with Lieutenant Blake Michaels, and she wasn't at all upset about it.

3

BLAKE TOSSED AND turned in his bed. Thoughts of Macy in those jeans and that lacy red top made it impossible for him to sleep. He'd wanted to kiss her as soon as he saw her lick the whip cream from her lips. That pink tongue had darted out and all he could think of was capturing it with his mouth. He'd wanted to cover her in the white confection and lick every inch of her.

Damn. He had it bad for her.

He sat up on the side of the bed. He needed a shower, a cold one.

Why did she have to be a reporter? If she had any other occupation he'd be doing his best to get in her bed. He couldn't remember when a woman had affected him the way she did. Her laugh, smile and the way she walked with those lovely curvy hips swaying back and forth held his attention.

He thought back over their conversation. Even though she'd pried, she did it respectfully. True to her word, she hadn't asked him a single thing he couldn't answer. And when she dug a little too deep, she'd backed off and made them chocolate chip cookie pies, her version of the whoopie pie.

She was hot. Smart and funny. The perfect combo.

But he couldn't risk hanging out with a woman who might reveal secrets he prided himself on keeping. He might slip up, get carried away. And the last thing he needed was for his superiors to see something like that in the newspaper.

He'd been thinking about taking the honorable discharge on offer, and maybe settling down like his friends Rafe and Will. They'd all met when Will was their captain on missions in Iraq and Afghanistan.

Will had retired and Rafe had been in charge the day of the ambush. Rafe had all points covered. There was no way they could have anticipated the assault. There would have been a lot more casualties if they hadn't been so prepared.

Before the memories pulled him into the darkness, Macy's smile flashed before him.

Damn. Damn. Damn.

He needed to go for a run, but the docs said it would be another three weeks before his leg could take the pounding.

The town might be small, but they did have a health club that was open twenty-hour hours, specifically for folks who worked shifts.

Grabbing his swim shorts, he pulled on a pair of jeans and a T-shirt. Throwing on his leather jacket, he was at the club in less than five minutes. A swim would be the only thing to burn off the excess energy. It was his substitute form of meditation since he couldn't run. The club was nearly empty at four in the morning, and for that he was grateful. He didn't have to make conversation or smile. The sleepy girl at the desk waved him by when he flashed his membership card.

Diving into the water he struck out hard, his arms and legs going at a blistering pace. After twenty or so laps, he slowed down and cleared his mind. The blank slate, his therapist suggested to calm his nerves, was hard for him to find some days. Tabula rasa, she'd called it. It was a challenge to find it when the sexy woman's face kept popping up over and over again.

Then there was his mother who had waited up to pepper him with questions when he'd returned the night before. Macy had nothing on his mom, who kept giving him strange looks and then smiled when he said he was tired and needed to sleep.

He'd never understood women, and his mom was the most confusing of them all.

"I don't know what that water ever did to you, but I hope you're never that mad at me." Macy's voice penetrated his concentration. He nearly gulped a mouthful of water as he stopped abruptly. He was at the end of a lap, and she stood above the lane in a formfitting navy swimsuit.

Hell. The woman was trying to kill him.

His cock was so hard it hurt. He leaned up against the wall and put his arms on the side of the pool to hide the evidence.

What was he, twelve?

Get yourself under control, Marine.

"I have to give up running for a few more weeks and this is the way I meditate."

She chewed on her lip. "I thought you did yoga, or sat and chanted to mediate."

He smirked. "That's awful closed-minded for someone who has traveled the world. Some people do. But I have trouble shutting off my brain if I'm not moving. When I sit still— Well. I have insomnia and sometimes exercise is the only way I can get myself to calm down."

She sat down and dangled her legs in the water. "I hope it's not because of what we talked about last night," she said worriedly. "It's my nature to push at people until they give me what I want. I tried not to do that with you, but sometimes I just can't help myself."

He couldn't tell her the truth, so he lied. "No, it wasn't that. Well, maybe a little. But not in the way you think." He'd made a fool of himself. "Why are you here?"

She pointed through the window where a man had Harley on a treadmill. "One of the trainers from the rescue shelter is working with Harley. The treadmill is made for people who have bad joints."

"She didn't seem to have any trouble running around the other day."

"No, but she shouldn't have done it. Running like that is bad for her. We're trying to teach her to walk at a fast pace on the treadmill. This was the only time Jack could do it. He's a vet tech at the shelter and his shift starts at seven.

"I thought while they worked out, I'd come do some laps. I didn't realize it was you until you made that last turn. I guess, though I never thought of it that way, swimming is my meditation, too. I do it more to make the puzzle pieces of my life and the stories I tell fit together. When I'm doing something physical, it helps me figure stuff out. And like Harley, I have a bad knee. I like running, but it doesn't like me."

He glanced at her left knee, there was a round puckered scar there, and then a long line that intersected it. His head snapped up, his eyes met hers. "You were hit."

She nodded. "About three years ago. It was a through-and-through, but did some ligament damage on the way out. Nothing like what you've experienced."

The thought of her being harmed brought out his protective instincts. He pulled himself up out of the water and sat beside her. "You don't have a limp."

"Nah. I had some great physical therapists." She traced the scar on his right leg. "Wow, that's nasty. Must really hurt."

Her touch had an instant affect on him. Thankfully her eyes were fixed on his right leg and knee. The scars went from his midthigh through his knee and calf. In all he'd taken three bullets in the one leg. And another one in his back. "It's a lot better than it was six weeks ago. What were you doing when you got hurt?"

"Researching a feature on the Arab spring. A demonstration I was covering got out of hand. Had to run for the border the first chance I got, and we were attacked. We were lucky that the marines were waiting on the other side.

"I got hit. They fired back. Luckily a navy surgeon fixed me up right away and then sent me to a good surgeon and physical therapist in Florida where he had a practice."

"You shouldn't have put yourself in danger like that." The words had more of a bite than he'd meant them to. "You could have been killed."

She pulled her fingers away from his leg as if he'd shocked her. "Uh, it's my job to report the tough stories. And trust me, I've been through worse."

Lifting her curls, she pointed to an ugly scar on the back of her neck.

The air left his lungs.

"That was the one that really scared me." She stared at the water.

He reached out and touched the wound.

She jerked away. "But that's a story for another day. I need to get my workout in. I'm sorry I interrupted yours." She stood and he noticed her toenails were painted a violet color. Something about that made him smile. Then he remembered what he'd done.

"Sorry I touched you. I can't stand violence against women. It—It's one of my triggers."

"Triggers for what?"

"A story for another day," he repeated the phrase back to her. Then he grabbed a towel and wrapped it around his waist. "Have a good swim."

4

When Blake touched Macy it was all she could do not to wrap her arms around him. No one had ever looked at her so tenderly or been so concerned. Her ex had been the one who sent her out on some of her roughest assignments. He'd expected her to be able to handle herself, and she did. But there was a small part of her that wished he'd worried about her once in a while. She should have known something was wrong when she called to tell him that she'd been shot and all he'd worried about was how she was going to get him the story.

She'd made the surgeon wait an hour so she could pound out ten pages and email it to the paper.

Blake would have been frantic worrying about her.

Hey, you are not turning into one of those women.

She refused to be the type of woman who needed the man in her life to save her. Macy prided herself on her independence.

Jumping into lane five, she sluiced through the water. When she thought of the marine, she tried to focus on the story she wanted to tell. But it was complicated. She didn't quite have all the pieces yet. She needed to talk to his mother and others who knew Blake. Well, duh, the whole town knew him.

She wanted a different perspective.

The idea was just out of her grasp. She pushed herself harder and harder until ten laps later she was out of breath and hanging on to the edge of the pool in the same way Blake had earlier.

She glanced through the window to see how Harley was doing. Jack gave her double thumbs-up and she smiled.

Why couldn't she go for a guy like Jack or even his boss, Josh? They weren't the subjects of a story and, as far as she knew, they didn't have any battle scars. Though, she sometimes wondered about Josh. He'd been wounded in some way. It was that haunted look in his eyes.

No one knew better than she did how those scars and secrets could weigh a soul down.

The treadmill slowed, and Jack gave Harley a treat. Climbing the ladder out of the pool, she dressed quickly.

Professional ethics kept her from loading Harley into her car and driving straight to Blake's house. She wanted to comfort him. To hold him in her arms and maybe even slip her legs around him and absorb some of the pain he'd experienced.

When would she realize, she never did simple.

After drying Harley off with a towel, she got her settled in the SUV without any fuss. The dog was too tired to fight her. She lay across the backseat look-ing exhausted.

As Macy pulled up the long drive to her house, she quickly slammed on the brakes.

Harley growled at her.

The marine plaguing her thoughts sat on the tail-gate of his truck more handsome than any man had the right to be.

What was going on?

Her body heated. One glance in the rearview and her cheeks were the color of primroses on a bright sunny day.

Every cell in her body screamed at her. She needed him just as much as he might need her.

Oh.

Cherie would start charging her by the hour.

But before she called her friend, she had to find out why the Blake was here in her driveway. His ex-pression said the weight of the world was resting on his shoulders.

She let Harley out of the backseat.

"Hey," she said as the dog ran up to Blake. He bent over and rubbed the animal's ears.

Macy tried her best not to be jealous, but it wasn't easy.

One small touch from Blake, and she already craved more.

"Hey," he said eyeing her warily. "Sorry I just showed up. We need to talk."

"About?"

"The fact that I touched you without your permis-sion. I was taught better than that. I can write you a letter of apology if you'd like, but I thought it might mean more if I said it in person."

She laughed. "Letters are so old-school. You could have texted me."

He shrugged. "I kind of like the old-school ways, besides, I didn't have your number. And there's something else."

"What's that?"

"I really want to kiss you."

She was in big, big trouble, she could confirm, because she wanted that, too.

"Wow. FOR A MARINE, you really aren't afraid to tell it like it is." Macy gave him a smile that didn't quite meet her eyes. He'd made her uncomfortable, but he had to speak his mind. If she told him off, so be it, but he had to let her know how he felt.

If he'd learned anything the past six months, it was that life was short. And from his therapist, that the truth was important.

"It's true. It's who I am. And I understand you and I can't— Well, that is, you have ethics. Some journalists don't anymore, but I can see that you do. We have a connection. I'm fairly certain you've noticed it."

She nodded.

Good, at least the attraction wasn't one-sided.

"But you're writing a story about me and that's a conflict of interest."

"Yes, it is."

"So, I think I have a solution."

She sat next to him on the tailgate and petted Harley.

"Don't write the story."

Immediately her back stiffened. "I can't do that."

"Why not? You're the publisher of the paper, right? Your uncle left you the whole thing, so you make the decisions. Or you could have someone else write the story, though, I'm going to be honest—I wouldn't trust anyone else."

She sighed. "Why do you have to be so—you."

He chuckled. "I'm not sure what that means, but do you agree with me?"

"The story is already compromised because you do strange things to me, Lieutenant Michaels."

He lifted her chin with his fingers and waited. She nodded her approval.

"Strange things?"

"Yes," she said softly. "I always seem to be too warm when you're around."

"Hmm. Maybe you have a fever." He held the back of his hand to her forehead. Then let his fingers trail down her cheek. He leaned in to kiss her.

Harley let loose with a harsh bark.

They broke apart chuckling.

A giant head was eye level with them. Harley's paws were up on the tailgate, and she gave them a look that said break it up.

"I think she's hungry," Macy suggested. "I should feed her."

The dog grumbled.

"Do you mind if I help?"

Macy pursed her lips.

"Hands off, I promise. I won't touch you again until you ask me."

"This isn't a good idea," she said.

"What? Feeding your dog? Surely she would disagree."

Since Macy didn't tell him to leave, he followed her into the house. Keeping his distance so she wouldn't feel pressured.

She needed time to get used to the idea. Hell, they'd only met a couple of days ago and here he was trying to kiss her.

He remembered about the ex. Maybe that wasn't over.

She winced. "I'm trying to fit in and I don't think dating the town hero will help my case."

"See, that's where you have it wrong. I could be just what you need to ingratiate yourself to the town. If I approve of you, well, it doesn't look so good on them if they don't accept you."

She placed the dog's water dish on a raised stand where Harley was mowing through her food. "I'll think about it."

He winked at her. "You do that. I'll pick you up at seven to take you out to eat."

"No," she said. "I mean it. I'll think about it. It hasn't been that long since I got out of a bad relationship. I'm not ready to date yet."

He shrugged. "Who said anything about a relationship? We're sharing a meal. We won't call it a date. We'll call it a mutual companion outing. Besides, you'd be doing me a favor. All the gray hairs keep throwing their daughters at me. You can be my shield."

That made her laugh. "I'm pretty sure you can

defend yourself just fine, Lieutenant Michaels. You don't need me."

He smiled. "But we had dinner last night. Why can't we do it again?"

"Last night it was about work. And frankly, I don't think it's a good idea to leave Harley alone while she's getting used to her new surroundings. I plan on taking her to the office with me so she doesn't feel abandoned."

Rubbing his chin, Blake eyed the dog. "If I can solve the problem with Harley, will you go to dinner with me?"

She bit her lip. He really loved when she did that.

"I'm not sure how many times I can say this isn't a good idea."

"Fine. I agree. It's not a good idea, but I'm having trouble focusing because I keep wondering what it would be like to kiss you. To hold your hand in mine."

"And spending time with me is going to solve that dilemma?"

"Maybe we'll get lucky and you'll bore me to tears. Or I'll be allergic to your perfume. You might like a movie I despise. I'm kind of a movie snob." That last bit was true. In college, he'd refused to date any woman who hadn't seen his two favorite films, *To Kill a Mockingbird* and *North by Northwest,* they were now followed closely by *Zero Dark Thirty.*

Movies were his favorite escape, and he took them seriously.

Shoving her curls behind her ears she stared at him.

"So, I'd really be doing you a favor by sharing

a meal at this mutual companion outing? We'll get
bored with each other and then we can move on,
right?"

"Exactly," he told her, but he didn't believe it for a
minute. She was bright, funny and beautiful. A triple
threat as far as he was concerned. Blake didn't want
to think about the future. For now he just wanted the
clever journalist with the curvy hips any way she'd
take him.

5

AMANDA PELEGRINE, the receptionist at *Tranquil Waters News,* put down her nail file and eyed Macy warily. For once, Harley was on her best behavior and strode in as if she owned the place. Macy was certain it had nothing to do with the giant box of dog treats and sack of brand-new toys she had in her hand.

Amanda, who was not Macy's biggest fan, sneered. "I'm allergic to dogs."

Good. Maybe you'll quit.

She'd wanted to fire the useless female since the day she took over the paper. But her uncle's will stated she had to wait three months before making any staffing changes.

He'd left her with an angry receptionist, who looked like something from the circus with her fuzzy raspberry sweater, two-inch-long green nails and fascinator that looked like a dead bird on a perch.

Having lived in big cities, Macy was used to all kinds of fashions, but she'd never seen someone like Amanda.

In addition to the snarky witch, she had one reporter, Darla, who was amazing, but eight month's pregnant with her second child.

The only columnist was Hugo, who was eighty, possibly ninety. Old enough that he couldn't remember what year he was born. He couldn't hear or see, but the man could write. He used an old manual typewriter, which meant someone else had to scan his stories into a computer.

Twice a week Macy stopped by to pick up his columns. She always had to make sure she scheduled an extra hour for each visit because Hugo was just as good at telling a story as he was at writing one.

He'd seen so much, and she enjoyed listening to him talk about the good old days.

"Well, Amanda, she'll be coming here with me every day. I'm happy to give you a severance package, otherwise, I suggest you invest in some antihistamines."

"Maybe I'll just talk to my friend the lawyer about working conditions." Her heavily colored eyebrow rose into her bangs. She wore so much makeup it was impossible to tell her age.

If Macy had to wager a guess, it would be somewhere around twenty-seven, but that was debatable.

She hadn't meant to sound rude, but she'd grown weary of the woman's constant negativity. "You do that." She only had to wait one more week before giving her the heave-ho.

"No reason to get testy. By the way, you have some messages." She stuck out her hand with a pile of pink notes.

"It's only nine in the morning."

The woman shrugged. "Some might be from the last couple of days. I cleaned off my desk when I was looking for my good nail file and I found them."

Stuffing the messages in her pocket, Macy's mouth formed a thin line. "In my office in fifteen minutes," she said through gritted teeth.

"But I have a—"

"Amanda, my office in fifteen," she said harshly as she entered her office. She slammed the door.

Harley whined.

"Sorry, old girl, but she is too much." Rolling out a furry mat that had gel on the underside, she put it behind her desk. Then she added a stuffed toy along with one of the chewies she'd bought at the discount store just outside of town.

Lucky for her, Great Danes were notoriously lazy. Once the dog was comfortable, she'd probably sleep most of the day.

Macy's phone rang. "Call from Boston," Amanda said snidely. "Same guy."

"Tell him I'm in a meeting."

She hung up before the receptionist could question her decision.

She had no interest in talking to her ex. The man had tried to apologize countless times. But she'd caught him red-handed, meaning in bed with his intern. Not one to give into hysterics, she'd turned on her heel, picked up her laptop and walked out with only the clothes on her back.

The week before she'd found him cheating, she'd received a visit from her uncle's attorney. At first, she thought she would sell her inheritance and use the proceeds for an amazing honeymoon.

But after what had happened, she decided it was a sign to move in a new direction. She'd been a high-profile, far-flung reporter for a long time. She had the awards and reputation to prove it.

So instead of planning a honeymoon, she gave two weeks' notice at the Boston paper and told HR she was taking two of the six weeks of vacation owed to her. She waited until she knew her ex was in a meeting, and went to the condo and packed up everything she owned.

A gypsy, always on the road, she didn't have much other than her clothes, shoes and a few pieces of art she'd picked up during her travels.

She then bought a car and drove to New York to visit Cherie. After a couple of days of being analyzed by her best bud, she knew her choice to move to Texas was a great one.

As soon as she saw her uncle's house, it felt like home, a feeling she hadn't experienced in years. It had surprised her how easy it'd been to walk away from the life she'd thought she wanted and the man she was supposed to marry. That was when she'd known—the obvious reason aside—he wasn't Mr. Right, after all.

Still, she had no desire to speak to him.

A knock on the door interrupted her revisiting the past.

"Come in."

Harley raised her head to see who entered and then lay back down. Amanda stood in the doorway.

"Have a seat." Macy pointed to the chair.

Eyeing her warily, she sat.

"As you know, the three months are almost up. I wanted to give you notice now so that you have time to find another job." Macy picked up a folder. "This is the severance package my uncle had in his files. I will honor it, even though—" She'd been about to say, "you don't deserve it." She shoved the folder across the desk.

"You're firing me?" Amanda's face crumbled. Huge black mascara tears dripped down her cheeks. "I knew it. Why don't you like me?"

Seriously?

"You've been hostile to me ever since I arrived. The missing messages today are just one in a long line of problems with you being inept at your job."

A good manager would have found a way to cushion the blow, but Macy was at the end of her patience with the woman.

"It is nothing personal. It's business. I need to employ people who are efficient and can carry extra duties when necessary. I can barely get you to answer the phone, and that's your only job. I've had to do all the admin, customer service and deal with circulation. That's on top of writing, editing and publishing the paper."

The woman sniffled.

Closing her eyes, Macy gathered her thoughts.

"I—thought you were going to get bored fast and hire someone to take over, so I didn't think it was worth getting to know you or impress you," Amanda said finally. "And you never asked me to do those things. You told me to answer the phone, so I did. I noticed the second week you were here that the accounts receivables were a mess, so I've been doing those. It takes me a little longer than it took Todd, but he'd been doing it for years. And I sort of had to teach myself those first few weeks. You never even said thank-you."

Her eyes popped open. "What?"

"That I was doing so much of the accounting. I'm pretty sure I've done it right, but you might want to have an accountant look over the books. My mom was able to help me with some of it, but once the treatments started, well. You should probably have the figures double-checked."

Macy groaned inwardly. She'd assumed her uncle used a firm to monitor the accounts receivable or payable. There was still so much she had to learn.

The first order of business was to find a good accountant to go over those books.

"We all thought you'd sell the paper, or quit and fold it up. So I didn't see any sense in putting forward any extra effort other than the day-to-day stuff until you figured out what you wanted to do.

"And you were so serious and businessy when you arrived. You didn't treat us any differently than the file cabinets, the gray ones you didn't like. I asked those first few days if I could help you with something, but you looked at me like I was a crazy person.

"I know I don't dress as fancy as you do. But clothes are how I express myself. And I've been studying so hard. I hid the books when you walked by because I was afraid you'd get mad if you saw me. I wanted to talk to you about it. I was hoping, since you were a woman, that maybe you'd give me a chance. But you make me so nervous, I don't know if I'm doing anything right and I sure don't want to ask for a favor."

Staring down at the files on her desk, Macy thought back. She'd been off on her own for so long that she was used to doing everything herself. When she was on assignment, it was expected.

And she'd been sullen and angry when she first got to Tranquil Waters. Had she taken it out on the staff? Did she have the scary face, her game face, on as Cherie called it, when she was walking around town? The same face she had when traveling, so that no one bugged her? No wonder folks thought she was some mean, Yankee shrew.

"That doesn't explain your hostility, Amanda, and what do you mean you've been studying hard? I've seldom seen you without a nail file in your hand."

"You know how you don't know how to act so you act like the other person even though you don't know why someone hates you…. I guess that's what happened. When a person is mean to me, I just do the same back. I'm kind of flaky. I'll give you that.

"You're some important war correspondent, I figured being professional maybe meant being mean. I saw that old movie *The Devil Wears Prada*. That editor was horrible."

Was the woman really taking her cues from a film?

"Yes, but that was fiction. I don't expect you to fall all over yourself, but I do insist on common courtesy." She held up the messages. "And this—this is bad."

The woman scrunched her face. "I considered

throwing them in the trash so you wouldn't find out. It took everything I had to give them to you. When you came in yesterday, you were in such a hurry that I didn't get a chance to pass them on. I stuck them under the phone so I'd remember, but Mrs. Dawes, the cleaner, must have moved them."

Macy gave her an incredulous look.

"I know, I know. But I mean it. I've been studying journalism at an online college. I have to do it like that because my mom is sick and I have to be home to watch my brothers at night when my dad's at work. So in the mornings, I'm tired and can barely keep my eyes open. The nail file thing is a kind of way to trick myself. I hate the sound, but it keeps me awake.

"I promise I'll try to be better. I'll do whatever you ask, just give me two more weeks."

Amanda folded her hands in her lap. The tears continued to roll down her face, and each one churned Macy's stomach a little more.

She felt sick. If the story was true, and her instincts said that it was, Macy had indeed been horrible with a capital _H_.

Journalism 101 was to find out the real story. Everyone had one, and most of the time they were fascinating.

"May I ask what's wrong with your mom? And you should know, as an employee, you do not have to tell me."

"Breast cancer. It's her third time with it. My grandma and aunts all died of it. But she's doing better. This last round of chemo and radiation has taken its toll, but the docs say her counts are good. Dad drives her to Houston once a week for treatment.

"She just doesn't have any energy. I'm the oldest of four, and all under sixteen. So I help out around the house and try to give them money when I can, since Mom can't work right now."

Shame on you, Macy Reynolds. Shame on you.

Dear God, she'd almost fired the poor woman and had the entire family out on the street.

The journalist in her told her to stop right there, that she was being too soft. If Amanda worked at one of the top one hundred papers, she'd be out. Everyone had to do the job of five or six people these days. When Macy started out as a reporter, she'd had to turn in only three columns a week. Her last job in Boston, she'd had to do a minimum of eight, and help with copyediting and online coverage.

But the *Tranquil Waters News* was not a top one hundred paper. She was certain it wasn't even ranked, though for a small paper, they had a good circulation.

"I see. That is unfortunate." Her words sounded cold, even to her. But she'd never been great at the touchy-feely stuff. Except when it came to Harley, that dog turned her into a pile of emotional mush.

"So, you've been studying journalism. What year are you?" She forced a smile.

"I'm a junior. I was all set to go to Texas State, but then Mom got sick again, so I enrolled online."

Rummaging through the old desk, Macy found her personnel file. She was only twenty years old.

Holy hell. That explained so much.

But they had to set some ground rules.

"Are you really allergic to dogs?"

The girl glanced at Harley. "No, but I'm scared to death of them. One tried to bite me once when I was a kid and I've never been able to get close to a dog since. I'm sorry, but that's the truth."

Macy nodded. "This one won't hurt you. She is the friendliest dog. Aren't you, Harley."

The dog lifted her head and cocked it sideways. A low grunt of what sounded like her agreement followed.

Amanda laughed.

"She'll hang out with me most days," Macy explained. "So it might be good if you two tried to be friends. I won't force it, but if you're going to make friends with a dog, this is the one to start with. I promise."

"I'll try."

"Okay. Well, if you're staying, we'll need some changes. Ones that you and I will decide on together."

"I'll do whatever you want, no problem." Amanda held up her hand as if she were swearing an oath in court.

"Good. To begin with, you'd better give me the lowdown on my other employees."

Macy listened carefully to each backstory. Amanda knew it all, which showed she had a propensity for getting the truth out of folks. Not a bad trait for a budding journalist.

"I'll come up with a code of conduct and expectations for you to sign off on. And we'll consider the next two weeks as a probation period," Macy said. "If that goes well, we'll extend it.

"As for your wardrobe, I don't want you to feel like you can't express yourself, but I do want to offer you suggestions on proper attire for the office."

Amanda made a weird face. "I don't have any old lady clothes or sexy librarian stuff like you wear," she said. "But I could maybe tone it down a little."

"How about we compromise with one bright color a day? And maybe jeans that don't show more than they should?"

"Fine by me. Would you like me to get you a coffee?"

Hmm. That sounded good. "Tell you what, you like those lattes from the café. Why don't you get one and I'll take a black coffee. Here's some cash. And then, please find out when everyone can come in for a staff meeting. We need to chat."

"That's going to be a bit tough on Hugo, but I can give him a ride from the nursing home if that's okay with him."

"We'll figure it out. I'd also like to talk to the printer, and before you leave today, I need access to those books. I'll hire an accountant this afternoon."

"Got it, Boss!" She hopped up. "Coffee, and then I'll make the calls. Thank you!"

Macy smiled. "You're welcome."

Amanda turned back when she reached the door. "Uh, there's one other thing."

Macy's eyebrow rose, but she didn't say anything.

"I have to write a feature story for one of my classes. I know it's a lot to ask, but if I can find the subject, can you just edit it for me? You know, like a real editor would?"

Someone long ago had done that for Macy, and life really was about karma. "Sure. Just bring it to me when you're ready."

A bright smile lit Amanda's face. "Wow. You really aren't the complete witch we thought you were."

When she shut the door, Macy snorted.

Well, at least there's that.

6

FOR THE PAST two days, a certain newspaper publisher had avoided Blake. She'd claimed that she was too busy with work. He didn't consider it stalking when he'd driven by the newspaper office on the way to the feed store and noticed her car was there.

No. It wasn't stalking.

For the life of him, he didn't understand why he couldn't get her out of his head.

Well, except for the fact that she was sexy as hell, smart and funny when she wanted to be. The waitress at the Lone Star Café had been gossiping about the new lady with the giant dog when he had his breakfast that morning.

"She's so uppity. Have you seen her walking around? That sneer on her face. I want to tell her that she'll catch more bees with honey, but she tips good so I ain't sayin' a darn thing," the waitress said.

Obviously, not everyone saw Macy the way he did. But then, he had heard her story. Orphaned, world traveler who was in search of a home. He knew that last bit because he felt the same way.

He was lucky that he had his mom, and that would always be home. Nevertheless, he was at a crossroads in his life. Again, he was lucky that he had many opportunities open to him. A marine to his core, the idea of desk duty didn't sit well with him. Pushing papers might be great for some folks; he liked to stay active and to be challenged.

There were a couple of business opportunities. He could take over one of the divisions of the security company he'd invested in with Rafe and Will. And his brother, J.T., had mentioned a number of other businesses that were looking to expand into Tranquil Waters. He liked the idea of being in on the ground floor of something and watching it grow.

His phone rang. He didn't recognize the number, but he picked it up.

"Hello."

"Lieutenant Michaels, this is Amanda from the *Tranquil Waters News* calling for Ms. Reynolds. She's in a meeting right now, but she wondered if you might be available to stop by the office either today or tomorrow afternoon."

Ms. Reynolds, eh. "Today is fine. What time?"

"Four-thirty will work well with her schedule."

"Fine by me."

They hung up.

She didn't call him herself, but she wanted to see him. Was she going to pawn his story off on another reporter?

He'd already told her that he wouldn't trust anyone else.

Glancing at the clock, he realized he had about an hour before the meeting.

She had a penchant for sweets. She said it was one of her few vices when she showed him her version of a whoopie pie.

Blake knew exactly what to do.

STANDING IN FRONT of the bathroom mirror at her office, Macy pushed her curls into some semblance of a style and reapplied her lipstick. She tried to convince herself that it wasn't for Blake's benefit.

Liar.

I need to look my best so I can convince him that my new plan for the story is a great one.

She wasn't sure he'd see it that way. Mentally, she prepared counter arguments for many of the points he might bring up.

Her eyelashes, which were much lighter than her hair color, were barely visible. She pulled out the mascara Cherie had insisted she buy on her shopping spree and applied a coat to one eye.

As she did the other, someone knocked on the door. She jabbed the stick into her eye, leaving a trail of black down her cheek.

"Banana shakes." Her least favorite flavor.

"Sorry, but your four-thirty is here. You told me to let you know as soon as he arrived," Amanda said.

"Thanks. I'll be there in just a minute."

Gathering up some tissues, she dabbed at the eye and did her best to remove the black makeup.

Most of it came off, but…that's when she remembered the sales woman telling her that she'd need an oil-based cleanser to remove it entirely.

Wonderful.

Both eyes were red now and watering. Why was it that if you poked one eye, both of them did that? This was useless. She could call out to Amanda and cancel the meeting, but Blake would know she was here.

She had no other choice.

When her nose started running, she did the only thing she could. Tucking a good chunk of toilet paper up her sleeve, she went to the reception area to meet Blake.

Concern etched his face when he saw her. "Did something happen?" He reached out to touch her, but then pulled back.

She remembered what he said about not wanting to touch her until she asked.

"I was going to lie and say allergies, but I'm not so good at lying. I stuck my mascara wand in my eye and now my face has turned into a faucet."

Blake coughed to cover a chuckle. But she knew what he'd done, and she smiled.

"Yes, I am beauty and grace." She curtsied.

"Do you want to postpone the meeting?" he asked.

"I'm okay, as long as you don't mind my weepy face."

"That face is beautiful no matter what is going on."

"Such a flatterer. I bet you say that to all the women."

"No, only one woman." He said it so low, she wasn't sure she heard him right.

Clearing her throat, she motioned to the chair across from her desk. She'd cleaned out all the file cabinets that had crowded the space and moved the heavy, carved desk so that it faced the door. She'd painted the dull army green a bright cream and brought in some art. She spent most of her days in the space and she liked that it was comfortable.

He set a box from the café on her desk. Then he pushed it toward her. "These are a peace offering for invading your space the other day. I should have called before I came by."

She grinned. "You surprised me, but I didn't take offense. I'm just not in a space where I can—" She lifted the lid on the box. "You got Mrs. Chesaline to make her éclairs? But she only does that on the second Tuesday of the month. I was waiting at the door last week at 5:00 a.m. when I found out what day she made them."

"I heard." He grinned.

She shook her head and frowned. "This town. I swear everything you do is circumspect."

"Yes, but it has its advantages, as well. When you need a helping hand, it's there. You'll see."

She wasn't so sure about that. It was easy for the handsome marine. The town hero home from the battlefield. Not so much for an uptight reporter who was too nosy for her own good.

"I appreciate you taking the time to come over. I've been tied up in interviews all day."

"Who were you interviewing? That is if you can tell me," he said.

"Oh. Uh. Actually, I'm hiring a couple of reporters. Well, I'm hoping I can find reporters who can also edit and lay out pages. I found an ad salesman, next up I need an accountant."

"Is that why you called?" He leaned forward and she caught his pine scent. It wasn't fair that he was beautiful and smelled so good.

"Excuse me?"

"About the accounting position. I don't practice but I do have my license."

She'd forgotten about him having an MBA. The man was so much more than eye candy, which made him so darn appealing. As if he needed any help.

"Well, you know. If you don't mind consulting until I can find someone for us full-time, that would be appreciated."

He nodded. "I can do that. I have something on for tonight, but I'll take a look tomorrow."

Wait, what kind of plans did he have? Was it a date? Why should it matter to her?

Because you know he wants to kiss you.

They had chemistry. But he was so hot he probably had that with every woman he met. He didn't seem like a player, but her track record wasn't the best when it came to men. She no longer trusted her instincts in that regard.

"Tomorrow. Yes. Listen, I appreciate you stepping in temporarily, but that isn't why I asked you to stop by."

He started to say something, but stopped.

Her eyebrow rose. "Please, go ahead."

"I was hoping you asked me for personal reasons."

She smiled. "I'm afraid you're going to be disappointed. It's about the interview. The one for your story."

He leaned back in his seat and eyed her suspiciously. "Are you doing the interview?"

"Hear me out, please."

Frowning, he stood. "Look, I understand this is what you people do, but I told you. I'm not interested in talking to anyone else."

"Why, because you like me?"

"I do, but it's because I trust you. And I've read your work. Whatever you wrote, it would be fair." His voice had grown raw and deep.

She'd touched a nerve.

"You're right. It would be fair if I did the article. And I'm flattered you know that. But what I have in mind goes far beyond just you. The person is someone you'll trust even more than me."

He crossed his arms. "Who?"

"You."

He huffed. "I'm no writer, and it doesn't make sense for me to do a story on myself. You should know I'm not a big fan of games." He was to the door in three strides.

"Hey, I'm sorry. I didn't explain it well. But I'm not exactly sure what it was I said that set you off."

He didn't turn around, but he didn't open the door.

"I thought it would be interesting if you interviewed other veterans, there are so many at the nursing home and the Lion's Club. Not really about war, but about what it's like to come home. How hard it is for families and friends who weren't there to understand what you've gone through." She stood, but didn't move toward him.

Instead, she continued. "The first time I came home from Afghanistan, I couldn't process what had happened. I tried to pretend like it was another life. But after a year of being stressed about everything, even if I'd ever live to write my next story—" She took a deep breath and pushed the painful memories away.

"I was in the newsroom in Boston. One minute I was packing up to go home and the next I was huddled, shivering at my desk unable to speak.

"My uncle Todd came to the rescue again. He'd covered Desert Storm. He got it. And he's the one who called my friend Cherie, who happens to be a psychiatrist. Between the two of them, I was able to talk about it.

"And Cherie taught me coping mechanisms. So thankfully I was able to go back. I had to go back. A lot of important stories needed telling. You get why I had to go back? You've done it time and again yourself, but many people don't. But what we don't always realize is that it not only takes a toll on us—you and I—it takes a toll on our family and our friends."

As he turned to face her, a myriad of emotions passed over his face. His knuckles turned white as he gripped the back of the chair he'd been sitting in. She didn't worry, though, and she certainly didn't fear him. This was his way of channeling anger.

"Being overseas in such conditions—it changes us, Blake. Sometimes for the better, other times not. As much as I'm a loner, I'm a lot more compassionate than I ever was. A journalist must be objective, but even I had to examine my life when I got home again."

She took her seat and gestured for him to take his. "I want to tell you something off the record. Something no one, except Cherie, has heard me say. I'm telling you because I know I can trust you."

"You can trust me," he said gruffly.

Why did she feel the need to confess? She didn't talk to anyone like this.

He sat in his chair. "You don't have to tell me right now," he said. "I believe you. And I'm sorry I—lost my temper. I'm trying very hard to simplify my life. Get up in the morning, do my job, go to sleep at night. I need that kind of routine right now. Things have to be easy."

"I get that. I suppose it's why I'm a workaholic. It happens to be the one constant in my life. We really are a lot more alike than either of us wants to admit."

A long silence followed before he spoke up. "Your idea for the veterans story and their experiences back home is a great one, but I'm not a writer. And you've been there, anyway. Seems to me you'd be perfect for the job."

"Thanks for that. But they'd still be talking to a reporter. I feel like…" She paused. Frustrated she wound a curl around her finger. "This might be really positive for them. I'll help you write the stories, but you need to be the one to do the interviews. How these men and women learned to assimilate back into society could be important for soldiers who are still coming home."

"They have programs," he said, crossing his legs. "Most branches of the military have a system in place where they work with families and do just that. Assimilate."

"Yes, I know, but how you'd write the story would be completely different. Everyone who comes home deals with it in his or her own way. That's why this will work. Readers will be able to say, 'Hey, that's the way I felt.' Or, 'No wonder my dad spent so much time alone in his study.'"

"It all sounds kind of therapist-like to me," he said.

She knew exactly what he meant. "It would be if I had a psychologist writing the stories. I tell you what, how about you do one or two interviews and see how it goes? If it's not your thing—I won't say another word about it."

Harley grumbled beside her and then made her way around to Blake where she placed her head on his lap. Her stomach made an appalling noise.

"Do you need me to walk her?" Blake asked as he stroked the dog's head.

"No, she only went out an hour or so ago. It's time for her dinner, though, and she gets two *c-o-o-k-i-e-s*." Harley's head popped up and she immediately began to drool on his shoe. "You cannot spell!"

Blake laughed. "I'm not so sure about that. I need to get going. I'll think about what you said. Maybe I'll have an answer for you tomorrow when I come check your books."

"You'll still do that?"

"Said I would, and I always keep my word."

"Thank you. I do appreciate it, and I promise I'll

do my best to find someone to help me on a more permanent basis."

"There's something else you should think about," he said.

"What's that?"

"The story you were about to tell me. I saw that look in your eyes. I know it well. If we eventually do this, you should share your own story with readers. It isn't just the military that is overseas and comes back wounded physically and mentally."

"That's true," she admitted. "But I'm not so sure people would be interested in my story, especially in this town. I'd kind of like to keep my head down low. Maybe at some point, fifty or so years down the road, they'll forget I'm the new girl."

"Like you said, the articles could shed some light on why certain people are the way they are. And how they deal with the day-to-day. I have a feeling if the rest of the town knew about what happened to you, it would change things."

Perhaps. But dredging up old memories was the opposite of what she needed. More than anything, she wanted to start fresh. That was what moving to Tranquil Waters had been all about.

7

"Hon, I hate to do this to you, but I need a big favor," his mother said as he walked in the house. The talk with Macy had him riled up and anxious. He wasn't exactly sure why. That look on her face when she thought back to her time overseas, he'd seen it one too many times in the mirror. It bothered him that she'd suffered so much. He wanted to sooth her, to help her forget.

"Blake?" his mother asked.

"Yes, ma'am, whatever you need." He rounded the kitchen and stopped when he saw her worried expression. She had a small suitcase packed.

"Mom? What's wrong?"

She put her hands on her hips. "Momma D isn't doing so well. Your aunt Eloise wants to put her in a rest home, but Momma isn't very keen on the idea. Right now she's in the hospital, and says all she wants to do is be in her own home. She's insisted that she'll heal better with her things around her and being close to her gardens. Even with the full-time nurse, Eloise thinks it's still too much for her at the moment. So I need to go down to San Antonio and look after her for a bit. See what's up."

"Do you need me to drive you? I can be ready in ten minutes."

She put her palm on his cheek. "You are such a good boy. I hate leaving you so soon after you've just got here, but it can't be helped, I'm afraid. I was hoping you could keep an eye on the store. Ray and Tanya pretty much run the place already, I do the books and talk to folks. You wouldn't have to do much. Make the bank deposits. Give Ray a hand with the inventory. You've done it all before when you were a kid. Nothing has changed, except it's all on computers now."

Well, he'd said he needed purpose and routine. Crazy how the universe worked sometimes. "When I saw Momma D on my way up, she seemed fine."

His mother waved dismissively at him. "She's old and a cold can turn into pneumonia in a heartbeat. But don't you worry about her. She's a tough old broad."

He frowned. "Seems like I'd be better off helping you guys down there than I would be here. Like you said, Ray has a handle on things."

"Oh, no, honey. I'll feel better if you're here. I'm going to sit around and gossip with her. And I'll make sure her gardens are ready for the winter. You know how much I love doing that stuff. She has only the one television, so I imagine we'll sit around watching her programs with the sound blaring."

There was that. When he'd stopped by on his way up to Tranquil Waters, he spent the day with this grandmother. She was his mom's stepmother. Her mom had died when she was only three, and Momma D had become the only mother she really knew.

She was nearly deaf, but she didn't miss much. When he visited her, she was in her parlor, which was what she called the living room, watching her afternoon soaps at an earsplitting octave.

But she'd taken one look at him and shaken her head. "Boy, you need a hug." Then she'd held out her arms. Damn if she wasn't right. He'd ended up spending the night there because he loved being in her presence. She was a positive light, and he needed that in his life.

"Your brother will be by in an hour. I asked him to bring you some dinner because I didn't have time to cook."

"Mom, I'm perfectly capable of taking care of myself. I've been doing it a really long time."

"Don't take a tone with me, son. Besides, I want you to grill your brother. Mona who works as a teller at the bank says she could have sworn she saw your brother in the parking lot, in his truck, with a woman in there. She had red hair. I never thought your brother would go for a redhead."

He snorted. In another five minutes, she'd have J.T. married off with five carrot-orange-haired kids.

"I'll take your bag to the car. Is there anything else you need?"

She scrunched up her face, and glanced around the kitchen. "No— Oh, if you don't mind, maybe you could take the sack of seeds on the workbench and put it in the car. And there are two rosebushes by the garage I'm going to take to Momma. They are heirloom, and you know how much she loves them."

It was a bit late in the fall to be planting, but it was San Antonio so the weather stayed pretty warm throughout the year.

Fifteen minutes after she left, his brother rolled up in the driveway in his truck. He didn't bother knocking, just walked through the back door like everyone else in town did. His mom's house was known as a gathering place.

"Stupid jarhead can't even fix a meal on his own." J.T. put a sack from the diner on the kitchen counter. Except for the paint color on the walls, which was a warm yellow, not much had changed in the light-filled kitchen since he was a kid. There were good memories in that kitchen of holiday baking, birthdays and his dad cooking dinner while encouraging Blake and J.T. with their homework. His mom was at the feed store a lot in those early years, so the men in the family had to learn to do for themselves, which wasn't a bad thing.

"Shut it, nerd. Did you bring me a chocolate donut this time?"

The nerd stuck two chocolate donuts on a plate.

"Why didn't you tell Mom you had already planned to come over and watch the game?" The first Mavericks' basketball game of the season started at seven.

"Brownie points, dude. It made me look good to bring dinner to the poor, broken jarhead."

"I'll show you broken if you don't stop calling me jarhead. Come on, nerd, I set up the TV trays in the family room. And thank you again for buying Mom that fifty-six-inch flat screen for Christmas last year. It's the best gift you've ever given her."

They chuckled at that.

"You could have come out to my place," his brother said.

"Not if I want to drink this," he raised one of the two beers he was holding in his hands. Earlier that day he'd visited the local doc for a checkup. He was down to half a pain pill a day. His leg continued to hurt like hell, but it only reminded him that there was still work to do on his body. The doc had given him permission to have one beer, maybe two, a day.

"I have a perfectly fine couch you could sleep on."

He shrugged. Time to have a little fun.

"So Mom says you're getting engaged to some redheaded chick. Who is she?"

J.T.'s beer spewed from his mouth onto his burger. "What the—?"

"Some lady at the bank saw you. Therefore, it must be true." Damn, he'd missed giving J.T. a hard time. The surprise on his brother's face was priceless.

He laughed so hard his gut hurt.

"Sometimes I hate this town," his brother growled. "She's not some chick. Her name is Anne Marie and she's a colleague. We were not on a date. We'd been at a conference in Houston. The rest is none of your business."

Blake held up his hands in surrender. "Hmm. I think he doth protest too much."

"Just watch the game, jarhead."

For the next two hours they did. Screaming at the

refs, who called fouls on everything. It was close but the Mavs won.

They clinked beer bottles.

Blake was relaxed, truly so. He almost felt like a normal human being. He'd been on for so long, he forgot what it was like to let go. Even in the hospital it had been one operation after another and then intense physical therapy.

He took a long breath.

The psychiatrist said he needed time. He understood now. Bit by bit it was coming back to him, how to live a life where he wasn't constantly looking over his shoulder or listening for changes in the wind. He'd never stop being a marine, but he could learn to be calm and enjoy things again. Maybe even sleep more than three hours at a time.

His mind wandered through his conversation with Macy. Could he do what she asked? It might dredge up a lot of issues he didn't want to think about. Then again, sometimes it helped to talk about what happened.

He sipped his second beer.

Then there was his other problem. The one that had kept him awake and unsettled ever since he'd seen her beautiful face in the pouring rain. Never in his life had he felt such a pull toward another person.

It was as if she had an invisible rope tied directly to his heart. He'd met her a couple of days ago, and he—what?

He'd almost lost his temper earlier, and she hadn't backed away one bit. She'd glanced at him, noticed his clenched hands and then looked him straight in the eye.

And she was right. They did have a great deal in common. What would it hurt to date? See her a few times, and get her out of his system. If he wrote the story she asked for, she couldn't use work as an excuse. He wouldn't take any payment for the accounting he'd do, or for writing the article.

So technically she wouldn't be his boss. She'd have to edit the piece, which might give her an out. But he'd find a way around that.

I know what I have to do.

8

THE SUN DIPPED below the lake and the wind gusted. Standing on the back deck of her uncle's place, Macy threw the ball for Harley. The dog loved to run, a little. It wasn't long before Harley kept the ball in her mouth and walked past Macy into the house where she dropped it into her basket of toys.

Chuckling, Macy shut the door and locked it. Using the remote, she turned on the fireplace, and padded to the kitchen to see if her marinara was ready. She'd made the sauce in the slow cooker earlier in the day. Her housekeeper had the next two weeks off while she cared for her ailing grandson, who had chicken pox. From what Macy could discern, the itchy disease had made the rounds of most of the elementary school and a number of day cares. They'd done a small feature about how to care for children and adults with the disease.

Macy didn't mind being on her own. If she had a choice, she'd let the housekeeper go. But she didn't. After setting a pot of water on the stove to boil, she picked up her cell phone to make sure she hadn't missed a call.

His call.

Blake had left a message at the office that he was busy at the feed store. He said he'd let her know when he could come by to do the accounting. It was almost five-thirty and he hadn't contacted her.

He was either really busy, or he might have forgotten.

Why was she disappointed? She'd heard through the Tranquil Waters grapevine that his mother was out of town for some reason.

"Cassidy Lee said she happened to spot Blake out behind the store, loading lumber into a truck." Macy had eavesdropped on the waitress's conversation as she lingered by the register at the café to pay for her lunch. The waitress in question had the rapt attention of a table full of women. "He had his shirt off, and she said it took everything she had not to walk up to him and start licking his abs. It's not a six, it's an eight-pack, ladies. And he has those sexy cut-ins on his hip. I asked her about the scars from his injuries, and she said, 'What scars? I was too distracted by those muscles.'"

The table of women whooped.

"Imagine how hot he must have been to take his shirt off when it's so chilly outside." One of the women fanned her face. "I think I might have to stop by the feed store to pick up some—" she paused for a few seconds "—seeds."

The other women tittered and joked.

Blake was a hot commodity in this town. Most of

the men his age and a little older were for one reason or another not available. She'd learned that bit of
news from Amanda, who said she went to Austin if
she wanted to dance because then she didn't have to
worry about some guy's wife giving her a hard time
the next day.

While Macy waited for the water to boil, she
cleaned up the mess Harley had made around her
food bowl. The dog had no manners when it came
to drinking and eating. She was well behaved otherwise, so Macy had no real complaints.

Once the noodles were ready, she put her meal together but skipped the garlic bread since her favorite
jeans were a little tight. She should probably up her
visits to the pool. She hated dieting and her knee still
bothered her, so running was out.

Taking a bite of spaghetti, she closed her eyes and
moaned about the delicious flavors. The sauce recipe
had come from a chef she'd met when she was in Italy,
covering the launch of a new political party.

Her cell vibrated on the counter.

Thinking it was Blake, she answered it.

"It's about time," Garrison, her ex, said. The man's
voice was as smooth as silk. But the instant she heard
it, she cringed.

"Don't hang up. I can hear you breathing. Look,
something's coming down the pike and I wanted to
give you a—"

"I'll make it simple for you. No. Whatever it is,
whatever you think you need to tell me, my answer
is no. Don't ever call me again."

She pushed the off button.

The nerve of the man.

Her phone buzzed again. She thought about ignoring it, but she knew he'd just keep calling.

"If I have to change my number to avoid you phoning me I will. I have no interest in anything you have to say. So take whatever is coming down the pike and toss it somewhere, away from me."

There was a long pause. Finally, she'd gotten through to him.

"Um, your receptionist gave me this number to call," Blake's whiskey-coated voice said.

Ahhh!

"Blake, I'm so, so sorry. I— The call before you— Uh, never mind. Yes, of course I wanted you to call."

"Are you okay?" he asked.

"What do you mean?"

"The call. Is someone harassing you?" His voice was measured, but she heard that protective side of him.

"Yes, but it isn't anything I can't handle. It's my former boyfriend. I really am sorry about that. I should have checked my caller ID."

"Do you still want me to look at your books?"

"Yes, but I'm at home. Do you mind coming here, or I can bring them to your house. I've got the ledgers. Everything else is on my laptop. My uncle kept two sets."

"Let me get something to eat, and I'll be over."

"I made spaghetti," she said quickly. "It's my special sauce. That is if you like spaghetti, if you don't—"

"That sounds great. But I have to warn you, I'm

pretty tired. I may not be able to go over everything tonight."

He'd worked hard all day at the feed store and he was still recovering from his injuries. What was she thinking? "I'm being selfish, Blake. You're so strong that sometimes I forget—"

"I'm fine." The steel in his voice made her smile. Never, ever talk about a marine's stamina. She should have known better.

Before she stuck her foot in any deeper, she opted for telling him, "I'll have your food ready when you get here."

"I'm about five minutes out. See you then."

Five minutes? She glanced at herself in the window. Sloppy sweats, mussed hair, her reading glasses on top of her head.

As she ran for the bedroom she gathered her hair into a messy knot on top of her head.

The washer dinged. All of her jeans were wet. She had a choice, flannel pajama bottoms with Dalmatians on them, or the sweats. She went for the dog pants. Then she tried to find a top that kind of matched. She found a black cotton cami that was a little tight, but it would do.

Harley watched her go back and forth as if she were playing both sides in a tennis match.

"I know. But there's no reason I can't look half-decent. It's not like I threw on a sexy cocktail dress."

She wiped the day's mascara off the under part of her eyes and swiped gloss across her lips.

Harley woofed. The truck could be heard pulling into the long drive.

Spritzing perfume, she dashed through it so he wouldn't know she'd only just put it on.

Running to the kitchen she filled a large bowl with noodles and sauce, and set it next to hers. When he rang the bell, she inhaled a deep breath and released it.

Before she reached the door to let Blake in, Harley was there with the handle in her mouth. The door opened about two inches.

"Macy," Blake called.

She cackled. "Harley opened the door, come on in."

He praised the dog every which way and followed Macy to the kitchen.

"Don't you dare tell her how smart she is," she said, laughing. "You could have been a serial killer. I'm going to get a bolt installed higher up, I guess. Or one of those locks that slide down from the top."

He chuckled. "I'm pretty sure she knows how smart she is."

She and Blake ate and chatted about his mom going to take care of his grandmother, and how the store was busier than ever this time of year because it carried hardware, seeds and gardening equipment, holiday decorating items, as well as the stuff for livestock and pets.

"Mom had this great idea to start a pumpkin patch in one of the outer buildings near the store. Normally the pumpkins would be outside, but with all the rain, she was worried about mold. I'll be happy when Halloween is over this weekend so we can get that building clean. We have to check every pumpkin every day to make sure they're okay."

They cleared the dishes, which she put in the dishwasher while he found containers and put the food in the refrigerator. He was a man used to working in a kitchen, and she liked that about him.

"If you're sure you aren't too tired, I've got the laptop set up in the family room. There's a table in there that I use as a desk so I can monitor you-know-who's television viewing habits."

"Now that I've eaten, I feel more awake," he said. "Let me take a look."

She sat on the couch while he sat at the table and wrote things down as he went through the computer files. Every few minutes she'd steal a glance at his profile. But she had to stop before her body overheated. The man made her feel crazy good.

Would it be such a bad thing to scratch the itch? He hadn't said he'd do the story, nevertheless she'd promised him no one else would get the assignment. That took the ethical problem out of the equation.

She had no desire for anything long-term. So far as they were discreet and no one in town would know. They could use his accounting for the paper as a cover. Friends with benefits. She'd never had one of those before.

"Why are you looking at me like that?"

She blinked and realized he was staring at her.

"Uh. You're very handsome."

That sly grin spread across his face. "Huh. Okay."

He turned back to the computer, but continued to grin.

He knew.

"You do bad, bad things to me, Mr. Marine."

The grin grew bigger.

"I haven't touched you," he said, still facing the screen.

"Oh, but you don't even have to," she whispered. Maybe she had one too many glasses of wine with dinner. The room seemed very warm.

That made him look at her.

"Ms. Reynolds, are you coming on to me?"

"Yes, sir. I believe I am. What are you going to do about it?"

He sat there for a few seconds, his dark brown eyes catching her gaze as if he were searching for answers.

"What about your ethical dilemma?"

"I'm not writing the story, so it's no longer a problem. I wouldn't be dating the subject of one of my stories. You'd just be another guy."

"So if I ask you on a date, you'd say yes?"

She nodded. "With a few conditions."

He leaned an elbow on the table, but didn't take his eyes off her. "I'm not surprised."

"They're nothing wild. First, we keep it simple. You mentioned that you need simple right now and so do I. So we set some ground rules, and everyone is happy."

"And those would be?"

"We are discreet and exclusive."

He frowned. "Why discreet? Are you ashamed to be seen with me?"

"Don't be silly. You're the hottest man I've ever seen. *Ever.* I'd be more than happy to show you off to anyone who would look. But I'm new to the town, and— I don't know. I just think it would be best. That is, since we are keeping it simple."

Now that she'd said it out loud, it seemed over the top.

"Listen, normally, I'd have no problem. But one of the benefits of our mutual companionship, other than the obvious, is that it would detract a lot of the ladies from pushing their single daughters at me. My brother saw a picture of me on a social media site today loading feed bags into a customer's truck. I didn't even know someone was taking pictures. And why would anyone care?"

She smiled. "Remind me to find out what site that is. I want a copy. I heard you had your shirt off."

He huffed. "This is what I'm talking about. How about we hold hands in public or something. Let me take you on a few dates. People date all the time. It doesn't have to mean forever."

"Okay. I see your point. And since I want this to be exclusive, for however long it lasts, it would make sense for others to know. And in this town, it's probably impossible to be discreet."

"Yep. So we're friends who date. Is there anything else?"

"Well, I was kind of hoping that there would be benefits besides dating."

He frowned. "Like what?"

She chewed on her lip. Did he really need her to spell it out for him? "When the time comes, if you're into it, maybe we could—you know."

He grinned and cocked the right side of his mouth. "I'd definitely be into that."

"Me, too." *In fact, we can start right now.*

"So will you go out with me on Halloween? A friend of mine is throwing a party."

She bit her lip. A movie or dinner date was one thing. Meeting his friends was another.

"You're going to say no, aren't you?"

"Uh, well, it depends. It seems a little fast to be meeting the friends. But that isn't the reason I'm hesitant. I promised to help out at the shelter that night. We're dressing up our pets in costumes and handing candy out to kids to raise awareness about the facility."

"Not a problem. I'll help you, and then we'll go to the party afterward."

"Deal. Is it a costume party?"

"Yes, but it doesn't need to be anything fancy."

"Okay. Cherie is sending me a costume to wear for the shelter event. She is really into Halloween and has a ton of stuff in storage. It will probably be a giant pink rabbit or something, so I apologize in advance."

He laughed. "That's some friend."

"You have no idea."

He stood and went over to the couch where he stuck out his hand. When she put hers in his, he pulled her to her feet.

"It's a bit preemptive, but I've wanted to do this since the day I met you."

His mouth was on hers before she blinked. His lips were softer than expected. When his hand cupped her chin, she sighed with pleasure.

"You taste so good," he said against her mouth.

"It's the sauce," she whispered back as he trailed kisses down her neck.

"No, babe, it's you." Then his mouth returned to hers and their kiss intensified, so familiar, so easy, as if they'd done this a million times before.

When he lifted his head, they both gasped for air. "I think I'd better go," he said, leaning his forehead against hers. "I'm not sure I can control myself much longer. I want you so bad it hurts."

She glanced down, reached out and caressed him.

Hissing, he broke away from her. "Macy, please. I—"

"I want you," she said. "Now." She met his gaze and smiled a warm, wide smile.

"But I planned to take you out and woo you," he said. His voice strained.

"Woo me? Do people still say that?" She undid the buckle on his jeans.

"Yes. I say that. Remember, this is Texas. We like to court our women." Even though he didn't have much of an accent he put an extra twang in there.

"I'm a Yankee woman. We don't need wooing. We just need hot, fit marines who make us think of naughty, naughty things to do."

He chuckled. "I'm beginning to like the North better and better every second. Are you sure?"

"Yes," she replied as she tugged his head down to hers.

9

AFTER THEY MADE sure Harley was settled with the largest rawhide bone he'd ever seen, Blake trailed the raven-haired siren to her bedroom. The rest of the house was decorated in rich leather and textured walls. But her room had white walls, white furniture and most of the bedding was the same color. Only the pillows on the bed were pale blue.

He was about to comment on her style, it fit her in a feminine but classic way, when she slipped off her top. A lacy black bra with a tiny red bow in the center cupped her lush breasts.

"You're beautiful."

Her cheeks turned pink. She had no idea how attractive she was.

She pointed to him.

"Your turn."

She was nervous, he could see the slight tension around her eyes and the trembling in her fingers. He was sensitive to her emotions. As if his body and mind had been tuned to her like a radio dial.

He slipped his T-shirt off.

Her mouth formed an O.

"Wow, you're amazing." She didn't hold back.

He liked that about her.

"You're gorgeous, so much so that I can't get you out of my head. You've been keeping me up nights. Once I saw you doing everything you could to heave Harley into the back of your car, I knew I wanted you."

She slipped her baggy pajama bottoms off, and he sucked in a breath. The panties matched the bra. A red ribbon bow on each hip held the tiny triangles of fabric together. Her long legs were those of a runner, strong and firm. Curvy hips, sparkling eyes, and those breasts, she was all woman, and his fantasy come true.

It occurred to him that in seconds she would see the evidence of that, but he didn't want to stop the game.

"Oh" was all she said as he undid his zipper and his hard cock revealed. "It's a— That is, okay, yes. It's really— Yeah. Impressive."

He chuckled.

"Beets!" she said suddenly and put a hand to her temple.

Was she ill?

"Beets?"

"We don't have condoms. At least, I don't." She shook her head. "Tofu turkey!"

"Do you always say food names when you're upset?"

"What? No, it's that I don't like to swear. My

mouth, uh, let's just say hanging out with military types and reporters has left me with a mouth like a—"

"A marine?"

She smiled. "Yelling curse words upset the animals, so I say foods I'm not super fond of to keep from saying the things I shouldn't. Do you have any condoms?"

"Not on me. But I have an idea."

She smirked. "It better not involve driving to a store and buying some. I don't think I can wait that long."

No way he could wait that long, either. Besides, he was worried that she might change her mind. He'd respect her wishes, of course, but he'd also be very disappointed.

"Hold that thought." He rezippered and left the house, heading for the driveway.

Opening the toolbox in the back of his truck he dug around for the first-aid kit. There he found two foil packages. When he'd gone through boot camp it had been drilled into his head that you always packed protection.

He kissed the packets before slamming everything shut and bolting for the door. Praying they hadn't lost the moment, he found Macy curled up in her bed with the covers to her neck.

He tossed the packets to her, and she caught them in the air.

"Quick reflexes," he said as he pulled off his boots and shoved away his jeans. "Is everything okay? You can still say no. You can always say no. I want you to know that."

She rolled her eyes and as a welcoming gesture tossed back his side of the covers. "Blake, I was freezing. That's why I got in here. I want you and I don't want to wait any longer." He slid in. She grinned as she ripped open one of the foil packages and leaned over him.

"Slow down," he said, coughing out a laugh. "You don't have to be in such a hurry."

"But I am." She palmed his erection. And he was about to lose that sense of control he'd warned her about.

"We've got all night." He struggled to get the words out without moaning.

"Yes, but I've been fantasizing about you, about us like this, for days." Before he could stop her, she rolled the condom down over him. When she had finished, he caught her wrist and brought her fingers to his mouth and kissed them.

Damn, that might have been the sexiest thing any woman had ever said to him, which made him all the more determined to make this last. Moving her onto her back, he propped her underneath him.

His right hand slid between them, his fingers seeking her heat.

She smiled and arched her back, clearly wanting and welcoming him.

"I want to do this. For you, Macy," he said, speaking softly into her ear. Her body arched again. "Knowing every inch of you is important to me." He rose up and sat back. It wasn't the most comfortable position for him, but he didn't care about the pain. "Put your legs over my shoulders, baby."

She started to say something, but she stopped. Taking one of the larger pillows, he tucked it under her. He intended to give her every pleasure he possibly could and this would make that easier.

"I—"

"What?" he asked, as he touched her breasts, teasing her.

"I haven't really…" she said, leaving the thought unfinished.

"That sounds like a challenge, Macy."

"No, it's—"

She drew in a sharp breath as his mouth stoked her rising passion. Encouraged by her growing cries and murmurs, he was intent on satisfying every inch of her.

When she called out his name, her body quaked in its release and she reached out for him. He gathered her in his arms and held her tight.

"I need you, Blake." Her body had almost stopped thrumming. "Now."

"Bossy, aren't you?" He dropped a quick kiss on her lips. Tossing the pillow aside, he rolled on to his back. With his leg the way it was, it would be easier if she was on top. His thigh was throbbing, but so were other parts of him.

A limp noodle, he drew her to him. Her soft thick hair had fallen from its messy knot creating a dark veil around her silver-green eyes and high cheekbones. She was so sexy.

His hard cock poked playfully at her belly. She smiled at him. "Finally." Lifting up, she positioned herself on him and sighed as she rocked back and forth.

He matched her pace. It wasn't easy with his beautiful nymph riding him with wild abandon. She increased their tempo and he groaned out his approval.

As her muscles contracted, he held on—barely—and told her to open her eyes.

The moonlight streaming through her window bathed her face in a gorgeous way, and her eyes met his.

"You're incredible," he told her.

She moved faster, pressing into him, never slowing until they'd lost their grip and climaxed together. Losing control had never felt so good.

"That was better than any dream," she whispered tiredly as she fell onto his chest.

He cradled her and murmured sweet words that made her sigh. In minutes, she was fast asleep.

A whine from the doorway had him sliding out from under his beautiful fairy, and pulling the comforter up to keep her warm.

She grumbled but her head stayed on the pillow.

He slipped on his jeans and T-shirt and let Harley out via the back door. He watched her as she ran around the yard a few times. The moon reflected off the lake, and he envied Macy this view.

At the thought of her name, something tugged in his gut, a warning that he might be headed for trouble.

Making love to her was definitely not going to scratch his itch. It only made him want her all the more.

Slow. He reminded himself. She'd just run from a

bad relationship, and he was in no shape to start anything serious. It wouldn't be fair to either of them.

Harley bounded inside and gulped some water. She then grabbed a chew toy and made for her bed. Lying next to the toy, she went to sleep.

What a dog.

He'd never seen anything like her, and he just loved her.

Her owner was equally unusual in a way that called to him.

Shutting off the lights, he considered his next move. He should go home, but it didn't seem right to leave Macy without saying goodbye.

Digging in his pocket, he found one of his pills. After breaking it in half, he drank it down with a glass of water. He slid back into bed with Macy.

"Thanks for letting her out," she said as she snuggled against his chest. He tightened his arms around her, bringing her close.

"No problem. Go to sleep, angel."

"You wore me out," she said quietly. "I don't have a choice."

That made him smile.

"You didn't have to stay, but I'm really glad you did." Her words were soft and heartfelt.

"I may be gone by the time you wake up for work. But trust me, I'd like to stay for the next couple of days. Right here in this bed with you."

"Mmm. I like having friends like you."

Friends? In the plural?

As far as he was concerned, he would be her only

friend like this for a very long time. The thought of another man's hands on her— Hell.

He'd already become one of those possessive blockheads.

She didn't deserve that.

He looked down at her sweet face.

But dammit. She was his.

10

WHEN MACY OPENED her front door to him two days later, Blake's jaw dropped open. He looked at her from head to toe, his eyes resting a bit longer on her midsection and breasts.

She scoffed and turned away. "I'm going to kill Cherie the next time I see her," she grumbled. "I can't wear this. It's—it's…inappropriate."

"Sexy as hell," Blake said at the same time.

"Maybe if it was only you and me, but I'm not wearing this genie costume to pass out candy to little kids."

Closing the door behind him, he followed her into the house. "It's not as revealing as you think," he said. "All of you is covered. It's that some of the material is flesh-colored. And you're not pretending to be from the Arabian Nights or something—that's a kids' story. Besides there are ballerinas, princesses and fairies running around all over the place."

She rolled her eyes. "It's not really a kids' story! A king kills a thousand virgins after he defiles them.

Most of the kids are under seven. And it's too late. I don't have anything else to wear."

"It's cold out, and the temperature might drop down to the thirties. Maybe you could just wear a sweater or something. The skirt isn't that bad with all the scarves." He eyed her appreciatively. "Do those scarves come off one by one?"

The man really did have a one-track mind.

She growled at him.

"That's good," he chuckled. "We can just paint your face to look like a tiger. By the way—hello. I missed you a lot today."

He snagged her and wrapped his arms around her. Instantly, she forgot her troubles as his tongue tangled with hers. Pressing herself into him, his hard cock poked back.

That she could do that to him pleased her. More than she wanted to admit. Every time he looked at her, she felt like the most beautiful woman in the world.

She'd smiled so much today that Amanda asked her if she was okay. When Macy gave her the afternoon off to get her brothers ready to trick-or-treat, the shock and gratitude on the young woman's face had been truly remarkable.

"As much as I want to stay here, I have to get to the animal shelter. I'm the only one who has a key to the locker where all the candy is stored. Mariel, the office manager, didn't trust herself with it. So I had to hide all the candy in my locker."

"We better get going. Where's the beast?"

"Outside. Chasing the geese dumb enough to land within her radius. She's been after them for at least an hour. I'm not worried about her catching one. Every time she gets close to them they honk at her, and she runs away. It's one of her games she's made up. I'll get her."

When she returned, he had Harley's leash and a few toys for the dog to play with while they handed out candy.

Blake had spent the past few nights here, rising early in the morning to be at the feed store. But their lovemaking in the evenings was epic. No man had ever taken her to such heights. She was kind of angry that she'd been missing out on so much.

In his arms, Macy knew it was the safest she'd ever felt. Even though it was only a temporary harbor, she enjoyed it. And he slept when he was with her. Plagued my insomnia and night terrors, he'd had neither since they'd been together.

He'd admitted as much the night before last. She'd laughed it off and said it was because she wore him out. But the look in his eyes, that deep, searching gaze of his, told her it was much more than that. She'd become his port in a storm, as well.

Scary how intimate and intense a relationship could become when both parties were in need of the same thing. They read each other on a more profound level. And he was kind and generous to a fault.

In a mere few days, her cold, jaded heart had realized it had been missing out on what a real relationship could be.

Except, that this was just a fling.

I must keep telling myself that.

Harley, who sat in the back of Blake's truck, on her

special blanket, licked Macy's elbow. It was almost as if she wanted to tell her, *you'll be okay. You have me.*

Reaching behind, she scratched the dog's ear.

And for that I'm grateful.

It didn't take them long to arrive at the animal shelter, but still, bunches of children dressed in an array of costumes had already climbed the hill and gotten there ahead of them.

Blake had assisted with the carving of several pumpkins, which adorned the front porch and the lobby. For safety's sake they had put battery-operated candles inside the jack-o'-lanterns. A good idea, since the first thing Harley did was step in one on the way into the building.

She freaked out until Blake was able to get her paw out of the offending orange ball. Harley growled at it.

"Bad jack-o'-lantern, bad." Blake wagged a finger at the pumpkin, which seemed to please the dog.

Blake put Harley's dragon ears and scales on her. They'd been another gift from Cherie. The scales covered the dog's back and buckled around her belly and neck. The ears were on a headband of sorts.

She pranced around as if she were the queen of everything.

"You are the cutest dragon I've ever seen," Blake muttered as he scratched her behind the ears.

Back outside, Macy kept her coat on. She got a kick out of watching Blake interact with all the kids. He'd worn jeans and a T-shirt that had the *Avengers* logo on it. He'd told her he wasn't much into costumes.

By eight, the crowds had thinned out. That was fine since they were almost out of candy.

"That went by a lot faster than I expected," he said.

"You were great. The kids loved you, and you definitely know your superheroes."

He laughed. "I love to read, and comic books were cheap when I was a kid. I had a habit of losing library books, so my mom only let me take one out a week. Comic books were a cheap alternative."

The man was nothing but contradictions. He was definitely more than a pretty face. He was as tough as they came, but he was also intelligent and thoughtful.

Everything a woman could want, and then some.

And he wanted her.

"What's going on?" he asked as he shifted into Drive and steered the truck away from the shelter.

"Hmm? Oh. Honestly, I'm sort of awed by how amazing you are. What I don't understand is why me? When you could quite obviously have a fling with any woman you wanted."

At the stop sign, he glanced over at her. "That you don't see how beautiful, smart and funny you are is one of the reasons I like you so much. Why would I want anyone else when I have you?"

If Harley's enormous head wasn't on the armrest between them, Macy might have moved into his lap right then and there. "You really do always know what to say."

The street he turned onto was crowded with cars on both sides. She loved this part of Tranquil Waters. Many of the houses had been built in the early 1900s. The neighborhood was decked out in fall colors and

Halloween decorations. People were out in their yards chatting while kids ran around in their costumes.

"It's going to be a hike to find somewhere to park. Do you want me to drop you off in front of my friend's place?"

Definitely not. The last thing she wanted to do was walk into a party where she knew no one—in a skimpy genie costume. "I'm up for a walk. I had my fair share of candy tonight. Are you sure it's okay to bring Harley?"

"Yep. Jaime loves dogs."

She'd never brought a dog the size of a horse to a party.

"No! I can't believe I forgot."

"What?"

"A gift. Your rule about always bringing a gift to a party. I've been rushing around and I didn't remember to get anything."

He grinned. "Don't worry. I've got us covered. I had flowers delivered earlier today from the both of us. One of those fall bouquets. Jaime loves flowers."

Wait. Jaime was a girl? He'd been telling her stories the past couple of days about how he and Jaime were always in trouble together as kids.

Before she could mention it, they were at the door of one of the largest homes on the block. A wrap-around porch and two-story columns gave it a plantation house feel.

The open door led into a foyer the shape and size of a rotunda. It was a fit for the Southern mansion. Dark wood floors graced the area, and a huge round table with a bouquet of flowers sat below a crystal chandelier. There were two staircases with banisters draped in magnolia garlands.

"Oh. My. God! It's my favorite marine." A woman in a formfitting Catwoman suit threw her arms around Blake and kissed him hard on the mouth.

And he didn't seem to mind a bit.

"Hey, stinky. What's up?"

"You're late," she said when she stepped back and eyed him up and down. "And you aren't wearing a costume. I told you that you had to wear a costume."

"You know I don't do costumes. I was giving a hand out at the animal shelter, which is why I'm late." That seemed to remind him that she was standing there. "This is my friend Macy," he said as he put an arm around her shoulders.

The happy smile faded from the woman's face as she gave Macy the once-over.

"You that Yankee newspaper editor?"

"Jaime, be nice," Blake warned, but with a playful tone to his voice.

Refusing to back down, Macy jutted out her chin. "Yes."

"This is who you're dating? Do we not have enough women in the South that you have to start in on the Northerners?"

Blake pointed a finger at his friend. "I *really* like her, so play nice. I mean it."

Her hero. Macy smiled up at him.

"What, for goodness' sake, is that?"

Harley cocked her head.

"That's Macy's dog, Harley," he answered.

Jaime glanced back at Macy. "Great Dane?"

"Yes."

The woman smiled at her. Then she put two fingers to her mouth and blew an earsplitting whistle.

A dark gray, almost blue, Great Dane with silvery eyes trotted into the room.

"Harley, this is Bruno."

"If you don't want that costume shredded in the next five minutes, I suggest you take if off of Harley. Bruno gets jealous when other dogs have things he doesn't. Though, I'm definitely going to get him a costume for next year because that dragon outfit is too cute."

Macy wondered if the dog might attack Harley, and she put herself between the two animals.

"Oh, don't worry. He wouldn't hurt a fly. But he would try to get that outfit off of her for himself. He loves everything with ruffles, patterns and either brown or green."

Blake took the costume off of Harley and she shook herself.

"Now, Bruno, play nice. Take her out to the clubhouse."

The dog glanced back at his owner and nodded.

Were all Great Danes so smart?

"Are you sure they'll be okay?" Macy wasn't worried about Bruno being with Harley, she was concerned as to how Harley would interact with him. She got along with the other dogs at the shelter, but she'd always been supervised.

"I'm sure," Jaime said. "Blake, go say hello to everyone. I want to speak to your Yankee lady."

Blake stared at Macy. "I think that might make her uncomfortable. It's probably best if I stick around."

Macy appreciated that he wanted to stay by her, but she wasn't a child.

"Don't worry, I won't bite her," Jaime promised. "Besides, anyone with a dog like that is okay in my book. Great Danes are sensitive and bright, and extremely needy. They take a lot of love, time and patience. That's something your Yankee will need if she's going to train you up, as well."

Blake rolled his eyes.

Macy laughed.

Jaime made a shooing motion with her hands. "Go on. She'll join you in a minute."

"I'm okay," she assured him. "I'll find you when we're done."

Curious about why Jaime wanted her alone, she encouraged him to go.

Jaime reached out to shake her hand. "Sorry about that. I'm a bit protective of him," she said. "He's like a brother to me."

Weird, she'd never seen anyone kiss a brother like that, but Macy kept her mouth shut. She shook the woman's hand.

"You have a great house," Macy said. Her mind was awhirl with questions.

"Belonged to my great-grandma. We've tried to keep the restoration accurate, but it isn't easy."

She motioned for Macy to follow her.

"We'll put your coat in here." Jamie stood in front of a long hall closet and held out her hand for the garment.

"I—that is, my costume's quite revealing."

The woman judged her warily. "It can't be any more revealing than mine, or some of the others in here. Tara has a French maid's outfit on. Every time she bends over to get some food, she flashes her red thong to the entire room. It can't be any worse than that."

Macy slipped off the coat, feeling exposed.

"Well, you are as pretty as he said. It's not fair that you have those legs and that chest."

She wasn't sure how to respond to that…compliment?

"He's head over heels for you."

"What?" The sudden change in topic had Macy's mind spinning.

"Blake. We've never seen him like this over a woman. He called every single person at this party and told them they'd better welcome you or else." She laughed at Macy's grimace. "I know. But he's protective that way. I like the fact that you stood up to me back there. I have a feeling you and I could be friends. But there's just one thing you should know."

"What's that?" Macy walked next to her as they entered the living room full of people.

"If you hurt him, I will do the same to you." The threat was undeniable. "And I always mean exactly what I say."

Macy was about to tell the woman to back off, but she was equally protective of Blake. "If it makes you feel any better, I think he's the most incredible man I've ever met."

Jaime seemed to be in shock. "Oh, you have it just

as bad for him. Interesting. I can't wait to see how this plays out."

She wasn't sure about what to make of that comment, but across the room she spotted someone she knew.

"Excuse me, I see a friend of mine."

Josh, the veterinarian from the shelter, stood by a bay window talking to another guest.

When he saw her, he smiled brightly. "Hey," he said and hugged her, "I didn't know you'd be here." He left an arm around her shoulders, which she didn't mind at the moment. She was grateful to have at least one other person, besides Blake, be nice to her.

She shrugged. "I'm on a date. He was the one who was invited."

Josh's eyes widened in surprise. "Good, good. Seems like you're assimilating into the town really well. Let me introduce you to Brendan Tucker. He and his wife, Jaime, are the hosts of the party."

Macy shook the man's hand.

"I met your wife," she said, searching for something polite to say.

The two men laughed. "She can be a bit much, but she's a sweetheart once you get to know her," Brendan said.

"I'll have to take your word on that. Frankly, I've dealt with insurgents who were less scary."

The men howled.

"So who's your date?" Josh asked.

"I am," a deep voice said from behind them. "And I'd appreciate it if you'd get your hands off my woman."

"Blake," Macy admonished. It made little sense. Why would he act so jealous? It was ridiculous. They barely knew each other and Josh was a genuine good guy.

"Who's going to make me?" Josh said with heat in his voice.

What was happening here?

Macy ducked away from Josh's arm and stood apart from the two men. They were glaring at each another.

"I am, jerk." Blake stepped forward.

"Now, fellas. You know Jaime will have a fit if you break anything. Everyone calm down," Brendan cajoled.

"Why did you have your arm around Macy?" Blake growled at Josh.

"She's my friend. We went out a couple of times when she first came to town. What's the big deal? You aren't still mad at me after all this time? I wasn't the one who made you write those letters."

"Wait a minute," Blake whispered harshly. "You two dated."

His snapped around to look at Macy as if she were some kind of traitor.

She'd had enough.

"I don't know what's wrong with the two of you, but you're embarrassing me."

"Answer the question, Macy. Did you date my former best friend?"

His former best friend?

Oh. Ohhhh. This must be some male feud and

she'd stepped right into the middle of it. "Two times," she replied.

"And that was it," Josh said. "We knew from the get-go that we weren't right for each other. But we are friends. She volunteers at the shelter so we see each other occasionally."

Blake's mouth formed a thin line. He focused in on Macy. "You never mentioned that you went out with anyone in town."

"You never asked. And anyway, nothing happened with your former best friend. You're acting so foolish. Both of you."

With that she stomped out in search of her dog. She would not put up with that kind of arrogant behavior from any man. She and Blake were causal. He had no right to—

She froze in midstep. Hadn't she felt the same about him when his friend Jaime had kissed him?

I was as jealous, just not as vocal about it.

"Hey, genie, why don't you come over here and grant me my three wishes?" a man in a Frankenstein costume called out. A crowd stood around him.

They all laughed.

She turned her back on them.

"Told you the Yankee girl was a witch."

These people were beyond rude.

"You know what, Frankenstein, so much for that Southern hospitality you folks talk about. I'm proud to be from the North. In fact—"

"George, are you giving Macy a hard time? Because if you are, I'm going to have some serious words with you," Jaime said as slipped her arm through Macy's in a clear sign of solidarity. "This is Blake's girl, so that means she's like family. And you know how I feel about my family. You all apologize right now."

Without hesitation, apologies were quickly issued.

"Forgive me, Macy," George said. "I'd blame the whiskey, but sometimes I'm simply an old fool. Just ask my three ex-wives."

The crowd chuckled, the tension evaporated instantly.

Macy looked to Jaime so they wouldn't see her smile. "You didn't have to do that," she told her.

"I meant what I said. I'm sorry about before. This couldn't have been fun for you what with friends fighting, George being his stupid self and me acting like, well, we know what I was acting like."

Macy shrugged. "I've been to worse parties."

Jaime guffawed. "You're all right. I need to check on the caterers in the kitchen. Come with me?"

What she really wanted was to go home, but she followed Jaime.

The kitchen bustled with servers and food preparers sprinting around and shouting.

"Pietro, those mushroom caps are a hit."

One of the guys in a chef's hat blew Jaime a kiss before opening one of the ovens to put in a tray of what looked like hors d'oeuvres.

Walking along the kitchen island, big enough for a dozen bar stools, Jaime inspected the food. Then she grabbed a plate and took food from several of the trays. She handed the plate to Macy. "This one's for you."

She loaded up another plate. "This one's for me. I

never get to eat when I throw parties, but I'm starved. Come on, let's go check on the dogs."

"Are Blake and Josh all right, do you think?"

Jaime laughed. "My husband is there, and they're scared to death of him. They won't get too out of hand."

"Why are they scared of him?"

"Because he's the only man who can tame me, so he must be one real son of a gun. And he is. I talk tough, but I'd do anything for that man. The love of my life, and he knows it."

Next door to the kitchen was the breakfast room, which looked out over a pool area. Macy could see Harley chasing Bruno around the cabana. The two dogs stopped for a second, and then Bruno began chasing Harley.

"They're pals already, see?" Jaime sat on one of the loungers and leaned back a heated lamp nearby. She put the plate of food on her chest and started eating.

Macy sat on a lounger next to her.

"Sorry," Jaime said after swallowing a bite-size quiche. "I haven't had anything but water and vegetables for a week so I'd fit in this damn costume."

Macy grinned. "Hey, it worked. You look incredible."

"Thanks for that. And I really am sorry about earlier. When we heard Blake was injured this time, well, we're all kind of protective of him. He's always been such a stand-up type of guy. And I didn't lie, he is like my brother. He has dated in the past, obviously, but—I've never seen him like he is with you. I noticed him when Josh hugged you. He'd been giving you the loving eyes from across the room, and then it was like a cartoon. I was surprised steam didn't come out of his ears when Josh put his arm around your shoulders.

"And shame on Josh for egging Blake on. That's one of those man things, pushing each other's buttons, I guess."

Macy should have seen this coming. It hadn't been that long since she'd been away from Garrison, although it sure seemed like it.

"I went on a couple of friendly dates with Josh, nothing happened," Macy offered. "But for some reason Blake seems to think I should have been a nun before I met him. Bunch of macho nonsense, if you ask me." Macy bit into something with bacon and cheese in the shape of a ball. It was heaven.

"Yes, it is. Things seem to be moving fast between you two."

Macy winced. "I'm not sure what I'm supposed to say. We both agreed that this would be a casual arrangement."

"Blake's way past casual," Jaime said.

"It's only been a couple of days. I mean, I've known him maybe two weeks. Don't get me wrong— I like him a lot." More than she would admit to one of his best friends. "I'm not sure what to do. Maybe I should slow it down until we both get our bearings."

"Good luck with that." Jaime pointed toward the house.

"There you are," Blake said worriedly.

"See ya, kiddies. I need to get back to my party. Blake, behave yourself. Macy, it was so nice to meet you. I mean that. I'm going to stop by the paper soon and take you to lunch."

"I'd like that," Macy said.

Blake took Jaime's place on the lounger, but he sat sideways facing Macy. They sat in silence for a full thirty seconds.

"I'd like to blame it on the pain pills or too much alcohol, but the truth is I haven't had any because I knew I'd be driving," he said quickly.

Macy stared down at her plate, no longer hungry.

"There's no excuse for that kind of behavior. I just saw his arm around you, and— I promise you it will never happen again."

"You embarrassed me."

"I embarrassed both of us. And I'm truly sorry, Macy."

She still didn't meet his eyes, but she noticed he wrung his hands.

Give the guy a break.

She lifted her head. "I should be flattered about the show you put on in there, but I'm not. I don't like bullies and I'm certainly not someone's possession. I don't belong to you, Blake. I'm an individual. I've been on my own for a long, long time."

He sighed. "You're right. It's a mess. Do you want me to have somebody drive you home? Or I'm happy to do it, if it's okay with you. I just don't want you to be afraid of me."

Macy shook her head. "I'm not afraid of you. I could never be afraid of you. You wouldn't hurt me, no matter what the circumstances. But it does bother me that you think I would be scared of you. You're one of the kindest men I've ever met. And so gentle with Harley…and me. And I don't think any of those guests would appreciate having a hundred-and-seventy-five-pound dog in their backseat, so yes, I'm okay with you taking us home."

"We're okay, then?"

"We are but you have to remember I'm not your favorite toy that you get upset when someone else touches it." She frowned. "That didn't come out right."

"You kind of are," he said under his breath.

"What?"

"Not a toy, but you are my favorite person. Ever."

She couldn't hide her smile. "Stop with the Mr. Charming routine. I'm supposed to be mad at you."

He smiled back.

They said their goodbyes, found Harley and climbed into his truck.

"I was beginning to worry, though. You did seem a bit too perfect," she finally said when they exited off the highway and turned onto her street.

"I'm a lot of things, Macy, but I'm far from perfect."

A few minutes later they were in her driveway.

"Thanks for the ride," she said. As he went to switch off the truck, she stopped him. "I'm really tired. I think Harley and I will say good-night here."

That emotionless mask slipped over his face, he nodded. "I understand."

"No," she said, as she opened the door for Harley, "I don't think you do. It's as much my fault as it is yours that this thing between us has been moving at the speed of light. You were the one who suggested wooing. I haven't forgotten that. A little space would be good so we can both think about what it is we want."

"You," he said. "I just want you."

She stepped up and leaned into the truck to kiss him lightly on the lips. "I want you, too. But with our recent histories, it's not such a bad idea to take a break."

He gave her a brief nod.

Harley ran over to the gate Macy used regularly to get into the house. It was the closest entrance to the driveway. The truck didn't move until she'd gone in and put on the lights.

He slowly backed out of the driveway and she sighed when the headlights hit the road.

Picking up her phone, she dialed Cherie.

"I'm the biggest idiot in the world," she said.

"Tell me something I don't know," her friend replied.

11

"I'M AN IDIOT." Blake stomped upstairs to his bedroom. "Certifiable." Stripping, he turned on the shower as hot as he could stand it. He'd gone and lost the best thing that had ever happened to him.

As much as he wanted to blame Josh, it was his fault for acting like a jealous goof. For the life of him, he didn't understand why he'd lost his cool.

That wasn't true.

He stuck his head under the water.

The woman tied him in knots; she was unlike anyone he'd ever met before. And he didn't know what to do with himself.

Hell, he couldn't even remember what he'd said to Josh. And for a few seconds, when he found out they'd been on a date, he'd been furious. The image of his friend possibly kissing her—or worse—had made him livid.

Because she was his.

He slammed a fist against the tile.

Get a grip, man.

You break something in your mother's house there really will be something to answer for. Leaning both arms forward, he let the hot water run down his back.

She'd just gotten out of a relationship with an idiot, and here he was acting like one. He didn't treat women that way, and if his mother ever found out she'd be so disappointed.

That was the answer. He had to talk to his mom. She'd know how he could persuade his favorite journalist to give him another chance. It meant confessing what he'd done, and she wouldn't be happy. But she'd give him good advice; she was always wise when it came to relationships. Until the day his dad died, his parents had had one of the best marriages he'd ever seen.

He wanted that with Macy. It was too fast, and his head knew it. But his heart told him she was the one.

Now he had to convince her of that.

After finishing the shower and checking close to make sure he hadn't broken one of the tiles, Blake picked up the phone.

"What were you thinking?" his mother bellowed, she didn't even bother to say hello. "I did not raise you to act that way!"

Someone, probably Jaime, must have already called her to say what a moron he'd been at the party.

"Yes, ma'am. I don't have an excuse."

"I agree, young man. If I were there I'd box your ears. That poor girl, in a house full of people she didn't know, and then you went all King Kong on her."

"Shame on you," he heard his grandmother say.

Why did I call? He glanced at the heavens.

"You aren't telling me anything I don't already know. I feel like the world's biggest jerk. And I swear it will never happen again."

"What have I told you about swearing?"

"Yes, ma'am. Please, tell me how to fix this."

"*That's* the most sensible thing you've said all night."

"Halleluiah!" shouted a chorus of women.

"Mom, am I on speaker? And who else is there?"

"Yes, and just a few ladies from Momma's quilting circle."

Blake palmed his face.

"You listen to what we have to say, boy," Momma D shouted. She didn't seem too sick to him. "We'll explain to you how to set things right with that Yankee, and you don't mess it up again. You hear me?"

"Yes, ma'am."

"Now get a pencil, this is going to be a long list," his mother ordered.

And a very long night.

THREE DAYS HAD gone by, and except for two texts, she hadn't heard from Blake or even seen him and it wasn't for a lack of trying. Twice she'd gone to the feed store to pick up food for Harley, and then later some nails that she didn't need, but he wasn't there.

The first text had been an apology. She'd already forgiven him so it wasn't necessary. At the end he had asked about the types of questions he could ask the servicemen and -women for the story. He'd said that he'd meant to tell her the night he worked on her books, that he wanted to do the articles, but he'd been distracted by other things.

By her throwing herself at him, she was certain.

She sent him a text back explaining that he didn't have to apologize, and she was looking forward to seeing him soon. She also emailed him a bunch of questions for the interviews and offered to help him in any way necessary.

He'd replied with, "Thank you."

That was it.

She reread her email again to make sure she hadn't said anything he could misconstrue, but she hadn't.

Stupid marine. She missed him. As much as she didn't want to admit it to herself, she had become quite attached to him.

More than likely she'd wounded his pride. What if he decided she was too much trouble and had moved on? She thought about the women at the café who were so enamored with the half-naked marine. He was bright, gentlemanly and as hot as they came.

And she'd been upset because why? Oh, yeah, because he'd cared for her so much that he went all crazy macho for her.

Cherie was right. She was a class A idiot.

"Some guy beats his chest for you, and you have to be all I'm Miss Independence and don't you dare like me too much," Cherie had chastised.

"But men should not be allowed to—"

"What? Be men. He was staking his territory. It's classic male behavior. Could he have handled it better? Yes. But they don't call them male rivalries for nothing, doll. There's history there. Probably a lot

of crap you know nothing about. He apologized pro-
fusely and you came back with you needed a break.
How else is he supposed to interpret that?"

"But he got so weird when he found out Josh and
I dated a couple of times. It was strange."

"Macy," Cherie scolded, "you are not this dense.
Oh, wait, you were attached to that boss of yours."

"Geez. All right. I get it. But explain to me how
I can feel so much for him so fast. I thought I was
in love with Garrison, but it doesn't come close to
what I feel for Blake. It scares me. And it's hot and
wonderful now, well, it was. But doesn't that kind of
thing burn out fast. Isn't it better to slow it down before we both get hurt?"

Cherie barked out a loud laugh. "Honey, when you
feel what you do, there's no meaningful reason to
slow things down. You said it yourself, you're afraid.
And you've been hurt, so your defenses are up. That's
actually a good thing. But from everything you've
told me, this guy's the real deal. If you get your heart
broken, at least it was by a guy who deserved you.
Oh, and the sex is great. Do you have any idea how
difficult it is to find a guy like your marine?

"I haven't found a single one and I've been looking. Trust me. You need to be a grown-up and reach
out to him."

Pursing her lips, she tried to forget the rest of her
conversation with Cherie and focus on the story in
front of her. It was deadline day and she didn't have
any more time to waste. An hour later, she'd edited
two pieces and had all but the ad pages ready to go.

The quality of talent in a town as small as Tranquil Waters had genuinely surprised her. It was full of artists and writers. Many of whom liked the idea of more reporting about the community writ large. She'd even found a good photographer to cover local sports.

High school football was a religion to many in this region and state. She'd discovered that if she had sports photos on the front page, then circulation went up. In turn, she'd hired a couple of freelancers to do personal stories on the most popular players and their families and neighbors. Next on her to-do list was to tap into other important local hobbies and interests.

Now when she went into the café, people actually smiled and waved at her. All it took was a little effort.

Everything at work seemed to be falling into place. Meanwhile, her heart was breaking.

This wasn't the first time and it probably wouldn't be the last that the aspects of her life would not be in harmony all at once.

Blake's friend Jaime had even called to find out whether she was okay. That was how Macy found out he was in a foul mood and that no one wanted to be around him. She'd advised Macy to sit tight and wait for him to realize what he'd done wrong, which was the exact opposite of what Cherie had said.

Amanda knocked on the door frame of Macy's office. "I'm running down to the diner to get a cheeseburger and some caffeine. Do you want anything?"

Turned out Amanda was a darn good writer. She made a lot of grammatical errors, but those were easy to correct. Teaching someone to have a voice that comes through in his or her writing was something else.

Amanda had it, and had created a column geared for students. It covered everything from homework tips to saving for proms to how to graduate without a load of debt. She referenced students of all ages and backgrounds, and even added personal tidbits from things that her family did and said.

"Yes, if you don't mind. And I'll treat."

Sweets were necessary if she wanted to survive the afternoon. She might as well wallow and get fat since she had abysmal luck with men. And really, after all the friendly advice she was more confused than ever about what she should do.

"I'll take a cheeseburger, as well. But get me whatever kind of ice cream they have. If they have pints or whatever, that will work. I just need something gooey and full of sugar."

Amanda smiled. "Have you ever had the chocolate fudge ripple from Dory's Dairyland?"

She shook her head.

"I've got you covered. Oh, by the way, your friend—the hot marine—dropped this by." She handed Macy a flash drive.

Macy gulped hard. "Did he say anything?"

Amanda thought for a minute. "Just that this was a sample, and if you didn't like it you can email him with changes." She turned to walk away, and then stuck her head back in the office. "And, Harley. He said to tell her that he missed her. A lot."

With that, Amanda was gone.

"Hmm, at least he misses one of us," she said as she plugged the flash drive into the USB port.

I just wish it were me.

12

Staying away from Macy was slowly killing him. He'd peeked through the window at the paper and watched her as she worked on her computer. He felt silly, but he couldn't help it. Before she turned, though, and saw him, he rushed to the front door to go in and leave the flash drive for her. His mother's advice was to give Macy what she wanted. Time and space.

But he worried each day that the longer they were apart, the easier it would be for her to walk away from what they had.

And they definitely had something. It wasn't just about her being his. He knew that now. His pride had felt threatened that night, but it was more about him finding the thing that made him whole.

He hadn't slept much since they'd parted. She calmed him and being in her presence had become a sanctuary of sorts. He hadn't fully recognized all she'd done for him.

She was the first woman who knew him inside and out, and still accepted him. Wanted him, in fact.

Which was probably why her rejection had felt like a fatal blow.

His mother said it was only a rejection, but it still felt like life ending to him.

After parking his truck behind the feed store, he went straight to the room in back. His mom sat there, reviewing something on the computer.

Taken by complete surprise, he blurted out, "What are you doing here?" Try that again, he told himself. "I mean—"

"Momma D is feeling better, and she insisted I was cramping her style. I came back for a couple of days and then I'll go down on the weekend to check on her again. You look awful, son."

"Thanks, Mom."

His cell rang. He frowned.

"Who is it?"

"Her," he said.

"Quick, answer it before she hangs up."

Blake stared at the phone for another second, and pushed Answer. "Hello."

"Blake." Macy sounded as if she'd been crying. "I need you to come to the office right away."

"What's wrong? Are you hurt? Is it Harley?" He picked up the keys he'd thrown on the desk and turned without so much as a see ya to his mother.

She cleared her throat. "No, I'm sorry. I didn't mean to worry you, but this is time sensitive and I really need to see you now if you can make it."

"I'll be there in five."

He was there in four.

Striding in, he bolted straight past the receptionist, who didn't seem shocked to see him, and into Macy's office.

She had her head down while petting Harley, who was sprawled out on the floor. When the dog saw him, she jumped up and then ran full force into him knocking him into the chair.

"Harley! Down, girl! Blake, did she hurt you?" Macy went to his side and grabbed the dog by the collar. "Sit, Harley," she commanded.

Harley obeyed immediately but kept her attention on Blake. He could have sworn she smiled at him, her tongue hanging out of the side of her mouth.

"No, she's okay. Hey, girl," he said and affectionately scratched behind her ears. She nuzzled his neck and he wrapped his arms around her. He'd truly missed the giant horse of a dog. She proceeded to sit in his lap like a human would and they nearly toppled over backward.

"That's enough!" Macy exclaimed, waving at the dog. "You really missed him, I get it. I missed him, too. Now get off of him and get back to your spot. Now."

Harley looked back at him.

"Better do what she says, girl."

The dog huffed and returned to her gel-pad dog bed.

"Sorry about that. She's excited to see you."

Macy grabbed a tissue and dabbed her nose. He remembered how she'd sounded on the phone. "Macy, tell me what's wrong."

"Nothing's wrong. I mean, yes, there are some things we need to talk about but—these stories you wrote—"

She paused.

Something *was* wrong with them. "I told you I'm not a journalist." He wasn't upset. Maybe a bit disappointed. He'd enjoyed meeting and talking to past military personnel, especially the older vets from long ago.

"Not a journalist?" she scoffed and then smiled. "They're brilliant. Choked me up a little they were so good. There are a few style points I'll need to fix, but other than that, they're okay to print. That's why I called you. I'm going to pull the front page. I'd like to run the first two stories right now. And then, if you're up to it, make it a weekly series."

She liked what he'd done. "Uh, I'm not sure they're front-page worthy," he said, "but thanks."

"I'm the publisher, I decide what is worthy of the front page. And for the record, this has nothing to do with you and, well, what's been going on with us. I want to make that clear."

So it was just business. "Sure," he said. "Feel free to make the changes you think are necessary. I'm glad you liked the stories."

He stood.

"Where are you going?"

He frowned, confused. "Was there more?"

Standing, she walked over and shut the door and the blinds. "Sit down, Blake."

He sat.

She picked up the phone and dialed.

"Davis, I'm sending you new copy for the front page." She paused to listen. "Yes, I know we already did the front page. But I have something better. Make sure you and Sam both look at it, and then send it on to the printer."

She hung up the phone.

Her longs legs moved in front of him, and she sat down on the edge of her desk. She wore dark denims that hugged her hips and were tucked into those stiletto boots he loved. She leaned over and her shirt gapped slightly, giving him a glimpse of purple lace.

"Are you seeing someone else?"

His head popped up. "Why would you say something like that?"

She bit her lip. "You haven't even tried to talk to me since what happened the other night."

He leaned back so he could focus on her face, because her breasts were distracting him.

"That's what you wanted. You said things were going too fast and that I was possessive. Time and space apart, I believe, was mentioned. So I've been doing that."

Crossing her arms, she stared at him. "I meant in regard to that one night. I was embarrassed and hurt. By the next day I was over it. But you didn't answer my question. Are you seeing someone else?"

"Who would I see?" he asked incredulously. "You've ruined me for anyone else."

It was the truth. No way in hell would he ever feel about another woman what he did for Macy.

She gave him a Cheshire cat–like smile. Then she

bent over so her arms were on the arms of his chair, her breasts eye level.

"You're seducing me," he said gruffly.

"Maybe." She slowly leaned in and kissed him.

"What would convince you? This?" She nibbled on his ear.

He coughed and kept his hands at his sides.

She edged her knees on either side of his legs in the large leather chair. Her heat rubbed against his cock. "Or maybe this," she teased and tormented, as her hand went to the fly of his jeans.

Gently, he seized her wrist and stopped her. "Macy, I'm going to lose it right here and now if you don't stop." Then he pulled her to him and ravaged her mouth.

"Not here," he said when he finally let her go.

"Why not?"

"Because when we do this, I'm going to make you moan my name so loud that everyone in town will know what we're doing."

She cocked an eyebrow. "Well, then. I suppose we'd better hurry home. I only have about an hour before the final proofs are ready."

"No. We aren't rushing this again. I'm taking you on a date. We'll have a nice dinner and—" She rubbed her heat over his strained cock.

"Stop distracting me."

She pouted. "What other things are we going to do on the date besides eat? Because I have food at home we can cook. And a soft bed where you can make me moan all night long."

Pulling away from him, she stood. "Unless you're not up for it?"

He chuckled. "When you want something, it's no holds barred, isn't it?"

"It is. So, Marine, I see this going one of two ways. I can make love to you in the restaurant of your choice in front of the customers, or you can come to my place and we can negotiate further."

He swallowed hard. "Will those boots be part of the negotiations?" He had a vision of her with nothing on but those damn boots.

"They could be, but before you leave, there's one more thing."

"Anything you want, babe, it's yours."

"From now on, if we have a disagreement about the terms of our mutual companionship, we discuss it. Calmly. And if I say I need a little time, I'm talking hours—at the most, a night. Understood?" She knelt in front of him and unzipped his jeans.

"Yes," he groaned. "Macy, I'm never going to be able to walk out of here if you keep doing that."

"By my clock we have an hour to fill before I look at those final proofs, so we're going to have some fun."

Her head dipped down and she slid her tongue along his shaft.

"Macy," he said, gritting his teeth, "this feels, you fee…"

Pushing her hair away from her face, she stared up at him. "I know, Blake. I feel it, too."

Before he could say another word, her mouth was on him again.

_13_

HAVING HER COFFEE in the backyard while tossing a chew toy to Harley, Macy was at peace. Even happy, maybe. When had she ever been able to say that? She had a home that was hers, and a dog that she loved and who loved her. It was like a dream that was never within reach when she'd covered so many stories and crisscrossed the globe.

Most of her adult life had been lived around some conflict. Adrenaline-fueled jaunts pursuing one lead and then the next. She accepted that was how she would spend the rest of her days, knowing that life might be cut short because of the job.

But now—that was no longer true.

Spending time in Tranquil Waters, learning to fit in, the intimacy with Blake—not just the sex—was beyond anything she'd ever experienced. All of these connections made her realize there was so much more to life than adrenaline and airports.

After the sixth throw of the toy, Harley ambled up to her. Macy sat down in a padded deck chair. Even in November, the weather was warm enough that she could be outside in a sweater and still feel comfortable. The same couldn't be said of what it was like in Boston at this time of year.

Her phone buzzed in her pocket, Harley lay at her feet. The dog had short spurts of energy and then she was tired for eight hours.

"You're up early," she said to her friend.

"It's your fault." Cherie yawned.

"Why is that?"

"Your ex won't stop calling me. He has something urgent he needs to talk to you about. He insists you call him now. And I'm supposed to tell you that it isn't personal. It's job related."

Macy frowned. "I don't want to hear anything from him, job related or whatever."

"Seriously, you need to talk to him. *Opportunity of a lifetime* was just one phrase he used. Said he owed you, and this was the big one."

"Last time I saw him, I seem to remember his 'big one' entertaining an intern."

Cherie coughed. "Hold on there. You made a joke."

"I discovered I have a sense of humor, go figure."

"Oh, Macy. Your marine must be something special if he's loosened you up enough to make jokes."

"He is something special," she said wistfully.

"You don't even sound like your old self. I thought you'd signed off on men for good?"

"I did. I have no clue how long this is going to last with the marine, but it's intense. I've— No matter what happens, it will have been worth the broken heart— At least in this case I've learned something about myself and what I want in a relationship."

"You have fallen in the deep end without your water wings again."

Definitely. But she hadn't lied. Nothing about the past few weeks would change if she had a chance to do them over again. Except perhaps, the three days they'd been apart. She was still ticked over the time they wasted.

"I always did like to take risks."

"So when do I get to meet him? You can and you will send me a picture."

"I promise, soon." Part of her didn't want to share Blake, it was new and seemed almost too good to be true. "Listen, I need to get to the office."

"Fine. Don't worry about me. I'm just the one waking up at the crack of dawn to give you news of limitless opportunities."

Macy laughed.

"Please, by all that you hold dear, call your ex. I wouldn't put it past him to hop on a private jet and fly down there to speak to you in person."

Ugh. Something she definitely did not want.

"Fine. And you know, Cherie, you can block his calls."

Cherie grunted. "I did, and then he called my assistant, which is the only reason I'm awake before ten."

AN HOUR LATER she was at the newspaper office. Harley was in her favorite spot sleeping. Deadline day was always a long one for Macy. She had to edit and

design the pages and make sure everything was elec-
tronically delivered to the printer on time.

In spite of the pressure, the new staff and other
changes had made a positive difference and everyone
had settled into a comfortable routine.

"Hey, I'm going to do a latte run. Do you want a
sandwich or something to go with yours?" Amanda
asked. Today she wore a pair of dark jeans, cowboy
boots and a T-shirt promoting a punk rock band that
had seen better days—the shirt, not the band. At least
the outfit was a step in the right direction and Macy
wasn't blinded by the color choices.

Glancing at her cell phone she saw that it was almost lunchtime.

"Yes." She pulled cash out of her purse. "And get
yourself and Lance something, as well."

"Do you mind answering the phones? Lance is upstairs installing the new computer equipment."

"Not a problem."

Harley barked. The dog grabbed her leash from its
hook and sat expectantly in front of Amanda.

Amanda rolled her eyes but smiled. "Yes, you may
come, but you have to stay by the bicycle rack and if
you try to trip me to get the food this time, there will
be no more walks for you."

"You don't have to take her with you. That's a lot
to juggle."

"It's okay, I know she just gets excited and can't
help herself. Besides, she's a guy magnet. Everyone
wants to know what kind of dog she is, because she's
so big."

Laughing, Macy followed them to the door.

She slipped her fingers around Harley's collar. The dog looked at her. "You behave, or no cookies for you tonight."

Harley did her signature move and cocked her head to one side.

"I mean it."

Harley grumbled, but licked Macy's hand.

The dog really did understand everything she said. It was spooky sometimes.

After washing her hands, she propped open her office door and the front door of the building so she could hear if someone walked in.

The phone rang as she was passing Amanda's desk. *"Tranquil Waters News."*

"I thought you owned the paper, why are you answering the phones?" The smooth voice of her ex was unmistakable.

Figures. As soon as Amanda leaves he would call.

"The receptionist is grabbing lunch. I don't have time to talk. I'm on deadline for our pages."

"Please! Don't hang up." She couldn't remember when he'd last used the word *please*.

"Whatever it is, Garrison, it can wait until tomorrow." She reached down to disconnect the call.

"The Henderson Paper Group wants you to be the executive editor of their online editions," he said quickly. "Aaron Henderson asked for you specifically."

She couldn't believe it. When she'd decided she was tired of traveling, she'd wanted to make a name for herself as an editor. In the six months she was at the Boston paper, which was one of Henderson's largest papers, she'd noticeably improved its bottom line. After streamlining the editorial process, the quality of the information had increased, bringing in more subscribers and consequently more advertisers.

"Are you still there?"

"Yes," she whispered.

"Henderson wants you back and he's bumping you up to executive editor. You're a hot commodity. The different papers in the chain all want you, they're fighting over you. I nearly got demoted when you left, because you had created such a dynamic online version that we were making more money than all the rest of the papers in the group combined."

She hadn't known that, but it pleased her. It meant that people were still interested in hard news, and not just what kind of underwear a celebrity might be wearing.

"You've worked with Aaron, and he's been watching what you've done with the paper there in Texas. From what we can tell, you've increased the ad revenue and circulation. And even though it's a small area without a lot of big news, the quality of reporting is exponentially better that it was six months ago."

"Did you do this?" If this was some bizarre plan to get her back to Boston, she wasn't interested.

This was beyond her dream job. To have creative and editorial input on an entire newspaper chain's online components was incredible. It also pulled at her heartstrings. Journalism, and the way it was reported. Ethics was the one aspect she felt strongest about. Good, objective reporting was needed in the world and this would give her enough influence to make that happen.

"No. In fact, I'd suggested another candidate. But Henderson only wants you. As far as he's concerned, there are no other candidates. He's in New York tomorrow and wants to meet with you personally. By the way, that's where the job would be."

Aaron Henderson had been her first editor, the guy who believed she was tough enough to be a war correspondent when no one else would give her a chance. She owed him. Big.

"That's really short notice."

"I've been trying to get in touch with you for two weeks. Did Cherie tell you I called?"

"Yes, but I've been busy." That was true.

The very least she could do was hear Aaron out. And she had to admit that it was a bit of an ego boost that they'd been watching what she did with the local paper.

"There's a first-class ticket waiting for you, all you have to do is claim it. The flight is at nine tonight. Once you land, a car will pick you up and take you to the hotel. You'll meet with Aaron there at ten the next morning. Are you in?"

Was she? Glancing around her office, taking in all the little changes that now made it hers…she knew it would be difficult to walk away. And what about her relationship with Blake? He had said he didn't plan on living in the small town for the rest of his life, but would he want to live in New York?

Before she spoke to him about it, she wanted to

know the fine print of what she was being offered. Then she'd make a decision.

"Yes. I'm in."

BLAKE HELD THE papers in his hand. An honorable discharge. There was a time he thought he'd go all the way and retire, but he was excited about new possibilities.

One of which was his mutual companionship with Macy. The other was figuring out his place in the world. He'd invested in his friends'—Rafe and Will's—security business. Anytime he wanted to step into a corporate roll it was there for him. He was already the CFO of sorts, overseeing most of the financials.

It meant a fair amount of travel, but that wasn't so awful. If he settled in Tranquil Waters, he'd need to let his soul free now and again. This kind of job might be the perfect answer. They had asked him to take over the rescue-operations department, as well. He'd coordinate search-and-rescue missions, which was something he'd always wanted to do.

His phone played Macy's favorite song. "Hey, beautiful, what's up?"

"How did everything go?" She didn't sound her normal self. There was hesitancy in her voice.

"Great. I've got my papers in hand, and I just landed at the Austin airport. How is everything with you?"

There was a long pause.

"Something has come up and I need to go to New

York for a couple of days. I could put Harley in a kennel, but I'd rather not."

What was in New York? Obviously she'd tell him if she wanted him to know. He guessed whatever it was was personal given the stress in her voice.

"I'll take care of her. What time do you have to leave?"

"My flight is at nine tonight, so I'd like to get out of here by seven at the latest."

"I'll be there by three. Do you want me to keep her at Mom's?"

"Uh, if you don't mind staying here, that would be better for her, I think. But I don't want to put you out."

"You aren't. Is everything okay?"

Another long pause. "Yes. It's— I've got a lot to process in a very short amount of time. Can we talk about it when I get back? I'll know more about the situation, and—we'll figure things then. Okay?"

Figure what things out? She said "we," so she probably wasn't going back to the ex. Besides, he was in Boston. Was it something to do with a job? He knew if he pressed her for details she'd see it as prying, even though her curiosity about everything was boundless. Macy had a double standard when it came to her privacy.

"Whatever you want." He tried to keep the sting of hurt out of his tone. That she wouldn't share what it was she had to figure out bothered him. Hadn't she been the one complaining that he never opened up?

"I have to put the paper to bed, but then I'll be out at the house. Thank you. I'm sorry I won't get to spend time with you. I've missed you."

Well, there was that.

"I missed you, too," he said.

"Bad timing that I have to leave tonight, but it can't be helped. This— It just came up this afternoon." There was a wistfulness to her words that pleased him.

Why wouldn't she just tell him?

"It's okay. You can make it up to me when you return, which is when?"

"I would imagine late tomorrow night or early the next day. Everything is kind of up in the air. And I'm sorry to be so vague. But I'll know more soon.

"Oh, and can you pick up another bag of food for Harley from the feed store? I'd really appreciate it."

"No problem."

By the time he picked up the food and dealt with a few things at the store it was almost four before he pulled up in front of Macy's house.

A large bark came from the other side of the front door, followed by the rattling of the handle.

"Harley, you stop that. No more opening doors, you brat," Macy chastised.

He chuckled. The dog never ceased to amaze him.

"She's keeping you on your toes," he said as Macy opened the door for him.

Harley held out a paw and he shook it. Then she nuzzled his hand.

"I'm glad to see you, too, girl." He rubbed her ears.

"And you." He kissed Macy as they jointly leaned over the dog's head.

He ended the kiss, but she captured his neck in her hand and held him to her where her lips devoured his.

When she finally broke the embrace, she stared deeply into his eyes. A storm brewed there, but he couldn't get a read on her.

"Are you doing okay?" He shifted the dog out of the way so he could put an arm around Macy's shoulders.

"I am. I don't mean to be so secretive, it's just— it's a job thing. A dream job, to be exact. At least that was what the ex told me."

The ex. At the mention of him, Blake's lips tightened into a thin line. "I see."

She didn't seem to notice the tension he felt, which was good. His ego, where she was concerned, had very nearly cost him their relationship. He wouldn't go there again.

"Yes, that's why I have to go. I don't know if he's telling me the truth or not about this job. But it's working with someone I like a great deal, and who gave my break in the business. I feel like I owe it to him to at least hear him out."

The ex, or someone else? He couldn't come up with a subtle way to ask, without sounding like a jealous boyfriend. They'd said from the beginning that this was a fling, even though it had come to mean a great deal more to him. But he was the last one to stand in the way of someone's dream. Whatever she decided, he cared for her enough that he would support her.

He was just grateful it was about a job, and not another man.

She moved away from him and headed for the bedroom. "I need to grab my carry-on, and then I'll—" She smiled sheepishly. "I was going to say I'd show

you where everything is for Harley, but you know all
of that as well as I do. The good news is I went on a
cooking binge while you were gone. There's a bunch
of stuff in the freezer, and I just put the King Ranch
casserole in the oven. It needs to cook about twenty
more minutes. The buzzer will ring."

"For someone who doesn't really cook, you've
been doing a lot of it lately." He smiled.

"It's your fault, making me watch all those cooking shows. I get inspired and then I get in there and
go crazy. It's one of the few ways I can settle my
mind. I guess, like running, it's my kind of meditation, only a lot more fattening. As soon as my knee
is back in shape, I'll have to start running again so
that my clothes will fit."

At the mention of food, Harley barked twice. Her
signal for feeding time.

He chuckled as he put his duffel bag on one of the
bar stools. "I've got her food in the back of the truck,
I'll go get it."

"There are a couple of cups left in the old bag,
but not near enough for her nightly feast. And watch
it if you eat apples, bananas or peanut butter. She'll
leave the roasted chicken on the counter but put one of
those down and it disappears in the blink of an eye."

"Noted. Do you need a ride to the airport?"

"Oh, thanks, but since it's such a fast turnaround,
I'll just take my car."

"If you get your carry-on, I'll put it in the SUV
for you."

She went to the bedroom and returned with the
suitcase. Dressed in an ivory sweater, dark jeans

and heeled boots, she took his breath away. Dammit. Whatever this business was, it was going to mess things up for them. He knew it instinctively.

And that hit him hard, as hard as any man could punch. He didn't want to lose her.

"What's wrong?" She touched his cheek with her fingertips.

"Not a thing. Though I'm worried slightly about you driving the hour into Austin. The traffic was a bear getting here, and you'll be right in the thick of it."

She kissed his cheek where her fingers had been. "You are the sweetest man ever. I'll be fine. Are you sure everything is okay with you? That was a big decision you made about taking the honorable discharge."

"A decision I'd been thinking about for the last six months or so. I'm good. Like you, I'm taking a look at my opportunities and trying to figure out my next move."

"I guess—it's good that we have so many opportunities. There are a lot of people who don't," she said.

"Yes, we're extremely lucky." He kissed her lightly on the lips. "Say your goodbyes to you know who. I'll go put this in the car for you."

Outside, he took a long breath.

Hell.

What if she got in that car and she never came back? It was hard for people to turn down dream jobs. She was talented, it was no wonder someone wanted her.

But no one wanted her more than he did.

Hauling the giant bag of dog food onto his shoulder, he grabbed the groceries he'd bought with the other hand.

When he got to the door, she was holding it open for him and trying to keep Harley inside. "Oh, I should have called and told you about all the food I'd made."

Once in the house, he set the giant bag next to the kitchen door.

"What? Oh?" He glanced down at his hand with the other bag. "These things aren't for me, they're ingredients for a new kind of dog cookie I wanted to try for Harley."

At the word cookie, the dog came sliding down the hall and stopped at his feet.

"She scares me sometimes," he said, nudging the dog out of the way so he could move things into the kitchen.

"You said it," she agreed. "I find myself being careful about what I say just in case I accidentally use one of her cues. But I swear she understands most of the English language." She sighed. "I guess if traffic is bad, I should get going."

He nodded regretfully.

Wrapping his arms around her, he kissed her.

Pressing her body into his, she intensified the exploration of tongues as if she were communicating something else, as well.

Before he could think too much about it, he was lost in her. Her touch did that to him.

They were panting when they finally separated.

"Never in my life has a man affected me the way

you do," she said softly. "And I don't just mean when we make love."

He sucked in a breath. He hadn't realized how much he needed to hear her say that. "The feeling's definitely mutual," he said.

"I don't want to go," she said softly. "I want to stay here with you."

"I want that, too. So hurry up and get back." He kissed her one more time.

Then he scooted her toward the front door and led her out to the car. Opening her door for her, he waited until she was belted.

"I have to kiss you one more time," he said.

"That's a good idea." She tilted up to meet his lips.

"Be safe."

She nodded and gave him a sweet smile. "Take care of my girl."

"Done," he replied, and he shut the door and waved.

Everything was about to change. He knew it in his bones. He waved again though her car was already where the driveway met the road.

Damn.

Harley whined beside him.

"I know, girl. I love her, too."

14

As Macy stepped out of the glass-and-marble shower in her hotel room, her phone beeped. Wrapping a towel around herself, she picked up the cell. A picture of Blake and Harley graced her screen. He had his fingers crossed, and the dog had one paw crossed over the other.

The text read, We're crossing fingers and paws that everything goes well for you today. No matter what happens, we are here for you.

The photo and message were the cutest things she'd ever seen and were exactly what she needed to help with jangled nerves.

The Henderson Paper Group had come to her, not the other way around, and besides, she didn't need the job. Still, she had a bad case of the jitters that the warm shower hadn't calmed.

Taking a deep breath, she texted back, You made my day. Thank you! I miss you!

For someone who didn't use exclamation points in her work, she meant every one of them today.

Do you have time for a call? he texted.

Hearing his voice would be the balm that she needed to make it through the next few hours.

Call me in ten minutes, she texted back.

Someone knocked on her door.

"Hold on," she called out as she yanked on the hotel robe and tied the belt around her waist.

Peeping through the peephole, she frowned.

"I know you're in there," Garrison said.

"Why are you here?" she asked through the door.

"Aaron wanted me to bring you to him. Thought you might be more comfortable if you showed up with someone you know."

"I'll be fine. Thanks, anyway. You can go."

"It won't look good. That is, it won't look good if we aren't playing on the same team. Your group will be answering to me. He needs to know we can get along."

Huffing, she opened the door.

The man always looked gorgeous in a suit. Nowhere as good as her marine, but he *was* a looker.

"Sit." She pointed to the sofa under the windows on the far side of the room. "Don't talk to me. Don't do anything. Just sit there until I get dressed." She scooped up her dress, tights and boots and headed for the bathroom.

Her phone rang as she was putting on her dress and she couldn't open the door.

Mortification set in when she realized Garrison had answered the call.

"She's getting dressed, who is this? What kind of

friend?" He sounded jealous when he had absolutely no right to be. That was so not what she needed.

Slamming the door open, she then rushed to grab the phone out of Garrison's hand.

"I told you to sit," she said, annoyed. She pointed to the sofa for emphasis.

He ignored her. "Sorry, I thought it might be the boss telling you the meeting was moved or rescheduled."

What a lie. He was just being nosy. You could take the reporter out of the newsroom and make him a vice president, but you could never take that need for information out of a journalist. That quest for knowledge never died.

"Blake?"

"Hey," he said hesitantly. "Everything okay there?"

"Yes, sorry. I was in the bathroom and someone decided he'd answer my phone, although I didn't ask him to. So, how are you and our girl?"

He chuckled. "I like that. A lot. We're good. She went for a fast walk with me, as fast as I could go with this leg, anyway. She's tuckered out and laying in front of the fireplace. She moved her sofa in front of it last night while I watched the game. I filmed it for you, but it's too big to text."

She laughed. That must have been a sight. "Oh, I really needed that. Thank you. Great Danes get cold. And their bones get achy. I bought some glucosamine tablets for her, but you have to coat the pills in peanut butter to get her to swallow them."

"Got it," he said.

"Uh, can I be the jealous boyfriend for a minute and ask who that guy was."

Get in line. On the one hand she didn't want Blake to get the wrong idea, but on the other hand she wouldn't lie.

"The ex. He's escorting me to the meeting. It's in the publisher's suite, so they wanted me to feel comfortable. Evidently." She moved into the bathroom when she spied Garrison listening to every word with a giant grin on his face.

"And are you more comfortable?"

She huffed and closed the door. "No. I'd rather not have to deal with him while I'm contemplating everything else that's happening. It's weird. I'm not angry anymore—just...irked because I don't like him much as a person."

Her marine let out a deep breath. "I have to admit, I'm glad to hear that. When he answered the phone—"

"I would have thought the same thing," she interjected. "But, trust me, you have nothing to worry about."

"Time to go," Garrison called to her.

"I heard him," Blake said. "Whatever happens today I support you and so does Harley. Right, girl?"

Harley barked in agreement.

That Blake was so supportive brought tears to Macy's eyes. Most of the men in her past were too competitive to be truly supportive, including Garrison. It wasn't until after she'd broken up with him that she'd seen their relationship had become a game of one-upmanship.

"I wish you were here with me," she whispered, not bothering to keep the want from her voice.

"Ditto, babe. Ditto. Call us and let us know how it went."

"Will do."

As she hung up, she heard Harley bark again.

She loved that damn dog.

And she loved the marine.

Settling down in a small town with them didn't seem like such a wild notion to her.

But the opportunity from Aaron tugged at her. A real chance to make her mark in this environment was so enticing. Still, she first had to listen to what he had to say.

She marched forward and opened the bathroom door. "Right. Let's do this."

"Uh. You might want to put shoes on." Garrison raised his eyebrow.

"Well spotted," she said with dripping sarcasm. "He does that sort of thing to me."

"*He* being the boy back home?" Garrison asked.

"He's a man—a decorated marine to be exact—and yes. Not that it's any business of yours."

"Ah. The lady is a little testy. Was he jealous about your ex answering the phone?"

"He has nothing to be jealous about."

Minutes later, they'd left her room and were in the elevator, heading for Aaron. Garrison used a key card in a slot beneath the row of elevator buttons, he pushed the *P* for penthouse.

They want me.

No need to be worried.

On the short flight up, she realized why she was worried. She was about to get the job of a lifetime, one she'd always wanted.

But there might be a big sacrifice in store for her to take the position.

No. I can't think about that right now.

Just listen to what the man has to say.

Then you can make an informed decision.

As the elevator doors opened, she steeled herself. Plastering a smile on her face, she left the elevator and approached the penthouse door.

This was it.

"You look beautiful," Garrison said behind her. "In fact, your small-town life seems to agree with you."

Forcing herself not to roll her eyes, she raised her hand to knock on the door.

"Say anything like that when we're in there, and you'll really regret it." She had no desire to deal with his games and meaningless flirtations.

"You were always a fierce one," he whispered in her ear. "And one of the biggest mistakes of my life was letting you go."

"You didn't let me go. I ran as fast as I could from your toxic, cheating self, which was one of the best things I've ever done. I've met a man's man, one who honors and respects me. A man who deserves me."

"Sounds boring."

She laughed. "Not even a little bit. He's taught me a lot about my body, enough that I know what I've been missing out on all these years."

She glanced back to see his eyes narrow.

Not her finest moment, to throw such a comment

at him, but maybe she'd save the next poor woman he got together with. Everything had always been about his pleasure.

Jerk.

The door opened and Aaron Henderson ushered her in. She'd been expecting one of his aides to answer and she nearly tripped as she passed by him. He steadied her and then guided her to a sofa in the living room.

"I'm so glad you're here," he said. Dressed in gray slacks and a cream shirt, he looked the epitome of classy casual. But she knew how hard he'd worked to own his newspaper group. At forty-five he'd accomplished more than most people did in double the years. "Can I get you some coffee?" He gestured toward a small tray on a table in front of the sofa.

"No, thank you." Her nerves were jittery enough.

"I'll leave you two to your meeting," Garrison said.

"No, please I'd like you to stay." Aaron nodded to a chair.

Aaron sat in the one opposite her.

Her ex hesitated for a moment, but then took one of the leather chairs to the side of the conversation area.

"Before I explain why I called you here, though I'm sure Garrison has mentioned a part of it, I need to know something. It's a touchy subject, but the truth is important to me if we're to move forward with this arrangement. It's personal and not something an employer would ever ask in the normal course of things. But this is a big step, so we need to be clear."

What the heck was he talking about? There was

nothing she couldn't answer. And Garrison didn't need to be here. What arrangement?

"I'll answer whatever it is," she said, defiant.

"Good. So explain to me why you broke your engagement to Garrison and ran off to the country to run your uncle's paper."

Crap.

AFTER MAKING SURE Harley was settled in the office at the feed store with his mother. Blake headed out to the barn where they kept the hay and fertilizers.

"Hey, Blake," Ray said. "What are you doing out here?"

He shrugged. "Need to work off some energy. Thought I'd help you with the bales."

The other man nodded. "Glad to have the help, but is your leg going to be okay?"

Blake patted his right thigh. "It likes a good workout now and then."

Sliding on his leather gloves, he picked up the first bale and walked it into the barn. After creating a stack of about ten, he worked on the next one.

What if she took the job? And really, why wouldn't she? From what her ex had told her, it was all of her dreams tied into one neat package. If she had to move to New York, what would she do with Harley?

What would she do with him?

No way could he lose her.

He could follow Macy, but would she want him to?

When her ex had answered the cell earlier, he was suddenly so angry. It scared him that his temper rose that quickly. That wasn't him.

You're jealous.

Hell. He'd never been jealous before the night of Jaime's party. He'd dated and even had a few girlfriends. But nothing like the connection he had with Macy. In such a short time she'd become everything to him.

He lived his days trying to find ways to please her and make her smile. And darn if that didn't make him feel good, as well. Being around her was the best therapy there was. She made him laugh and look at the world through her curious eyes. Having seen more than his fair share of the dark side of things, he'd become jaded.

The past few weeks, she'd shown him that yes there was darkness, but there was also light. Her articles and features about the local folks had warmed his heart. She understood the true essence of people.

She'd gone a step further and shared some of the stories of people she had met during her travels. Many of them had the same problems as folks here in a small Texas town. Ultimately, they all wanted the world to be safe for their children, put food on the table and have a decent roof over their heads.

No longer did he think of people as us and them. There were evil people in the world, but there were a lot of good people, too. People he would gladly die to protect. When he was in the thick of it, he hadn't been able to see the truth.

Macy wrote that the world was a melting pot and that everyone was more the same than they were different.

That was one of the ideals she could pursue on a

higher level if she took the job. He knew that before she had any of the details. She had a voice that should be heard, and he would not in any way hinder that.

"Not sure what those bales of hay have done to you, but throwing them around is getting messy," Ray's voice cut through his thoughts.

Blake's eyes took in the chaos around him. Two of the bales had busted and there was hay all over the floor.

"Sorry," he said as he reached for the broom. "I'll clean it up."

"Don't worry about it. Let's get the rest of these bales into the loft. It looks like it's about to rain. Mind if I hand them up to you?" Ray asked.

Stepping up on the ladder, Blake climbed into the loft. A half hour passed before the storm hit, and water poured down on the tin roof of the barn. Normally, it was a comforting sound.

But his mood was no better than it had been before he'd started. Though, his muscles certainly ached now. He'd be lucky to get out of bed in the morning.

"Go on," Ray coaxed him. "I'll clean this up. I'm betting that horse of a dog of yours is giving your mom hell about the thunder."

Damn. He'd forgotten about Harley and loud noises.

Running through the rain and into the back of the store, he slid to a stop outside his mother's office door. She sat on the floor reading a book to the dog.

Blake chuckled. She'd done the same for his little brother who'd missed being struck by lightning by mere inches when he was six, and had been afraid of storms most of his childhood.

The crazy thing was the dog hung on her every word.

"Go check on Tanya at the register. There's news the river might flood. Folks will be stocking up. I'll be there once I get her to sleep." She rubbed Harley's head.

He nodded. Still soaked to the skin, he found Tanya had a long line in front of her.

Entering his code, he quickly opened the second register. "Next in line, please."

Grateful for the distraction, Blake's mind never wavered far from what Macy might be doing. Would she go out with the ex to celebrate?

Stop it. He forced himself to smile as he rang up the total for the nails and plastic tarp old Mr. Davis was buying. He did the same for all of the following customers, too. After the initial rush, the crowd thinned out.

He went to the office to check on his mom and the dog.

"You go ahead and take the dog home. She'll be more comfortable in a familiar place," his mom said.

The dog's head was in her lap on top of the small pillow his mother used for her back when she sat in the office chair too long.

"She looks pretty comfortable to me." He smiled.

She smiled back. "Yes, but my legs are numb from her overly large head, and I'm too old to be sitting on the floor."

After scooting the sleeping dog off his mom, he helped her up.

She stretched. "That's a smart dog you have there."

"That she is."

"For a monster, she kind of grows on you."

He laughed. At the sound, Harley glanced up and gave him the evil eye for waking her from her nap.

"Yep. She's too smart for her own good."

"Well, then. You two should get along just fine," his mom said as she patted his shoulder. "Any ideas on what your next move is? Are you sure you don't want to buy the store? You'd mentioned it when you were in the hospital, but we haven't talked about it since you got back."

That was before he met the woman who'd come to mean everything to him. And he'd also been told there was the possibility that he might not be the same again physically.

That wasn't an option for him, and he'd shown everyone, including himself, that he refused to allow his injuries to dictate the rest of his life.

"While you're gone, Mom, I do enjoy hanging out here, but this is your passion. I think mine is elsewhere. The guys have asked me to take a more active part in the security firm. They have some new ideas that might be beneficial to rural areas especially. So I'll probably be helping them grow the business. As soon as I know my next step, you'll be the first one I tell," he promised.

Giving him the mom-knows-all stare, she said, "You haven't heard from her yet, have you?"

"Mom," he warned.

"Son, I'm not saying anything except that her meeting was this morning and it's nearing five."

"I'm aware. Let it go—please."

She shrugged. "Whatever you say. I'll go help Tanya close up. You're soaking wet, get home before you catch your death."

Home. It hit him that it was Macy's house where he now felt at home.

Yes, ma'am. He was in big trouble.

15

As he braked in the driveway and put the truck into Park, Harley woofed. "Let me turn off the engine at least." He patted her back. As soon as he opened his door and got out, she leaped past him and ran for the house.

She must be hungry.

The dog opened the front door before he could get there. That wasn't right. He was certain he'd locked the door when they left earlier in the day.

"Hello, pretty girl. I missed you, too," Macy said as she greeted Harley. "I was a little concerned about you two. I tried to call, but no one answered."

She glanced up at Blake. He could see the concern on her face.

"You called my cell?" He went to take the phone out of his pocket, and discovered it wasn't there. "Well, that explains it," he said. "I must have lost it when I was working with Ray in the barn this afternoon."

Harley soon had her pinned against the fridge de-

manding to be fed. He grabbed the towel he'd left by
the garage door and wiped the rain off of the dog's
coat before she ruined the sexy dress Macy wore.
She had on high-heel boots, and her hair was done
up in that haphazard way that made her look like the
sexy librarian.

Though, they'd never had a librarian in Tranquil
Waters that ever looked like that.

"I missed you," she said. There was something
in her expression that he couldn't quite understand.

"And I missed you. I'm surprised you're here."

"Where else would I be?" She smiled but it didn't
quite meet her eyes.

Hell. She was going to take the job.

She held up a hand. "I haven't made a decision
yet," she said as if she could read his thoughts. "In
fact, I don't want to think about anything right now.
The flight into Austin was one of the bumpiest I've
ever been on, and I've flown on a lot of planes. Then
the traffic this time of day getting out of Austin
through the rain was enough to turn me into one of
those road-rage maniacs. I could never understand
how people got so angry in the car, but I do now.

"All I want is a hot bath and a glass of wine, and
I want you to join me."

His body was instantly at attention. Who was he
to question if she needed some time?

"Red or white?" he asked. He had a bottle of champagne in the fridge, which he planned to surprise
her with if she took the job. But now wasn't the right
moment.

"You pick. And do we have any chocolate? I really, really, really need chocolate."

He laughed. "You go start the bath. I'll bring in the treats."

"Deal," she said. "Come on, Harley, have a seat on the couch. *Bad Dog!* is just starting."

"Make sure it's not one of the animal rescue episodes. It upsets her when she sees other animals in pain," he said. He'd made that mistake the night before and ended up sleeping next to her on the floor. It was the only way she'd calm down.

"I should have told you about that. In my rush, I must have forgotten."

As he opened the cabernet sauvignon, he tried not to think about Macy. But he knew the truth.

Finding the box of chocolate truffles he'd bought for her to celebrate, he placed them and the wine on a serving tray he found next to her fridge.

As he passed Harley on her couch she glanced up at him. "Tell you what? You stay there for the next hour or so and behave, and I'll give you two more of these." He put a dog cookie down in front of her. Harley cocked her head and he swore she winked at him. Then she settled back on her sofa to watch her favorite channel.

Balancing the wine, glasses and chocolates again, he found Macy already to her neck in bubbles.

He placed the drinks and plate on the small round table next to the tub and poured the wine.

Handing her the filled glass, he smiled when she moaned with the first sip. His cock twitched, as well. Indeed, one small moan and he was hard.

"Are you sure you want to share the bath, you look pretty comfortable."

She reached out and tugged on his jeans. "Hey, these are already wet."

"I suppose you may not have noticed, but it's raining outside, and wrestling with your dog to get her into the truck was no easy feat. I am grateful that the thunder had stopped by the time we got home. I had to tell her a story on the way as she tried to hide from the noise.

"What kind of story?" She pointed to his shirt as if to say, "Hurry up and strip," so he did.

Her eyes followed him appreciatively as he slid into the tub across from her. Even with his size, he could stretch out his sore legs. His body warned there'd be a steep price to pay for lifting all those bales of hay.

"Mom watched her while I was out in the barn. When I came back, she was reading a romance novel to her. Harley hung on her every word. I swear she understood her."

Macy popped a chocolate in her mouth, and then she shook her head. "I'm not surprised. She's so smart. Sometimes I forget that she's a dog. I talk to her like I would any friend."

"If it makes you feel any better, I do the same thing. But don't tell anyone I said that."

She watched him for a moment from under her lashes. "Tell me about your day," she said before having a large sip of wine.

As he shared the minute details, she shifted around so that she rested against his chest. His legs stretched out along hers, his hard cock pressing into her back. He put his arms around her and drew in her scent.

She was his.

No matter what she told him, he had to find a way to stay in her life. Compromise wasn't one of his strong suits, but he could learn if it meant being closer to her.

"Weren't you afraid of hurting your leg?" she asked.

"Huh." Then he remembered what he'd been telling her about loading hay into the barn. "No. It's good to work out once in a while and push harder than I normally do. Helps build up strength." At least that was what his PT had told him a few months ago.

"So you're feeling okay?" As she asked she turned to face him. She was on her knees, the bubbles creating a pretty swirling design across her breasts.

"Right now, I feel great," he said as he reached out and rubbed his thumb across one of her taut nipples. It hardened even more at his touch.

"I need you," she whispered.

Not nearly as much as he needed her. Leaning down, he teased her sensitive skin with his tongue.

She hissed in a breath.

"I've wanted you since I heard your voice on the phone this morning," he said and raised his head to kiss her. As his tongue played with hers, his fingers found her sex. He stroked her until she arched back and cried out.

"Yes," she moaned. "Yes."

Then she gently moved on top of him.

He shifted forward so she could wrap her legs

around him. She gripped his shoulders as she rode him, his arms strained to keep them as one.

Their bodies rose and fell, and the water sloshed around them. The overwhelming sensations as he filled her had him gritting his teeth for control.

"Please, Blake. Don't hold back. I want to feel all of you."

He smiled and upped their rhythm. He savored every word, every sound that came from Macy's lips.

Throwing her head back, her face radiant, her body began to quiver. Her muscles tightened around him as the orgasm rocked her, and he could hold on no longer.

"Mine," he whispered fiercely as he climaxed.

"Yes," she said. Her lips on his.

When he tilted her forward, so he could see her eyes, a tear streamed down her cheek.

"What is it baby? What's wrong?"

Chewing on her lip, she shook her head.

"You took the job." It was more of a statement than a question.

"Not yet. I— We need to— What we have is so intense. I don't think I can live without it. We said that this was a fling. That we weren't serious."

"We ran past serious the first night we made love," he said as he moved a damp curl from her eyes.

"I thought so, too. That's why I don't want to make this decision, and it really is a life-changing one, without discussing it with you. I have no right…"

He smiled. "I love you, Macy," he told her. "I'm with you no matter what you choose to do."

It took a minute for his words to register. "I love

you, too." She put her arms around his neck and hugged him. "This is strange, right? We've only known each other a few weeks."

He agreed. "But I don't think that's anything we can control."

She shivered.

"Let's move to where it's comfortable," he said. "I think this conversation is going to need more wine, and maybe some of that casserole you made."

She frowned. "Except for the chocolates and wine, I haven't been able to eat all day," she said as he helped her up and into the large walk-in shower. The glass curved so that there was no need for a door.

"Well, no decision should be made on an empty stomach—at least that's what my mom always says." As the warm water sluiced down their bodies, he gathered her close to him. "We will figure this out. I promise."

She smiled and squeezed him tight. "Why does life have to be so hard?"

He kissed the top of her head. "Got to get through the bad to get to the good," he told her. And he meant it.

Could he support her if she went off to New York and left him and Harley behind? It was no place for a dog as big as she was.

It wasn't lost on him that he was prepared to sacrifice a great deal for that damn dog—and even more so for the woman in his arms.

AFTER A GOOD MEAL, which Blake insisted Macy eat, they snuggled on the couch. Automatically, she changed the channel to Nova. The dog watched entirely too much television, but she'd probably done so with her former owner.

There had been times when the television popped on while Macy had been in the bath, or outside in the backyard or garage. And the channel always seemed to land on one of Harley's favorites. When Macy arrived back in the room, the dog would look around as if she had no idea how it had happened.

"This is where I want to be," she said. "Next to you, with the dog watching our favorite shows. Well, her favorite shows." She grinned as she looked up at him.

"I'm kind of fond of our time together, as well," he said. "But being comfortable isn't the same thing as being happy. I care for you too much to let you turn down a lifelong dream."

She gathered her knees up under her and rested her chin on them. Could she handle a new relationship, and a very time-consuming job? What would she do with Harley? The thought of giving her up was just impossible. She loved the dog.

"Tell me what the job entails."

She explained that she would be in charge of all of the online components for the publishing group's papers. They would use a specific strategy to grow their online content, and use a more uniformed format. She'd have almost a hundred people on her staff located across several countries. Henderson wanted to bring her old-school principles to their online content, which was sorely needed.

Stories went up too fast, a lot of facts went unchecked. They'd all agreed, after the very uncomfortable conversation about her ex and why she left, that it was time for them to create a place in Henderson Newspaper Group where people could go to find solid journalistic principles and legitimate stories online, in a timely manner.

Blake whistled and put a hand on her shoulder. "That's impressive. And you have to know it's a huge honor that they think so much of you."

She nodded. Her ego, in between bouts of bone-crushing insecurity, had been buffed more than once during the meeting in New York. She questioned whether she was up for the job, but they believed in her so much that she stopped doubting herself. "Yes. But I'm really torn. I love the life I've created here with you and Harley. The town has even begun to accept me. And I feel like I've made a real difference with the paper."

"True, though now you can take your plans and strategies and ideas out to the wider world," he encouraged. "Talk about making a difference."

She cocked her head to the side and glared at him. "I want you to say, 'you can't leave. You're my woman.' All cavemanlike." She frowned.

"I will, if that's what you actually want. But what kind of man would I be if I kept you from fulfilling your dreams?"

"The kind of man I usually fall for," she snorted. "Many guys wouldn't want their significant other running off to parts unknown to manage a company—at least, part of it, that is."

"Macy, if we've learned anything over the last few weeks, it's that there's nothing *usual* about us."

"You're right." She imitated her receptionist's gesture and bumped fists with him.

He chuckled, but it wasn't a happy sound.

"This relationship is just beginning," he said. "We fell fast for one another. But maybe, like you said, it's good that we slow down to figure out what we want to do next. I'm not sure myself. Moving to New York would be somewhat easy for me, since I own part of a security firm there. But I feel like my next step should be my own."

"So you think it would be good for us to be apart?" She chewed on the inside of her lip.

He frowned at her. "No. I can't stand the idea of being away from you, but I think it's important that you at least try to do this. Dreams change, but this kind of opportunity is something that you've been dedicated to for a long time. There will be serious regrets if you don't get out there and give it a chance."

She sighed. "Why do you have to be so smart *and* handsome?"

He gathered her into his lap. "You're the good-looking one. I'm going to check into chastity belts online. You can find almost anything on the internet these days."

She sputtered and laughed. "Trust issues, dude. Trust issues."

He winked at her.

"There's only one man allowed to touch me," she whispered as she kissed his neck.

"And who's that?"

"A certain marine who has me going every which way so that I'm constantly confused."

He tapped her chin with his fingertip. "Hey, I'm trying to make this easy on you."

She put her palms to his chest. "It would be easier if you'd just tie me to the bedpost and make me a kept woman."

"Hmm." He looked as if he were genuinely contemplating the idea. "I didn't know you were into that, but I'm sure we could work something out."

Suddenly, she hopped from his lap.

A moment of clarity hit her. "I'm scared," she said.

"You wouldn't be human if you weren't," he spoke softly.

"No, not about the job. About losing you." How long would he wait while she was supposedly achieving her dreams?

"Hey, I'll be here. And maybe at some point I'll join you. That is, if we can sort out what to do with you know who."

Macy's heart jumped to her throat. She'd momentarily forgotten about Harley, she'd feel awful leaving the poor dog behind. They really had become family.

"That's going to be hard. I don't think there's a dog park big enough in the city to contain her."

"Well, you won't have to worry about it for a few months. Take the job, and give yourself time to get settled. Once things are in order, then we'll discuss what happens next for us."

"You always say you aren't so great with compromises," she said as she kissed the stubble on his chin. "And yet, you're a lot better at them than I am."

"Only when it comes to you. So, are you going to call Henderson?"

She shrugged. "I will call him, but not tonight. This is our time, yours and mine. His newspaper can wait. In fact, I have until Friday to let Aaron know of my decision and I'm going to take those days. Once I say yes, things will move very fast."

"We have two whole days?" His eyebrows waggled. She didn't have the heart to tell him that a lot of those hours would be spent trying to make sure she had the Tranquil Waters paper seen to. She wouldn't allow it to fail, especially since they'd all worked so hard. Her gut churned. There was so much here that she'd have to leave behind now.

Blake might believe her mind was made up, but she wasn't so sure. There had to be another answer, she was just too tired and wired to think clearly.

"Yes!" she said and kissed him smack on the lips. "So have your wicked, wicked way with me, Marine."

"How about those ropes and bedposts you were talking about," he joked and sent her a naughty grin.

"Oh? What would your mother say?"

"Are you going to tell her?"

She lifted her T-shirt over her head. "Do I look like a girl who would kiss and tell?"

And with that, she was lost in the sweet company of the man she loved.

16

WHEN HE JOINED the marines any hint of a distracting emotion was driven out of him. The words, "Separate yourself from the situation and get the job done," had been seared into his brain.

But that concept wasn't working so well today. While Macy packed, he'd made her eggs, bacon and waffles. He'd taken Harley out for a walk, and added a new playlist to her phone.

He did these things to keep his mind off the fact that in ninety minutes he'd be driving her to the airport, and there was every chance it'd be a month, maybe more, before he could see her again. The gnawing in his gut reminded him of those timely words from the military, even though he was trying to ignore the raw tension.

Whenever his brain began playing the what-if game, he occupied his mind by thinking of other gifts Macy could unwrap when she got to New York. She'd been given a corporate apartment in a fancy building with a doorman, so at least her place would have proper security. And Henderson had insisted she accept the car and driver he provided. He didn't want her wasting valuable time in the subway tunnels with no internet. The car had been specifically outfitted to be a mobile office for her. In the first few weeks she's be traveling to New Jersey, Upstate New York, Virginia and D.C., and after her most recent flight home, she wasn't thrilled about all the travel.

Henderson arranged for the car, and told her when she had to go to the Midwest and Pacific Northwest, she'd have use of the company jet. She had her boss on speakerphone when all of this was discussed, so Blake couldn't help but listen in. He'd never seen someone's eyes almost pop out of their head, but hers were close.

"So, Ms. Corporate Executive how does it feel to be traveling in style?" he asked after she hung up.

"Weird. I'm used to being the one in the middle seat in coach between the lady with the snotty two-year-old and the guy who's decided to be my new best friend on a fourteen-hour flight because the paper didn't have it in the budget and my reservation was made at the last minute. I've been in a jeep with no air-conditioning outside of Iraq when it was nearly a hundred and twenty degrees. There was about two years early in my career, when I didn't come back to the States. I existed with two pairs of khakis, four T-shirts and one pair of boots. I'd start every day not knowing where the story might take me. I usually had to bum rides and barter for taxi rides.

"So yes, it's weird." Then she'd taken his hands in hers. "Everything is changing so fast."

He'd kissed her fingers and smiled, even though it was forced. "Yes, but we have each other. And we're good."

She looked as if she were searching for courage. "I've never really had someone I could depend on before. It's—hard for me to—"

"Trust," he finished her sentence.

She nodded.

"After what you went through before you came here, it's understandable. But you have to realize, I come from a mind-set that we are a team. Harley and I are here for you. We'll video chat and text. And we'll both be so busy we won't even notice how long we've been apart."

"Do you genuinely believe that last bit?"

"No. But we can pretend our hearts aren't breaking while we're apart." He'd taken her in his arms. "There's a lot going on here, as well, but I'll find a way to come see you."

As it had done so many times in his life, opportunity was knocking. When he talked to Rafe and Will a few days ago he'd learned about their new idea that involved protection for wireless service in rural areas.

Their strategy was attractive to him, especially after listening to a frustrated Macy grumble about bad connections and loss of online access.

"Promise to never leave Harley on her own?"

He laughed. "Wherever I go, she does. I don't think I'd have a choice. We've seen what she does when she wants something."

"It's a big responsibility to dump on someone," she said guiltily. "I'm the one who adopted her."

"You did, and she's grateful. And I have lots of dog sitters if I ever need a break, though I doubt that will happen. We've become pretty good friends."

Macy snuggled into his chest. "Hold me really tight," she said.

He did.

She kissed him hard. "You are the most thoughtful man. And I saw the songs you added to my phone. I'm going to cry all the way to New York."

He stroked her back and recognized her sweet scent again. Though he doubted he'd ever forget it.

"I don't think I can do this," she choked out.

A lump of emotion sat in his throat. He swallowed hard, it didn't work. "You can, and you will. When you get scared, call me or focus on the adversity you've known in the past and overcome."

Her exploits seemed legendary to him. He had such respect for her and he knew she felt the same about him.

"Got your bags, ready to go?"

There was a tiny sob against his shirt.

Damn. He was just grateful it wasn't him doing the crying.

"Hey," he murmured, and he affectionately tapped her chin.

"I feel like I'm abandoning both of you," she said, glancing down at the dog. Harley was never more than two feet away from Macy since she'd brought her suitcases out of the closet.

"No. Don't think of it like that. You're going on your best adventure yet. You live for that sort of thing.

You'll call us each night and tell us about everything that happened, and we'll do the same."

Her phone rang. She handed it to him, too choked up to answer.

"Hello?"

"I'm calling for Ms. Reynolds," a man stated.

"Yes, she's indisposed at the moment, can I help you?"

"This is Mr. Henderson's assistant. He has sent the jet to pick her up so that she doesn't need to fly commercial. The plane is at a small private airfield about four miles outside of Tranquil Waters. The thing is, it's there now, waiting for her. So if she wouldn't mind bumping up her schedule to accommodate—"

The assistant left the rest up to him to decipher.

"We'll get her there as soon as possible."

"I'll text the address," the assistant said and hung up.

"Macy, there's good news and bad news," he told her. "The good news is you don't have to worry about any plane with crying babies or folks who want to adopt you. The bad news is that Henderson's jet is waiting for you out at the Jones airstrip. They'd like you to leave right now."

Her eyes flashed big. "But—but I'm not ready. I wanted to stop by the paper and make sure—"

"The gang has it handled and I'll be checking in with them often. Come on. I'll get your cases. We'll bring Harley with us."

A half hour later they drove straight up to the plane in his pickup. The sleek jet was luxurious and impressive.

The pilot met them at the door, and the steward took her luggage to stow in the back. The interior had rich leather seats and the walls had dark wood paneling. It reminded Blake of the exclusive club in London where he and Rafe had had Will's bachelor party. Coincidentally, the club wasn't far from his soon-to-be-wife's modeling show. They'd given him a hard time about modeling the jeans in the finale of her show, but he'd said there was nothing he wouldn't do for his woman.

At the time, Blake hadn't understood Will, but he did now. He would do anything for the woman he'd followed into that jet. Harley barked at the bottom of the steps. She and Macy had already said their good-byes. She was probably worried he was leaving, too.

"Wheels up in ten," the pilot said. "There's a storm brewing over the Atlantic, and we want to get you there before it hits."

That was the last thing poor Macy needed to hear.

"Sit here," he encouraged, and she claimed one of the cushy chairs. Her pink cheeks had gone pale at the mention of the storm. "You're going to be fine. You'll get there before the storm, that's why you have to leave now."

"It's going to be okay," she said as if she were trying to convince herself.

"I love you," he said as he knelt down on his good knee.

"I love you, too." She gathered his hands in hers, and he passed the small gift into her palm.

"What's this?" She opened her hand and revealed a silver chain with four charms on a ring.

"The Great Dane charm is self-explanatory. The saber represents me. The typewriter—I looked for a computer but they didn't have one—represents you. And then the heart is us." He turned the heart over so she could read the inscription. "'You are mine.'" He slipped the necklace over her head.

"This way, we'll always be with you, no matter where you are."

Tears streamed down her cheeks. She threw her arms around him and kissed him.

"This is the nicest, most beautiful gift anyone has ever given me," she croaked.

The tears were almost his undoing.

"I got you something," she said and dug into her tote bag. Holding out a small package, she handed it to him. "You've been so wonderful. It's not much, but— Just open it." She smiled through her tears and put the handkerchief he'd handed her to her nose.

"You didn't have to do this," he said as he ripped off the navy-and-red paper. Inside he found a scuba watch. It was the exact one he wanted. He'd been planning on replacing the one he'd broken when he was injured. He just hadn't gotten around to it.

"Read the inscription on the back." She grinned.

"'You are mine,'" he read out loud and then he chuckled.

"Great minds, right?" She laughed, but it sounded weak to his ears. He smiled, anyway.

"You're amazing. I love you so much," he said.

"Five minutes," the captain called to them.

"I better get going. I don't want Harley to hear the engines."

She frowned. "Yes, she won't like that at all. I don't want you to go."

He cupped her chin in his hand and kissed her lightly. "I don't want to, either, but it's okay. Now that we know we have each other."

He held up the watch. "Call me when you land."

She nodded, the tears falling faster down her cheeks.

The jaded journalist never cried, so he had a good idea how much this parting hurt her.

"I love you," she repeated as he headed to the exit.

"Be safe, you're my heart." Then he turned quickly so she wouldn't see the hurt in his eyes. She seemed to read him so well.

Is this what love did to people? Because it was painful.

Took everything he had to walk away from her when she was like that.

Harley whimpered as he hit the last step.

The plane made a high-pitched whining sound.

"Let's go girl, we have to be a safe distance away."

The dog didn't hesitate. She jumped into the cab of his truck. Then her paw pushed the button to close up the passenger-side window.

Backing the truck up first, he then drove out onto the dirt road that lead to the small airstrip.

The ground vibrated as the jet rumbled to life and soon gathered speed down the runway.

Harley barked as the jet was lost in the cloud cover.

"I feel the same way," he said.

Obviously pouting, the dog rested her jowls on the front dash.

"She'll be back." At least he hoped so.

He hadn't lied; it did feel as if his heart was flying away to New York City. He wasn't sure how he'd live without it.

_17_

FRIDAY COULD NOT come soon enough, although Macy had to work through the weekend, she could do most of it in her apartment. She'd forgotten what a rush a busy newsroom could be, but it was also draining.

Her team had accomplished a great deal in a short amount of time. The first two days, she put together a top gang of editors, columnists and reporters. Not one of them had turned down the opportunity when she explained her mission.

Not a single one. Jobs were scarce, but it was clearly more than that.

"This could revitalize the industry," her friend Jill, had said. They'd worked together to cover stories in Pakistan and Afghanistan. "Everyone will want in."

Jill was right. If Macy had any doubts about what they were doing, they were gone. By Thursday, she had a long list of everyone she wanted on her team. Most of them had to give two weeks notice, but luckily enough some of them were between jobs and started the day she hired them.

Henderson and Garrison had helped, going out to some of the bigger-name columnists and bringing them in.

Together with the other editors, she'd set up a stylebook and code of ethics. They hired some of the best fact checkers in the business, and nothing made it on the website until it had gone through three editors and at least one of the fact checkers. Every source was vetted.

Closing her laptop, she stuck it in the messenger bag. The lovely leather case had been waiting for her in her apartment when she'd first arrived. A gift from her marine. She'd received one at the apartment each day when she returned home. They had a routine that after dinner, they'd sit down and watch one of Harley's shows while they video chatted.

That hour each night had been her saving grace. It was almost like meditation, separating her from the stress at work and the time she needed to sleep. Not that she did much of that. After they signed off each night, she'd crash. Then she'd wake up at three in the morning to get to the office for the morning edition. There were a couple of nights when she was still at the office at nine. Still, she'd opened up the chat line and she and Blake had talked for more than an hour.

As she punched the button on the elevator, she realized she'd forgotten the flash drive of the confidential employee reports Henderson had given to her. She grabbed it quickly, she didn't want to keep her driver waiting downstairs as it was beginning to snow. Everyone had warned her that with the Thanksgiving holiday coming up in two weeks, and the weather, the weekend would likely turn a bustling Manhattan into a mess. The group's offices were located at Central Park West. She had a small space, but it had a prime view of the park. She didn't care about the size of her office. She'd expected to be in the middle of the newsroom.

But it was nice to have her privacy. By the time she returned to the elevator, it'd moved on. Being so high up it took a while—especially at the end of the day—to get an elevator.

Pushing the button again, she waited.

This time when the doors opened, Garrison stood there.

"Excellent. The boss wants to see us upstairs." He reached out and tugged her into the elevator. She landed against his chest.

"Hands off," she bit out.

"What? Does my intense charm send your senses reeling?" His mocking tone only annoyed her more.

"Uh, no. It definitely does *not*." She stepped to the other side of the elevator.

"You probably don't want to hear it from me, but you've done an amazing job this week." He sounded almost sincere.

"I appreciate your help with Appleton and Carter," she said, mentioning the two popular columnists he'd brought into the fold.

"Didn't have anything to do with me, it's this *mission*—there's no better word for it—that you're—we're—on."

She shrugged. "We're all fed up with the way things have been going with online journalism the past ten years. I only hope a lot of other online publications follow what we're doing."

The elevator doors slid open at the top floor. She and Garrison made their way to the double-etched glass doors that led to Henderson's sanctuary. That was what he called it. It was part office, part art gallery. The man had a passion for painting and sculpture. He'd insisted the arts get equal coverage as the headline grabbing news, which was fine by her.

"And here she is," Henderson said as they entered his inner office. He was there with some of the board members and a couple of vice presidents. He oversaw an entertainment conglomerate that had everything from television shows and films, to online video streaming sites, radio stations and a lot more.

He'd told her, that by hiring people like her, he was able to juggle so many things. "Hire the best," he said. "A hard worker is worth their weight." He had a soft spot for newspapers, which was why he was so interested in investing in the online industry.

Those assembled clapped as she joined them.

Okay, she should have dressed nicer. She'd run out of skirts and tops, and had worn her dark jeans with a T-shirt and jacket. The people around her were in suits, and the women wore dresses that weren't off the rack.

"You've made a tremendous difference and only a week's gone by," Henderson said as he handed her a glass of champagne. "If you folks will excuse us for a minute, I need to speak with our golden girl— pardon me—golden woman," he corrected when one of the women tsk-tsked.

"Sorry. You're a powerhouse. I didn't mean anything derogatory."

"No problem," she said as he ushered her into a conference room adjoining his office. It was almost as large as the reception area outside. The room had the same view as her office, although this was much more expansive.

"I have an instinct when it comes to people," he said as he motioned for her to have a seat at the table. "I was surprised when you left the Boston paper so fast. You were kind last week when I asked you about why. In the end, I found out the truth from one of the other interns who was working there at the time."

She started to speak, but he held up a hand.

"None of it matters now. But I've been doing a little more digging, and before I bring you into this next project, I have to ask you something personal again."

Great, now what? He was a handsome man, she only prayed he didn't hit on her.

He smiled as if he'd read her mind. "Don't worry. It's not like that. I just need to know if there's anything coming up in the next year that might pull your focus."

She frowned. "I'm not sure I understand."

"The marine? Great guy if the reports are to be believed. He's keeping an eye on the paper, oh, and your dog, while you're here, right?"

Chewing on her lip, she thought for a moment. "This is invasive, Aaron, Mr. Henderson. Would you ask a man the same thing?"

He chuckled. "Actually, I would. I have big plans for you, Macy. Your vision and leadership as well as your management skills are outstanding, and we'd like to take them—you—to the next level."

She blew out a breath.

"Over the next year, the plan is to transition you into a vice president's position overseeing your own division."

Wow.

"I'm not really the executive type." She glanced down at her jeans. "I—"

"*You* are perfect because you care about what's important, and we have a serious lack of people like you in the world. So then, you'll understand why I need to know if you're planning to get married and have children.

"And yes, I'd be asking the same if a man were sitting in your seat. This next year is key if we want to successfully implement a number of changes and do so as fast as possible. A vice presidency will mean a lot of travel for you and long days."

Marriage? Geez. She'd only known Blake for a month, though they both admitted they couldn't ever remember not loving each other.

"Some day, maybe," she said hesitantly. "But not anytime soon."

"Would it make it easier if we moved him here and offered him a position?"

That made her laugh. "Uh, no. That isn't a good idea. He has his hands full with a couple of businesses already, one of which he's responsible for getting off the ground. We're committed to one another, but that's all I can say for now. He's incredibly supportive of my choices. At some point, when I figure out the lay of the land here, I'll think about finding more permanent digs so at least Harley can join me."

"That's the Dane?"

She nodded.

He got out his wallet. "These are mine," he said, pointing at a photo of a pair of Irish wolfhounds.

"Amazing. They're bigger than Harley."

"Not by much, I'm sure. Those two keep me sane, and they go everywhere with me, even overseas."

She paused, about to speak.

"With enough money, you can make anything happen," he said, laughing as he pocketed his wallet.

"What I'm trying to say—although I'm not doing a very good job of it—is that we'll work with you when it comes to the personal business. If you need to fly your marine and Harley in for a visit, or have them travel with you anytime, that won't be a problem."

"But this kind of thing just doesn't happen to me. Ever," she said. What he was proposing seemed so surreal to her. "I'm the one who gets the rotten assignments, pinches her nose and moves on to the next story. I'm not used to being treated—"

"Special." He grinned.

"Yes. And besides, I don't understand it. We've recently hired a slew of talented journalists, why me? I asked you that question when you offered me the job, but I really need to know the answer."

He crossed his arms, and glanced out the window. "Because none of them have your passion for what we're doing. They want to be involved, but it takes someone like you to get others to take action. Not everyone has that. You do, and you have more potential than anyone I've ever hired. I wouldn't be surprised if you were doing my job some day."

That made her laugh. "As if." Then she covered her mouth with her hand. "Sorry."

He smiled warmly. "You have only one flaw. You're too hard on yourself. You've put in the hours, done a good job and now opportunity has come your way. How you handle your new responsibilities is up to you. Just remember, we're all human. And even the best of us make mistakes."

She wasn't sure why the conversation had taken this turn. "Did I do something wrong?"

He chuckled again. "No. But you have some tough decisions to make. I know it's a lot to take in your first week around here, but I wanted to make sure you were aware of what's ahead. That way you can plan your strategy. Will you be one of those people who have to decide how to wear many hats? Or will you be married to the job like me? And for the record, there's no wrong answer. I just want you to go forward fully informed of what's expected."

By the time she finished her glass of champagne and snuck out of the reception he'd thrown for her, it was nearly nine. She returned to her office, dealt with a few emails, collected her things and was completely and supremely grateful for the waiting chauffeur when she spotted him.

In the car, she called Blake, but he didn't answer. He was probably in the shower or out walking Harley. When she walked into her apartment, she smiled. There two dozen red roses with a card.

You made it to Friday. We knew you could do it.
Love B & H

She so appreciated Blake's thoughtfulness. After
a quick shower, she checked her phone. He hadn't
called or texted her back. After ringing the landline
at her house and getting no answer, she pulled back
her covers and snuggled into bed.

Too much information today. And more than anything she wanted to speak with Blake about it all, especially Henderson's plans for her. She texted Blake
one more time and then put her headphones on. Opening her laptop, she began editing a long column about
medical research funding.

By eleven, he still hadn't contacted her. It was only
ten in his time zone, but she worried that something
might be wrong. He was usually so good at returning her calls and texts.

She was about to call his mom, when her phone
rang.

"Hello, gorgeous woman of mine!"

"Hey, Marine. Thank you for the flowers."

She could hear a lot of people in the background.
Was he at a party?

"You deserve them. I called earlier but your assistant said they were throwing you a reception. I wanted
to let you know that I'm at a birthday party for my
brother. And don't worry about Harley. She's here
with me. She's the belle of the ball. Everyone keeps
telling her how beautiful she is. And of course, she
treats them like the adoring fans they are. We got a

great picture of her wearing a birthday hat. And Jaime made dog cupcakes for Harley and Bruno.

"Dog cupcakes. Can you believe it? What is the world coming to?"

That made her grin. "Why am I not surprised?"

"Sorry I didn't notice your first couple of texts. It's so loud. I couldn't hear my phone. I came outside with Harley, and noticed them. Is everything okay?"

He was out having a good time, and the last thing she wanted to do was ruin his fun with a heavy talk about their future.

"Yes, I just missed you. I want your arms around me."

"We are like-minded that way," he said.

"Blakeeeee, it's your turn," a woman's voice called out.

Blakeeee? Her stomach dropped.

"Well, I guess I better get going. I don't want to hold up the game. Can I call you in the morning? Or maybe we can V-chat?"

"Absolutely," she replied, forcing herself to sound positive. "Have fun tonight."

"I love you," he said, but he hung up before she could say it back.

It was silly for her to be upset. It was his brother's birthday party.

When had she become a woman who was jealous of someone having a little fun? If she'd really needed him, he would have dropped everything to talk to her. That knowledge should have been enough.

But how long could they do the long-distance relationship? So many times the past week, she'd wished he were there for her to come home to. Selfish, perhaps, but she'd never really been in love. She thought she was in love with Garrison, but now she knew it wasn't anywhere close to the real thing.

It's been only a week, and already you have doubts? You're tired. Go to sleep.

But her dreams were filled with Blake dancing with a bevy of sexy, sultry women. She woke up cranky and when Blake called, she didn't answer. After going for a run and working out at the gym, she realized how ridiculous she'd acted.

It had only been a week. She needed to get a grip. Walking away from her marine was not an option, but she also wouldn't give up the incredible chance she'd been offered.

Picking up the phone, she called Blake.

"WELL, BABE, IT'S no wonder you feel overwhelmed," Blake said as he listened to Macy vent. Between her job and everything else she had going on, she needed him.

He'd hop on the first plane, but he had half a dozen important business meetings set up over the next few weeks.

"Thank you," she said. "I'm sorry it all kind of poured out. I'm embarrassed about feeling so insecure last night."

"Don't be. By the way that was Tanya from the feed store giving me a hard time at the party. She knew you were on the phone. There's only one woman for me, and that's you. In fact, every time I walk down the street, people ask how you're doing. You definitely left an impression."

She laughed. "I needed to hear that. And tell Tanya I'm going to get even with her when I see her."

"Noted," he said and laughed with her. He was glad to lighten up her mood.

"I am not this woman," she proclaimed and then sighed. "You know the one who gets jealous and is whiny. It's so selfish of me to want you here when you have a lot on your plate, and besides, I'm so busy that I fall into bed every night and get up before the sun. I think I might be addicted to you. I need those arms around me when I go to sleep."

"Hey, I feel the same. And if you were here, Harley would be less likely to crawl on your side of the bed in the middle of the night. I woke up this morning and couldn't breathe. Her head was on my stomach. Oh, and this is where I found her yesterday afternoon."

She put him on speaker and opened the text when it arrived. The bed was made, but Harley's head was on her pillow.

"I think she might miss you a little." Blake chuckled. "Every once in a while, I find her in your closet. She's just lying in there on a pile of your clothes. I kept washing stuff, but finally gave up. I found some of your old pj's and sweatshirts and made a small pile in the middle of the closet for her."

"That's sweet. I miss you both so much it makes my heart hurt."

"I'm right there with you. Give yourself some grace. Any job is tough that first month, but it's obvious given what he's offering you after one week, that they really believe in you. I know I do. Is this a crazy route to starting a relationship? Yes. But we aren't like everyone else. And honestly, if I stayed in the marines, we would have had to have been separated even longer."

"True. I feel better just talking to you."

"Next time you feel like you did last night, don't be afraid to tell me that you need me. You're there for me and I'm here for you. Don't forget that. Also, any hope of you getting away for Thanksgiving?"

"I hadn't even thought about the holidays much. They're coming up fast—maybe I'll be home for Christmas. But there's still a lot to do here the next couple of weeks. And I've never been a huge fan of Thanksgiving. My parents didn't really do holidays."

Another hiccup. He'd promised his mother he'd be home for this Thanksgiving. It would be the first one in eight years he'd make. He wouldn't disappoint his mom. But even though she put up a good front, Macy needed him more.

"No problem. Christmas will be great," he said without enthusiasm.

It wasn't his favorite option, but that was the way things were.

"It isn't lost on me how lucky I am to have you in my life," she said softly.

"I know and I feel the same, Macy." But he was worried that the longer they were apart, the more she'd withdraw. She was so used to being on her own that she didn't feel comfortable coming to him when she was stressed or having a bad day. Clearly, she thought she should only show him the good side.

No way would he let her do that. It would mean sacrifice on his part, but Macy was worth it. He thought they could wait it out longer. But she needed him now, if for no other reason than to have someone be there for her at the end of the day. And he was the only someone who would be doing that.

After they hung up, he called his brother.

"We need to talk."

18

"Do you need me to stay?" Joe Pollack, Macy's assistant, glanced at the heavy snow falling outside her office window. She knew he had plans to catch a train and travel upstate to see his family for the holiday.

"No, you go ahead. I'll do a final check on the new sites to make sure there are no bugs, and then I'll be leaving, too."

"Thanks. You do know that Stu and Margaret have been through those sites multiple times today? They're clean, and they even added several upgraded firewalls to make it tougher for the hackers."

Shuffling papers on her desk, she looked up at him. "You know how I am. Once I feel like everyone really understands how important speed *and* accuracy and all of this is, I promise, I'll cut back on the micromanaging."

Joe didn't seem convinced. "Right. That's never going to happen."

She smiled. She couldn't help it. "I've been a bit on the loony side, have I?"

"I wouldn't say loony, more like determined. Uh, very determined."

"Always a diplomat. That's why you are such a super assistant."

"Yes, that and my ability to know when you are in need of coffee. Oh, and let's not forget my special talent to keep you from chewing out those who displease you," he joked, taking the bite out of his words. She'd had run-ins with a few reporters who hadn't double-checked their facts. The stories had been minutes away from going up on the site, when one of the fact checkers had called her to relay the news that there was something wrong.

Macy understood and appreciated the fact checker speaking up, but she made it clear, anyway, that those kinds of mistakes wouldn't be tolerated. Joe had remained at her side just to make sure she didn't actually throttle the reporters.

Admittedly it had been a good idea. One incorrect story could ruin everything they were all working so hard to achieve.

"Don't stay too late. Are you sure you don't want to come with me? My mom's always insisting there's room for one more at the table. She'd love to meet you."

"That's so nice of you, Joe. And I'd love to meet your mom. Be sure to arrange it if she's ever here visiting you. Thanks, anyway, but I'm looking forward to sleeping for a good twenty-four hours. I can't remember the last time I slept in."

He nodded. "You're always the last to leave and

first to arrive. There's been gossip that you actually live here."

"Sometimes it feels like it."

"Did you know, that if you were so inclined, your office has a perfect view of the Thanksgiving Parade?"

No, she didn't know that. Maybe she would come into the office, after all. Other than sleeping, she really didn't have anything else to do. "Cool. Now go on. The crowds at the station are going to be horrible. I don't want you to miss your train."

After he left, she sat back in her chair and blew out a breath. Everyone had worked so hard earlier in the week so they could be with their families. Even Henderson had taken off for Barbados to get away from the subzero temperature.

Even Cherie had abandoned her. She was on a book tour in Europe. Macy had seen her friend only once since arriving in New York. Cherie's book about relationships had hit the bestseller lists and she was more popular than ever.

Macy's cell rang. She glanced at the picture that came up on the mini screen and smiled.

"Hello, Mr. Marine."

"Hello, yourself. Are you still at work?"

"I am, though I did promise myself I'd leave before it gets too late. The weather is taking a turn for the worse."

He coughed. "I heard. I was worried about you getting home."

"Ah, you're too kind. Tony will be here to pick

me up. You don't need to worry. How is everything going with you? Is your mom fixing a huge feast?"

He snorted. "You said, 'fixing.' Our Texas words have seeped into your vocabulary, as for Mom, enough food for five or six families. We were over there the other day and discovered that Harley has a thing for apple pies."

"Oh, no. She didn't."

"She did. But we caught her before she ate the second one off the counter. She didn't feel so good for a day or two, but the vet says she's fine. I was going to tell you about it, but you had so much going on that I didn't want to possibly add to your concerns."

"You have a ton of patience. I don't know how you put up with her like you do."

"I don't consider her a chore. She's fun to have around."

She could hear Harley barking in the background as if confirming the fact.

Macy froze. She wanted to be there with them. Her mouth watered at the idea of homemade apple pie. It was stupid of her to stay in New York. Most of what she had to do was online. She could have gone home.

But it was too late now.

It was the day before Thanksgiving, no way would she be able to find a flight. And the company jet was in Barbados with Henderson. Even if a flight was available, with the snow the way it was, she had little chance of getting out of the city.

"Hey, did I lose you?"

"No. Sorry. I was just thinking how silly I am for

not coming home to see you at Thanksgiving. Work is busy, but—"

"Don't beat yourself up," he said. "If I hadn't promised my mom that I'd spend the holiday with her, I'd be dragging you out of that office right now."

Harley barked again.

"What's going on?"

"She needs to go out. Can I call you back? Or call me when you're on your way home so I know you're safe." He sounded distracted. Well, he probably was. Harley was likely dragging him to the door.

"No problem. I'll call from the apartment once I get there. Love you."

"Love you, too."

Chewing on her lip, she decided to pack it in. Poor Tony probably had a family he'd like to get home to, as well. She could work from her place. If she wanted to. After texting Tony, to let him know that she was ready to leave, she headed out.

In the lobby, she ran into Garrison, who held two bags of food. "Macy, I was just bringing these things up to you. I found this Thai restaurant still open nearby. Your assistant told me you'd be working tonight."

Her ex had been a little too nice the past few weeks, which made her suspicious. But he'd kept it professional, and Henderson had mentioned that his reports about her had been complimentary.

"Can I ask you something?"

He looked surprised. "Sure."

"What's up? Why are you being so considerate, when you've always been so competitive? I half expected you to tell Aaron that I was doing an awful job."

He shrugged. "I may be a cheating jerk, but even I can't deny you're as talented as they come. Besides, he doesn't need any reports from me. The evidence is out there. It's admirable what you've done. And honestly, I've been nice, because I have this horrible fear that you might be my boss some day. He's that impressed with you."

She laughed. "Oh, geez. You're serious aren't you?"

He nodded.

"Well, you don't need to worry. I forgive your past transgressions. I'm in a really good place. I'm happy in my relationship right now. It isn't easy, us being apart so much, but we're making it work."

He smiled. "I'm truly happy for you. Really. You deserve happiness. He's a fortunate guy."

"Thanks. Sorry about dinner, but I'm on my way home." She stared at the bags. "I have plans."

This was Garrison's life. Take-out Thai food the night before Thanksgiving while he worked. All of a sudden she knew that wasn't the life she wanted for herself. It was so clear to her now.

Henderson had asked if she'd be the kind of person who would learn to wear many hats. She was. Because she didn't want to end up lonely like the man in front of her, or like Henderson, for that matter.

"With who?"

"Huh?"

"Who are your plans with?"

The thought struck her as funny because it was so

glaringly obvious, and she laughed. "Don't look so surprised. My boyfriend."

"I thought he was in Texas." He seemed confused.

"Have a good Thanksgiving, Garrison. See you Monday."

With that she was out the door. Maybe she couldn't be in Texas, but they could share a virtual Thanksgiving. It was better than nothing. She couldn't wait to get back to the apartment and tell Blake her idea.

The snow was pretty, though it fell fast and didn't look to be letting up anytime soon. It took an extra half hour to reach her building.

"Tony, stay in the car. You don't need to open the door. And thank you. Have a wonderful holiday."

He turned to face her. "Won't you be needing me?"

She shook her head. "Not this weekend. You take some well-deserved time off. Enjoy."

He tipped his hat to her, and the doorman opened the car door. "Mind your step, miss. It's very slick on the sidewalk." He carefully led her to the front door. The soles of her boots were smooth, and made the slippery walk treacherous even with his help.

"Thanks," she said as she entered into the lobby. The marble floors proved to be as slick as the sidewalk. Just inside the door she slipped, and would have fallen if strong arms hadn't held her up.

"Whoa," a deep voice said.

It couldn't be.

Her marine smiled down at her. Had she fallen and woken in a dream? This could not be real.

"You— It's not—"

He kissed her then, and she lost herself in his embrace.

Harley barked and barked beside them.

"Ah, sweet girl." Macy bent down to put her arms around the dog's massive neck. "I've missed you."

She stood and stared at Blake, her heart soaring. Blake touched her cheek. "How is it you haven't been sleeping, yet you're still so damn beautiful?"

"Also sweet. But how did you get here? Not that I'm complaining." Macy wished the doorman a happy Thanksgiving and she, Blake and Harley headed for the elevator.

"Well, you couldn't come to Thanksgiving, so I brought Thanksgiving to you." He gave her that sexy smile of his and inside she melted a little. She loved this man.

"I can't believe you're here. I feel like time has stood still or something and suddenly I'm going to find out that none of this is really happening. And I do so want it to be happening."

He chuckled. "Let's get upstairs and I'll show you just how real it is," he whispered.

She sighed happily. "How was she on the plane?" With the loud noises, Macy was surprised the dog still wasn't sleepy.

"We drove," he said. "I didn't have the heart to put her in the cargo hold. And I had some business in North Carolina. We've been on the road the last few days."

"Why didn't you tell me!" she said as she pushed the button for her floor. "I was searching for flights while we were on the phone, but it was ridiculous considering this is the busiest day of the year."

"That and the airports are shut down." He gathered her in his arms. "We wanted to surprise you."

"You did." Her heart felt light. She was excited and at peace all at once. "Surreal. This is what it feels like. There's no better word for it. Wait, Harley's on the elevator, but pets aren't allowed in the building."

"She is. Evidently, she's the exception."

"I bet Henderson had something to do with that. He's a big fan of dogs."

"She did get me into your apartment. I hope that's okay. I had some things to drop off there before I could find a place to park and walk the dog."

"Make yourself at home. Whatever I have is yours."

She opened the door and was assailed by the smell of delicious food.

She turned to glance at him, and he shrugged. In her kitchen, she found his mother and brother, up to their elbows in dressing.

Throwing her arms about their necks, she kissed each of them on the cheek. "I'm so happy you're here. I can't believe you guys did this. Thank you, thank you."

"It's nothing, dear," his mother said, smiling. "Let me get my hands out of this corn bread, and I'll give you a proper hug."

She looked up at Blake who smiled at her.

"You did all of this. How?"

"Harley and I drove, but Mom and J.T. flew in this morning. We knew about the weather. They've been cooking all day. You're a part of the family now, and it wouldn't be right to celebrate without you. Besides, we heard you have an excellent spot to watch the Thanksgiving Parade. Mom's a fan, so she had no problem packing everything in dry ice and shipping it here."

Macy put her hands to her cheeks. "No one's ever done anything like this for me. You guys are incredible."

"It's what families do," J.T. said as he nudged her with his shoulder.

"Why don't you and Blake relax? Dinner should arrive in just a bit," his mother said.

Macy was baffled.

"All of this," J.T. said, waving at the cluttered counter, "is for tomorrow's lunch. We ordered pizza for tonight. It's a family tradition, or at least it was when Blake and I were kids. Mom was always too busy getting ready for the big day to take time to cook dinner the night before, so our dad would order pizza. And there's no better place to carry on that tradition than here."

Thankfully, the kitchen was well stocked with dishes and pots and pans, none of which had been used since she'd moved in. Most of her meals were eaten at work, and then she'd order in most nights.

But sitting around the dining room table with Blake's family, well, it was the best gift anyone could have given her. The brothers gave each other a hard time, their mom butting in to tell them to behave. They were a proper family.

Her parents loved her and cared about her, but they

didn't understand the importance of having this kind of time together.

She wouldn't make that mistake. Macy wanted it all. The family squabbles, the general silliness that came with hanging out with people who knew you better than you knew yourself—and the love.

A few hours later, she and Blake were in bed. Harley had passed out in the living room, and Blake's mom and brother had gone to their hotel.

"I know I keep saying this, but I still can't believe you are here."

He put an arm around her shoulders and leaned over for a kiss. "Believe it," he said and he kissed her again. Desire pooled in her belly. Yes, this was the way one should end the day.

His hand curved around her hip, and he drew her nearer. Wrapping his arms around her, he held her tight.

"This is home," she said against his chest.

He kissed her mouth, her cheek, behind her ear. "Yes, that's the way I feel. It doesn't matter where we live, as long as we're together." He went back to kissing her lips.

"I've got to tell you something, Blake, so just listen, okay? You don't have to say anything."

Blake tensed.

"I mean it. Just listen to what I have to say." She poked his chest as she glanced up at him. "I need to do this before I chicken out."

"Okaaaay," he said slowly.

She met his eyes. "I love you, Blake Michaels. And I want it all."

As her words sunk in, a slow smile split across his face.

"That's a good thing, since I love you and I want it all. In fact, I'm willing to do whatever it takes to make that happen."

"Wait." She lifted her head. "What are *you* saying?"

He gave her a sheepish grin. "I've been making a lot of changes over the last few weeks. I wanted to tell you, but it wasn't until a few days ago that I knew everything was going to fall into place the way I wanted it to. As long as you're all right with what I'm about to ask."

What was he talking about? What kind of changes? "You can ask me anything," she said honestly.

"How would you feel about Harley and I moving here full-time?"

Uh, it would be a dream come true. She slugged his arm. "How do you think I'd feel?"

"Hey, no need for violence." He rolled over and pulled her on top of him.

"I can't believe you were making all these plans and didn't tell me. I've been devising all these scenarios trying to figure out how I can split my time between here and Texas." She sat up straighter, fully aware that he was hard as a rock underneath her.

"So you like the idea."

She laughed. "Of course. It's what I've wanted all along, but I didn't feel right asking you to give up everything you had there to move here with me."

"If you'd asked, I would have done it. But a couple of weeks ago when you were so sad, I realized I didn't care if you wanted me to be here or not, you needed me. I'd do anything for you." He took her wrist and brought her forward and kissed her.

"I want and need you," she whispered, "more than you will ever know."

"Trust me, I do know. I'll have to go back and forth for a while. J.T. will help me out. I'll be based here, though. And it's good timing, too, for the security business my friends and I have. We're thinking of expanding and opening an office here. Besides my financial duties, the guys want me to take charge of implementing the new ideas we've got going and do a forecast for a possible office here. It's a lot, but as soon as I made the decision to be here with you, it all fell into place."

She kissed him, lightly at first, and then she deepened the kiss, putting everything she had into it. "I'm so glad. And what about you know who?" she asked.

He twisted one of her curls around his finger. "You know who will be happy having us and her toys. At some point we should maybe consider trying to find a house outside the city, but there's a great dog park not far from here. She loved it."

"You really have thought of everything."

Something was still making her nervous, and she realized it was because she was so happy.

"You don't think it's too soon for us to cohabitate?" he asked, his expression serious.

She shook her head. "You know it isn't. Like you said, there may be some bumps along the way, but if you're riding over them with me, we can cruise through life together."

"That was a terrible metaphor." He laughed.

"Yes. Yes, it was."

"Have I mentioned how much I love you?"

She glanced at the nonexistent watch on her wrist. "It has been a good ten minutes since the last time. I was beginning to wonder."

Growling, he reversed their positions.

She smiled, and put her hands on either side of his face to hold him close. "Show me, Blake," she said, "show me how much you love me."

Capturing her lips in a long and passionate kiss, he left her breathless. Just from the kiss alone she was ready for him.

"Not so fast, sweetheart," he said as he nuzzled her neck. His mouth paid equal attention to each of her breasts. As he moved down, kissing all the way, she cried out. Having him here with her meant everything to her.

He caressed her, tempted her, touched her exactly as she wanted to be touched. He was amazing, so strong and also so tender.

Her orgasm was searing and swift. She felt it from her head to the tips of her toes. It made her shudder and call out his name.

"Now," she said, shutting her eyes, anticipating him.

"No." He teased her into yet another orgasm. This one robbed her of all control. "Blake, Blake..." she whispered.

He stroked her thighs, moving onto his knees. The intensity of passion in his gaze was enough to make her shudder again.

He entered her slowly, carefully, filling her, completing her.

"Yes," she said, matching the intimate movement of his hips.

As they raced to the edge together and leaped, he kissed her thoroughly. Every bit of love he felt for her was in that kiss, and she returned it.

He was her marine, body and soul.

19

HARLEY BARKED AS Santa passed by the window. Blake's mom clapped, and the woman wrapped in his arms laughed so hard he couldn't help but smile. They were all in Macy's office enjoying the parade.

J.T. shook his head in wonder. "How does she know it's Santa?" he asked.

"Who knows? But she does have a thing for presents and toys," Macy answered.

They laughed.

"Dear girl, that parade was too exquisite for words," Blake's mom said. "So much better in person and beyond anything I could imagine. I am surprised that even with all the snow on the sidewalks, so many people showed up."

"Yes. It was fun and nice to be able to watch it here in my office where it's warm and comfortable. More snow is expected later this afternoon. I'm just glad the skies cleared a bit so they could have the parade. It would have been awful if you came all this way to see it, and then it didn't happen."

His mother pulled her out of Blake's arms and

hugged her. "Macy, sweetie, we didn't come for the parade. We came to see you. No one should be alone on Thanksgiving. I've had a few too many of those myself, and I didn't want that for you." She kissed Macy's cheek. "Let's roll, J.T., we'll take Harley for a walk. You two be back at Macy's place by one so we can eat."

She paused in front of Blake and touched his hand. "It's wonderful to see you so happy, son. It's about time."

He held his mom's hand and squeezed. "Mom, you are the absolute best. I love you."

"Love you, too, son. Don't be late for dinner." She followed J.T. and Harley out the door.

Blake sat on the edge of Macy's desk. She pushed his legs apart and slipped in between them. He leaned toward her and she put her arms around his neck and kissed him.

"This has been on of the best days of my life and it's still early."

He held her close. "I agree. Are you sure you're okay with my family invading your space unannounced?" He'd kept an eye on her throughout the morning. It was almost as if she were afraid of offending someone or saying the wrong thing. He didn't want her to feel that way.

"Blake, I so appreciate what your mom and brother have done for me this Thanksgiving. It's been great. I've never felt like—I was a part of a family. Years on my own, well, you know how it's been. Now that I see what I've been missing out on, I want to make up for lost time. So there's no invasion. I'm ecstatic that you and your family are here."

He kissed her nose. "Good. Because my mom is

very excited about shopping tomorrow. I was hoping I could count on you to handle that one."

Macy laughed. "Always with the ulterior motives. I should have known. But if I'm going out in the wilds of Manhattan and facing all those shoppers, then seriously, you're coming with us." She tugged on his arm and they left her office.

"I had a feeling you'd say that." At the elevator, he helped her on with her coat. He thought about that and all the other things in future that he would want to help her with. Big and small. He planned to spend the rest of his life loving this woman.

She was his everything.

One day he'd ask her to marry him, but not until he knew she was ready. The year ahead represented a lot of change for her. He'd be there for her. He wanted her to achieve her dreams. In fact, he couldn't think of anywhere he'd rather be.

"Hey, Mr. Deep Thoughts. What's going on in that brain of yours?" She was standing in the elevator, waiting for him.

No more living day to day, wondering if it might be his last. From now on he and Macy lived in a world of possibility.

"I'm thinking about the interesting things I can do with you after everyone leaves tonight."

Her cheeks turned a bright shade of pink as she yanked him into the elevator. "Now that's all I'm going to think about during dinner."

He waggled his eyebrows. And then he kissed her.

This was only the start of a long and happy life together.

* * * * *

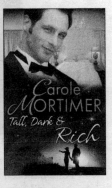

Her only weakness, his deepest desire

Nora has been kidnapped by Marie-Laure, Kingsley's sister and Søren's wife, whom everyone had presumed dead thirty years ago. Betrayed by her brother and the husband she once madly loved, now she is out for revenge.

Kingsley, Søren and Wes—all foes to some degree—must work together to figure out how to save Nora.

Are you ready for Book 4?

Welcome to the world of the #OriginalSinners...
The Siren • The Angel • The Prince • The Mistress

3/MB449

Meet The Sullivans...

Over 1 million books sold worldwide!

Stay tuned for more from **The Sullivans** in 2014

Available from:

www.millsandboon.co.uk

B